ARENA THREE

(BOOK #3 OF THE SURVIVAL TRILOGY)

MORGAN RICE

vowed (book #7)
found (book #8)
resurrected (book #9)
craved (book #10)
fated (book #11)
obsessed (book#12)

PART ONE

CHAPTER ONE

I thrash against the struggling current, lungs bursting, desperate for air. I try to propel myself to the surface, kicking furiously, treading for sunlight. I don't know where I am or how I got here—but I know I can't breathe, and I can't last much longer.

With one last kick I finally manage to break the surface. I gasp, gulping the air, never having felt so dead—and so alive.

As I bob in a fast-moving river, I catch a glimpse of someone standing on the bank, looking down at me. Before a wave crashes over my head, I realize: my dad. He's alive.

And he's watching me.

His face is hard, though, too hard. No warmth is there—not that he was ever warm to begin with.

I push up to the surface again, fighting the power of the current.

"Dad!" I shout, fighting against the raging current. "Dad, help me!"

I'm overwhelmed with joy to see him, but there's no emotion on his face at all. Finally, he locks his jaw.

"You can do better than that, soldier," he barks. "I want to see you fight!"

My heart constricts. I look around me, disoriented, and it's then that I see them: rows of spectators behind him. Biovictims with melted, tumorous faces. They are braying for blood.

I recoil in horror as the crowd begins to chant.

"Fight! Fight! Fight!"

I suddenly realize: I'm in another arena, its floor made up of water. It's as if I'm in a giant fish bowl, with all the spectators high up on bleachers, all chanting for my death.

My fighting instinct kicks in and I tread with all I have, trying to stay above the surface. I scream soundlessly, no noise coming from my mouth at all.

I suddenly feel an icy hand on my ankle beneath the surface, trying to drag me down.

I look down and am stunned to see, beneath the clear waters, a face I'd never thought I'd see again.

Logan.

He's alive. How can it be?

He holds onto my ankle with a viselike grip. His eyes are locked onto mine, boring into me as he pulls me deeper into the water, down into the depths.

"Fight!" my dad screams.

1

The crowd joins in, and as I am dragged down, I can hear their chants beneath the water, like a tribal drum pounding in my skull.

Panicking, I kick and writhe, trying to get away from the nightmare that is unfolding before my eyes. The water makes everything seem to move in slow motion, and I look down at Logan, his hand latched to my ankle and his sorrowful gaze still fixed on me. He looks at me forlornly, as though realizing that to hold onto me would be to kill me.

"I love you," he says, his voice etched with pain.

Then he lets go, drifting away, and quickly disappears into the black depths.

I scream so loud it wakes me up. I sit bolt upright, my heart thudding so fast in my chest it feels like it could burst. I'm trembling all over. I touch my body all over as though checking that it's real. My skin is clammy to the touch, and I'm drenched in a cold sweat.

Reeling from the horror of the dream, I wait a long while for my heartbeat to slow. It's only then that I realize I have no idea where I am. I listen, immediately on guard, trying desperately to remember, and hear a soft beeping noise in the background. I smell the stench of antiseptic in the air.

I look around me and discover that I'm in some kind of hospital. Dawn is breaking, casting a pale red light on the clean walls, and as I look around I see I am lying in a bed, a blanket over me and a pillow beneath my head. I feel a tug on my arm and look down to see an IV, while a machine to my left beeps in time to my heartbeat.

The entire scene seems unbelievable, a place so quiet, so clean, so civilized. I feel as if I've gone back in time to the world before the war. I can't help but think I'm having another dream, and half expect it to turn into another soul-crushing nightmare.

Cautiously, I get out of bed, surprised to find my legs sturdy beneath me. I rub the puncture wound on my leg, from the snake bite I got in Arena 1, now mostly healed. So this is real.

The IV is attached to a metal stand with wheels. I hold on to it and pull it toward the window with me. I open the blinds, and as they inch up, I take in the sight and gasp.

There, sprawled out before me, lies a perfectly preserved town. It looks impossibly pristine, untouched by the war. All the buildings are intact, their clean windows shining. There are no bombed out buildings, no rusting, abandoned hulls of cars.

Then my heart quickens as I see that there are people milling about, leaving buildings that look like homes, heading down paved

2

streets toward fields and farmyards. They look carefree, clean, well fed, well dressed. I even see one smile.

I blink several times, wondering if I am dreaming.

I am not.

A rush of hope hits me as I think of the rumored town in Canada, the one Charlie and Logan both believed existed. Have we made it here?

It's then that I think of the others. I realize I am completely alone in this hospital room. I spin around and of course see no sign of Charlie or Ben, no sign of Bree.

Fear takes hold of me. I rush to the door and find it locked. Panicking, I wonder if I'm a prisoner. Whoever put me here decided to lock me in, which doesn't bode well.

Just as I'm rattling the handle and pounding frantically against the door, it swings open, and I stagger back as a small group of people enter.

They wear strange uniforms, and there's something militaristic about the way they move as they swarm into my room with a brutal sort of efficiency.

"General Reece," a woman says, introducing herself as she raises her hand up in a salute. I notice her Canadian accent. "And you are?" she demands.

"Brooke," I say. "Brooke Moore___." My voice sounds startled and breathless, weaker than I would have liked.

"Brooke," she repeats, nodding.

I stand there, stunned, not knowing what is going on.

"Where am I?" I say.

"Fort Noix," she replies. "Quebec."

I can hardly breathe. It's true. We really made it.

"How?" I stammer. "How do you exist?"

General Reece looks at me expressionlessly.

"We are defectors from the American and Canadian armies. We left before the war, because none of us wanted to be a part of it."

I can't help but think bitterly of my dad, of the way he volunteered to join the war before he was even called. Maybe if he'd been idealistic like General Reece and the other soldiers here we'd never have gone through everything we did. Maybe we'd all still be a family.

"We've created a safe society here," she continued. "We have farms to grow food, reservoirs for water."

I can't believe it. I sit back on my bed, overwhelmed, feeling relief wash over me. I'd given up all hope of ever being safe, of ever living a life again where I wouldn't need to fight.

But she isn't about to give me time to bask in the moment.

"We have some questions for you, Brooke," she says. "It's important that we know where you heard about us and how you found us. Staying out of sight is paramount to our survival. Do you understand?"

I take a deep breath. Where do I even begin?

I recount my story for the General and her troops, beginning with the Catskills, the house Bree and I shared on the mountains, before going into the trauma of the slaverunners. I tell her about escaping Arena 1, about rescuing the girls who'd been taken to become sex slaves. She watches me with a grim expression as my story unfolds, our capture and ordeal in Arena 2. The only thing I leave out is Logan. It's too painful to even say his name.

"Where are my friends?" I demand when I'm finished. "My sister? Are they okay?"

She nods.

"They're all fine. All recovering. We had to speak to each of you in turn, separately. I hope you understand why."

I nod. I do. They had to make sure our stories corroborated, that we're genuine and not slaverunner spies. Suspicion is the only thing that keeps you alive.

"Can I see them?" I ask.

She puts her hands behind her back, a position I remember my dad adopting all the time. It was called "at ease" even though it doesn't look remotely relaxed.

"You can," she says in her clipped, emotionless voice. "But before I take you to them I need you to pledge to never speak about what you see here to anyone. Absolute secrecy is the only way Fort Noix can survive."

I nod.

"I will," I say.

"Good," she replies. "I must say I admire your bravery. Everything you've been through. Your survival instinct."

I can't help but feel a swell of pride. Even though my dad will never be able to see me and tell me he is proud of my achievements, hearing this from the General feels almost as good.

"So I'm not a prisoner?" I say.

The General shakes her head and opens the door for me. "You're free to go."

4

In my thin hospital gown, I begin to take small steps down the corridor. General Reece and her soldiers escort me, one wheeling the IV on my behalf.

Just a few rooms down, the corridor opens up into a small dormitory. The first person I see is Charlie, cross-legged upon a bed reading a book. He looks up, and the second he realizes, his eyes fill with relief.

"Brooke," he says, discarding his book, standing from the bed and coming toward me.

Movement from the other side of the dormitory catches my eye. Ben emerges into the brightening dawn light. Tears glitter in his eyes. Beside him, I see the small figure of Bree, with Penelope, her one-eyed Chihuahua, in her arms.

Bree begins sobbing with joy.

I can't help myself. Tears spring into my eyes at the sight of them all.

The four of us fall into an embrace. We made it. We really made it. After everything we've been through, it's finally all over.

As I cling to Charlie, Bree, and Ben, I let my tears consume me, shedding them cathartically, realizing this is the first time I've cried since the war began. We've all got a lot of healing to do. For the first time, I think we're going to get the chance to mourn.

Because we may have made it, but the others didn't. Rose. Flo. Logan. Our tears aren't just from relief, but grief. Grief and guilt.

I realize then that the horrible nightmare I had last night is just the beginning. All of us have tortured, traumatized minds; all of us have endured more than anyone should ever have to. In some ways, our journey hasn't ended.

It's only just begun.

CHAPTER TWO

Our embrace is interrupted by a gentle tap on my shoulder, and I pull back from the others and turn to look behind me. General Reece is standing there stiffly. Her expression reveals to me that our outpouring of emotion has made her feel awkward. My dad was the same—he was always teaching me not to cry, to hold everything in.

"Now you're all back together," she says, "I'll need to escort you to the Commander. It's up to him to make the final decision."

"The final decision about what?" I ask, confused.

Emotionlessly, as though it's the most obvious thing in the world, the General says: "To decide if you can stay."

My stomach twists at her words, at the sudden realization that we might be forced back out. I'd been an idiot to assume our staying at Fort Noix was automatic. Of course we wouldn't be accepted just like that.

Ben's hand reaches for my arm and squeezes and I realize he must be thinking the same thing. Likewise, Bree grabs the fabric of my gown, twisting it anxiously into her fist, while Charlie stares at me with wide, terrified eyes. Penelope whines with anguish. None of us want to go back out there. None of us can leave this place now that we've seen it. Even the thought of it is too cruel.

A nurse, tending to someone on the far side of the dorm, looks over and scowls at General Reece.

"My patients are still weak," she said, glancing at my IV line. "They need to be allowed to rest for a few days. Sending them back out there like this would be a death sentence."

It would be a death sentence in any state, I think.

Almost as soon as she says it, I become immediately aware of all the aches and pains in my body. The adrenaline of finding myself alive and safe, of being reunited with my friends and sister, has been the only thing carrying me this far; being reminded of everything my body has gone through brings the pain flooding back.

"Then they will die," General Reece replies firmly, matter-of-factly. "The decision lies with the Commander. I follow the Commander's orders. You follow mine."

The nurse looks away, immediately obedient, and the General, without another word, turns on her heel and marches out.

We all look at each other anxiously and then, prodded by the soldiers, we follow the General, flanked by her equally obedient soldiers.

It's difficult to walk down the corridor. There are aches in muscles I never knew I had, and my bones seem to creak and grind as I walk. Sharp pains race through my neck and spine, making me wince. Moreover, I'm absolutely famished. Yet I don't feel able to ask for food, worried that it may sway General Reece or the Commander, make them think that we're demanding or spoiled. If we want to survive, we need to give off the best impression we possibly can.

Ben keeps glancing at me with a worried expression, and I can see his anxiety, his fear that we might be expelled from Fort Noix and left to fend for ourselves all over again. I share his fear. I'm not sure any of us would survive that again. It's as if I'd been bracing myself all these years, steeling myself to survive this world, knowing that no other option existed. But now, seeing all this, seeing what is possible, the thought of going back to it is just too much.

We reach the end of the corridor, and as General Reece pushes open the two double doors, morning light floods in so bright I have to blink.

As my eyes adjust to the brightness, Fort Noix appears before me. It's a fully functioning town, filled with people and buildings, military trucks, bustle, noise, and laughter. *Laughter.* I can't even remember the last time I heard that. I can hardly believe my eyes.

It is the most beautiful thing I have ever seen.

The General's voice breaks through my reverie.

"This way."

We're led along a sidewalk, past groups of kids around Charlie and Bree's age playing in the streets.

"We don't have many children at Fort Noix," the General tells us. "The ones that are here are educated until the age of fourteen. Then we sort them according to their abilities and assign them work."

Bree looks at the children with longing eyes: the prospect of four years of school is beyond tempting for her. Nestled in her arms, Penelope immediately reads the change in Bree's emotion and licks her face.

"What kind of work?" Charlie asks, curiously.

"All forms of labor are needed to keep this fort operational. We have farmers, fishermen, hunters, builders, tailors, and then we have more administrative duties, like assigning rations, taking registers, and the like. We have professionals, too: teachers, soldiers, doctors, and nurses."

As we're led through the town, I find myself more and more impressed by what I see. Fort Noix runs on solar power. All the buildings are only one story high, so as not to be visible from afar or attract any attention. Most of them have grass on their roofs—something the General explains is for both insulation and camouflage—and tree branches covering them.

As we stroll along, the sunlight grows warmer and brighter, and the General explains the history of the place. It seemed to come about through a combination of fate, chance, and a whole lot of luck. There were already a number of military bases peppered along the powerful Richelieu River. Due to its geographical location between New England and New France, the river had been a key pathway in the French and Iroquois Wars in the seventeenth century and, later, the French-English battles of the eighteenth century__. Because of its rich military history, those who, like General Reece, opposed the brewing American civil war were drawn to it, and helped turn it into a safe zone for defectors.

The second bit of luck was that the river flowed from the distant Green Mountains bordering Vermont. When the war finally broke out in New York, the mountains sheltered the fort from the winds carrying nuclear radiation. While the rest of the population succumbed to the radiation and disease that resulted in the biovictims, the military personnel hiding out in Fort Noix were protected. At the same time, the good source of clean running water provided them with an abundance of fish, so that when supply routes were blockaded, bridges blown, and villages leveled, the people in the fort survived.

The wars that had raged around these parts had another unlikely outcome. Since most of the local towns were flattened, the surrounding forests had a chance to grow. Soon, a thick barrier of evergreens surrounded Fort Noix, reducing its chances of being found to virtually nil, while providing wood for fires and game for hunting.

Once the sound of bombs stopped and the fort's residents knew the war was over, they sent out scouts and quickly realized the human race had obliterated itself. After that, they cut themselves off completely and set to work expanding the fort into a town, and building civilization again from the ground up.

By the time General Reece has finished her story, I'm in awe of her. Her calm and military steeliness reminds me of my dad.

As we walk, I can't help but feel overwhelmed by every little detail. It's been so long since I've seen civilization. It's like stepping back in time. Better, even. It's like stepping into a dream come true. The people milling around me look healthy and well cared for. None of them have endured starvation. None of them have had to fight to the death. They're just normal people like the ones who used to populate the earth. The thought makes a lump form in my throat. Is it possible to start again?

I can tell the others are as overwhelmed as I am. Bree and Charlie stay close together, side by side, looking around with awe. They're both clearly excited and happy to be in Fort Noix, yet also anxious at the thought of it all potentially being taken away from us.

Ben, on the other hand, seems a little dazed. I can't blame him. To step out of our brutal world and into this one is beyond disorienting. He walks slowly, almost as though in a trance, and his eyes glance furtively from side to side, trying to take everything in. I realize as he walks that it's more than just being overwhelmed. It is like how my body could only reveal to me how exhausted it was once I was safe. Ben's mind, I'm sure, is revealing to him just how much he's been through: the death of his brother, fighting in the arena, every near-death experience. I can almost see that his mind is preoccupied with thoughts as he sifts through his memories. I have seen people suffer from post-traumatic stress, and his face bears the same look as they'd had. I can't help but hope that his appearance doesn't hamper our chances of being accepted here.

Soon, we're off the main street and walking down some smaller, winding roads that lead through the forests. This time, it's Charlie who starts hanging back, trudging a little way behind the rest of us. I drop my pace and draw up beside him.

"What's wrong?"

He looks at me with terrified eyes.

"What if this is a trap?" he says under his breath. "What if they're taking us to another arena?"

His question makes me wonder whether I'm being too trusting. I think back to the man who stole our supplies when we were on the run from the slaverunners. I'd trusted him and I'd been wrong. But this time it's different. There's no way Logan would have directed us toward danger.

I put my arm around Charlie's shoulder.

"We're safe now," I explain. "You don't have to be scared anymore."

But as we go, the canopy thickens above us, blocking out the daylight and making dark shadows crowd in around us. Something about walking this long, dark path reminds me of the arenas, of walking those corridors knowing that a horrible, painful death was all that awaited me. I can feel my heart begin to hammer in my chest.

The sky gets darker and darker as we go. Bree must notice something is wrong, because she snuggles into me.

"You're sweating," she says.

"I am?"

I touch my brow and find that I've broken out in a cold sweat.

"Are you okay?" Bree adds.

But her voice sounds strange, distorted, like it's coming from far, far away.

Suddenly, there's a hand on my arm, and I scream as I see Rose's black, wizened hand latching onto my arm. I lash out, pushing her away, scratching at her hand with my fingernails.

Then all at once the panic is gone. I come back to the present and realize that it wasn't Rose's hand on me at all. It was Ben's. He's cradling it against his chest, and deep scratches run along it. He looks at me with an expression of pure anguish while Penelope yap-yap-yaps her distress. The soldiers around us politely avert their gazes.

I look down at Bree and Charlie, my heart hammering.

"I'm sorry," I stammer. "I thought... I just..."

But my words disappear.

"Maybe we should take you back to the hospital," Ben suggests in a soft, persuasive voice.

"I'm fine," I say, sternly, frowning at their worried expressions. "I thought I saw something is all. It's no big deal. Come on."

I stroll ahead, leading the pack, trying to gain back some sense of myself. I'm not the sort of person who crumbles in the face of adversity and I'm not about to become the sort who is haunted by the past.

Yet as I continue to walk, I'm not so sure I can leave the past behind.

We turn a bend, and I see it: the short, squat building that must contain the Commander's office. I brace myself, heart pounding, as we walk.

The outcome of this meeting, I know, will determine if we live or die.

CHAPTER THREE

The Commander's building is buzzing with life. Military personnel march quickly by, while others sit around conference tables looking at blueprints, discussing in loud, confident voices the benefits of building a new granary store or extending the wing of the hospital. It feels like a real unit, a team with a purpose, and it feels good.

And it makes me all the more nervous that we won't be allowed to stay.

As we pass along the corridors, I see a sprawling gymnasium, people training with weapons, firing bows and arrows, sparring and wrestling. There are even little kids being trained how to fight. The people of Fort Noix are clearly preparing themselves for any kind of eventuality.

Finally, we're led into the Commander's office. A charismatic man in his forties, he stands and greets us each cordially by name, clearly already having been briefed. Unlike the General, he doesn't have a Canadian accent; in fact, he surprises me with a strong South Carolina twang, which tells me he's one of the defectors from the American side of the opposition.

He turns to me last.

"And you must be Brooke Moore." He cups his hand around mine and shakes, and the warmth from his skin seeps into mine. "I must say I'm impressed by your experiences. General Reece has filled me in on all you've endured. I know it's been hard on you. We don't know much about the outside world. We keep to ourselves here. Slaverunners, arenas—that's a whole different world to what we're used to. What I've been told about you is really truly incredible. I'm humbled to meet you all."

Finally, he drops my hand.

"I'm amazed by what you've done here," I say to the Commander. "I've dreamt of a place like this ever since the war. But I never dared dream it was true."

Ben nods in agreement, while Bree and Charlie seem completely entranced by the Commander, both gazing at him with wide eyes.

"I understand," he says. "On some days it's hard for me to take in, too."

He takes a deep breath. Unlike General Reece, who is a bit on the bristly side, the Commander is warm and pleasant, which keeps me hopeful.

But now that the formalities are over, his tone changes, darkens. He gestures for us all to sit. We sit in our chairs, stiff-backed like kids in a principal's office. He looks us over as he speaks. I can feel that he's judging each of us, summing us up.

"I have a very serious decision to make," he begins. "Regarding whether you can stay at Fort Noix."

I nod solemnly as my hands twist in my lap.

"We've taken in outsiders before," he continues, "particularly children, but we don't do so as a matter of course. We've been tricked in the past by kids your age."

"We're not working for anyone," I say, quickly. "We're not spies or anything like that."

He looks at me skeptically.

"Then tell me about the boat."

It takes me a moment to understand, and then I realize: when we'd been rescued, we'd been traveling in a stolen slaverunner vessel. I realize that they must think we're part of some kind of organization.

"We stole it," I reply. "We used it to escape from Arena Two."

The Commander regards me with suspicious eyes, like he doesn't believe that we could have escaped from an arena.

"Did anyone follow you?" he asks. "If you escaped an arena and stole a boat from slaverunners, surely they'd be pursuing you?"

I think back to the time on the island in the Hudson, of the relentless game of cat and mouse we played with the slaverunners. But we'd managed to get away.

"There aren't," I say, confidently. "You have my word."

He frowns.

"I need more than your word, Brooke," the Commander contests. "The entire town would be in danger if someone had followed you."

"The only proof I have is that I've been lying asleep in a hospital bed for days and no one's come yet."

The Commander narrows his eyes, but my words seem to sink in. He folds his hands on top of the table.

"I'd like to know, in that case, why we should take you in. Why should we house you? Feed you?"

"Because it's the right thing to do," I say. "How else will we rebuild our civilization? At some point we need to start taking care of each other again."

My words seem to anger him.

"This is not a hotel," he snaps. "There are no free meals here. Everyone chips in. If we let you stay you'll be expected to work.

Fort Noix is only for people who can contribute. Only for the tough. There is a graveyard out there filled with those who couldn't hack it here. No one here rests on their laurels. Fort Noix is not just about surviving—we are training an army of survivors."

I can feel my fighting instinct kick in. I pull my hands into fists and thump them on the table. "We *can* contribute. We're not just weak children looking for someone to take care of them. We've fought in arenas. We've killed men, animals, and monsters. We have rescued people, kids. We are good people. Strong people."

"People who are used to doing things their own way," he contests. "How can I expect you to alter to a life under military command? Rules keep us alive. Order is the only thing stopping us from perishing like the others. We have a hierarchy. A system. How will you hack being told what to do after so many years running wild?"

I take a deep breath.

"Our father was in the military," I say. "Bree and I know exactly what it's like."

He pauses, then eyes me with dark, beady eyes.

"Your father was in the military?"

"Yes," I reply sternly, a little out of breath from my outpouring of anger.

The Commander frowns, then shuffles some papers on his desk as though looking for something. I see that it's a list of our names. He taps mine over and over with his fingertip then looks up and frowns.

"Moore," he says, saying my surname. Then he lights up.

"He's not Laurence Moore?"

At the sound of my father's name, my heart seems to stop beating entirely.

"Yes," Bree and I cry at the same time.

"Do you know him?" I add, my voice sounding desperate and frantic.

He leans back and now looks at us with a whole new respect, as if meeting us for the first time.

"I know of him," he says, nodding with clear surprise.

Hearing his tone of respect as he talks about my father makes me feel a surge of pride. It's no surprise to me that people looked up to him.

I realize then that the Commander's mood is shifting. Coming face to face with the orphaned children of an old acquaintance must have stirred some kind of sympathy inside of him.

"You can all stay," he says.

I clasp Bree's hand with relief and let out the breath I'd been holding. Ben and Charlie audibly sigh their relief. But before we even have a chance to smile at one another, the Commander says something else, something that makes my heart clench.

"But the dog has to go."

Bree gasps.

"No!" she cries.

She wraps her arms more tightly around Penelope. Sensing she's become the subject of attention, the little Chihuahua wriggles in Bree's arms.

"No one stays at Fort Noix who cannot contribute," the Commander says. "That goes for animals as well. We have guard dogs, sheep dogs, and horses on the farms, but your little pet is useless to us. She absolutely cannot stay."

Bree dissolves into tears.

"Penelope isn't just a pet. She's the smartest animal in the world. She saved our life!"

I put my arm around Bree and pull her close into my side.

"Please," I say to the Commander, impassioned. "We're so grateful to you for letting us stay, but don't make us give up Penelope. We've already lost so much. Our home. Our parents. Our friends. Please don't make us give up our dog too."

Charlie looks at the Commander with concern in his eyes. He's trying to read the situation, to work out whether this is going to escalate into a fight like it always did back in the holding cells of Arena 2.

Finally, the Commander sighs.

"It can stay," he relents. "For now."

Bree turns her tear-stained eyes up to him. "She can?"

The Commander nods stiffly.

"Thank you," she whispers, gratefully.

Though the Commander's face remains emotionless, I can tell he's moved by our plight.

"Now," he says quickly, standing, "General Reece will assign you quarters and take you to them."

We all stand too. The Commander clamps a hand down on Bree's shoulder and begins steering her to the door. Then all at once we're shoved out into the corridor.

We stand there, shell-shocked, hardly comprehending what just happened.

"We got in," I state, blinking.

Ben nods, looking equally taken aback. "Yes. We did."

"This is home now?" Bree asks.

I squeeze her close into me. "It's home."

*

We follow General Reece outside past rows of small brick buildings, one story high, covered in branches to camouflage them.

"Males and females are separated," the General explains. "Ben, Charlie, you'll be staying here." She points at one of the brick buildings covered in thick ivy. "Brooke, Bree, you'll be across the street."

Ben frowns. "Don't people live with their families?"

The General stiffens a little. "None of us have families," she says, a hint of emotion in her voice for the first time. "When you desert the military, you don't get a chance to bring your husband, kids, or parents with you."

I feel a pang of sympathy in my gut. My dad wasn't the only person who deserted his family for a cause he believed in. And I wasn't the only person to abandon their mother.

"But hasn't anyone formed a family since?" Ben asks, pressing her further, as though oblivious to her emotional pain. "I thought you said you began repopulating."

"There are no families at the moment. Not yet, anyway. The community has to be controlled and stabilized to ensure we have enough food, space, and resources. We can't have people breeding whenever they want to. It must be regulated."

"*Breeding?*" Ben says under his breath. "That's a funny way of putting it."

The General purses her lips. "I understand that you have questions about how things work here, and I appreciate it may seem unusual to you from the outside. But Fort Noix has survived because of the rules we've put in place, because of our order. Our citizens understand and respect that."

"And so do we," I add, quickly. I turn and put an arm around my sister. "Come on, Bree, let's get inside. I'm looking forward to meeting our new housemates."

The General nods. "They'll show you the ropes from here on out. Follow them to lunch when it's time."

She gives us a salute, then walks away, taking her soldiers with her.

*

A cheerful American woman named Neena shows us around our new home. She's the "mother" of the house, which consists, she tells us, of a group of teenage girls and young women. She explains that the rest of our housemates are out working and that we'll meet them in the evening.

"Give you time to settle in," she says, smiling kindly. "A house full of twenty women can get a little much at times."

She shows us into a small, simple room with bunk beds.

"You two will need to share a room," she says. "It's not exactly a five-star resort."

I smile.

"It's perfect," I say, walking into the room.

Once again, I'm overwhelmed by the sensation of peace and safety. I can't remember the last time I stood in a room that smelled clean, that had been dusted and polished and vacuumed. Light streams through the window, making the room look even more welcoming.

For the first time in a long time, I feel safe.

Penelope likes it, too. She runs around happily in circles, jumping on the beds, wagging her tail and barking.

"I must say it's so exciting to have a dog in the house," Neena says. "The other girls are just going to love her."

Bree grins from ear to ear, every inch the proud owner.

"She's so smart for a dog," she says. "She saved our life once, when—"

I grab Bree's arm and squeeze it to quiet her. For some reason, I don't want what we've been through spoken about within our new home. I want it to be a new beginning for us, one free from the past. More than anything, I don't want anyone to know about the arenas if they don't have to. I've killed people. It will change the way they look at me, make them more cautious, and I don't know if I can cope with that right now.

Bree seems to understand what I'm trying to silently communicate. She lets her story disappear into the ether, and Neena doesn't seem to notice.

"There are things for you on the bed," she says. "Not much, just a few bits to tide you over."

On each of our beds are neatly folded clothes. They're made from the same dark material that General Reece and her army were wearing. The fabric is rough; I figure it must be home-grown cotton, colored by naturally made dyes and stitched into a uniform by the tailors she'd told us about.

"Do you girls want to wash before lunch?" Neena asks.

I nod and Neena takes me to the small bathroom that serves all twenty of the house's residents, before leaving me be. It's basic and the water is cold, but it feels amazing to be clean again.

When Bree comes back into our room after her own shower, she starts laughing.

"You look funny," she says to me.

I've changed into the stiff uniform that was left for me. Tendrils of hair hang over my shoulders, making wet patches in the fabric.

"It's itchy," I say, wriggling uncomfortably.

"Clean, though," Bree replies, running her fingertips against the fabric of her own uniform. "And *new.*"

I know what she means. It's been years since we had anything that was *ours*, that wasn't stolen or found or recycled. These are our clothes, never before worn. For the first time in a long time, we have possessions.

Along with the new clothes, we are also given towels, shoes, nightwear, a pencil, a pad of paper, a watch, a flashlight, a whistle, and a penknife. It's like a little welcome package. From what I've learned about the place so far, the contents seem very Fort Noix.

Neena leads us out of the house and along the street, and after a short stroll we come to a larger building. I look up. It has the air of a town hall, yet simple, anonymous.

We go inside and immediately the smell of food hits me. I start to salivate, while Bree's eyes widen. The room is filled with tables, most taken up by farm workers, recognizable from their muddy clothes and sun-blushed skin.

"There's Ben and Charlie," Bree says, pointing to a table.

I notice that both of them have plates piled high with food, and both are gorging themselves.

Neena must notice the look of want on my face because she smiles and says, "Go sit with them. I'll bring you over some food."

We thank her and go to sit with Charlie and Ben on a bench filled with farm workers. Everyone nods politely to us as we take seats. For a community that doesn't usually take in outsiders, they seem pretty accepting about the sudden appearance of four bedraggled, half-starved kids and a one-eyed Chihuahua.

"Someone's feeling more at home," I say to Ben as he rams another mouthful of food into his mouth.

But that same haunted look has returned to his eyes. He may be clean on the outside, but his mind appears to be polluted by the things he's been through. And though he's eating, he's doing so mechanically. Not in the same way Charlie does, as though he's relishing every single bite. Ben eats as though he can't even taste the food. What's more, he doesn't say a word as we take our places beside him, almost as though he hasn't noticed we're there. I can't help but worry for him. I've heard about people going through terrible ordeals only to then fall apart as soon as they reach safety. I pray that Ben won't be one of them.

I'm distracted when Neena returns with two plates of food, one for Bree and one for me, heaped with garlic-buttered chicken with roast potatoes and some kind of spicy zucchini and tomato side dish. I can't remember the last time I saw food that looked like this. It looks like something you could order in a restaurant.

I can't hold myself back. I begin wolfing it down, making my taste buds come to life. It's absolutely delicious. For so many years I subsisted on the plainest of foods, the tiniest of portions, and trained myself not to want more. Now, finally, I can let myself go.

Bree is a little more restrained. She gives a generous portion of chicken to Penelope before seeing to herself. I feel a little embarrassed by the way I devour my food as if my life depends on it, but table manners aren't exactly my priority right now.

Down the table, across from us, I can't help noticing a boy who looks a little older than me, feeding strips of meat to a pit bull terrier. The boy looks exactly like the type who'd own a pit bull. His head is shaved, and he has dark eyebrows, brooding eyes, and a cocky smile.

"Who's this?" he asks Bree, nodding at the Chihuahua.

"Penelope," she says. "And yours?"

"Jack," the boy says, rubbing the dog's neck playfully.

"I thought animals weren't allowed here," I say.

His eyes meet mine, smoldering, intense.

"He's a guard dog," he replies. Then he looks at Bree. "Do you reckon Penelope and Jack might want to be friends?"

Bree laughs. "Maybe."

They both set their dogs down on the ground. Straightaway the two begin to play, chasing each other and gently pawing at each other's face.

Then, to my surprise, Jack bounds right over to me, leaps into my lap, and plants a big, slobbery, hot lick across my face.

The others laugh, while I can't help laughing myself.

"I think he likes Brooke more than Penelope," Bree says with a grin.

"I think you might be right," the boy replies, fixing his gaze on me.

I finally manage to shove Jack off me, and as I wipe his drool from my cheek with my sleeve, the boy watches on, seemingly amused. He breaks apart a piece of bread with his strong fingers, and taps one edge into the juices on his plate.

"So," he says before taking a bite, "I'm guessing Brooke is your sister."

"Yes," Bree says. "And I'm Bree."

Even though his mouth is full, he says, "Ryan," and slides down the bench and stretches his hand out and shakes Bree's.

Then he offers it to me. I look up. His dark eyes bore into me, making a pit swirl in my stomach. The sensation reminds me of the first time I saw Logan: not the warm, slow-building feeling I got with Ben, but an instant, heart-stopping attraction. I don't want to touch him, worried that I'll somehow betray my attraction.

Immediately, I feel guilty for having any kind of attraction to him at all. It's only been a couple of hours since my dream about Logan. I still miss him.

I look at Ryan's outstretched hand suspiciously. I have no choice. He's not going to just put it down. I grasp it, hoping I can get the shaking over quickly. I turn my gaze back down to my meal, hoping he doesn't notice the blush in my cheeks.

Ryan's gaze stays on me as I eat. I can just about see his crooked smile from the corner of my eye. He's looking at me so intensely my heart begins to flutter.

"Your sister has a healthy appetite," he says, speaking to Bree but looking at me the whole time. "And butter on her chin."

Bree laughs but I feel self-conscious, my blush deepening.

"I was just joking," Ryan says. "No need to look so angry."

"I'm not angry," I reply sharply. "Just trying to eat in peace."

Ryan tips his head back and laughs; I'd been trying to get him off my back, but it seems as though my words have only encouraged him. His dark eyes twinkle.

"So *you're* the one from the arena," he says.

I swallow hard. "Who told you?"

Then I notice Charlie looking guilty beside me. He must have already spilled the beans about our ordeal. So much for a fresh start.

I don't say anything.

"I'm not judging you," Ryan says. "Actually, I'm impressed."

At these words, Ben looks over. He'd been in his own world this whole time, seemingly lost in his own thoughts, but now he's suddenly alert, a flash of jealousy in his eyes as he looks over at us.

"Have you just come back from the fields like the others?" I ask Ryan, trying to steer the conversation toward safe territory.

Ryan smiles to himself, as though pleased to finally have my attention. "Actually, I've been on guard duty this morning."

"Really?" I ask, genuinely interested. "How does that work?"

Ryan stretches out in his chair, making himself comfortable, as he begins his explanation.

"A group patrols the outer borders at all times, while a second group patrols inside, making sure everyone's keeping to the rules. And to make sure no one gets too power crazy, we take it in turns, in a rotation. Everyone has to do it, even the kids. I mean, you won't have to do it for a while since you're recuperating, but—"

"I want to," I say suddenly, interrupting him.

The idea of sitting around doing nothing fills me with horror. If I sit around idle, my mind might start playing tricks on me again. I'll see Rose and Flo. I'll see Logan. I don't know if my heavy heart could cope with seeing him again.

"Well, you will eventually—" Ryan begins.

"Now," I say, firmly. "Can I come on your shift with you?"

Ryan gives me a curious look, and I can see his eyes are filled with intrigue and respect.

"I'll see if General Reece is okay with me having a tagalong."

"Make that two," Ben says suddenly.

I look over at Ben, and for the first time since we got here, he seems to be fully lucid.

"You sure you're up for it?" I ask.

He nods, sternly. "If you think you're well enough to patrol, then I definitely am."

Ryan nods, looking equally as impressed by Ben as he did by me. But I'm not entirely convinced Ben is well enough to come. He looks haggard, his eyes rimmed with dark shadows, and I can't help but suspect that he only wants to come along because he doesn't want to leave me alone with Ryan.

And it's then that I wonder: what have I just gotten myself into?

CHAPTER FOUR

Ryan leads Ben and me across the length of Fort Noix, heading for the arsenal, and as we go, I feel satiated for the first time in months. My stomach is almost uncomfortably heavy. It feels good. It also feels good to be heading to guard duty, to have a mission, a purpose, and something to take my mind off everything. Without it, I think I might go crazy.

We pass plenty of people, all as clean and well fed as Ryan is; none have radiation scars or melted flesh from nuclear fallout. None are missing limbs or teeth or dragging a deformed leg behind them as they walk. I haven't seen so many healthy-looking humans in one place since before the war. It's almost disconcerting.

Ryan walks beside me but Ben lingers a few steps behind. There's an undeniably tense atmosphere, one I attempt to ignore by focusing all my attention on Jack the pit bull, who has been tagging closely at my heels as if I'm his master rather than Ryan.

"He's taken a shine to you," Ryan says with a chuckle.

Ben's head immediately snaps up. He frowns. I can't help but wonder why Ben insisted on coming with us. I don't want him lingering around me like a dark storm cloud, casting suspicious glances in my direction. We're on the same team, we always have been, and I don't like seeing him like this. It reminds me too much of the way he acted with Logan; jealous, wanting more from me than I am able to give.

At least Ryan doesn't seem to pick up on the tension. He strolls confidently across the compound, like someone who has never seen real death or destruction. Not like Ben and me, whose very steps seem to reveal our past torments.

"Here we go," Ryan says with an air of pride as he hauls open a huge steel door.

A cloud of dust swirls into the air, obscuring my vision. As it settles, I get my first glimpse of the treasures inside the arsenal. My mouth drops open as I step inside and take in the sight of pistols and sniper rifles, automatic crossbows and AK47s. I feel like a kid in a candy shop.

As I scan the walls, something catches my eye. A shotgun. It reminds me of the antique one Dad used to have displayed behind glass at home. I go over to it and pick it up.

"Are you sure you want to take that thing?" Ryan asks, as I test the weight of it in my hands. "Something smaller would be better for your stature."

In a matter of seconds, I lock and load the shotgun, before hitching it on my shoulder in firing position. I go through the motions expertly; thanks to Dad, I'm at ease with a shotgun.

"I think this one will suit me just fine," I say.

Ryan's eyes widen with surprise. He seems impressed by my knowledge of the weapons and I can't help but feel a surge of pride.

Ben narrows his eyes and grabs his own weapon, a rifle.

"So you guys have used guns before?" Ryan asks.

"Of course," Ben replies, a little too harshly.

I think back to the first time I met Ben, when we were speeding through the frozen wastelands chasing after the slaverunners who had kidnapped our siblings. He'd been useless with the gun, and had even dropped it at one point.

"Ben's more of a bow and arrow kind of guy," I say, gently mocking him, trying to coax him into the conversation.

Ben frowns, clearly not taking the joke well. Ben's always been sensitive, but he's clearly feeling more sensitive than usual. I remind myself to be more careful with him. I don't want him to think I'm making a joke at his expense or that I'm letting Ryan's jovial attitude rub off on me.

"No problem," Ryan says. "We have plenty of bows and arrows if you'd prefer."

"I'm fine with this," Ben answers tersely.

Ryan shrugs, once again seemingly oblivious to the building tension in the air.

I then notice a wall display of knives. I go over and see the same kind of knife my dad had when I was a kid, with a military insignia brandished into the handle. A wave of nostalgia washes over me.

I touch my fingertips to the cool metal blade. "Can I take this too?"

"Of course," Ryan replies, suddenly coming up very closely behind me. "Take what you want."

I can feel the warmth radiating from his body as I snatch up the knife, holding the weight of it in my hand. It feels like mine, like it was always supposed to be in my grasp. Then I dart out of Ryan's shadow, stashing the knife at my hip as I go. I load up with the gun on one shoulder, and a bow and arrow slung across my back.

Ryan whistles as he takes in the sight of me.

"Ready for duty," he says, giving me a light-hearted salute.

I can't help but smile to myself. I feel every inch a guard and I'm practically itching to get out there, to learn the ropes and prove to the Commander that I deserve my place here.

Ben, on the other hand, is fumbling around and getting frustrated with a twisted strap. Ryan goes over to help him. As he tightens his straps, I can't help but think that Ben looks like a lost, vulnerable child being dressed by his parent on their first day at school.

We head out of the arsenal and my stomach swirls with anticipation as I catch sight of the group of ten other guards up ahead that we'll be patrolling with. They've congregated by one of the huge iron barbed-wire-topped gates. A few dogs mill around, pawing tufts of grass at the base of the fence, sniffing the air, cocking their heads at every noise. It occurs to me that they've all been trained to help with patrolling and to offer protection against attacks. The Commander was right when he said everyone at Fort Noix has a job to do—even the animals. I'm grateful again that he conceded to keep Penelope, and I hope she gets a chance to prove that despite being the size of a cat and having only one eye, she's the smartest dog he'll ever meet.

Jack breaks away from us and rushes up to the other dogs, barking excitedly. His presence alerts the group to our approach. Heads begin to turn in our direction, taking in the sight of Ryan leading two strangers toward them. I can't help but feel like I'm being scrutinized, sized up, and I try to calm my racing heart. After all, this is nothing compared to the leering eyes of the biovictim spectators in the arenas.

Ben doesn't seem to be faring as well as me, though. As we get closer to the group, I can see his face becoming paler. He's not ready for this at all. Being with strangers, packing weaponry—it's all too much for him, like being back in an arena. I don't get a chance to tell him to turn around and go home, though, because we're suddenly at the entrance. Ryan's clapping people on the back, reeling out names that fly in one ear and out the other. The only one that sticks is Molly, because the girl it belongs to has shockingly ginger hair.

She looks over at me.

"You're living with Neena, right?" she asks with a friendly grin. She looks about my age, with bright green eyes and freckles across her nose.

I nod, a little overwhelmed by all the names and faces.

"Me too," she replies. "I guess that makes us roomies."

Roomies. The word seems alien to me, like it's a term that belonged to an old, ancient world that I thought had ceased to exist. Not for the first time since arriving here, a wave of happiness washes over me. I have a feeling she might become a friend. *Friend*. A word I had never thought to use again.

The group begins to move and we follow, sticking close to Ryan and Molly. We pass through several layers of fencing, guards stationed at the gates of each one. The amount of security they have here is crazy, but I understand their need to be so heavy-handed. The only way to keep the people inside Fort Noix safe is by making it impenetrable to all the monsters lurking outside.

Between one row of fencing and the next, nestled in the trees, I see a row of wooden cabins.

"Do you guys stay in those overnight?" I ask Molly.

She shakes her head. "No, people live in them."

"Really?"

Before Molly has a chance to reply, Ryan speaks up, practically salivating at the opportunity to impart his wisdom.

"We call them the Forest Dwellers," he says. "They're sort of a part of Fort Noix but not at the same time."

"Why?" I ask.

"Well, not everyone wants to live by military command. They want to structure their lives differently. They want to have families, homes, pets, that sort of thing. You know, the whole men and women being separated thing isn't so great for that." He smiles and wiggles a knowing eyebrow. I blush and avert my gaze as he continues. "Anyway, they've all taken the pledge to keep the fort secret, so they're pretty much a part of us really, especially as they are within our perimeter. They're just not on the same job rotation system—and they don't get rations."

Just then I notice a barefoot young girl sitting on the wooden doorstep of one of the cabins. In her lap sits a huge rabbit with light brown fluffy fur, which she strokes gently. As we pass, she looks up and waves. I wave back. She must take it as an invitation to come over, because she places the rabbit on the ground, leaps to her feet, and bounds over. Her patchwork dress swishes as she skips toward us, and her blond ponytail bobs.

"Oh, here we go," Molly says under her breath while rolling her eyes, giving me the distinct impression that she's not much of a maternal type.

"Trixie," Ryan says in a gentle warning tone as she draws up beside him. "You know you can't come on patrols with us. It's far too dangerous."

"I just wanted to say hello to the new people," the little girl says breezily.

24

She's absolutely adorable. I can hardly believe that such a smiley, carefree child can exist in our brutal world.

"I'm Brooke," I say to Trixie. "And this is Ben."

I look around for my companion, realizing he'd been so quiet I'd completely forgotten about him. The whole time that I've been chatting with Molly and Ryan he's been silent, just taking it all in. As I look at him now, I can see how distracted he seems, looking over his shoulder, flinching at every noise. My worry for him magnifies.

"Do you want to come to my house to play?" Trixie says to me, breaking through my thoughts.

Her sweetness and innocence warms my heart. She can't have seen any of the atrocities of the war, or have the constant terror of being kidnapped by slaverunners at the back of her mind. She's carefree, just as a child ought to be.

"I'd love to," I say, "but I'm on guard duty. It's my job to protect you."

Trixie beams up at me. "Well then maybe another day," she says. "My mom will make you soup if you like. Dad made a Scrabble board out of wood. Do you like Scrabble? My sister's better than me at it but it's still my favorite game."

The thought of hanging out with a family playing games and eating soup seems like a dream come true.

"That sounds like a lot of fun," I reply, feeling a strange pang in my stomach as I realize that I haven't played a game since before the war, that my childhood, and the lives of many, many others, was cut short by all the fighting. "Maybe I'll be able to come back and see you," I finish.

This seems to placate Trixie. She trots off back to her home, although not before stroking each one of the guard dogs.

"She's so cute," I say to Ryan as I watch her skip away. "I can't believe she lives out here with her family. She seems so carefree."

"She is," Ryan replies. "That's part of our job. We're not just protecting the fort, we're protecting everyone we can."

A strong wave of happiness washes through me, telling me I'm exactly where I need to be.

Finally we pass through the perimeter fence and head farther into the woods. It's colder out in the open and the ground beneath my boots is frozen, crunching underfoot. The new boots Neena gave me prevent any of the cold seeping in like my old, worn leather ones used to. The strange uniform is pretty good at keeping out the cold too.

"So, where is it that you guys are from?" Molly asks Ben and me, sounding genuinely interested.

She has a soft Canadian accent, which invites me in and tells me I can trust her. But I'm reticent to tell her about the arenas and everything we've been through. The thought of making a friend, a real friend, is so tempting. I don't want to scare her off by revealing my gladiatorial past. No one wants to make friends with a killer.

"The Catskills," I reply. "New York."

Her eyebrows rise with interest. "New York? How did you end up in Quebec?"

Logan. That's the real answer. He always believed in this place and urged us to come here. But I can't tell Molly that. I can't even let his name pass my lips.

"There was a rumor about Fort Noix, about survivors," I say. "We thought we'd risk it."

Ben looks at me inquisitively, silently noting my inability to utter the name of our dead companion.

This time, Molly's eyes widen. "You'd better not tell the Commander that there are rumors about this place. He's terrified about anyone finding out about us. I mean you guys are the first outsiders we've welcomed in a long, long time. He seems to think the whole fort will implode if anyone finds out about our existence."

"He's right to think that," Ben says, a little too abruptly. "You'd all be in danger if the slaverunners found out about this place."

Molly gives him curious look, one that seems to suggest that she's seen through him, into his soul, and has glimpsed the darkness inside. But she doesn't challenge him, and I'm grateful.

The outpost is a little ways away from Trixie's cabin. It's a tall metal structure that stretches far up into the canopy. The climb is at least thirty feet. Molly enthusiastically begins to scale the ladder, showing off her strength. But I falter. Because as I stand at the base of it, I get a sudden flash of memory of the horrible sand dune we had to climb in Arena 2.

"You need help climbing up?" Ryan asks.

I shake my head, dislodging the memory, then grip the rungs. I'm determined not to be weak, not to let the things I've been through in the past affect me now. I take a breath to steel myself and begin to climb, Ryan following right behind. My muscles protest but I push through my pain, and after a few moments I'm at the top.

The effort was worth it. Up here at the top, there's an amazing view all around. The mountains look beautiful, with their snow-capped peaks glittering in the midday sunlight. I let the air stir the hair at the base of my neck, cooling the sweat from the effort of climbing. I completely tune out the sound of the rest of the guards clambering into the outpost, and revel in the tranquility of the moment.

Far in the distance, I can see huge craters in the earth where the bombs hit. It makes me so sad to think of all of the needless destruction, all the death and pain, and I wonder if our world really ever can recover. But then I realize that the craters are overgrown with vegetation, as though nature is trying to eradicate the disastrous effects our war has had, trying to heal the scars and gashes our bombs created. The sight gives me hope for a better future. All at once, a smile bursts across my face.

From the corner of my eye, I can see Ryan watching me intently. I squirm under his scrutiny and let my smile fade. For some reason, I don't want him encroaching on my private moment. When he approaches I don't look at him, keeping my gaze steadily ahead.

"I don't think your friend is enjoying the view as much as you are," his voice quips into my ear.

I look behind and see Ben, his gun huddled in his arms, looking overwhelmed.

"It's the height," I say, knowing exactly why Ben is freaking out, knowing he must have had the same horrible flash of memory as I had. "We had to climb up a mountain in one of the arenas. It was full of spikes that bludgeoned kids to death."

I shut my mouth immediately. I don't know what came over me, what made me blab about such a painful secret from my past to Ryan like that.

"Oh," he says, his mocking smile immediately disappearing. He looks suddenly serious for the first time since I've met him. "Sorry, I didn't realize."

A feeling of intense awkwardness overcomes me.

"You couldn't have known," I reply quickly, trying to end the conversation.

On the other side of the post, Molly takes a seat beside another guard and pulls out a pack of cards. I'm shocked and a little taken aback to see her, and the other guards around her, looking so lax. No one seems to be alert at all. The Commander made it seem as though everyone at Fort Noix was as serious and militaristic as he is, but here are his guards lazing around.

"Don't worry," Ryan says, clocking my expression. "Nothing ever happens on guard duty. There were attacks at the beginning but these days it's calmed down a lot."

But it's not enough to placate me. Everyone back at the fort is relying on these guys to do their job and here they all are sitting around like it's a big game. Even the guard dogs are slacking off, play fighting with one another rather than looking out for intruders. So much for everyone has a job to do! Only Ben and I seem to be alert to the possibility of lurking danger.

Just as those thoughts are crossing my mind, I notice movement coming from the distance. In the area pocked with bomb craters there's a patch of trees and shrubbery, and it seems to be rustling.

"Do people live over there?" I say, nudging Ryan.

He peers out where I'm pointing.

"In the bomb craters?" he says. "No way. The radiation levels are too high."

Every muscle in my body tenses. "There's someone there," I say.

I bring up my shotgun. The motion alerts Ben. He comes to my side, poised with his rifle.

"Whoa, whoa, whoa!" Ryan cries. "You guys are getting a bit trigger happy. I'm sure you're seeing things. It's probably just a deer."

Molly notices the commotion and comes to my side.

"What's going on, Brooke?" she asks, her expression serious and intent.

"There are people in the trees," I say, not looking at her, my body still positioned to fire, my eyes still locked on the foliage, seeking out possible danger.

Unlike Ryan, Molly doesn't contest me. She seems to have understood me straightaway. She raises her own gun, taking position beside me.

The trees continue to rustle. Then all at once, something huge and black billows from the foliage. I let off a shot, the noise splintering the air. It's only after I've fired that I realize my evil predator was a flock of innocent birds.

The tenseness leaves my body in one go, replaced by embarrassment. Molly gives me a sheepish look, as if she's embarrassed on my behalf by my overreaction. Ryan just grins, amused by the whole thing.

"Told you there was nothing to worry about," he says, arrogantly.

But no sooner are the words out of his mouth, than the sounds of screaming and frantic barking come from behind.

I spin and my heart drops as I see that, just on the other side of the outpost, near the ladder leading up, a group of crazies are thundering out of the vegetation. They're heading right for us.

Ryan's slow to react. "Breach!" he finally shouts.

Immediately, I fire my gun at them, but my angle is off and I miss my target. The guards seem stunned, like they were never expecting such a thing to happen. They take far too long to react. By the time they join me, I've finally managed to hit one of the crazies, and he goes down like a dead weight.

At last, guns begin firing off all over the place. The noise is so loud I wince. The air becomes thick with smoke from the shots we're firing and the smell of sulfur.

The crazies start to drop, but some are getting dangerously close to our outpost. I adjust my position and begin firing as they ascend. Ben stands beside me but I realize he isn't firing his gun at all. His hands are trembling and sweat is pouring down his face. He's as white as a ghost.

"Ben!" I cry. "Help me!"

But he's completely frozen. It's Ryan who sidles up to me and helps me take down the group, one by one, while Molly flanks my other side, firing expertly, too.

Suddenly, I hear a shrill scream from behind and swirl on the spot. One of the crazies must have taken a different route than the others and has gotten up the outpost without anyone noticing. It dawns on me that not a single one of the guards thought to cover us from behind, leaving us completely exposed.

The crazy's arm is locked around Molly's throat and he's dragging her back toward the ladder. I watch, horrified, as Jack bounds forward and locks his jaws around the crazy's leg. The man roars in pain and loosens his grip on Molly, leaving just enough for her to run away. But now Jack's the source of his hatred. He grabs the pit bull and yanks him off, bringing him over his head, ready to hurl him off the outpost. The whole world seems to slow down as I notice the terrified dog's expression as he hangs helplessly over the edge of the outpost. The thirty-foot drop will certainly kill him.

Without even thinking, I pull my knife from its sheath and race across the length of the outpost. With every ounce of strength in my body, I stab the crazy straight in the heart.

The crazy's eyes roll back in his head and he falls backward. I manage to wrench Jack from his grasp before the crazy plummets over the side of the outpost and hits the ground with a sickening squelch.

My blood-soaked knife clatters to the floor, and then, all at once, quiet descends. I stand there panting, Jack whimpering in my arms, the warm blood of the crazy dripping down my face. Slowly, I turn back to face the other guards.

They're all looking at me in disbelief, as though they can hardly comprehend what I just did. I can't tell if they're scared of me or in awe of me, but the main thing is that my secret life as a killer can no longer be hidden.

I cradle Jack in my arms then slowly approach Ryan. I place the dog in his arms. His cocky expression has completely gone. His arrogance seems to have faded, too, leaving behind a stunned and slightly alarmed expression.

"Thank you," he says, quietly. But I think what he really means is, "I get it now." For the first time he understands what sort of world we really live in, and what sort of person it has made me.

Everyone else seems too stunned to move. I feel I have no choice but to take control of the situation.

"We should report back to the Commander," I say, trying to hide the tremor in my voice. "That attack wasn't accidental. It was planned. That means there might be more to come."

CHAPTER FIVE

Twilight is breaking by the time we make it back to the fort. Up ahead I see a group of guards who must have returned from guard duty before us sitting around a bonfire, chatting away without a care in the world. They begin whispering when they notice us trudging wearily toward them.

A tall, lanky man with a goatee comes up to us.

"What happened to you lot?" he says, smirking.

"A breach," Molly explains.

Immediately, the man's expression changes. "What do you mean?"

"We were attacked," Ryan adds. "By a group of crazies."

The rest of the group begins to take notice of the conversation. They stand up from their positions around the bonfire and come over, listening intently, looks of concern on their faces.

"Did anyone get hurt?" the man with the goatee asks.

Ryan shakes his head. "Thankfully not. But if it hadn't been for Brooke, there might have been fatalities."

I shift uncomfortably as everyone's attention turns to me, the stranger, taking in the sight of my blood-splattered uniform. But rather than looking scared of me like the others who'd seen me kill the crazy at the outpost, they look at me with respect. People start congratulating me, clapping me on the shoulder. Zeke, the man with the goatee, salutes me.

I can't believe it. I'd been so worried about people finding out about me being a killer and judging me for it, it's quite a relief for it all to be out in the open. I can't remember the last time I felt accepted like this.

"Someone get this girl a drink!" Zeke says, before adding, "We don't have liquor, I'm afraid, so I hope you like mint tea."

"That sounds great," I say, but I'm still in fight-or-flight mode. "But we should report to the Commander."

Zeke shakes his head and rests a hand on my arm. "Don't. It will just make him more paranoid."

"But…" I begin, but he interrupts me.

"Honestly," he says, passing me a mint tea. "The Commander is becoming more and more isolated. We take in fewer survivors every year. To be honest, I'm surprised he even let you guys stay. We've kicked kids out younger than you before. If he knows the attack came so soon after you arrived, he'll probably blame it on you, saying you led them here. So if I were you, I wouldn't give him more reasons to turn people away."

The heat from the tea seeps into my skin as his words seep into my mind. It hadn't occurred to me that not everyone within Fort Noix would be on board with the way the Commander chooses to run things. But, like the Forest Dwellers I saw earlier, it seems as though not everyone is happy with how things work here, with the Commander's stance on not taking in outsiders. My gut instinct back when I'd met him in his office earlier this morning had been revulsion—to not take in outsiders is the equivalent of sentencing them to death. But then I'd gotten so caught up in it all, in being a guard, in protecting this precious place, that I'd let myself forget how cruel that policy really is.

Just then, I hear a voice calling me from far away.

"Brooke!"

It's Bree. I turn and see her running along the path toward me, Charlie just a few steps behind. Neena walks a little way behind them both with Penelope on a lead. Some of the girls and women from our house are walking beside her, and the boys from Ben's house are also coming toward the bonfire.

Bree reaches me, flies into my arms, and hugs me tightly. I hold her close.

"What happened?" she cries, moving out of the embrace. "You were gone for hours. I was worried."

I smile at her reassuringly. "I'm OK."

"Is Jack okay?" Bree asks, bending down to stroke the pit bull at Ryan's feet.

"He's fine," Ryan says to Bree, but his eyes are locked on me. "Thanks to Brooke."

Over Bree's crouched figure, Ryan's smoldering eyes burn into me. Before, I wasn't sure what he thought about me, but now I do. He admires me. My stomach flutters at the thought.

"Where's Ben?" Charlie asks.

Immediately, I feel guilty for letting myself feel anything toward Ryan at all. I glance around, searching for Ben. I see him sitting on a bench, alone, beside the fire. He looks just as lost back at the fort as he did out in the forest.

"There he is," I say to Charlie. "Why don't you go and get him some tea?"

"I'll get it," Ryan says, his intense gaze still fixed on me.

I falter. "Okay… thanks."

I watch, my stomach roiling, as he disappears into the crowd.

Bree grabs my hand and drags me toward the bonfire. Charlie follows, and the three of us sit down beside Ben. Despite the danger we've just been in, we're all still overjoyed to be at Fort Noix. To be warm, clothed, and cared for. To be amongst allies. But Zeke has planted a seed of doubt in my mind. Is it enough for just *us* to be warm, clothed, and cared for? Is it okay to sit on our laurels when others like us die out in the wilderness at the hands of slaverunners, biovictims, and crazies?

Ryan comes back with more mint tea and some chicken soup for us all.

"Do you want to join us?" I ask him.

I want to speak to him about the Commander's isolationist position, about his hard-line policy on not letting in survivors. But Ryan casts his eyes over at Ben, and I look over to see that Ben's watching us, his expression a mixture of anger and sadness.

"Not tonight," Ryan says. "You guys should probably spend some time together."

So Ryan's starting to figure it out, to understand that there's something between Ben and me, or at least, that Ben feels something for me. He's not prepared to tread on Ben's toes when he's in such a fragile state, and I'm grateful for his thoughtfulness. It seems there's more to Ryan than meets the eye.

I nod and watch him take the bench opposite with Molly, whose ginger hair matches the color of the flames.

The soup tastes absolutely delicious. The heat from the bowl and the fire, along with the fresh, healthy food, rejuvenates me. I feel like I'm coming back from the dead, not just physically but psychologically too. For years I've been in battle mode. For years I've felt completely alone. But now I have people around me, people who will fight beside me. And it's the greatest feeling in the world.

I look over at Bree and Charlie laughing happily, as carefree as Trixie had been when I met her earlier. Finally they're getting to be children. But Ben is a different matter altogether. He seems even more withdrawn.

"Ben," I say cautiously. "Is everything okay?"

He looks at me slowly, a little dazed. "It's just being around all these people," he says. "It's a bit overwhelming."

I know it's more than that, but I don't want to push him to speak when he doesn't want to.

Everyone finishes their soup.

"I think you kids should be heading home now," I say to Bree and Charlie. They both look exhausted, like they're fighting to stay awake so they can be part of the festivities.

Bree pouts. "Can't we stay up a little longer?"

I shake my head. "It's been a long day. Ben will take you home."

Ben looks over at me and frowns, like he thinks I'm trying to get rid of him, when really I just want him to get a good night's sleep and rejuvenate. But he doesn't argue; he just stands, as though hypnotized, and leads Charlie and Bree back home.

I watch them go. But as soon as I'm alone, I feel suddenly out of place surrounded by the other guards, all laughing and joking easily. For me, smiles come rarely. The past constantly lingers in my mind like a storm cloud, only parting occasionally to let in a ray of sunshine. None of these people have the same darkness inside of them. I should be feeling peaceful and happy right now, but I can't. I can't just see the crazy attack as a one-off to be forgotten, because for me it was just the latest battle in my long, never-ending fight against the world we live in. And while we won that particular fight, somewhere in the world, another group of children loses.

Ryan must notice my change in mood, because he comes over and extends his hand to me.

"Come on," he says.

"Where are we going?" I reply, looking at his outstretched hand.

"For a walk." He beckons, urging me on. "Come on," he presses.

I don't feel like I have much choice but to take his hand and let him guide me to my feet.

We walk. It's pitch black and the stars are twinkling above us as we stroll away from the light of the fire and out into the compound.

"Brooke, I know that you think the way the fort works isn't fair," he begins.

"What makes you say that?" I reply. "I understand why it has to work this way. I just don't think that it's enough for me."

"What do you mean?" he asks.

I pause, trying to gather my thoughts in such a way that I can articulate them. "I mean I have to do more," I begin, carefully. "I can't live with myself knowing others are out there dying. I need to do something. I can't be part of a place that doesn't do more to help people. It would make me a hypocrite."

"Does that mean you want to leave?" he asks, frowning.

I turn my face, unsure myself what I really want. It's true that I've started to question whether I've made the right call by coming here. Can I really sit back, after everything I've witnessed, and live out my life in peace, knowing that there's a thousand more Roses out there who need saving, a hundred more Flos trapped in the arenas, a dozen more Logans who have been forced into policing a city they loathe? But at the same time, how could I force my friends and my sister back out into that world? I couldn't. If I left, I would have to go alone. And that would mean leaving them behind.

Ryan gently touches my arm. Warmth radiates from the place where his fingertips touch me. "I don't want you to leave, Brooke," he says. "Will you stay? For me?"

I move my arm away, a little startled by the contact, by the intensity of what he's asking me.

"I can't promise that," I say, not meeting his eye. But I know it's not enough, that I owe him more of an explanation. I take a breath then turn to meet his gaze. "Bree and I survived in the mountains for years. So did Ben and his brother. There are thousands more kids out there who don't have anyone to help them. There are so many more survivors."

"And you think it's our responsibility to be out there looking for them?" he challenges me.

"Don't you?" I say, my tone becoming more heated. "Don't you think we ought to help the innocent survivors of the war?"

I sigh, frustrated by the fact that Ryan and the rest of the people at Fort Noix have no idea at all what the real world is like now. It's not their fault that they've been completely protected from it all, but I can't help but feel the sting of injustice. That one random crazy attack can shake them to the core when for me, it's an everyday occurrence.

Ryan gives me a steely look. "I understand why you're angry. And trust me, you're not the only one who thinks that way. It's a controversial topic around here. But the Commander is an isolationist. It's what he fundamentally believes. It's kept us all alive so far, so why would he ever change it?"

He sighs when he sees that I'm still frowning.

"We do what we can, Brooke. We found you, didn't we? We took you in."

"That's not enough," I contest. "Four kids and a dog, when there's thousands out there. There are girls being kidnapped for the sex trade. There are kids fighting to the death for the entertainment of others. You're an army, trained fighters. You could make a difference."

His mouth twists to the side in consternation. I can tell that my words are getting to him. But at the same time, I know he's not going to change his mind. And why would he? Fort Noix is paradise for all who live within it. No one wants to rock the boat, or risk losing it all. Fighting off a bunch of crazies is one thing—willingly seeking them out is quite another.

Ryan lowers his voice and looks around cautiously, as if debating whether to tell me something.

"There are people who want to help others outside Fort Noix," he says. "There's actually a group who meet to discuss it."

"There is?" I say, relieved to hear that.

He nods.

"Zeke and Molly are among them. But you have to keep it quiet. The only way the Commander can keep the peace is by maintaining everything exactly as it is."

I understand the need for secrecy, but I'm intrigued and want to know more.

"So what's their plan?" I ask. "What do they propose to do? Bring survivors back to Fort Noix?"

Ryan shrugs.

"I don't know. They're not rebelling or anything like that. They're just trying to build their numbers in order to persuade the Commander that it's what people want. If there's enough, he might listen."

"Do you think that will work?" I add. "Is he the sort of man who can be persuaded?"

He shrugs.

"It hasn't worked so far," Ryan replies.

I think about my meeting with the Commander earlier in the day. He'd been hard-line about us not joining Fort Noix, but I'd managed to convince him to change his mind. About Penelope too. There's leeway in him, definitely.

"I'd like to meet them," I say, "the others who want to search for survivors."

Ryan nods. "I'll take you to a meeting," he says. "If it's a way to get you to stay." He suddenly shoves his hands into his pockets and looks shy.

"Thanks," I reply, grateful for the darkness that is hiding my blush.

"Brooke," he says hurriedly, "I know it's early but…I wanted to ask you if maybe one day you'd want to go on a date with me? I mean, I know 'date' isn't really the right word for it anymore, but I just mean, well…you know what I mean."

His voice drops as he speaks and his gaze falls to my lips. I realize he's thinking about kissing me.

I want to say yes to a date, want to consent to a kiss, but something inside is holding me back. It's the shadow of Logan in my mind. It's the echo of Ben's kiss on my lips. And it's the horror of everything I've been through.

Ryan must sense my hesitation because he starts to rub his neck awkwardly. "Sorry, bad timing on my part, right? I mean we almost all died today and here I am asking you on a date."

"I'd love to," I interrupt him with a hurried whisper. "But I can't. Not now. Not yet."

"Because of what you went through in the arenas?" he asks.

I glance away, feeling suddenly uncomfortable and embarrassed.

"I have to figure out how to live in this new world first," I say. "I've spent so long fighting, I don't know who I am anymore. Do you understand?"

He looks a little hurt, but nods all the same.

Just then, I feel something cold land on my nose. It feels like rain, but softer. I look up and see that it's starting to snow.

"Winter comes early in Quebec," Ryan explains.

I keep gazing up, watching the snowflakes fall. I feel happy and content, grateful to be alive and well fed. But I also feel like staying at Fort Noix forever just won't be possible.

Out of the corner of my eye I can see Ryan watching me, studying me, trying to work me out.

"Will you at least stay for the winter?" Ryan says. "After everything you've been through, you deserve that much, don't you? It's not selfish to want to recuperate and rest. And you can help far more people in the spring. You don't know what our winters are like here."

I don't answer, but keep looking up at the falling snow, reflecting the twinkling starlight. I don't want to promise Ryan anything I won't be able to give.

"If you won't stay for me," he adds, quietly, "stay for Ben."

Finally, my head snaps over to look at Ryan. "What do you mean?" I challenge him.

"I've seen guys like that before," Ryan says. "I'm worried he might have PTSD."

I nod. I'd been thinking the same thing.

"You know everyone has to work here, right?" he adds. "The Commander isn't particularly kind when it comes to things like that."

"What do you mean?" I whisper.

"I mean the Commander wouldn't keep a useless soldier around. He doesn't have the resources or the motivation to rehabilitate damaged people."

My insides turn to ice at the thought of Ben being turfed out of Fort Noix and left to fend for himself when at his most vulnerable. If I'd had any concerns about leaving my friends and sister before, they're now magnified by ten times. If the Commander finds out about Ben's PTSD, he'll be kicked out for sure.

Which means for now, I have no choice but to stay and look after him.

I'll stay, I realize.

At least for now, I'll stay.

SIX MONTHS LATER

CHAPTER SIX

"Brooke! Brooke! Brooke!"

The crowd is cheering my name. My heartbeat races. My palms are sweaty. I start to tremble as I raise my bow. I poise, holding my stance, whispering a silent prayer under my breath. Then I let my arrow fly.

Bull's-eye.

I hit my target dead center. Flooded with relief, I turn to face the audience and squint against the spring sunshine. As my eyes orient to my surroundings, I remember where I am. Not in an arena, but on the firing range in Fort Noix: a big grassy field, beautiful and tranquil, peppered with the first flowering buds of spring. I'm not fighting to the death, but taking part in Fort Noix's annual shooting competition.

Beside me, Molly takes her own shot, hitting the bull's-eye too.

"Molly, Molly, Molly!" the crowd chants.

My competitiveness is set alight. Molly and I are the last two left in the knock-out competition. Now we have to go head to head, taking on an assault course, shooting moving targets that pop up as we go. It's made up of cars, tires, ropes, and climbing nets and has become my favorite thing to do in training. In fact, I've done it so many times now, I know how to jump and weave like a ninja.

A horn blares and we're off. I leap from one car hood onto a net, swiveling around to fire a shot at the target that's just popped up behind me. I get it right between the eyes and it pops back down again.

I quickly climb up the rope and heave myself onto a platform. Immediately another target pops up down below me. I crouch down and fire. I hit my target and it pops down again. The crowd starts cheering.

I shimmy down the netting on the other side and race past the tire stack. A target appears the other side. I can just about see it through a gap in the tires. I shoot through the hole and it disappears. Straightaway, another appears at the end of the stack, just by the finish line. I race toward it and shoot it out of my way, not even slowing down in the process. The crowd screams and cheers as I pass over the finishing line.

I've won.

"Brooke! Brooke! Brooke!"

Panting, I bend forward, exhausted from my run, and let the sound of the cheering crowd filter into my mind, reminding myself that it is not the braying cry of biovictims but the cheer and support of my friends and allies. I catch sight of my instructor, General Reece, standing in her typical arms folded pose. There's a sliver of a smile on her lips, one that tells me she's pleased with my performance.

"The winner of our annual shooting competition," she announces, "is Brooke Moore!"

In the audience I see Bree and Charlie going wild and feel a swell of pride. Over the last six months that we've been in Fort Noix, they've both grown. Bree celebrated her eleventh birthday and is looking more like a teenager every day. It's amazing what a healthy diet of vegetables and meat can do to a girl.

Neena's also in the audience, looking on proudly like the surrogate mother she has become to me. Neena's one of the kindest women I've ever had the pleasure of knowing. She takes good care of all the girls in the house, making sure our bedding is clean and our clothes are mended, and though she can be fierce, life is harmonious.

But then I catch sight of Ben. He's clapping in the muted, emotionless way I've come to now expect from him. I feel a knot form in my stomach. I'm surprised that he even came to watch me compete since he's been doing everything he can to keep his distance from me.

Molly and Ryan come over to congratulate me on my win, quickly distracting me from my thoughts.

"And this is the girl who said she wasn't going to compete," Ryan says, kissing me on the cheek cordially.

It's true. It took General Reece more than a bit of encouragement to get me to compete. I was terrified about standing in front of an audience again after everything I've been through in the arenas, worried it would cause another flashback. But having people cheer me for my skill rather than bray for my blood is beyond healing. My only wish is that she could have convinced Ben to take part as well, but he hasn't touched a weapon since that first night at the outpost.

"Typical," Molly says, rolling her eyes playfully. "Even when Brooke doesn't want to do something she's still better than the rest of us!"

I can't help but smile. Their support means the world to me. Since Ben seems to be drifting further and further away from me, sometimes I think their friendship is the only thing that's keeping me going.

"So," I say, "do I get a medal or anything?"

Molly laughs. "It's not quite that easy to become a decorated soldier at Fort Noix," she tells me, knowingly. "Your reward is just to bask in your own triumph."

"That's good enough for me," I reply, jovially.

It's not just my mind that's been rejuvenated by the last six months living and working in Fort Noix. It's my body. I've put on weight, my muscles are stronger, and all my wounds are healed. The snake bite is now nothing more than a cool silvery scar on my calf.

Bree and Charlie run over to me, Penelope yapping at their heels. When they reach me, they throw their arms around me and Penelope licks my hand. Watching them flourish is the best reward of all.

"Want to come to Trixie's?" Bree asks me once she releases me from her bear hug. "Charlie and me are going to play Jenga."

Charlie and Bree have been spending all their free time with the Forest Dwellers, particularly Trixie and her family, learning how to forage and playing games. Trixie's dad carved a Jenga set, which has been well played ever since.

"I'd love to," I say. "But I have plans."

I glance up at Ryan shyly. He smirks. Bree looks from me to Ryan then nods knowingly at Charlie. They think something romantic is happening between us, but really it's not. At least, I don't think it is. It's just that we've been spending a lot of time together out in the forest, hunting and fishing together, as well as discussing our positions at Fort Noix, and the Commander's isolationism. Because while I love seeing the kids thrive, I also know in my heart that I can't stay here forever. I need to go out looking for survivors. I have a moral duty. Ben's been safe under the radar for six months. I can't put my life on hold for someone who doesn't seem to want to know me anymore.

"Shall we?" Ryan says, gesturing toward the path that will lead us into the forest.

I can practically feel Ben's glare from here. I don't like hurting him, but I can't just stay on pause forever. He's the one pulling away from me, not the other way round.

I nod, and leave with Ryan.

*

The woods have become my favorite place. As much as I love Fort Noix and how well it runs, like a well-oiled machine, nothing can beat the peace and tranquility of the forest. If there's any good to have come out of the war, it's that nature is getting the chance to reclaim the earth. My only wish is that if civilization ever recovers, we don't destroy the environment again.

Ryan and I go straight to the river to check on the poles. Eating the food supplied by Fort Noix is one thing, but catching our own fresh food and cooking it on the bonfire is quite another.

We find that we've both had catches. I tug on my line and pull out a trout, its scales glistening in the spring daylight.

"Nice catch," Ryan says when he sees it.

He's smiling, but I don't feel like returning the gesture.

"What's wrong?" he asks, when he notices my lackluster expression. "Anyone would think you'd just lost the shooting competition!"

I take a deep breath. "Spring is here," I say. "And I think it's time to leave."

Ryan's expression falls. He always knew this day would come, but I think he's been hoping that I'd change my mind.

"Is that still what you want?" Ryan asks.

I turn back to the water. It's clear and glistening. The beauty of it is astounding. I wish I didn't have to leave this peace and tranquility behind when I've only just found it.

"It is," I say, hesitantly.

"But?" he presses, picking up on my undercurrent.

"But." I pause. "But what exactly will the future hold? The country. Civilization. Will we ever get that back?"

Ryan shakes his head and lets out a little laugh. "Saving people's lives isn't enough for Brooke. She needs to save the world."

I know he's only joking but I can't help but feel a little riled.

"Well, why not?" I demand. "What's so bad about wanting everything back to the way it was before? Fort Noix is basically a normal town in many ways. If they can do it, we can do it somewhere else. Replicate the model."

"I think you're getting a bit ahead of yourself."

I huff and bend down to check my pole again. There's another trout wriggling on the end. I scoop it out of the water and lay it on the bank. It gasps its last breaths before falling still.

"Maybe I am being idealistic," I say, "but saving a few lives here and there isn't going to make a huge amount of difference. We need to start rebuilding the country. I wish..." I pause, struggling to get out my feelings. "I wish you would support me."

"Hey," Ryan says softly. "I'm sorry. I just don't want you to die. Is that so bad?" Then he rests his hand on my arm. "How about we deal with the future when we get there?"

I fall silent and we stand there side by side. Then I feel him slide his hand down to my hand. For a brief moment, I let his fingers lace through mine. Then I pull away.

Ryan doesn't say a word. He doesn't question me or press me. He hasn't for the last six months.

I look at him. His eyes are burning with desire, his gaze fixed on my lips. I'm overwhelmed with the desire to kiss him.

All at once, we hear a twig snap and the sound of pounding footsteps. We leap apart as Molly appears, frantic, running through the shrubbery, her cheeks as red as her hair.

"What is it?" I ask, suddenly terrified.

"A message!" she says, panting.

Ryan frowns. "A message? What do you mean?"

"A transmission," Molly says again. "On the radio. Someone's contacted us from a camp in America."

Ryan and I exchange a disbelieving look. I can hardly believe it to be true. A survivors' camp in America?

I turn and race up the bank toward Molly, stashing my fish in a bag as I go. Ryan follows, leaving the kiss that never happened on the bank of the river.

And as I run, I sense that everything is about to change.

CHAPTER SEVEN

My heart's pounding as we tear through the forest. A message from America? What could it be? Molly must have alerted the Forest Dwellers to the news as well, because they're all racing a few paces ahead of us, heading into the compound.

Trixie sees me and bounds over.

"What's happening, Brooke?" she asks, clutching onto my arm. "Is it something bad?"

I shake my head. "Not bad at all. Someone's made contact with us. From another camp in America."

Her eyes widen with astonishment.

As we race through the gates, I see that literally everyone from Fort Noix is gathered in the main square where we hold our bonfire parties. With all the Forest Dwellers crammed in as well, it's completely packed. There are so many people all squashed in together, some are spilling out into the side streets. I don't think I've seen so many people in one place since before the war.

Someone's made a small makeshift stage and other guards are busy hooking up some speakers. They're going to use solar power to broadcast the message for us all to hear. The benches that are usually around the bonfire pit have been stretched out in front so that some people can sit, but no one does. They're too busy pacing restlessly, or standing around looking concerned. Everyone's feeling disconcerted by the news. But while most are reacting with anguish, the main emotion coursing through me is excitement. This could be the trigger, the moment I've been waiting for, to begin my search for survivors.

Trixie, Molly, Ryan, and I weave through the crowds. I search for Bree, knowing she'll be here somewhere, but there's too many people and I can't see her.

Suddenly, the crowd falls into a hushed silence. I look up and see the Commander take to the stage.

"I believe most of you have heard the news in some form or another," he says. "So I'm here to confirm that yes, we have indeed picked up a radio transmission from America."

The crowd gasps. There's a hum as people start whispering. Someone moves through the crowd and slips beside me. It's Zeke. I can tell the instant I look into his eyes that he's thinking the same thing as me—that this could be the catalyst that turns the tide, that makes the majority of people realize that we have a duty to go out and look for survivors. Because here, at last, is the definitive proof that they exist.

The Commander tries to quiet the crowd down with his arms. "It is a recorded message," he explains. "We can't establish how long ago it was made. It could even have been from before the war."

I catch Zeke's eye.

"What did the message say?" someone cries.

"The frequency wasn't clear," the Commander replies. "And at times the message cuts out. But we will play it for you."

He nods to one of the guards, who goes over to the radio that's been hooked up to the loudspeakers, and flips a switch. Immediately, the crowd groans and covers their ears as a high-pitched squeak blasts out of the speakers. The guard quickly adjusts the volume to cancel out the horrible noise. Now the sound of crackling fills the square. It's intermittently punctuated by silence from where the transmission cuts out. Everyone listens intently.

"This is -- of the -- battalion. Our base -- Texas. -- survivors. -- -- -- more."

My heart clenches. That's all there is. A garbled message about battalions, Texas, and survivors. But two things strike me more than anything else. The first is that this message has come from another military compound. The second is the last word: more. Because I can't help thinking it wasn't "more," but "Moore." The voice is too distorted to work out if it belongs to my dad. And though there's no way of making out the words that filled the silence before it was spoken, the person could easily have said, "there are many more," but he also had time to fit in, "This is Laurence Moore."

The message repeats again. I strain to hear the words, to recognize the voice, to fully understand what is being said and by whom. But it's no use. The volume of the crowd has notched up another level, there's too much interference, and the silences cut out the most important words. All I know for sure is that somewhere in Texas there's a military faction that survived long enough to send out a message about survivors and, though it would be a huge coincidence, there's a small chance that it could be from my dad.

"Have we been able to message them back?" a woman shouts.

"Do we have any idea who sent it?" another cries.

"That's not the point," someone else shouts. "The point is that there *are* other camps! We're not the only one."

It feels like pandemonium is descending on the compound.

The Commander waves his arms, trying to get everyone to shut up. "We have not been able to make radio contact with them. As I said, the message is recorded and repeats on a loop. There's no way of knowing if the people who sent it are even still alive."

"We've been combing the airwaves for four years!" Zeke shouts from beside me. "Wouldn't we have heard it before now if it was old?"

The crowd agrees and the Commander looks flustered, like he's starting to lose control. Everyone begins shouting at once.

"We need to make contact!"

"Can we send a search-and-rescue team?"

Suddenly I feel it, that the tides of opinion are changing. Never before have the people of Fort Noix received a direct call. Before, it was easy for them to sit back idly because there was no real proof that there were other survivors' camps out there. But now the proof has arrived, and people are becoming unsettled.

Ryan gives me a mournful smile. He knows full well what I'm thinking: that I want to leave in search of the Texan survivors. He knows that he is finally about to lose me. I feel terrible for him, but when I look over at Molly's and Zeke's triumphant expressions, my resolve returns. The turn of the tide is exciting for all of us. My dream of rebuilding civilization might be about to happen. Now, I just need the people of Fort Noix to demand that the Commander use his resources to start helping those in need.

But there's still a strong isolationist faction arguing against those who are challenging the status quo.

"We can't risk being found!" they cry. "It would be a suicide mission!"

Everyone's shouting. The voices that are demanding that the Commander help become louder, bolder, stronger. More forceful. They start drowning out the shouts from the isolationists and any of the supporting voices of the Commander.

"We made an agreement years ago," the Commander cries. "Fort Noix does not seek survivors. Our own survival depends on us remaining secret and hidden." But as he looks out over the crowd, his expression changes, like he can see that it is not enough anymore, that many, many people no longer agree. "I ask of you all, please, that we sit down and talk about this. Democratically."

People begin to fall silent, taken aback by the mention of democracy, something that a fort run on military command doesn't usually get to experience. I catch sight of General Reece's distasteful expression, as though she certainly would have preferred this not have been resolved diplomatically at all.

"There is no need to shout and argue," the Commander adds. "I'm not going to force people to do things they don't want to. But we need a frank and honest discussion about what it entails, how these decisions may impact the rest of the group. The security of Fort Noix has always been, and will always remain, my paramount concern."

We all settle down, sitting on the ground and benches. It reminds me of kids at kindergarten sitting on a storytime rug, only we're soldiers, and we're discussing something far graver than a five-year-old could ever imagine.

"Say the message is recent," the Commander begins, "we can take it as fact that there are indeed survivors out there. Who feels that we should be searching for survivors?"

There's a show of hands, and I look around to see that far more people than just our group have raised their hands in support. I feel a swirl of happiness in my stomach to know that so many people share my belief about looking for survivors.

"And what do you people propose we do with them?" the Commander asks calmly.

Nicolas, a man in our group, begins to speak. "We want to go on short missions to rescue them and bring them back to the fort."

General Reece shakes her head. "That would be out of the question. It would alert slaverunners to our presence."

"Then what about creating a safe place for them nearby?" Molly asks. "We can train them to guard and patrol like we do."

People murmur in agreement, as though this is indeed a good idea. It would make Fort Noix a town of separatists rather than isolationists.

"How many people would be willing to set up this new fort?" the Commander asks.

Many of the people I've been speaking with over the last six months volunteer themselves, including Trixie and her family, and a large number of the Forest Dwellers. The Commander nods, though he looks a little stung to see so many wishing to leave.

"Then, please," he says, "know you have my blessing to do what you think is right. But let me make it clear right now. If you leave, you cannot come back. It's too risky."

General Reece nods. "I agree. If you're going to be going out on multiple rescue missions, you're bound to be noticed by someone sooner or later. You cannot lead those people here."

"I understand," Nicolas replies. "We're all aware of the dangers."

Molly nudges me and gives me a thumbs-up. What we've wanted for months is finally coming to fruition. People will be saved, given a chance at life like me, Bree, Ben, and Charlie were.

But something is still niggling in the back of my mind. The message. The American military base.

"What about the radio message?" I say. "Can we send a team to Texas to make contact with the survivors there?"

Silence falls across the crowd.

The Commander looks at me. "We don't know for certain if the survivors there are still alive," he says. "And Texas is a very long way to travel on the off chance that they are."

"It's a chance that many of us are willing to take," I say, confidently.

But when I look around, to my dismay I find that no one is agreeing with me. I realize in that moment that they've changed their minds. Making limited local runs to rescue people is enough for them. Heading across the length of America is too much. Traveling all the way to Texas was never the plan. I feel deflated.

"Like I said," the Commander replies, noting the complete lack of support anyone is giving me, "you're free to leave. But you cannot come back."

I know I should just be happy that, at last, there will be a group of people searching for survivors.

But it's not enough. Because I can't help thinking that the person trying to contact us could be my dad, that he could have survived the war just like the Commander did, and started his own group. Even if there's only a million to one chance that it is him, I have to find out.

And that means leaving Fort Noix.

And if need be, alone.

I breathe in deeply.

"In that case," I say, "I want to leave."

The silence would be deafening if it weren't for the shrill cry of a young girl coming from somewhere at the back of the crowd. It takes me a second to realize that the cry is coming from Bree.

I look over my shoulder and see her pelting through the crowd, making a beeline for me. Guilt swirls inside of me. I once made a promise to her that I would never leave her, and here I am, breaking it to her in the least sensitive way ever, that I'm going to do just that.

She reaches me and flings herself into my lap.

"I don't understand what's happening!" she sobs into my chest. "You want to leave? But you'd never be able to come back!" She pulls away, her tear-stained face bright red with emotion. "What about me? Charlie? Ben? What about us?"

I'm about to soothe her and explain my theory about Dad, when Neena pushes her way through the crowd and puts a maternal arm around Bree, as if trying to shield her from the pain I'm causing.

"Come on," Neena says in hushed tones as she heaves her to her feet. "Let the grown-ups talk. This is no place for a child."

Bree looks at me through red-rimmed eyes, her bottom lip trembling, then lets Neena lead her away. Ben and Charlie follow them through the crowd, both glaring at me darkly.

My heart breaks as Bree disappears. I feel awful to have caused her pain. I need to explain to her about Dad, about my gut feeling that the message is from him. Once she understands that, she'll see why I have no choice but to leave.

"Brooke," General Reece says, "I think you should reconsider leaving. You'd be going to Texas on nothing more than a hunch. I don't want to lose my best shooter."

"It's more than a hunch," I reply. "Zeke's right when he said we would have picked the message up sooner if it had been recorded years ago. I'm absolutely certain that message has only just been sent, that they're all alive. I want to find them."

"I'm with Brooke," a voice says and my heart skips a beat

I turn and look over at Ryan. All these months that we've been debating isolationism and rescuing survivors, he's been the person most opposed to my views. He's always wanted to stop me from leaving, to convince me that it's better just to stay. Yet now, he's the first to volunteer to come with me.

"Why?" I ask, astonished.

He smirks. "Because the chances of you changing your mind are nil," he says. "And I'm not about to let you walk out alone into your death. So that leaves me no other option."

My stomach flips. That Ryan would do that for me, it's more than my heart can handle.

"I'm coming too."

I turn and am floored to see Molly smiling back.

"Unless I'd be a third wheel," she adds wryly.

"You won't," Zeke adds. "Because I'll be with you all."

I look from one to the other, relief swelling inside of me that I'm not doing this alone. And gratitude. I am touched that they care about me so much that they'd all risk their lives for me.

"Brooke," the Commander says, "come to my office tomorrow morning. All of you," he adds, addressing Zeke, Ryan, and Molly. "We'll formulate a plan for your departure."

My stomach flips again at the thought that this is really happening, and that the Commander is going to help me. My whole body is a mixture of excitement and anticipation. After six months of dreaming about leaving this place, it's finally about to happen.

But there's something else there too, a deep, hollow sensation inside of me. I realize it's the thought of leaving Charlie, Ben, and Bree behind. I know they won't come with me. Bree loves Fort Noix too much, Charlie is her hopelessly devoted shadow who will do anything she asks, and Ben's too unwell to come even if he wanted to.

But I cannot change my mind now—and I don't want to. Other survivors might be out there. And among them, I even dare to hope, my father.

I have sealed my fate.

CHAPTER EIGHT

When I enter my room, Bree, sitting on the bottom bunk bed, puts her book down and stares at me. That look kills me. She's annoyed at me for rocking the boat, for bringing disorder and chaos into her previously stable life, but I decide not to sugar coat it. Bree's matured a lot over the last few months. She deserves the truth. I sit beside her on the bed. She looks so serious, so grown up. I feel a pang of loss for the little girl she used to be.

"Bree, I'm sorry," I begin, but she cuts me off.

"I think the Commander's right," she says, seriously. "Fort Noix is the first place we've been safe. We don't have to worry about slaverunners or going hungry. Have you already forgotten what it was like out there? Don't you remember how it felt to be starving? I never want to feel that again." There's accusation in her tone.

"But there are other people out there," I argue gently. "Other survivors. Don't you think we should find them?"

Bree just shakes her head. "No. I don't. The Commander would let them in if they made it here just like he did with us. But I don't think we should go looking for them. It's way too dangerous."

"What if one of them was Dad?" I contest.

Bree frowns. She looks even madder than before.

"We don't even know if Dad's alive," she says.

"We don't know for certain," I admit. "But I have this feeling deep inside of me that he is. Like if the Commander can survive this long, then why not Dad? He was one of the best in the platoon, you heard the Commander say that."

"But what does your thinking Dad's alive have to do with going to Texas?"

I know she's going to think I'm crazy, but she has to understand why I'm so adamant about leaving. "The radio message. I think it was from Dad."

Bree looks at me sadly. "I see Mom all the time, too. It's just part of grief."

"It's not like that," I snap. "I'm not seeing ghosts." She goes to roll her eyes but I grab her roughly by the shoulder. "Listen," I demand. "The message is from a military base. Dad was in the military. It's in Texas. Dad trained in Texas. He said 'Moore,' right at the end!"

Bree wrenches her shoulders from my grasp. "And that's enough for you to just up and leave?"

"That and a feeling right in here," I say, touching my heart, "that Dad is alive out there somewhere and now that we're strong enough to find him we should."

Bree sighs heavily. "Nothing I say will change your mind, will it?"

I look down into my lap, ashamed. "You know I don't want to leave you."

"Do I?" she snaps.

"Of course I don't!" I cry. "You're my sister. I love you."

She flashes me a haughty look. "You left Mom."

The words sting more than a slap to the face. My little Bree, whom I did everything in the world for, is challenging me over one of the hardest decisions I ever had to make, one that I made to make sure she stayed alive.

I'm not prepared to argue with her. It feels as though being at Fort Noix has turned her from a helpless kid into an independent one. She's acting like she doesn't need me anymore. Maybe she doesn't.

I stand from the bed and climb into the top bunk. With an angry sigh I stare at the ceiling.

"I love you, Bree," I say. "Whatever happens, remember that."

She doesn't say anything back.

*

I pace down the darkened corridor, tiptoeing so no one can hear my footsteps. I'm deep in the bowels of Fort Noix, though I can't quite recall how I got here.

At the far end of the corridor, light seeps out from beneath a door. It's one of those big steel doors like in a submarine. I realize then that I'm far, far underground.

I creep up to the door and press my ear against it. Inside, I can just about make out a deep rumbling voice with a strong South Carolina accent. It's the Commander.

I can only hear some of the words he's saying but it's enough to gather that he's speaking to someone about the radio message, about the group of survivors in America. Then I pick out something that makes my heart stop.

"Laurence Moore."

That's my dad's name. What's the Commander doing talking about my dad?

I shove the door open. The Commander's back is to me. He's bent over a large machine which I assume to be some kind of radio device. It takes up the whole other half of the room. A single light bulb hangs from the ceiling, casting a dirty dark yellow light over the room, making the shadows stark.

When I barge into the room, he spins around to face me. But it's not the Commander I come face to face with. It's my dad.

He's in full military gear, looking exactly like he did the last time I saw him. Behind him the radio bleeps and crackles.

Confused, I start to stagger back, but all at once, the ground beneath my dad gives way. The entire floor to the secret bunker room is collapsing. He screams as he plunges down, with bits of the huge radio machine falling after him.

"Dad!" I cry, reaching for him.

It's no use. He's fallen a good thirty feet to the bottom of a long pit. The wires of the device have snapped and dangle against the wall. Every time they touch, electricity zaps across them, sending sparks down on my dad. He peers up at me, terrified.

That's when I realize I'm not alone. All around the perimeter of the room, looking down at my dad in the pit, are hundreds upon hundreds of biovictims. They shout and jeer, waving their fists in the air.

My dad is in an arena.

From the far end, a door opens and a huge spider, at least ten feet tall, crawls into the arena. Its legs are as thick as tree trunks. It scuttles toward my dad as fast as a tiger. The spectators go wild.

He looks up at me. "Brooke!" he cries. "Brooke! Help me! You have to come to me!"

I start to scream.

I wake, screaming, and look all around.

I realize I'm back in my room, in my bunk bed. Daylight is streaming through the curtains and Bree snores softly in the bed beneath me. My heart is beating fast. I take deep breaths to try and calm myself down. It was just a dream, I tell myself. Just a dream.

But it felt like a dream that was telling me something. Urging me to find my dad. To help him.

Telling me that he's alive.

Quietly, I climb down the ladder of my bunk bed and land softly on the ground. I take the fresh uniform Neena cleaned and ironed for me and slip it on, feeling the rough fabric against my skin. It's a sensation I've become familiar with over the last six months at Fort Noix. As I sling the backpack over my shoulder, I hear Bree's voice coming from behind me.

"You're an idiot, Brooke," she says.

54

I tense. I hate hearing my sister so angry, and I can't help but draw painful comparisons to the way I left Mom, the last bitter words I said to her.

Without looking back, I say, "I'm sorry, but I have to do this."

I take one more step, stop, and add: "I love you. Don't ever forget that."

There comes silence in return.

Then, without another word, I step out of this room, out of this new life, for what may be the very last time.

CHAPTER NINE

Molly, Zeke, Ryan, and I watch quietly as the Commander spreads a map out on the table in front of us. We're in his office in the busy main building, the one where he'd first decided to let us stay all those months ago. Now, here he is, helping me to leave.

The map looks incredibly old. People stopped making physical maps because technology surpassed the need for them, and most of the ones still in existence would have been poached from museums around the early twenty-first century. There's no doubt in my mind that this map is an old, historical relic, stolen in a raid years ago. There's no way of knowing for sure if the roads depicted on it will still be there, or that there won't be extra settlements on the way not shown, places where unsavory people might dwell.

General Reece leans over and taps a spot on the map. "This is us," she says. Then she runs her finger down the length of the map all the way to Houston, Texas. "And here is where the signal came from."

I frown and lean forward, looking more closely at the map in the dingy yellow light. It looks like such an enormous distance to cover. The thought is daunting.

"I would recommend you stick to the waterways wherever possible," she continues. "It will be safer. Faster. And will require less fuel. Stay far from the shores. Take the Lawrence River and head west as far as you can."

I'd been planning on leaving by the same route I arrived, traveling alongside the Hudson toward New York. It seemed logical to me to retrace my steps, to tread familiar ground, at least for the initial part of the journey. But looking at the map makes me realize that my plan is too risky. New York is crawling with slaverunners, and is the site of Arena 1. She's right: passing through it via land would be incredibly dangerous. By sticking to the waterways and following the river for as long as possible, we'll be able to bypass many of the main highways and cities.

"There's just one snag," I say. "I don't have a boat."

It's the Commander who answers.

"We'll give you a boat, Brooke," he says, almost matter-of-factly.

My mouth drops open at the news. I can hardly believe it. Molly and Zeke are both wide-eyed in disbelief, too. My first instinct is to ask him why, why he would choose to help me by offering up a precious vehicle like a boat, but I decide against it.

General Reece taps the map again, pointing to a place in Ohio on the banks of the river.

"If you survive that far," she adds, "the water can take you all the way to Toledo. There's an old train station there, built during the war as a way to transport coal down south. There are tracks running all the way to Texas."

"Really?" I gasp, my voice rising several pitches at the stroke of luck.

She nods in her typically emotionless way. It takes all my willpower to contain my excitement. General Reece and the Commander have no idea how grateful I am to them for the information.

The tracks aren't on the ancient map, so General Reece leans forward and draws a straight red line from Toledo to Chicago, then all the way down to Houston, Texas.

"This is your first main danger point," she says, tapping Chicago. She runs her finger down to St. Louis, Missouri. "This is your second one."

"Why?" Zeke asks.

"They're both major cities and the tracks run straight through them," the Commander explains. "And where there are cities, there are arenas."

I shudder at the thought.

"So we go around them," I say. "Adds a day or two to the journey, but it's not worth the risk."

General Reece frowns. "You can't go around them," she states, blandly. "You'll be on a train."

I pause and draw my eyebrows together. "We will?"

"Well yes, of course," she replies. She taps Toledo again. "The train station is relatively new. It operated throughout most of the war. The chances of it still being operable are highly likely. Especially since all you need is coal. You'll just need to find an engine still on the tracks, fire up the coal, and you'll be away."

Molly lets out a little squeak of surprise. I shake my head, unable to comprehend.

"I'm sorry, you want me to drive a *train*?" I stammer.

"A coal-powered train," General Reece says with a nod, as if that makes any difference.

I take a seat as I try to catch my breath, completely stunned by the enormity of the journey ahead of me. This journey is going to take me entirely out of my comfort zone.

The Commander looks at me curiously. "If you don't think you can handle it, Brooke," he says, "maybe it would be best not to go at all. You've made a decent life for yourself here. There's a group about to head out looking for survivors to start their own colony. You could always go with them. Take your sister. Your friends."

I shake my head, determined. "No," I say, forcefully. "I can do this."

"You can," Molly agrees.

"We can," Ryan adds.

I look up at my friends' faces. They all seem to have so much faith in me, so much belief. They're willing to leave their home to help me follow my dream.

"Any of you guys ever driven a train before?" I ask.

Everyone breaks into a smile.

*

My arms ache as I heave the last of the supplies into the thirty-foot sailboat, making it rock on the banks of the river. We have a huge stash of weapons; plenty of dried food provisions like cured meat and pickled vegetables; changes of clothes; and a medical kit containing slings, bandages, and antibiotics in case of emergencies.

I then reach over and begin loading the thirty-gallon drums of fuel, knowing how precious each one is as General Reece hands them to me.

"We can only spare four," she explains, as I load the last one. "You'll need to sail as much as you can. Use the fuel sparingly, only if you're in trouble or in bad weather. That engine is really meant for backup, anyway. Remember, this is primarily a sailboat, not a yacht."

I nod, taking it all in. The Commander's map is safely stashed in my pocket. Of all the items on board the boat, it is by far the most precious. Without the map, we'll just be four people wandering through America.

Jack jumps excitedly into the boat, kissing me first, as he always does, and I feel reassured to have the pit bull with us.

Four people and a dog, I think to myself.

"You ready for this?" Molly asks, coming up to my side.

Her question makes me aware of the flutter of panic in my chest. "I guess," I reply. Then I look at her and frown. "Why did you decide to come with me?"

The corners of her lips turn up. "You might be the best shooter in Fort Noix, but you're not going to get very far without the second best watching your back."

She says it in her usual dry way. But I read between the lines of her sarcasm. She's coming because I'm her friend and she wants to help me. The thought is beyond comforting.

Jack starts barking at something in the distance, and I look over to see figures approaching.

"Looks like our farewell party has arrived," Ryan says.

A group of guards comes up to Ryan, clapping him on the shoulder and embracing him. There are people there for Molly and Zeke as well. My stomach drops at the realization that no one has come to say goodbye to me. A part of me understands Ben not being here. His PTSD has driven a wedge between us and we've grown apart over the last six months. And Charlie, of course, won't be here unless Bree is. But it's Bree's absence that hurts me the most. I know she's mad at me but I wish she would at least come to say goodbye. It reminds me, painfully, of the way I let my dad walk out of my life all those years ago. I'd refused to say goodbye to him because I'd seen him hit my mom and was mad about him leaving us for the army. In my darker moments, that memory has haunted me.

As I'm dwelling in my emotions, I suddenly catch sight of a figure standing a little way behind the others. It's Ben.

My heart leaps at the sight of him. I always thought Ben was handsome, with his soft features and gentle eyes, but right now he looks beautiful, standing so still like a statue in the midday sunshine.

He notices me looking but doesn't approach. I wonder if he was planning on just watching me leave and think maybe I shouldn't say anything to him. Then I decide that I don't care about his poignancy, and head toward him.

"You came to say goodbye," I say as I walk up to him.

He shakes his head. "I came because I wanted to come with you."

His words shock me. We've barely spoken for six months and now he's telling me he wants to up and leave Fort Noix to be with me.

"You do?" I stammer.

He nods, his expression pained. "I did. But this was as far as I could go."

I look him up and down, frozen to the spot as though with fear. The group of well-wishers are down by the shoreline. Ben's PTSD has stopped him from getting any closer.

Once again, I feel guilty about leaving him here. He's managed so far to just about present himself as well enough. He's kept himself beneath the radar. But what if my leaving triggers something in him, makes him worse?

"Are you going to be okay, Ben?" I say.

He nods, but I can see tears glittering in his eyes. The sight of them makes my own emotions threaten to choke me. Ben's been by my side more or less since Bree was kidnapped. We've been together through everything. The last six months as he's pulled away from me has made me unaware of just much I will miss him.

Suddenly, I realize how much of a jerk I've been to Ben. I've been pushing him away for months, unable to deal with his detached, grief-stricken ways. I'd run to Ryan like a moth to a flame, wanting to be with someone who wasn't so damaged, to have a friendship where for once I didn't have to be the strong one. Bree's right. I am an idiot.

I fly into Ben's arms and hold him tightly, so tightly I can feel his heart beating against my chest.

"Come with me," I whisper into his ear. "Please."

He shakes his head. "I wish I could," he replies, his voice tremulous. "You have no idea how much I wish I could."

I pull away from the embrace, feeling like my heart is splintering into a thousand pieces.

"Look after Bree," I say, quickly wiping the tears from my eye.

Then I turn and head back to the boat.

"You ready?" Ryan asks, offering his hand to help me into the boat.

I don't take it, just step onto the boat beside him.

"Let's do this," I say.

We raise the sails together. I yank on the coarse lines and already my palms are burning; it takes more power to raise the sails than I'd imagined. They rise slowly, one foot at a time, and I must use all the leverage of my body to get them up. Molly helps beside me, while Ryan leans over the hull and raises the anchor. Zeke secures the lines and turns the rudder, and a moment later, I experience the most incredible feeling: we are moving. The wind catches our sail, and foot by foot we begin to leave shoreline and gain momentum.

I look back, taking one long, last look. I wonder if I will ever see this place again. My heart aches from my goodbye with Ben, from knowing I can never come back.

"Look, Brooke," Molly says.

I see all the people amassing on the shore, standing on the banks, saluting. The four of us salute back. I wish my dad could see me now.

We stand there, saluting each other, as the boat drifts farther and farther away. Then, farther down the shoreline, we see another group of people. It's the Forest Dwellers. They wave, clap, and cheer. I see that Trixie is there at the front, her giant bunny in her arms. The sight of her reminds me why I am doing this; to make the world safer for everyone.

We wave back, feeling like superstars. The sounds of the cheers make me smile.

That's when I notice that one person isn't waving or smiling like the others. It's Bree. She's standing beside Trixie, with Charlie clutching her arm on the other side. She watches me, silently, her chin tipped up.

I let my waving hand drop. As the boat sails past, we continue to watch each other, our gazes locked together. I watch the figure of my little sister grow smaller and smaller as the distance between us lengthens. I watch until she is nothing more than a smudge on the horizon. My heart breaks as it never has, as I am filled with waves of self-doubt and guilt.

Then I turn around and face the open water, ready to take on the rest of my life.

Ready to find my father.

PART TWO

CHAPTER TEN

Ryan sits in the stern___, steering the boat, Jack beside him, paws up on the rail, his tongue lolling. I lean back, letting the wind catch in my hair, tousling it behind me. It is surprisingly windy and because of the speed, the wind is bracingly cold. My nose is stinging and my cheeks are frozen.

It feels good to be on the move, to know my journey has finally begun. After all these months thinking about this moment, it has finally arrived. It's especially great to be on the water, away from the cities and destruction. Out here, you can almost pretend the war didn't happen.

The water sparkles beneath us as we cut through it at speed. I let it relax me. If it weren't so cold, I'd almost be tempted to sunbathe.

"Take a look at that!" Ryan calls over his shoulder.

I sit up and see where he's pointing. Up ahead are lots of small islands dotting the water. Some are filled with trees, like mini floating forests. Some are linked by bridges, now rusted and falling apart. On others there are houses; big, grand buildings that are beginning to crumble into the water.

"Did people live in those?" I say, surprised.

Zeke holds up the map and points to the St. Lawrence River, which we are currently sailing down. "Must be the Thousand Islands," he says, tapping the blobs of green that run along the length of the river.

I watch, awestruck, as we weave in and out of the islands. I can't even begin to imagine the sort of community that would have lived here, needing a boat to get to their neighbor's house, or to the mainland for school and work. The houses are very plush, making me think that they must have been inhabited by rich people.

We pass a house that would have been a mansion in its heyday. It's covered in thick ivy that strangles all the windows, turning it into something out of a children's fairy tale. For a moment, I wonder what it would be like if we all pulled over and moved into one of these mansions, lived out our days here, in crumbling opulence. I wonder if anything inside is still intact. Chandeliers? Marble fireplaces? Priceless rugs? Antiques?

All of that, if not looted, would surely be ruined by now. We'd be living in a hull of a mansion, unheated, without food or running water. I shake my head. It is a mirage of opulence, a dream from another era.

"This is where the others should bring the survivors," Molly says with a laugh. "Can you imagine?"

I cast my mind back to the moment we were rescued in the Hudson River. After our horrendous ordeal, finding Fort Noix was like stepping into paradise. But finding this place would have been like stepping into another world, a dreamland.

"Too bad we can't go back and tell them about this place," I say, with a hint of bitterness in my voice.

Molly picks up on my tone. "Are you pissed with the Commander for saying we can't go back?"

I shake my head. For all his faults, the Commander really came through for me in the end. Without him we wouldn't have the map or the boat.

"It's not that," I say, gazing out over the crystal blue water.

"Is it Bree?" Molly probes.

My heart squeezes at the memory of her watching me silently from the shoreline. She truly believes that I've left her forever. She has no faith in me to find our dad. In my mind, I'll make it to Texas and send a radio transmission home, calling to her. Or drive one of the military tanks up and collect her myself. But in her mind, I've left her behind, just like I left Mom. Just like Dad left us. What she thinks I've done to her is unforgivable.

When I don't say anything, Molly puts her arm around my shoulder. She holds me like that, not saying a word, just letting me be present in my pain.

Just then, the clouds start to darken.

"Looks like rain," Zeke says, gazing at the sky.

We all look up at the graying clouds starting to crowd above us.

The boat is completely exposed. Depending on how bad the storm is, we could be soaked to the bone if we keep going. But I don't want to have to stop so soon after leaving.

"Why don't we stop off there?" Molly says, pointing up ahead to where an amazing castle stands on one of the tree-covered islands.

My mouth drops open. "It's beautiful," I gasp.

Ryan, at the helm of the boat, looks over at me and raises an eyebrow. "Well? Time for sightseeing?"

Just then, the rain begins to fall. It's a cold, hard rain that lashes us.

"Pull over," I say. "Let's shelter in the castle."

Molly pulls the line on her side, and we all duck as we tack and the boom swings, while Ryan steers us toward the little island that houses the castle. He steers us expertly to a stop by the small jetty.

Jack's the first off the boat, jumping off and running onto the steady ground and barking his excitement. He pees, then rushes off toward the castle, taking in all the new smells of grass, mud, and stone.

Molly and I leap off while Zeke ties up the boat. As soon as he's done, Ryan follows, and the four of us race into the castle.

We're soaking wet by the time we're inside. The castle has seen better days, and parts of the ceiling have caved in. Water drips down, pooling in the middle of the large, marble floor.

There's a spiral staircase leading up, a broken piano in one corner of the hall, and a grandfather clock that's no longer ticking. Black mold spots the walls and there's a dank smell.

So much for my fantasy of opulence.

"Where's Jack?" Ryan asks, peering through the gloom.

"He ran off that way," Zeke says, pointing down one of the corridors.

We begin to walk down the corridor, our footsteps echoing across the marble tiles.

"Jack!" Ryan calls. "Where are you, boy?"

There's the sound of barking from far in the distance. We head toward the sound.

"Hey," I say as we go. "What's that up ahead?"

Everyone looks, peering through the darkness. There seems to be something glowing in the distance, like some kind of source of light. But it's too yellow to be daylight. It looks more like a flame.

"A fire!" I gasp, suddenly alerted to the fact that someone else is here.

Immediately we draw our weapons. My mind races. Who could be here? A crazy colony? A group of slaverunners camping out on their way to the cities?

A lone survivor?

Suddenly, Jack emerges from the shadows. He leaps up at Ryan, licking him.

"Whoever it is," Ryan says, "Jack seems to think it's safe. He's usually a good judge of character."

"Who is there?" a voice calls from the darkness.

We all freeze, our guns poised, ready to fire. Shadows leap across the stone walls as a figure slowly shuffles toward us. As he gets closer, I see that it's a young Hispanic boy, maybe fifteen. He's thin with a baby face.

"Don't come any closer!" I shout, jabbing my gun forward for emphasis.

The boy holds his hands up. "That's not a very polite way to treat your host," he says. "You are in my home, after all."

My eyes dart right and meet Molly's. She's pulling a bemused expression.

"You live in this castle?" I say to the boy. "Alone?"

"All alone," the boy replies. "You're the first people I've seen in four years." He looks away as though pained. "I'd started to think I was the last."

"The last what?" I ask.

"The last human on earth."

My heart aches for him. To have spent all those years alone, thinking he was the only one left. It's a thought too horrible to bear.

I lower my gun.

"I'm Brooke," I say, holding my hand out to shake his.

He looks at me, guarded, unsure whether he can trust the girl who moments earlier was pointing a gun in his face. In the end he takes my hand.

"Emmanuel," he says.

He peers over at the others, their guns still trained on him. The rest of the gang take my lead and lower their weapons.

"You got any food in there?" he asks, eyeing my bag.

"If you've got a fire we can dry ourselves by," I reply.

He nods. "This way."

We follow him down the corridor and into a large hall that resembles a ballroom. The mold smell is even worse in here. There's a large marble fireplace in one of the walls with a small fire burning in the middle. We all rush over and begin to warm ourselves.

I notice that Emmanuel is eyeing my satchel.

"Help yourself," I say, knowing there are enough rations in the boat to last us for weeks.

He opens up the bag and pulls out some dried meat strips, then starts to eat them ravenously. The sight of him gorging reminds me of the hunger that was a constant fixture in my life in the mountains. Thanks to being regularly fed in Fort Noix, I'd let myself forget what it felt like to starve. I feel a sudden pang of empathy for the boy.

"How did you get here, Emmanuel?" I ask him.

His mouth is stuffed with dried meat, but he speaks anyway.

"I'm from Toronto," he replies. "When the rebels came and took it over, my family and I had to flee the city. There were loads of other people with us, maybe a thousand. Maybe even two." He pauses, swallows, then takes another huge mouthful of meat. "We had to go on foot. It was a long journey. We were following the river because we didn't have a map or compass or anything. We'd got as far as the Thousand Islands when the bombs fell. They were killed."

"Your family?" I ask gently.

"Everyone," he replies. "I was the only one who didn't die."

I gasp, trying to imagine a group of two thousand people obliterated in one bomb strike, leaving just one boy alive.

"I don't know what made me jump in the water," he adds. "I guess it was some kind of instinct to just get away from it all, from all that death." He shudders as he relives the moment. "I just jumped in the water and started swimming. Then I ended up here."

"And you've been here ever since," I reply.

I'm amazed by his story. If he is indeed fifteen, and has been here for four years, he was Bree's age when everyone he knew was killed in one second. How he found the strength and resolve to carry on, I don't know.

Molly whistles. "That quite a story, Emmanuel," she says.

He glares at her, at her insensitivity. I can almost feel him screaming in his mind that it's not a story, it's his life. Molly's my friend and I have to remind myself that she hasn't seen the same kind of pain and devastation as we survivors have. It's harder for her to empathize with someone like Emmanuel than it is for me. In fact, none of them do. Not Molly, Ryan, or Zeke.

Suddenly, I feel the absence of Ben like a hole in the heart. He'd get it right away. His sensitivity and understanding would be really welcome round about now. But I know that's not going to happen, so I'm going to have to try and do it myself.

"I'm a survivor too," I say. "I lived in the mountains in New York. Just me and my sister."

"Is she dead?" Emmanuel asks.

I shake my head. "No. She's safe. Happy." At least, I hope she will be eventually, once she's gotten over my betrayal.

The rain lashes outside, and the sky is starting to darken. It makes me feel uneasy. With nightfall comes extra danger. Us not being able to see properly gives predators—be they slaverunner, wild creature, or crazies—the advantage. But Emmanuel has survived here alone for years, so it must be safe. Still, the thought of us having to camp out overnight here doesn't exactly thrill me.

"Why did you leave New York?" Emmanuel asks.

"We had no choice," I reply. "Slaverunners found us."

Emmanuel looks confused. "What are slaverunners? Are they the deformed people?"

It takes me by surprise that Emmanuel's hideout is so cut off from everything that he doesn't even know what slaverunners are.

"Slaverunners control the cities," I explain. "They go out looking for survivors to put to work or..." My voice trails away. "To use for entertainment."

I can feel everyone's eyes on me. Of all the things that interest my new friends, it's my time in the arenas that intrigues them the most. I've never fully spoken about it as it hurts too much to think of. Recalling memories of Logan is still excruciatingly painful.

"There are still cities?" Emmanuel asks. "With survivors in them?"

"Yes. But they're dangerous places now. The only safe places are the military-run survivors' camps. There's one just north of here. You should go. You'd be safe there."

"I'm safe here," Emmanuel replies. "No one bothers me. The only thing that worries me are the deformed people, but they just sail right past."

I pause, my attention suddenly alerted. "Wait," I say. "What do you mean they sail right past?"

Emmanuel prods the fire with a stick nonchalantly. "Well, they don't know I'm here. It's not like I have a boat or anything that would draw their attention to me."

Molly's eyes suddenly snap wide open as she comes to the same realization as me. Our boat is tied to the jetty in full view. We didn't even think to hide it. But if there are crazies in this area, they will surely have spotted it.

I leap to my feet and grab my gun. At the same time, somewhere from down the long winding corridor comes a strange sound, like a slamming door.

Molly looks at me.

Silently, I nod. Ryan and Zeke also leap up, their hands on their weapons. Emmanuel looks terrified.

"What's happening?" he asks.

I press my finger to my lips. "Be quiet. And put out the fire."

He does exactly as I say, rushing over and kicking the flames until there's nothing left but smoldering coal. In the pitch blackness, we all stand completely still, listening to the shuffling, pattering sounds coming from the other side of the castle.

I curse myself for having been so stupid as to leave the boat in view. We'd been so distracted by the storm we'd been thinking only of finding shelter. That lapse in judgment might have cost us dearly.

"Emmanuel," I whisper to the terrified boy, "we're going to try and get to our boat, okay? We'll get you out of here and head to safety."

I'm thinking of Nicolas and the Forest Dwellers' new survivors' colony. We can send Emmanuel in that direction. It would probably take little more than a day to reach on foot.

But Emmanuel is shaking his head. "I don't want to leave the castle," he says stubbornly. "This is my home."

"Not for long," I reply. "Listen. You hear that? Footsteps. There are people here. People who want to hurt you."

He frowns, suddenly angry. "You led them here," he accuses me.

There's nothing I can say to refute it. He's right.

"And that's why I'm going to do everything I can to keep you safe," I reply, sternly.

I feel someone move beside me in the darkness. Even without being able to see, I can tell that it's Ryan.

"I'm sending Jack ahead," he whispers. "We can follow his route."

"Good idea," I reply.

I can just about make out Jack's white fur as he trots quietly across the large ballroom and out into the corridor.

"Come on," Ryan whispers.

We creep silently across the room, putting all our faith in Jack like he's a guide dog for the blind. We make it to the corridor and skirt along, our backs to the damp stone walls. After a tense few minutes, we emerge into the main chamber with the piano, staircase, and grandfather clock.

A stream of weak moonlight comes through the hole in the ceiling. Jack's only fifty paces away from the open door when he stops. His head darts up, picking up a sound that none of us can hear. Then he begins barking shrilly, as though instructing us to run, leave, get out.

Without a second's hesitation, we race forward, heading straight for the door. At the same time, shadows lurch out of the corridor.

Crazies. At least ten of them.

They race toward us, their faces melted, their deformed hands stretching out for us. I'm ready for them. I start shooting before anyone else has even had a chance to draw their weapon. My first shot is so precise it only just skims past Ryan's face before meeting its target.

Emmanuel screams and freezes on the spot. I have no choice but to grab him and start dragging him, making me unable to fire my weapon. I just pray the other three can cover me.

Ryan, Zeke, and Molly shoot their guns desperately at the crazies but none of the bullets find their destination. They're panicking too much. Finally, Molly gets herself together and manages to shoot one of the crazies dead. He falls directly in my and Emmanuel's path. Emmanuel trips over the corpse and goes flying across the slippery marble floor, right into another crazy. The deformed man snatches him up in his arms, ready to whisk him away. But there's no way I'm going to let that happen. This whole thing is my fault. Emmanuel was safe before we turned up. I won't let him die because of me.

I aim my gun up and blast the crazy right in the face.

Blood explodes all over the place and the crazy falls to the floor dead, releasing Emmanuel, who crumples into a heap, shivering, staring at the place where the crazy's face used to be.

"GET UP!" I cry at him. "MOVE!"

He drags himself to his feet and runs toward where Jack is barking by the door, ready to lead the boy to safety.

With Emmanuel safely out the way, I wheel and direct my gun at the shadows, at the figures darting around in them. Molly's gun cracks out another bullet, hitting a crazy in the chest. She fires two more times, and he finally falls. Ryan and Zeke both fire on a second crazy and he collapses to his knees before falling face first onto the marble with his arms splayed either side of him. I turn my gun on the last standing crazy and fire. My bullet hits him right between the eyes. He pauses momentarily before falling to the ground.

Panting, blood-splattered, we look around at the fallen group of crazies. Ten of them lie dead on the floor. That was way too close for comfort, but we did it. We killed them all.

Suddenly, I hear the sound of Jack's barking coming from outside the castle. If Jack is barking, that means there's more danger. My mind immediately thinks of Emmanuel, who followed the pit bull outside. He's completely defenseless.

Ryan, Zeke, Molly, and I exchange a quick glance before rushing out of the castle doors. And that's when we see them. Through a gray sheet of rain, we take in the sight of more crazies. A whole gang of them—on our boat. The ones inside the castle were just an offshoot of this main group, a distraction used to give these crazies the opportunity to steal our boat. And there in the center sits

Emmanuel. He's been completely bound in rope. His frantic gaze locks with mine.

"NO!" I scream.

The engine of our boat thrums and the black water churns as the propellers turn. The boat starts to move away, taking our weapons, food, and medical supplies with it.

Flooded with anger, drenched by rain, I raise my gun. But what can I do? I can't get a clear shot of the crazies driving the boat because Emmanuel is in the way. If I shoot it to sink it, that would be no help either. We'd lose everything, including Emmanuel, who wouldn't be able to swim to safety. There's nothing I can do. I'm completely defeated.

Suddenly, I feel something grab me from behind. I scream and thrash around frantically. Beside me, Molly, Ryan, and Zeke have all been grabbed as well. As I finally catch a glimpse behind me, I realize that the whole island is filled with crazies. There are at least fifty of them surrounding the castle. The ones in the boat were just a decoy. We're trapped. There's nothing we can do.

I'm certain I'm about to meet my death when the sudden blast of a shotgun splinters the air. Something whistles past my face and immediately the arms that were latched tightly around me release. The crazy who'd been holding me falls into the wet, muddy earth, dead, with a neat bullet hole in the side of his face.

I touch my cheek and feel warm blood mingling with the ice cold rain drops. The bullet grazed me. Whoever just fired that gun was a millimeter from blasting my face off.

I don't have time to think about the fact I'm still alive or how. I dart forward with my gun, spin on the spot, and start shooting the crazies. I free Molly first, knowing full well that she's a better shot than either of the guys. She looks completely startled as she wriggles free from the dead crazy who'd been holding her. She's soaking wet from the rain. Her uniform weighs her down and her ginger hair is plastered to her head.

"Save Emmanuel!" I shout at her.

She nods and splashes through the muddy puddles as she races toward the jetty, where the small boat is rapidly disappearing across the water. It's only then that I notice the other boat, the one that's coming toward us, the one containing three silhouettes, one of whom is holding a gun.

Out the corner of my eye I have time to see the silhouetted figure shoot his gun. Again, the bullet just skims me. For a second, I wonder if I was the intended target. But then a dead crazy flops to my feet and I realize I'd been mere seconds from being attacked by him. Whoever it is in that boat, they're trying to help us.

I have no time to think about the mysterious people who are helping us; I have to focus on freeing Zeke and Ryan, on neutralizing the threat. I turn back and see that Jack is attacking the crazy holding Ryan, gnashing with his jaws. The crazy tries kicking him off but it's no use. He finally lets go of Ryan and falls down in the mud.

Ryan, now free, grabs his gun and fires a vengeful bullet straight into the man's head. When he looks up at me, his jaw is set firmly. The expression on his face chills me to the bone much more than the pounding rain that soaks me. It's a murderous look.

As though fueled by revenge, Ryan grabs his gun and begins firing round after round at the crazies. They begin dropping to the rain-drenched ground, falling face first into the mud and dying undignified deaths. My heart pounds as I fire too, and kill the crazy holding Zeke.

Now that there are three of us on the island shooting the crazies, plus the mysterious stranger on the approaching boat, the crazies begin to fall more quickly. Soon there's only a handful left, the ones that were clever enough to take cover behind walls and trees. Ryan stalks over to one, seemingly without any recognition of the danger he's in by exposing himself, and fires at the crazy, killing him at point-blank range.

With Ryan on his murderous rampage and Zeke covering him, I decide to help out Molly. I can hear her gun firing as she tries to kill the crazies taking away Emmanuel, and every time she pauses to lock and load, she curses, and I know she's having no luck. I race to her side but it's no use. Our boat and Emmanuel are far away. There's no chance of rescuing them now.

Suddenly, the sound of gunfire ceases. I glance behind me and realize that Ryan has shot the last of the crazies. We did it. But we lost Emmanuel and our boat containing all our supplies. It hardly feels like a victory.

For the first time, I let myself fully look at the other boat, the one with the strangers who were helping us. It's a boat just like the one we'd just lost, but smaller. A sailboat, its small engine is nonetheless whining as it's being driven like a motorboat. Even in the gloomy moonlight, and obscured by the sheet of pelting rain, I can tell that they are not strangers at all. The three figures on the boat are in fact so recognizable to me as to be family.

It's Bree, Charlie, and, holding the gun, the gun that saved my life twice in the last five minutes, Ben.

*

I stare at them as if I've seen a ghost. The small boat reaches the jetty and Jack bounds over. Penelope leaps ashore and the two dogs race around in circles, happy to be reunited.

The rest of us just stand completely still, too shocked to move.

"Is that…" Molly begins.

"Yes," I reply.

Suddenly, I find my feet. I race toward them full speed through the squelchy mud, not caring about it splattering all over my clothes. When I reach them, the kids grab hold of me and pull me into an embrace. I'm filled with relief.

"Bree," I stammer, staring into my sister's face cupped between my hands. "You came."

She nods. "I'm sorry. I should never have let you go like that. Without saying goodbye."

"Shh," I say, hushing her. "No sorries. If anyone's sorry it should be me. We're together now, and that's all that matters."

I pull her into my arms again and hold on tightly, while Charlie's arms circle tightly around my waist.

"You're bleeding, Brooke," he says, sounding worried for me.

"I'm fine," I say, touching my wound as I remember the bullet that whizzed past my cheek and saved my life, the bullet that was shot by Ben.

I look over the children's huddled figures at Ben, who is standing a few paces back from the rest of us.

"How did you…" I begin, a million questions entering my mind, not even knowing what to say next.

"We begged the Commander for another boat," Ben said. "We had a feeling you might need us."

I smile.

"Nice shot," I say, knowing full well that it's the first he's made since that day at the outpost when his PTSD stopped him dead in his tracks.

Ben looks at me intently with his soulful blue eyes. "I don't know how," he says. "But when I saw that you were in danger I could just suddenly shoot again." He sounds confused, like he doesn't fully understand it himself.

"Well, I'm glad," I say. "And I'm glad you came."

"Me too," he says quietly.

73

Just then, the other three come over. Everyone hugs, shakes hands, pats each other on the back. But my joy and relief are only short-lived as I remember Emmanuel and our boat.

"What do we do now?" I say.

We all look at Ben's boat. It's even smaller than the one the Commander gave us, and there's no way we'll fit comfortably in there. And they don't have any supplies or weapons to speak of.

But we have no choice. The seven of us huddle into the boat, the two dogs squeezing in too. It might be cramped but the important thing is that we're all together. Everyone I love is in this boat. Everyone but one person... Dad.

"I'm coming, Dad," I whisper under my breath.

CHAPTER ELEVEN

The boat, its engine off, now at full sail, sways and lurches in the water as Zeke consults the map.

"We've reached Lake Ontario," he announces.

I look out, as do the others, shocked by the sight ahead. It looks more like an ocean. The waves are huge and rock our overcrowded boat violently. I cling on for dear life, praying that after surviving an attack from crazies we don't meet our doom in the water. I would hate to drown like Logan.

The rain is still pounding and we're all completely soaked and shivering. But we need to keep going, plowing onward, putting as much distance between us and the crazies as possible.

The entire way I kept my eyes peeled for the crazies, for our old boat, for Emmanuel, desperate to save him. But to my horror and guilt, they were nowhere to be found.

Suddenly, a sound dawns on me, one that had been nudging at my consciousness and growing louder with each minute.

"Uh-oh," Zeke says. "Looks like danger ahead."

I huddle forward and peer at the map. He's pointing to something. I read *Niagara Falls*.

"Oh," I say, apprehensively.

That was the sound: rushing water, distant, yet growing closer.

It's a testament to the dangers of the cities that the Commander and General Reece thought it would be safer to direct us via Niagara Falls than have us go by foot for any significant portion of the journey.

"What do we do?" Ryan asks.

"It's the only way to get into Lake Erie," I reply. "Toledo is on its west bank. We'll just have to be careful."

The tension is unbearable. Not only do we have poor weather and overcrowding to contend with, but now we have to maneuver past a waterfall. I feel Bree's small, cold hand slip into mine.

"It will be okay," I say. Then I look up at Ryan, who is steering the boat. "Won't it?"

He nods grimly, his expression not exactly filling me with confidence.

"We don't have much gas," Ryan adds. "And we'll need as much power as possible to counteract the force of the falls, to get us to shore before we go over."

"Use it all if you have to," I tell him. "We can sail the rest of the way. Just don't let us go over."

He turns back to the tiller___, his features transforming into complete concentration. I hold Bree close to me and whisper a silent prayer under my breath. She nuzzles her head into my chest and squeezes her eyes shut. Penelope sits in her lap, shivering from the rain.

The boat chugs along, churning up water as we go. Ryan steers us smoothly along, trying not to fight the power of the water while also using it to push us forward. I can hear the engine struggling in the choppy water, and then a new noise makes me even tenser. It's the rising sound of the waterfall, of thousands of liters of water plummeting down a cliff face, crashing on the rocks. And we're heading right toward it.

I grip the sides of the boat even tighter. Beside me, Molly is doing the same. Zeke has practically turned green. In complete contrast to the others, Ben sits serenely, his gaze locked on me. I can't help but feel calmed by his presence. We've gone through so much together and are still standing; it's almost like he's a good-luck talisman. He nods as if to say, "We've got this. We've been through worse." Despite my fear, I find myself smiling back at him.

The boat carries on forward and the sound of the waterfall grows even louder. The amount of water spray kicked up by the power of it is immense. It drenches us as much as the rain.

The sound and feel of the engine beneath me changes. I look over to Ryan and see that he's giving the boat more power. And that means that the pull of the waterfall is starting to take effect. I can't help but visualize our little boat being sucked into the stream and splintering to a thousand pieces on the rocks on the way down.

I catch my first glimpse of the waterfall's edge. How strange to think of all the tourists who gathered here and took tour boats across the water. They will all be dead now, all those people whose lives consisted of day trips to beauty spots. They could never have imagined as they stood here looking at the breathtaking sight of nature at its finest that in a few hundred years our species would have almost entirely annihilated itself.

I push the thoughts from my mind and keep my gaze on the lip of the waterfall as we skim past it. I feel like every muscle in my body has tensed up and that I've turned to rock. I've never been at someone's mercy like this. It's almost unbearable. Usually when I'm in danger I know I can fight and get myself out of it. Now, I have nothing to do but hope and wish and pray we make it out the other side.

The end of the waterfall's rim is just in sight.

And then a strange *putt-putt-putt* noise makes me frown. I look at Ryan. His expression instantly tells me it is bad news.

"The engine," he says. "We're running out of gas."

As soon as he says it, the whirring of the propeller starts to slow. Instantly, the power of the waterfall can be felt beneath us. The boat starts to be pulled toward it by the force.

"ROW!" I scream. "EVERYONE! NOW!"

We grab the oars from beneath the seats and frantically begin rowing. My arms ache with the power of my movements. I grit my teeth with determination and put everything I've got into forcing the boat away from the waterfall's edge. But despite all our strength, we continue to veer closer and closer to the rim.

There's just five meters or so to push through before we clear the edge. The engine hasn't died yet and Ryan's able to keep it turning over, giving us just a fraction more power.

"Head for the shore!" I cry to Ryan.

With the combined efforts of all of us, and what little power we have left in the engine, we manage to just reach the shore.

I heave a sigh of relief, as do the others, all of us drenched.

The second we touch land, I leap off and extend my hand to Bree. She grabs it and I haul her up onto the solid land. I heave Charlie out next. Jack and Penelope leap up on their own, and Molly, Ben, and Zeke are able to heave themselves out of the boat and onto the land. Together we grab the ropes and hold on for dear life as Ryan makes the leap out and onto land.

"Now what?" Molly cries, fighting against the power of the boat.

"Now we pull the boat onto land," I shout back.

She gives me a look like she's less than thrilled, but she doesn't argue. Zeke, Molly, Ben, Ryan, and I begin heaving with all our strength. After rowing for so long, my arm muscles scream in pain. But I keep pulling. Finally, we edge the boat out of the water and onto the strip of land.

I fall back, exhausted, aching, relieved. We're still alive. I can hardly believe it.

"That was a close call," I say to the gray, drizzly sky.

Ben's face appears above me. "Come on," he says, extending his hand to me.

I take it and let him pull me to my feet, overwhelmed once again by the mere sight of him. Ryan must notice the way I look at him because he shoots a glare my way. He's probably thinking that he was the one who just saved all our lives, that he was the one who came with me in the first place, and yet here I am swooning over

Ben, the boy who barely spoke to me for six months and let me head off alone. I know it's not fair, but I don't fully understand my feelings toward either of them.

Zeke pulls out the map the Commander gave us.

"We should walk the boat to Lake Erie," he says. "There's three more waterfalls to get past in this part of the lake. We won't have enough gas to power past them all."

He's right. Once in Lake Erie, we'll be able to sail all the way to Toledo, but we won't have the strength to pass any more rapids.

Despite our complete exhaustion, no one is prepared to take a break, especially when we're on land and completely exposed. We all feel much more comfortable on the water where the chances of crazy and slaverunner attacks are closer to nil. Plus, we're nearing Buffalo, which was a densely populated city before the war. If there's going to be any slaverunner activity in these parts, that's where we're likely to find it.

We trudge along the road, weary, shivering, soaked to the bone. A rest would be welcome around about now, but we have to keep going. Apart from the kids, we all take it in turns carrying the boat. It's heavy, and what with our muscles already aching, it starts to really slow us down.

After an hour of walking, I'm completely spent. I stumble, my legs giving out beneath me.

"We can't stop here," Zeke says. "Buffalo is just ahead."

He nods toward the horizon, where a collection of skyscrapers and tall buildings make up the skyline. I drag myself to my feet and begin trudging along again. To make matters worse, my stomach feels completely hollow. We lost all of our provisions when the crazies stole our boat. We're going to have to hunt sometime soon before we all collapse from exhaustion. But I keep telling myself "not yet." Once we've made it past Buffalo and are back in the water, then I can start worrying about things like sleep and sustenance.

The city looms up ahead of us. I get an unpleasant feeling in the pit of my stomach. But it's not the feeling that tells me danger lurks nearby, it's a different feeling. It's the feeling of death. Of ruin. The entire city is empty, deserted. A once bustling metropolis has been left to decay because of a pointless war that killed its inhabitants.

Night is starting to fall, making stark shadows across the streets, turning the houses into skeletons. I shiver and draw my arms across my chest for protection.

"Looks like there's nothing to worry about here," Zeke says.

The abandoned city is good news. It means no slaverunners. But it makes me think dark, depressing, hopeless thoughts, and that is definitely not good. The sooner we get out of Buffalo the better.

"This way to get to the water," Zeke says, pointing to the dog-eared map.

"Here," I say, going up to Ryan. "I'll take the boat for the next stretch."

He swaps out with me. Then Ben comes over and swaps out with Molly. For the first time, Ben and I are walking together. We don't say a word, we've never had much need to. Without him having to utter a single syllable, I can tell that the gesture was a symbolic one, one that says he won't leave me again, that we'll be walking side by side forevermore. The thought comforts me.

We get to the lake's edge and nudge the boat into the water.

I heave a sigh of relief, completely spent.

"Lake Erie," Zeke announces, like some kind of tour guide, as we begin to clamber on board. "Three hundred twenty miles to Toledo."

My legs shake from fatigue as I clamber aboard. The kids practically fall asleep the second they hit the deck.

"We'll need to take this in turns then," I say. "Get some sleep in shifts. Ryan, why don't you sleep first since you steered us through Niagara Falls and all?"

I'm expecting to see his cocky smile at my quip but he just looks at me with pained, haunted eyes. It occurs to me that the last twenty-four hours have probably been the most traumatic in his life. He's become a shell of himself. But he nods, accepting my urging.

"Just twenty minutes," he says. "Then wake me up."

I agree, though I have no intention of waking him for at least two hours. Zeke decides he'll take the first sleeping shift as well. Then I turn to Molly.

"Do you want to sleep on the first shift too?" I ask.

She looks from me to Ben with a curious look in her eye. I can tell she doesn't think it's a great idea for me and Ben to be left alone together, and I wonder if it's because she doesn't yet trust him or because she is suspicious of there being something between us and feels loyalty to Ryan. Whatever it is, she finally agrees to sleep.

Everyone apart from Ben and me curls up on the floor of the boat, leaving the two of us to set the sails and steer out into the expanse of water.

We head southwest, keeping the banks in our sight line at all times.

I look over at Ben. He looks stunning in the dawn light.

"I'm glad you're here," I tell him, speaking quietly so as not to wake anyone up. "I missed you."

"We were only apart for a few hours," he replies.

"That's not what I mean."

He looks down, embarrassed, as it dawns on him that I'm referring to our time in Fort Noix, and the way he cut me out of his life.

"Where did you go?" I ask him. "Why didn't you speak to me for six months?"

He can hardly meet my eye. "I didn't want you to know how weak I'd become."

I frown. "And why would that matter to me? You're my friend, Ben, I care for you no matter what."

"That's just it," he replies. "I'm your friend. Your weak, sensitive friend. Rather than the sort of strong, confident guy who could one day become more than your friend." His eyes skim over Ryan's sleeping form.

"Are you telling me you ignored me for six months because you're jealous of Ryan?" I'm almost too angry to speak.

"It's not just Ryan," Ben says. "It's Logan too. The second we reached Fort Noix you never spoke of him again. Never even said his name. You were in love with him, weren't you?" His eyes burn into me.

"I don't know," I say, squirming.

"Well, I do," Ben says. "You were. And even after he died I still wasn't good enough for you."

"Ben," I say, pained. It hurts to hear him talk like this, especially when it couldn't be further from the truth. I do have feelings for Ben, I just don't fully understand them.

"You have a type," Ben adds. "Strong. Confident. Accomplished."

"You're all those things," I reply, a little exasperated.

He just shakes his head. "It doesn't matter. I know my place now, Brooke. Because you see, I tried to let you go and it didn't work. I came running straight after you. My place is beside you. Whether you want me there or not."

"I do want you there," I say. "Always."

Ben turns his face from me and looks out over the sparkling water. He doesn't believe me and my heart deflates. I wish I was better with words, and that I could make him see how much it means to me that he's here. But I don't get the chance because Molly stirs.

"Brooke," she whispers. "Why don't I take this shift?"

It occurs to me then that she's heard everything, that she hasn't slept a wink. Like a good friend, she's trying to protect me from my pain.

"Thanks," I say. "I could do with the sleep."

As we swap places, she squeezes my arm, as if to tell me that everything will be all right.

"Good night, Ben," I say.

He doesn't say anything back.

*

I'm woken by a jolt. I sit up sharply, and realize it's morning. I must have slept all night. No one woke me to take another shift.

I drag myself to sitting and look around. The boat is lurching violently.

"What's happening?" I shout.

Above me, Zeke, Molly, and Ryan are fighting with the sail.

"Storm!" Zeke shouts down.

I finally make it to my feet. The water is dark, churning violently. Waves several meters high rise up, dragging our little boat helplessly along with them. My stomach turns as we plummet down the side of a wave.

"I'm scared!" Bree cries.

I look back at her clutching the sides of the boat. She looks terrified, as does Charlie.

"It's going to be okay," I tell them hurriedly. "We can handle it."

I help the others with the ropes and sails. There's very little we can do, though, other than sit it out. We're at the mercy of the water and can only pray that it doesn't capsize us.

The sensation is horrible, like being on a terrifying rollercoaster or an airplane in turbulence. Molly loses her footing and gets catapulted across the boat. Zeke grabs her just in time to stop her falling overboard.

"Everyone hold on tight!" I cry, reaching for my friends.

We huddle together, keeping vigilant of any danger as our little boat is buffeted by the waves and thrown around. Even though my stomach is empty, I still feel like I could throw up.

The dogs whimper as we lurch sideways. Bree begins to cry. For the first time I wonder if we made the right call taking the river route. If Buffalo was completely deserted, maybe all the big cities along the lake's edge are deserted as well. But just as I'm thinking it, I catch sight of a city on the banks, and what I see chills me to my core.

"Zeke!" I cry as the boat bobs up and back down again. "Where are we?"

"Must be Cleveland," he replies.

"Do you see it?" I shout to Ben, my eyes transfixed on the city that the lake seems to be pushing us toward.

"I see it," he replies.

There, in the distance, looming up in the middle of bombed out buildings, is the unmistakable outline of an arena.

"We have to MOVE!" I cry. "There are slaverunners in that city. If they see us, we're dead."

I remember the powerful speedboats the slaverunners chased us with before. Our little boat will be nothing against them. If we're spotted, we'll be captured in a matter of minutes.

"There's nothing we can do!" Ryan shouts back as the boat makes another huge push up, followed by a stomach-churning plummet down.

I know he's right but I just can't accept it. There must be something we can do to put a bit more distance between us and the city crawling with slaverunners. We seem to be forced closer to the banks. From here, I can even make out the sight of the bright yellow school buses that are used to transport young girls to the sex trade. We're far too close for comfort.

"Is there any gas at all?" I cry to Molly, who's sitting by the engine throttle.

She tries it, and to my relief, the engine sputters alive.

"There must be a tiny bit left," Ryan says.

"Good. Then use it!"

He powers the boat forward, heading away from the coast and farther into the middle of the lake. The waves here seem even stronger, and with the forward motion of the boat as well, we seem to be bobbing up and down even more violently. Charlie begins retching in his hole at the bottom of the boat. Bree holds onto him to comfort him.

"Come on, Ryan," I urge, willing him to go faster, to get us out of sight of the dangerous city.

At last, the distance between us and Cleveland seems to grow. I can no longer make out the buses, and the tops of the buildings disappear over the horizon. The only thing that's left in my sightline is the roof of the huge arena.

Just as the waves begin to lessen, the engine of the boat finally splutters to death. We're sitting ducks again. Only at least this time we're nowhere near the dangerous city of Cleveland. Instead, we're closer now to the northern bank of Lake Erie. From here we can see the derelict city of Detroit. It's another grand city reduced to nothing more than rubble. I shiver, desperate to make it to Toledo soon and put the danger and horror of mass destruction behind us.

But I have a feeling it's only just beginning.

CHAPTER TWELVE

"So this is Toledo," I say, looking around at the decaying harbor we've landed in.

Finally, we touch the shore and disembark. It feels strange to be back on solid ground after so long at sea. I am not sure whether I am relieved to be off the violent waters, or anxious to be back on dry land.

I look around. Toledo is more or less intact, but completely empty. It's a ghost town, eerie in the pale morning light. The place is so thoroughly deserted, I can't help but think slaverunners must have been through here, picking off all the survivors. The thought makes me shudder.

Zeke consults the map. "It's this way," he says, pointing ahead.

We all stop and turn and look at the boat. I have mixed feelings, knowing we are abandoning it. I can only hope and pray we find the train soon. And I can't help but feel a sense of victory that we made it this far by water.

We turn and walk. We trek down a narrow road, tall trees growing on either side. There are young tree saplings that have clearly grown since the war because they look healthy and untamed. But the road itself has been ravaged by bombs. Every few steps we pass another crater, another burnt out car, and bits of twisted metal all over the asphalt from an explosion that ripped vehicles right apart from its force. Nature has attempted to reclaim the road. Tufts of grass spring out of cracks, and vines twist around street signs, hydrants, and lamps.

After a while, we turn onto a main road. Here there are houses dotted either side of the road, the wood siding rotting and falling off in places, their front gardens completely overgrown. Some of the houses have endured fires and have huge black smoke marks above the grubby windows. Others look almost completely intact, the bombs that fell here missing their properties by mere feet.

We pass a gas station, with a raggedy American flag still blowing in the wind. There are rusted trucks sitting in the parking lot, abandoned. We check them all for gas, to see whether we can use them to reach our destination more quickly, but they've all already been siphoned. It's a sign that people lived around here after the war long enough to scavenge, but there's no one to be seen now. No sign that anyone's set foot on this road, in this part of America, for years and years and years.

Beyond exhausted, we trek all day. Finally, night begins closing in. We're all famished. The only upside is that there have been no more attacks from crazies, and no sightings of wild animals, despite the Toledo zoo being just a few blocks from where we're heading. I'll never forget the time I came face to face with a wild lion that had broken free from Central Park Zoo. It's an experience I hope never to repeat.

The air is heavy with dust. The houses become more dense, as does the destruction. There are whole streets where the front parts of the buildings have been blown off, like the door to a doll's house being taken off and exposing the whole house inside. Each house tells the same story: of everything of worth being looted, of the building being left in disrepair with wallpaper peeling from the walls, plaster and wiring falling from the ceiling, the stairs caved in, of nature trying to reclaim what was taken from it. Rats have nested in the old family homes, as have birds.

I'm on even greater alert here than before. Anywhere that was once more populated is more dangerous. Not only are there more places to hide but there's more chance that people survived the war and got left behind. At least there's no sign of slaverunner activity. I'm certain that this area must have been amongst the first to be raided by the slaverunners. They probably haven't been here for years now, discarding the place after taking what they needed, leaving a ghost town in their wake.

Finally, I see the huge rust-colored bridge where the train tracks pass over the roads. For the first time in a long time, I let a flicker of hope lift my spirits. I even find enough strength in my limbs to run.

"Guys, come on, this way," I call to the others.

With tired, heavy footsteps, we dash across the last bit of open land and into the train yard. But the moment we get a clear view of the station and tracks, my stomach sinks with disappointment. The whole place is destroyed. Explosions have melted the metal of the tracks and twisted them up at strange angles. The train cars that were on the tracks must have been blasted off, because they lie on their sides, scattered across the yard.

And of course, there is no coal.

They've all been looted.

I'm devastated by the sight I see before me. The Commander's historic map was right, it led us on the right path to the right place, but we're here years too late. The map has led us to a place that's been completely obliterated. The only things still standing are the bridge across the road and the small metal station house.

Molly is the first to speak.

"Now what?"

It's a good question and one I can't answer. When we left Fort Noix, there was no plan B.

"We'll need to find another vehicle," I say.

"Way to state the obvious," Molly says. "But we've been checking pretty much every car we've passed. There's nothing."

I really don't appreciate her attitude right now.

"We can't stand here," Ben says.

He's right. Darkness is crowding in on us, and that means danger is getting ever closer. Slaverunners, crazies, escaped animals, if they wanted to attack, now would be the time to do it, while we're all standing here in the middle of an open train yard.

I look back at the ragtag bunch of followers. Bree and Charlie are clasping hands with each other. They look completely exhausted, with dark circles under their eyes and downturned mouths. Molly appears to be fuming, but getting angry and hostile has always been her reaction to negative experiences. Ben looks frantic. Even Zeke, the only actual adult here, looks like a tired, vulnerable infant. Ryan's the only one who looks like he has any fight left in him at all.

I realize then that they're all looking to me. They need me to tell them what to do, to make the decisions, to lead them.

"Let's head for the train station," I say, agreeing with Ben. "We can hide out there until we figure out what to do."

We begin walking past the rail yard toward the small station house. Zeke leads the way, zigzagging through the fallen train cars, assuming the position of leader just like he used to when we had our meetings. But leading a discussion around a table and leading a mission are two completely different things. He's not being cautious enough, just plowing ahead. Some instinct tells me to reach for my gun.

All at once, there's an almighty noise of screeching metal. Everyone freezes as one of the train carriages ahead of us appears to start moving. It rocks side to side, light glittering off the metal, and in the darkness, I can see movement coming from under it. Like a swarm of ants under an overturned log, crazies start crawling out of the train carriage.

I don't have any time to think. I start to fire straightaway. Ryan takes up his firearm, his gunshots joining the cacophony of noise. Beside me, Ben and Molly start shooting too.

The crazies surge forward, charging at the closest target: Zeke.

"Run!" Molly shouts.

We run, jumping over bits of blown-up train carriage, dashing across the yard. The only place that offers any kind of protection in the near vicinity is the station house, and that means racing round the perimeter of the yard in a full circle. It's impossible to go straight ahead because that's where the mass is coming from.

Without question, everyone follows me.

"Don't look back!" I shout.

Then I hear a scream, one that makes my bones turn to ice. It's Bree.

I don't even stop to think. I turn on the spot.

"Brooke! What are you doing?" Molly cries, coming up to me, trying to shove me on.

But it's no use. I barge past her easily and run back to where Bree is right at the back of the group. The crazies are so close to her they're barely an arm's length away.

Like a relay race runner preparing to receive the baton, I stretch my hand back for her and get in a stance ready to run. She sees me and stretches her hand forward. The second her fingers make contact with me, I yank her forward, pulling her with me. We pelt across the yard, heading for the station house where the others have already made it.

"Run! Brooke, run!" they're all screaming from the door.

I can hear the sound of hundreds of crazies' footsteps pounding after me. There's so many of them I can smell their odor, feel the heat coming from their skin. Bree stumbles as she runs beside me, but I won't let her fall.

We're almost there. Fifteen feet. Ten feet. Five feet.

Then we catapult in through the open door and collapse onto the ground. Ben slams the door shut behind us, locking it with bolts. We hear the sound of the crazies as they blast into the side of the building, thudding one after the other.

Bree and I sit up, panting. She clasps onto me just like she used to when it was just the two of us in the mountains. We hold each other close in the center of our group. Everyone's huddled into the middle of the room, looking out at the windows, where the silhouettes of the crazies bob around, banging their fists against the glass.

We're completely surrounded.

CHAPTER THIRTEEN

The sound of pounding is like a drum in my brain. The dogs are barking feverishly.

We're trapped in the station house. I'm still clutching Bree in the middle of the dark room, sitting on the dusty floorboards. My friends seem frozen with fear around me. The same thoughts must be running through all of our minds: this is the end, this is how we die.

The fear I'm feeling is so consuming, I don't even realize that Bree is trying to break free from my clasp.

"Brooke," she's saying. "Brooke, look, look there."

Finally I let her go and turn to see where she is pointing. She scrabbles up from me and rushes over to a small hatch in the ground. I have no idea how she managed to see it in the dim light, but the relief as I pull it open and see stairs leading down into blackness is all consuming.

"Quick," I shout at everyone.

Ryan is the first to rush over. He races down the ladder, disappearing into the blackness. Molly gestures for Bree and Charlie to go next, ushering them in, then dropping down after them. Zeke is quick to follow.

Ben appears, his gun drawn and pointing at the door as he edges backward.

"Brooke, go," he says. "I'll cover you."

But some sense of responsibility is stopping me from saving myself first. It would be like a captain abandoning a sinking ship.

"You first," I cry out. "Come on."

I grab him by the shirt and pull him toward the hole. Just as he starts descending, one of the windows smashes. I flinch at the noise and turn to see crazies climbing over one another in their haste to get to me.

"Brooke!" Ben screams up from the hole.

I clamber onto the ladder, pulling the heavy wooden trapdoor down with one hand and fumbling with my gun with the other. I get out four shots at the advancing crazies before disappearing into the hole and yanking the trapdoor firmly into place.

From below, the hands of my friends reach for me. I'm lifted clean off the ladder by Zeke and Ben, and set on the ground. Above us, the crazies pound on the trap door.

My heart beats wildly as I look around. Molly's lit her flashlight and is shining it around, lighting up the place. We're in a tunnel, stretching on as far as the eye can see. It seems like some kind of storage place, with wooden crates stacked haphazardly around. It's made of brick and is dank, molded with mildew. It stinks of rat and death down here.

Though we have no idea where it is leading us, we have no choice to but to follow the tunnel. The crazies will get through the trapdoor sooner or later. Going forward is the only way to avoid certain death.

We run through the tunnel as fast as we can, our flashlights lighting the way, bouncing and making shadows dance all around us in a crazy flashing pattern. It's like we're in some kind of nightmare discotheque.

From the other end of the tunnel, the way we'd just come, we hear the sound of cracking wood, followed by thuds as the crazies drop through the trapdoor to the ground. Once again, the hunt is on. I can only pray that there isn't more danger at the other end of this tunnel.

I can hear the crazies' footsteps gaining on us. My whole body is tense, pumping with adrenaline. I don't want to die down here in this dark, smelly tunnel.

As my feet pound against the cement floor, I feel something brush past my leg. My first instinct is a rat, but it was far too big for that. It's then that I realize Jack is heading back the way we came, running straight for the crazies. Penelope is running right after him, eager to join the fight too. I turn my flashlight on them and see them both baring their fangs, aiming for the crazies' throats. The sight is so gruesome it turns my stomach. I'm also terrified for their safety. They're both so small and fragile in comparison to the crazies.

I fire off some rounds of ammunition to help out, but I know it's not enough. If I want to stop the crazies from pursuing us, I'll have to think of something drastic.

"Guys!" I shout ahead. "We need to create a blockade with the crates."

"We can't stop!" Zeke shouts back. "They're too close."

But I know we're not going to make it if we keep running. We still can't see the end of the tunnel. We don't even know what's at the end of it. It could be leading us to a brick wall for all we know.

Ignoring his warning, I start knocking the crates with my arm as I go. They tumble down to the ground, splintering and spilling their contents onto the floor. Coal. Stacks and stacks of it. Seeing it gives me my second burst of inspiration.

I keep knocking down the crates, hoping that the crazies will find it harder to reach us with the obstacles in the way. At the same time I rip a strip of cloth from my uniform, hold it between my teeth, and fumble in my bag for matches. Finally, I find them. I light the end of the fabric, stop, turn, and throw it into the strewn coal and splintered wood. The splinters act like kindling and the fire spreads quickly. But it's too low. The heat might slow the crazies but it's not enough to stop them.

Jack and Penelope dart toward us, sprinting past the fire and back to the group. They've managed to cause a lot of damage between them, but there are still crazies standing and they're getting very close. I grab one of the crates and throw it with all my might at the fire.

The others finally realize what I'm doing. They all stop too, quickly building a waist-high barricade with spare crates. The fire catches, and at last we have a barrier. Some of the crazies run straight into it, setting themselves alight.

"Come on," I say. "Let's keep going."

We leave the flaming barricade behind us and sprint along the tunnel. Jack is right by my heel and I'm so grateful for his bravery back there. He slowed the crazies down long enough for me to collect my thoughts and come up with a plan.

Smoke is starting to thicken in the tunnel as more and more coal starts to smolder. It's thick, making it difficult to breathe. The kids start coughing.

"We have to get out of here!" I yell.

"I can see a ladder!" Zeke shouts from up ahead.

We all hurry toward him and see a rusty, half falling apart metal ladder screwed into the wall, leading up to a round metal cover. It's a manhole, presumably leading out to the streets of Toledo.

Zeke's up it quicker than I can blink, slamming his shoulder into the cover at the top. It opens and cold evening air blasts us. He disappears out the top, then his face reappears.

"Come on!" Zeke cries, holding his hand down.

We pass up Charlie and Bree. Molly starts climbing, with Penelope under one arm. The ladder groans under her weight. The screws in the wall seem loose and they rattle with every step she makes.

"Brooke," Ben says. "You're the lightest, you should go next."

I look from him to Ryan. I can't go up knowing one of them will be last, that the ladder might not hold out for one of them and send the other plunging to his death. But I don't get a choice, because Ryan suddenly sweeps me up in his arms and shoves me onto the first rung. He pushes from behind, and I have no choice but to climb.

I grab Zeke's outstretched hand and he yanks me up into the street through the hole. The cold air shocks me after the stuffy, stinking, smoky tunnel. I start coughing, and Bree runs over, flinging her arms around me. But it's not over yet. Ben and Ryan are still down there, down in that horrible, dark place.

Black, acrid smoke billows out the hole as I race over beside Zeke and stretch my hand down. Jack is shoved into my arms by Ryan. I heave him out and plop him down behind me. He runs over to Penelope and Bree for some much needed pampering.

Ben is next. I help pull him from the hole. He's completely soot covered, his face streaked with black, looking like a miner emerging from the mines. But as he pops out the hole, the ladder screeches and disintegrates behind him.

"Ryan!" I scream, as twisted bits of metal fall down around him, clattering to the ground.

From the bottom of the hole, Ryan looks up at me, looking lost and terrified.

"Grab my hand!" I scream.

"No!" he shouts back. "I'm heavier than you. I'll just pull you in."

I turn to Zeke and Ben. "Hold my legs, I'm going in."

I don't give them a chance to protest. I fling myself forward into the hole and they grab me, pinning my legs against the asphalt. I'm hanging into the hole by my waist, stretching forward for Ryan. He's still a good few feet below me.

"Jump!" I shout.

The smoke is so thick now it's starting to obscure my view of him. For a second, I lose sight of him. My first fear is that he's passed out.

"Ryan!" I scream. "RYAN!"

Suddenly, he reappears, making the smoke swirl around him. He's got a crate. He coughs as he positions it on the ground, covering his face with his sleeve, then clambers onto it. It gives him just enough height to reach my hands. I grip him as hard as I can.

"Pull!" I shout at Zeke and Ben.

Molly comes over to help, and between the three of them, they heave me up with Ryan dangling from my arms. We get him through the hole then flop back against the ground. I take in a huge gasp of air, lying sprawled on my back, gazing up at the black sky.

My first instinct is to laugh. We made it. We're alive. But when I turn to Ryan, expecting to see his cocky smile, instead I see that his eyes are closed. He's not moving.

"No, no, no," I say, dragging myself onto my knees and crawling over to him.

I rest my head on his chest. It's not rising or falling. He's not breathing.

Everyone begins to realize what's happening. They crowd over, looking anxious and pale. The kids cling to each other, unable to look as I begin performing CPR on Ryan. Jack howls into the night, and Penelope joins in.

"Come on!" I shout as I pump down on Ryan's chest.

He's completely covered in black smoke. When I push my lips to his they taste of coal. I will Ryan to breathe again. He can't leave me. Not now. I don't know what I'd do without him.

Suddenly, Ryan takes a sharp intake of breath. He's breathing again, but he's still unconscious.

I sit back on my heels, feeling overwhelmed. What are we supposed to do now? We're in the middle of the street, completely exposed. We don't have the train anymore, and Ryan's out cold.

"We need to find shelter," Molly says, taking me by the arm and leading me to my feet. "In case there are any crazies left alive around here."

"Shelter where?" I cry, glancing around at the derelict buildings. None of them seem to offer adequate protection; they're all falling apart.

Just then, I realize the dogs have disappeared. Once again, they've hurried off, sniffing the air, searching for danger on our behalf. Then from somewhere far away, Jack starts barking and Penelope joins in with her high-pitched yapping.

"I think the dogs might have found somewhere," Molly replies. "Come on."

She takes my hand, not wanting to let me go, even when I pull back to try and get Ryan. So I let her lead me away in the direction of Jack's and Penelope's barks, while Ben and Zeke carry Ryan's unconscious body.

Penelope and Jack lead us all down a road that runs parallel to the train tracks. Up ahead is a strange-looking building that looks like it might have been some kind of power station once upon a time. It's made of a series of buildings like silos. Beside them is a pyramid-shaped building that is completely rusted. There are no windows and the only way in is up a steep, narrow ladder. I'm so glad the dogs managed to find this place; it will certainly offer us protection for the night. With only one way in, we'll be able to guard the door.

"Come on," I say, scaling the ladder.

I push open the door at the top and step inside the strange building. I realize then that it's not a power plant at all, but an enormous grain store. I've never seen anything like it before. Zeke, Ben, and Molly manage to carry Ryan up the steep stairs and into the grain store. Bree and Charlie come inside last. Zeke slams the door shut, plunging us into darkness. Then we all sink to the floor, exhausted.

I help settle Ryan into a comfortable position and wipe the soot from his face. He's still unconscious and the sight terrifies me.

"I think a few of us should go back to get the boat from the harbor," I say to the group.

"Why?" Molly questions me.

"Because the river runs all the way to Indiana and we know we're safest on the water."

Zeke consults the map. "She's right. The Maumee River would take us on for miles but it goes through some built-up areas." He points to where the river diverges at a place called Grand Rapids, heading due south almost all the way through Ohio. "This river would avoid all the large towns."

"I don't want you to leave, Brooke," Bree says, her bottom lip quivering. "And what about Ryan? What if he wakes up while you're gone?"

"She's right," Ben says. "We shouldn't split up. Not while there might still be crazies out there."

"Well then what's your plan?" I say with a harsh tone.

"How about," Molly says, acting as the peacemaker, "we all get some sleep? Eat some food? Talk about this in the morning?"

I shake my head. "We need to have a plan."

"And we will," she says sternly. "Tomorrow. The kids need to rest."

She gestures toward Bree and Charlie. They both look terrified and exhausted and I know Molly's warning me to calm down, to not look so desperate and frantic in front of them. But I can't help it. I can't bear the thought of not knowing where we're heading next, not knowing what the next step of the plan is. We were supposed to be on a coal train right now, hurtling through the open countryside, not cooped up in a grain store.

"No," I snap back. "Tonight. We'll work out what we're doing. As soon as Ryan's awake, we leave."

Molly narrows her eyes. She doesn't appreciate my attitude or being bossed around by me. But I feel like I'm losing my mind right now. Plotting our next steps is the only thing that will stop me from worrying.

"You know what, fine," she says gruffly. "Since none of my opinions seem to matter, I'm going to go and see if there's anything edible in this place. You guys sit around talking in circles."

She stomps off. I feel bad for making her annoyed, but she has no idea how much danger we're in, in the middle of nowhere, completely off course. The quicker we plan our escape route the better.

Zeke spreads the map out on the floor and Ben and I peer over it.

"Do you really want to go all the way back for the boat?" Ben asks.

"What other option do we have?" I reply. "It's our only transportation. We can't get to Texas by foot."

"She's right," Zeke replies. "The boat is integral here. We could even head all the way west then row it down the Mississippi."

"But that would mean going via Chicago," Ben says. "There's bound to be an arena there. And that's not to mention how far we'd have to carry the damn boat in the first place."

"Do you have a better idea?" Zeke asks.

Ben shrugs. "I don't know if it's better or not, but I think we should leave the boat behind. The chances of us finding one at the other end are pretty high, wouldn't you say? And it would mean we weren't being slowed down the whole time by carrying the boat."

I'm about to launch into another argument when I suddenly hear a shrill scream.

"Molly!" I cry.

Jack and Penelope bound off into the darkness, ready to play the heroes again. We stand, prepared to follow them.

"Stay here!" I cry at Bree and Charlie. "Look after Ryan, okay?"

Then we run, Zeke first, then me, then Ben. The metal grating clangs underfoot as we hurry after Jack and Penelope.

"MOLLY?" I cry, but there's no response.

I'm terrified for my friend. What could have happened to her? Did she fall over one of the balconies and hurt herself? Was she attacked? If so, by who, or what?

I can see Jack and Penelope draw to a halt up ahead, but I can't see Molly at all. We race toward the dogs and see why they've stopped. There's a large door that's sealed shut. The dogs scratch at it, whining.

"She must be in there," I say.

Zeke and Ben start ramming their shoulders against the door. I join in too, and before long, we manage to pry it open just a little.

"Molly?" I shout through the gap. "Where are you?"

Again, there's no response. We manage to make a gap just big enough for Penelope to get through.

"Please find her," I tell the one-eyed Chihuahua.

The little dog tips its head to the side as though she understands what I'm asking of her, then disappears through the gap.

"She'll be okay," Ben says, wrapping an arm around my shoulder. "Penelope will find her."

I fold into him, remembering how safe and comforted I feel in his arms.

Finally, we hear Penelope's familiar *yap-yap-yap*. She leaps back through the hole, tail wagging, and a moment later, the door creaks open, and there stands Molly.

"Oh God," I cry, flying into her arms. "I thought something terrible had happened to you."

But that's when I realize she's not moving, not reciprocating the hug. I open my eyes and discover that I'm starting straight down the barrel of a gun.

I jerk back and hold my hands in a truce position. As I move away from the door, I catch sight of Molly's captor. He's a young guy, maybe nineteen years old, with a guarded expression. One of his arms is tight around Molly, the other clutches the gun, pointing it at us.

"Who are you?" he demands.

"Just survivors," I say. "Just people like you."

He glares at me, untrusting.

"Why are you here?" he snaps. "No one's been in Toledo for years. Why did you come here?"

"Why don't you put the gun down so we can talk properly?" I say.

"No way," he says, shaking his head. "Tell me why you're here."

"We're trying to get to Texas," I reply. "To an army camp there. We were supposed to take the train all the way down but the tracks were damaged and we were attacked by crazies."

He pauses and a little flicker of interest crosses his face.

"An army camp?" he says.

I feel like I might be getting somewhere. The mention of the military camp has piqued his interest.

"Yes. We received a radio message from a survivors' camp. A military one. We're going to check it out."

He studies my face as though trying to work out if I'm telling the truth or not.

"I'm Brooke," I continue, trying to lure him into security so he'll put the gun down. I point to each of the guys behind me. "Ben. Zeke. And that's Molly." I point at my friend, who is trembling, the gun poised at her temple. "I'm also here with my little sister, Bree, her friend Charlie, and there's one more of us, Ryan. He's unconscious. Then there's Jack the pit bull and Penelope the Chihuahua, who you've already met. And that's it. That's everyone. You don't have any reason to be afraid of us. We just wanted somewhere to shelter until Ryan wakes up, then we'll be off."

"You're really going to Texas?" he asks, his tone closer to curiosity than aggression. But his eyes are still narrowed, telling me he's not quite sure if he can trust me.

"Yes," I reply.

"What if..." he begins, then pauses. I can tell he's hesitating, deliberating. "What if I told you I know the best way to get to Texas from here? Would you let me come with you?"

I can feel Zeke and Ben tensing behind me. We don't know this guy. All we know about him so far is that he has a gun and he's pointing it at Molly's head.

"I would," I say, trying to sound as honest as possible. "The bigger the group, the stronger we'll be. Survivors need to stick together."

He narrows his eyes. "How can I trust you?"

I shrug. "You just have to make that leap of faith."

There's a long moment of stillness. Everyone holds their breath. Molly's eyes are squeezed tight. Her skin is drained of all color.

Then suddenly, the boy releases her. She flies forward into my arms. I grab her trembling body and hold her tightly, exhaling all the tension I'd been trying to hide from the boy.

Everyone's relief is palpable.

"I'm Stephan," the boy says, still looking guarded but showing no guilt or shame at all for having held Molly hostage.

"Nice to meet you, Stephan," I say, trying to sound cordial rather than angry.

I hold out my hand for him to shake. But as his gaze darts down to my outstretched hand, I turn it into a fist and slam it under his chin. It knocks him out cold.

His gun clatters to the floor. I grab it and stash it in my belt. Everyone stares at me, open-mouthed.

"What?" I say defensively. "He deserved it."

No one argues with me.

"You'd better tie him up before he comes to," I tell Zeke.

"I'll go and raid his food supply," Ben adds.

"Good idea."

I loop my arm through Molly's and begin leading her back to the others. She's still trembling.

"So you were just lying when you said Stephan could come with us?" she asks.

"Oh no, he can come with us if he wants," I say with shrug.

"Then why did you punch him?!"

"I just felt the need to put him in his place. No one points a gun at my best friend's head."

Molly locks her green eyes on me.

"Thank you, Brooke," she says under her breath. "And I'm really sorry about our argument."

"It's okay," I say. "Already forgotten."

Molly and I have never been into mushy displays of affection. It makes me uncomfortable to talk like this. Thankfully, we've reached the others and Bree runs up to me.

"Where have you been for so long?" she cries.

"We found a survivor," I reply.

Bree frowns. "You did? Where?"

"Oh, Zeke's just tying him up."

Her frown deepens. But before she gets a chance to fire another question at me, I'm distracted by a noise that comes from behind her. I look over and see that Ryan is stirring. He's waking up. Molly loosens her grip on my arm and gives me a little shove, as if to say, "Go to him."

Quietly, I head to where Ryan is starting to bring himself up to a sitting position. He looks disorientated, and his cropped hair is still filled with soot. He manages to prop himself up against the wall, and hunches his knees to his chest.

"Brooke," he says when he sees me approaching. "What happened?"

I crouch down beside him and put my hand gently on his shoulder. "Nothing happened. You're safe."

He shakes his head. "No. No. Something bad happened. I died, didn't I?"

I falter, unsure as to how much I should really tell him. "You stopped breathing," I explain. "But it was just for a little bit."

"It being for a little bit doesn't make it any better."

I look away. My voice is quieter. "No, I suppose not."

"Sorry," he says. "I didn't mean…" He pauses, frowns, stares at me intently. "You brought me back to life, didn't you?"

I can feel the emotion lodging in my throat. The fear when I'd thought I'd lost him. The panic. The utter relief when he came back to me.

I nod, slowly.

Ryan looks down at his lap, frowning as though some deep thoughts are consuming him. Then he looks up at me again, leans forward, and quickly kisses me.

I'm completely taken aback. It was the last thing I was expecting him to do. But it felt wonderful, like electricity in my body.

The pleasant sensation doesn't last long, though, because I'm suddenly hit by a pang of guilt. Ben. Ryan. I don't know what I want or how I feel.

"It's okay," he says, studying my expression. "I'm not expecting anything from you. This world is too insane for relationships or dating. I just wanted to do something a normal eighteen-year-old guy would do, you know? Just in case I die properly next time."

I let out a small laugh and smile shyly. "Okay."

Just then, Zeke and Ben return with Stephan. He has a huge bruise from where I punched him, and looks incredibly angry. They're carrying a box filled with cans of food. At last, we'll be able to eat. Molly looks at Stephan coolly, as if to warn him that she has neither forgotten nor forgiven the gun incident.

"You must be the survivor," Bree says with a friendly smile.

Stephan gives her a moody look. "That's me."

"Well, thanks for letting us stay here," she adds, brightly. "We appreciate your hospitality."

Stephan touches his jaw and winces. "I didn't exactly have much choice."

"Come on," I say, peering into the box filled with can of beans and fruit. "Let's eat."

We gorge ourselves on the provisions, and as we do, we look over our map again, plotting out our route. Between mouthfuls of canned peaches, I look at Stephan.

"You said you knew a good route to Texas," I say. "So, tell us."

"The Mississippi is by far the safest route," Stephan explains, pointing it out on the map. "You can follow its path all the way to Baton Rouge in Louisiana."

"We have a boat," I explain as I pop another piece of peach into my mouth. "It's in Toledo Harbor. It would only take a couple of hours to head back and get it. We could send a small group."

"A boat isn't going to do you any good," Stephan says, his laugh closer to a scoff.

"Why?" I ask, frowning.

"Because there's no water in the Mississippi anymore. The riverbed is completely dry."

"What?" I snap. "Then why would we even bother going that way?"

"Because it's still the best route," Zeke says gently. "And at least this way we won't have to go back for the boat."

I chuck my empty can down on the ground, making it clatter. Everyone jumps at the sound. I don't know why I'm so angry, it's just that fate seems to be throwing every obstacle it can at us.

"You really need to chill out," Stephan says.

"Chill out?" I say, getting more irritated by the second. "What about this scenario do I have to be chilled out about?"

"Well," Stephan says, haughtily, "how about the fact that I know somewhere nearby where we can get motorcycles?"

I stare at him, my mouth agape. "Why didn't you say so?"

He gives me a smug look. "Maybe something to do with you punching me out cold. It didn't exactly warm me to you."

"Brooke!" Bree chastises me. "You didn't, did you?"

"He was pointing a gun at Molly!" I cry, defending myself.

"Stephan," Bree snaps at him. Then she looks at each of us in turn. "Can we all please stop arguing? It's not doing any good. We're all in this together so we may as well start acting like friends."

I fold my arms and stare Stephan down. He gives me a fake smile, one that says we will probably never be friends. But if he knows how to get us bikes, and as long as I'm in possession of his gun, then we're sticking together.

"Fine," I say, relenting. "Let's get some sleep. We leave for the Mississippi in the morning."

CHAPTER FOURTEEN

"Ta-da," Stephan says, gesturing to the open garage door.

I peer into the gloom. Inside I see several old vintage motor bikes and choppers, covered in thick dust and cobwebs. They look like they could have belonged to a gang of Hells Angels once upon a time. They've certainly seen better days.

"And these things work?" I ask, incredulous.

I can't help thinking that Stephan's led us on a wild goose chase.

"Oh, they work," he replies.

He walks into the garage and toward one of the choppers, then retrieves the keys from inside its seat compartment. He twirls the keys around his fingers, showing off. I roll my eyes.

"Hurry up, please," I say. Stephan's really testing my patience.

He grins and finally puts a key in the ignition. The bike thrums to life, its engine roaring and throwing out fumes.

"I don't believe it," I say, pacing forward and drawing up beside the bike. "How much gas is in this thing?"

"It has a full tank," Stephan replies. "They all do. I've been siphoning gas for years, filling them all up, just in case."

"In case of what?"

"In case I ever found somewhere to go."

For the first time since I've met him, I feel bad for Stephan. He's a survivor like me, who's done morally questionable things to survive just like I have. Making Molly a hostage was just a desperate act on his part. Can I really say I wouldn't have done the same if our positions were reversed?

"Thanks," I say, trying to sound sincere. "We'll get to the Mississippi in no time at all with these. Come on, guys, grab a bike."

Everyone enters the dark garage and chooses a vehicle. I make sure my bike has a sidecar so that Bree can travel with me with Penelope on her lap. It makes me feel better to have her close. Charlie chooses to ride in a sidecar with Ben. As Ryan attempts to mount a bike, I rest my hand gently on his arm.

"I don't know if it's a good idea for you to be in control of a vehicle after what happened yesterday."

"I'm not an invalid, Brooke," he replies. "I'm fine now."

"I know, I'm just being cautious. And anyway, you should be in a sidecar with Jack really. You are his master, after all."

He finally agrees to get in the sidecar with Molly driving.

Before we set off, Zeke pulls out the map.

"It's four hundred miles direct," he says. "But that takes us straight through Chicago."

I shake my head. "No way. We need to avoid Chicago entirely. There'll be an arena there. I'm certain."

He nods in agreement. "Then how about we take this route, heading slightly southwest? We'll avoid Chicago completely, but it will add an extra three hours to the journey."

"Three more hours?" Ryan repeats. "That's a hell of a lot more gas used up than needs to be."

"I think we should take the direct route," Molly says, joining in the debate.

"I think we should take the safest route," Ben contests.

I sigh, my head filled with thoughts that swirl around. "Is there anywhere to stop off midway?" I ask Zeke. "We could do with hunting and picking up some more provisions."

Stephan makes a scoffing noise. "Yeah, great idea, since you've eaten all my rations."

Even though it's true that we finished up the last of his rations over breakfast, I shoot him a glare and he quiets down.

Zeke shows me a spot on the map that's meant to be a wooded area. It's on the direct route, close to Chicago. It would be risky to go that way but I'm starting to think it's our best bet.

"Remember this map is about a hundred years old," Zeke reminds me. "Whether that wood is still there or not, there's no guarantee."

I nod, understanding that it would be a risk to head somewhere we can't be certain exists, especially when it's so close to a major city.

"Molly and Ryan are right," I say finally. "We need to head the most direct route. We can stop off here in the forest, pick up some provisions, have a rest. Then we'll detour a little south so that we miss Chicago entirely."

I look up at my friends, hoping for confirmation. Ben's the only one who doesn't look impressed. He must think I'm siding with Ryan when I'm really just trying to do what's best for everyone.

Zeke folds up the map and puts it away safely in his pocket. "That's settled then. Let's go."

We mount our bikes and head out of the garage and onto the main road, leaving Toledo and the destroyed rail yard behind us, venturing out on a new path, with a new plan, into the unknown.

*

Since there's no one else on the freeway, we can use as much of the road as we want. It feels freeing, like we're breaking all the rules of our old civilization.

It's a cool spring morning. By the color of the sky and the position of the sun, I would guess it's only slightly after 6 a.m. We all managed to get a decent night's sleep last night and, along with filling our stomachs with Stephan's canned food, we've all woken up feeling rejuvenated.

It takes four hours of solid driving to reach our stop-off point in the woods south of Chicago. To my great relief, the drive is uneventful. After about two hours of cruising, the engines whining in my ears, my friends at my sides, I finally stopped bracing myself for catastrophe.

I slow my bike to a stop beneath a patch of trees. The others draw up beside me and kill their engines. Silence descends. By the time we turn off the main road, fatigue and hunger have set in.

After a moment, birds start singing in the trees.

"Dinner," I say, dismounting my bike.

I look over at Ryan. The two of us spent months hunting in the forests of Fort Noix, and I've been missing those quiet, peaceful moments. I'm expecting him to jump at the opportunity to come hunting with me, but he doesn't look like he wants to go anywhere at all.

"I'll come with you," Ben says quickly.

I look from one to the other as it dawns on me what is happening. The jealousy between them is growing, causing a rift. Before, Ben was the weak one, the distant one, and Ryan was right by my side supporting me. But now, after his near-death experience, Ryan's the one who's becoming withdrawn, and Ben isn't hesitating for a second to step into his shoes.

"You know, there's a lake a little farther north," Zeke says. "Maybe we should send someone to fish as well."

"I'll go," Stephan says. "I know how to fish."

I look at him skeptically. I still don't trust him, even after he led us to the motorbikes and let us eat his food.

"I'll go with him," Zeke says.

"I don't need a chaperone," Stephan replies.

"You don't get a choice," I say to Stephan. Then to Zeke, I add in a hushed tone, "Don't let him out of your sight."

Ben and I collect the bows and arrows and head into the forest. The thick canopy of trees above us provides a nice, cool shade.

We walk quietly through the forests, making sure not to startle any birds. The silence between Ben and me has never been awkward. Our friendship has never needed many words spoken. Ben feels like my companion, like an extension of myself. He's been there since the beginning, since everything changed for me and Bree. He helped me through some terrible times. He's seen me at my absolute worst and he's always been by my side. If he wasn't there, I wouldn't feel right.

I pause and gesture for Ben to do the same. He freezes and we both listen to the twittering coming from the trees above us. I recognize it as the call of grouse.

Slowly, imperceptibly, we both move into position with our arrows poised and ready to fire. The second the grouse take flight, we let the arrows go. They sail through the air, side by side, and each one hits its target.

Elated, I swirl on the spot and embrace Ben. His arms encircle me, holding me close. It feels so good to be reunited with him. Being in his arms feels so right.

I hear a twig snap and leap away from Ben, suddenly filled with guilt. I look up and see Stephan standing there, his eyebrow raised, a row of fish hanging from his line. Zeke's a few steps behind.

"Don't let me interrupt," Stephan says, amused.

"You're not interrupting anything," I mumble, feeling uncomfortable and awkward, putting some extra space between me and Ben. I don't meet anyone's eye as I add, "Let's get the food back to the others."

Ben and I grab the grouse from where they fell, then the four of us head back, not saying a word as we go.

We make it back to the place at the edge of the forest where we pulled over to find that Ryan and Molly have made a sort of camp. Charlie, Bree, and the dogs are all sleeping curled up around each other beside a fire pit lined with hot rocks.

"Grouse," I say to them, holding up the two dead birds. "The others caught fish."

They all look thrilled.

It takes a few hours to cook the fish and birds on the hot rocks. The smell while we're waiting makes us salivate. But the results are better than I expected and everyone sits around munching on the tender meat, relieved to finally be resting and filling their stomachs.

Soon, the light begins to fade.

"Should we set up camp for the night?" Molly asks.

"No," Ryan says. "We should get a move on."

I'm inclined to side with him; the longer we stay out here in the middle of nowhere the more likely we are to run into danger. But there are risks to driving in the darkness as well. We're so close to Chicago we'll have to drive without headlights so as not to draw any attention to our whereabouts. That will make it far more difficult to navigate and far more dangerous to drive. But despite the danger, I'm certain it would be better for us to keep going, albeit slowly and cautiously, than risk being discovered or ambushed in the middle of the night.

"Ryan's right," I say. "We should pack up and ride through the night."

"I think we should stay," Ben says, challenging me.

I frown, looking at him with confusion. I'd assumed Ben would be on my side—he's seen firsthand what the slaverunners can do after all. A part of me wonders if he's saying that just to start an argument with Ryan.

Whatever his reasoning, it works. I can't tell whether Ryan's making up for lost time or just being overzealous because he has an opposing opinion to Ben, but he pushes his point rather aggressively.

"We'd be sitting ducks!" he cries. "We're far too close to Chicago."

"We'd be driving blind," Ben counters. "It's too dangerous."

"Hardly," Ryan scoffs. "It's not like we're going to run into anyone else out on the road. But if you're worried that your driving skills aren't up to the challenge—"

"My driving skills are fine," Ben shoots back.

Stephan starts laughing, seemingly finding the two boys bickering a source of amusement. I decide that things are getting too heated and step forward to intervene.

"Guys," I say, holding my hands up. "Arguing isn't helping anything."

"But you're siding with him," Ben says.

I can see the hurt in his eyes.

"It's not about sides."

Molly steps in, again trying to be the peacemaker. "We need to do what's best for the kids."

"What's best for the kids is not getting kidnapped by slaverunners," I say. I look at Ben, appealing with my eyes. "You know that. You're just being argumentative."

Ben looks down at the floor. He knows I'm right. He knows the fight he's picking with Ryan isn't about whether we drive through the night or not, but about me.

"Ben, I'm sorry," I say. "But there's plenty of bikes. If you want to stay back and sleep the night, you can. Ryan and I can just go on ahead and meet up with you later."

His gaze snaps up. "No way."

Once again I know he's arguing against me and Ryan being alone together more than anything else.

"There has to be some kind of compromise," I say diplomatically.

Bree, overhearing the dispute, comes over.

"Brooke's right," she says. "We have to keep going. If we stay here we'll get caught by slaverunners."

Ben folds his arms. "I'm not just going to change my mind because an eleven-year-old girl has told me to. That's not how democracy works."

"Who said this was a democracy?" Bree says haughtily. "Brooke's leader. It's her plan. She gets to decide."

Everyone looks at me. I curse silently in my head. I wish Bree hadn't put me in such a difficult situation. I know Ben's going to read more into my answer than he ought to, that he's going to think that I'm choosing Ryan when really all I'm choosing is common sense. But right now staying alive is more important than not hurting Ben's feelings.

"I'm sorry," I say to him. "But we're driving on. It's only a couple more hours before we reach the Mississippi. We can rest there."

Ben shakes his head and looks so disappointed it makes my stomach ache. The atmosphere is beyond tense. Then suddenly, Stephan starts clapping.

"I'm so glad you guys brought me along for the ride," he says. "This is so entertaining."

Molly shoots him an angry glare.

With a heavy heart, I get back on my bike and try to kick it to life. But nothing happens. I check the gas gauge and realize that it's practically on zero.

"Um, guys!" I call out. "I'm out of gas!"

One by one, everyone checks their own bikes and realizes that the same fate has befallen them. Every single one of our bikes has run out of gas.

I turn on Stephan.

"I thought you said the tanks were full!" I snap. "You said we could make it all the way to the Mississippi."

He looks sheepish. "They were. I guess they just… well, the bikes are really old, you know? Maybe there were leaks in the tubes or something."

Furious, I run over to the road that we'd come along. Sure enough, there are little droplets of gas all along the road. I run back to the others.

"Okay, now we really have to get out of here," I say, urgently. "We've made a trail with gas all the way here. If there are slaverunners on that road, we'll lead them right to us."

Everyone looks terrified.

"You want us to walk?" Bree says, trembling. "In the pitch black?"

"We have no choice," I say, marching ahead. "Come on! Everyone, get a move on!"

I'm starting to lose my cool. But the rest of the gang knows I'm right and they start to follow.

As the night grows darker and colder I curse under my breath. Our two-hour drive has just turned into a twenty-four-hour trek.

*

The sun starts to rise. We've been walking all night. As the black nothingness I'd found comforting disappears, I'm now faced with a sight of destruction and devastation.

Up ahead a rusted metal sign reads Galesburg, but it's the only thing left standing. The rest of the town has been reduced to a huge crater. Someone dropped a bomb here so powerful it wiped the entire town off the face of the earth, leaving behind nothing but a welcome sign teetering on the edge of the crater.

It's heartbreaking to think of what this place once was. To think of all the innocent families blown to pieces, their lives cut short in one catastrophic moment.

"I don't believe it," Ben says, breaking through my thoughts.

I look up. Just ahead, the only thing standing beside the long, straight road, is a used car yard, still filled with cars.

I try not to let myself feel too hopeful, but as the gang rushes over, the dogs barking excitedly at our heels, I start to feel that we might have had our first stroke of luck in hours.

Together we rush across the street to the auto salvage yard. They cars look like ones from the 1950s. The doors, thankfully, are unlocked.

Zeke climbs in the front driver's seat.

"You're not going to believe this," he says. "It has a full tank of gas."

I can't believe our luck. But no sooner do we get the good luck than we're immediately hit with the bad luck.

"Damn, no keys," Zeke says.

"That's not a problem," Molly replies. "I can hotwire a car."

I raise my eyebrows at her. She shrugs.

"We all have pasts, Brooke," she says with a haughty little smile.

She gets the car started then does the same with another. Bree jumps in the back of the other car. Of course, Charlie joins Bree, and Penelope, too, wanting to be with her favorite human, clambers in. Then Jack starts barking at the kids and dog in the back seat, making it very clear that he wants to ride with his furry companion.

Ryan beelines for that car. "I should stay with Jack," he says. "Plus, I want to drive."

Molly takes the passenger seat in the other car next to Zeke. Ben takes the backseat behind Zeke and Molly, then it's just me and Stephan.

"After you," I say, trying to get him to take the pressure off me over whose car I get in.

He laughs and shakes his head. "No way. I wanna see who Brooke is going to choose!" He makes a kissy face.

"You're a jerk," I hiss, looking from one car to the other, from Ben to Ryan, torn, not knowing what to do.

Thankfully, Bree leans out the window. "Come with us, Brooke!" she cries. "Please, please, please!"

I smile. "Of course."

I turn and clamber in the seat beside Ryan while Stephan waltzes to the other car, whistling nonchalantly as he goes. I don't look for Ben's expression. I don't want to know how angry he is with me for choosing Ryan over him once again.

Once we're all strapped in, Ryan guns the gas pedal and reverses out of the lot. Zeke does the same. At last we're on the road, in vehicles. For the first time, the chances of us making it to Texas don't seem so small.

"Let's get to the Mississippi already," I say.

Our two cars cruise along side by side, heading west. As we go, we try to avoid any of the towns or cities, cautious about how close we get to built-up areas. There's no knowing whether they'll be in enemy hands, crawling with slaverunners ready to kidnap us and bring us to their arenas. So we stick to the open roads wherever possible, the ones that cut straight through barren landscape.

Darkness falls like a blanket of black. We can hardly see anything beyond the hood of the car, and we certainly can't see Molly, Zeke, Stephan, and Ben's car behind us.

Ryan's a careful driver but I know in another life he wouldn't be. In another world, a world without the war that's ravished everything, Ryan and I probably wouldn't even get along. He'd be the cool senior boy, a bit fringe, a bit tough, driving some beat-up piece of junk and never seen without his trusty pit bull. I'd be... I don't know what I'd be. I can't even imagine who I'd be without all the terrible things that have shaped me.

At last, we reach the Mississippi and ride down the slope into the bone-dry riverbed.

Seeing the impact that the war has had on the Mississippi is truly awful. I hate what our species has done to the world, the ways in which it has destroyed nature. My only hope is that one day our country will recover, that the Mississippi will be the beautiful, life-giving river it once was.

"What's that noise?" Ryan says, breaking me from my thoughts.

I strain to hear over the rumble of the engine. I can just about pick up a noise, a sort of whining. It sounds like a vehicle revving.

"It's the other car, isn't it?" I say.

Through the darkness, I can just make out Ryan shaking his head. My blood runs cold.

All at once, a blinding light suddenly appears in the rearview mirror. My heart clenches as I realize we're not alone, that someone's been following us.

Suddenly, our car's shunted forward. I scream and grab hold of my seat as we jerk roughly around. Ryan fights to keep hold of the steering wheel, to keep control. But whatever hit us rams into us again. I can't see through the bright light, I can't tell what's hitting us. But there's no chance to work it out, because we're hit again and suddenly we're spinning, up and over, round and round.

Charlie and Bree are screaming as we spin. My body feels like it's being hurled through the air.

Then, suddenly, my head slams against the window. I hear a crack. Before I get the chance to work out if it's the glass or my skull, everything turns black.

PART THREE

CHAPTER FIFTEEN

I groan. My head is pounding. I manage to open my eyes a sliver. The daylight is stark and bright, making me wince. I realize my face is against a hard cement ground covered in sand.

Memories of the car crash come back to me in a rush. I sit up, startled. As I do, I hear the distinctive clinking noise of chains.

I look all around. I'm in a bare cell filled with other people. We're all sitting on the dusty ground, chained to the wall. There's a window set high in the bricks, letting in the blistering sunshine. We're definitely still south, but where exactly is a question I cannot answer.

I notice Charlie curled up in a ball opposite me. He's covered in the sandy-colored desert dust, but other than that, he looks like he got out of the crash unscathed. Then I see Bree slumped against a far wall, unconscious. There's crusted blood all over her clothes and matted into her hair. My heart clenches at the sight of her. An instinct in me makes me reach for her and my chains jangle loudly as I move. But they hold me back, stopping me from reaching her.

"Brooke?" I hear someone whisper.

I look left. It's Ryan. He's one of the few prisoners who's awake, and must have been drawn by the sound of my clanking chains.

I'm relieved to see him alive, and glad to know that everyone from our car made it out of the crash. But at the same time I feel frantic, desperate, and distraught. We've been captured. Again. Once more, my freedom has been stolen from me. And I have no idea what happened to the other car, to Molly, Zeke, Stephan, and Ben.

At the thought of Ben, my heart constricts. We parted on bad terms. What if that ends up being the last time I see him alive? How could I have let him get into the other car like that, with so much left unspoken between us?

There's no time to dwell. Though my heart aches with worry over what could have happened to my friends in the other car, I have more pressing matters to deal with in the immediate moment: escape.

"Are you okay?" I say to Ryan.

He nods but he's gritting his teeth and I know something is causing him pain. It's then that I notice Jack isn't with him. His trusty best friend, who has been by his side since forever, has been taken. I look back at Bree and realize that Penelope is missing too.

Rage swirls through me at the thought of what might have happened to them.

"What are we going to do?" I say to Ryan.

He shakes his head. "I don't know. Wait. See what's what then come up with a plan."

My stomach drops. I know all too well what's what. I've been in this situation before. There's only one thing that awaits us, and that's an arena.

Just then, the sound of footsteps comes from the other side of the cell door. Then there's a rusted, grinding noise as someone turns a key in the lock. The door swings open and bangs against the wall, making a cloud of dust whirl into the air.

Many of the prisoners who've been sleeping jerk awake. One of them is Charlie. He looks around, disorientated and panic-stricken. I catch his eye and nod to him, trying to reassure him. But his large, fearful eyes keep being drawn to the figure that just entered the room, a man dressed in a long, black robe, with a large hood that completely obscures his face.

"Morning, sleepyheads," the man says in a thick southern accent. He uses a cheerful tone but I can hear the undercurrent beneath it, one that tells me this man is anything but friendly, that he is cruel and mean. "Who's hungry?"

People begin to moan, stretching their hands out desperately for food. The other prisoners must have been survivors before they were kidnapped, living out in the harsh desert wasteland.

More people enter the room behind the black-clad man, all in similar attire. They're carrying buckets. The buckets are dropped in front of us, one bucket to three or four prisoners. Breakfast. But when I look inside, I recoil. They're filled with dead cockroaches.

"Come on, slaves, eat up!" the man cries sadistically. "We gotta get y'all strong for a day's hard labor!"

I look up at him sharply, trying to make eye contact with him through the slit in his hood.

"Why don't you just take us to the arena and get it over with," I bark at him. "That's why we're here, isn't it?"

There's a pause before the man walks over to me slowly, his heavy boots clunking. He bends down at the knees and gets close to my face.

"That's not why you're here at all, missy," he hisses. "We don't have any arenas here. We've got much better things for y'all to be doing. You see, the other biovictims, they're jealous of y'all, with your pretty features and your healthy bodies. All they want is to eradicate you. Not us. We know that God chose us. We're biovictims because of his grand plan. This new world, the one that exists after his Armageddon, it's a world made for *us*."

He pulls his hood off in one quick movement. In spite of myself, I flinch. His face is horrific. It looks as though half of it is melting, with one of his eyes dropping down his face at an awful angle. His teeth are exposed on one side of his face where the flesh is no longer there, and there are places on his bald head where the skin has bubbled and burned.

"You don't like the look of God's new creatures, do you?" he says, so close his spittle hits my face. "Well, you listen to me, missy. This is how it's going to be now. You all had your chance and you blew it. Literally. We're the ones who own the earth now. And that means you gotta work for us."

"You're making us slaves?" I say.

The man stands at last and puts his hood back on. "God said that he put the animals on the earth for us to use. And that's what y'all are to us, nothing more than animals. So we're going to use y'all, just like He said we're meant to. We're going to work y'all to death."

The people who'd brought in the buckets begin hauling prisoners up to their feet, locking them into a row with chains. Ryan gets yanked up and cries out in pain. I can see now that his shoulder has been dislocated, probably from the crash.

I watch helplessly as people are dragged to their feet and added to the chain. Charlie, despite his young age, is shown no mercy, and neither is Bree, who only wakes up, finally, once she's shaken roughly to her feet. I try to get her attention, to calm her down, but she's so frantic she doesn't see me. I can't imagine how frightened she must be feeling to have woken up to this horror.

Finally, I'm added to the row, right at the front. A heavy metal collar is placed around my neck. The chains weigh so much it's hard to even stand upright.

"This way," the hooded man says to me.

When I don't move he gestures to one of the other robed men, who then pulls a long whip from his belt and strikes me with it. The pain is so sharp I'm momentarily winded. I gasp and feel tears spring to my eyes.

"I said, 'this way,' missy," the leader snarls.

I don't argue again. I begin to trudge through the cell, following his lead out of the prison cell, along the corridor, then finally out the cell block and into the bright sunshine.

It takes a moment for my eyes to adjust. When they do, I gasp in horror. As far as the eye can see are groups of slaves, other people like me, chained together, moving heavy blocks and stones to make buildings. They're all painfully thin and barely clothed. Many of them are bright red, sunburned from the harsh glare of the sun. I can see why our captors wear the robes now, to protect their skin from the UV glare. Black-robed slavers ride about on motorbikes, making clouds of dust fly into the air. They whip the prisoners as they go, seemingly at random.

Enormous structures like temples are dotted around, made of huge stone bricks. Some stones stand several feet high, while others have intricate patterns, statues and columns carved into them. It reminds me of pictures of Ancient Egypt that I learned about in school. The slavers are building a new city in the crater where another city once stood. It's like being in a valley, only this one was man-made, created by bombs, bombs that were far more destructive than anything I saw in the north. These bombs have created a wasteland, a brutal landscape of desert. There's not a tree or body of water as far as the eye can see.

"Welcome," the robed man says in his fake cheery voice, "to Memphis, Tennessee."

*

We trudge along, me leading the way, following the robed man. The whole time, my eyes are darting around me, taking in everything, seeking a way to break out of this nightmare. We're so close to reaching Texas, there's no way I'm giving up now. I'll do whatever it takes to get out of this place.

My heart soars when I catch sight of bright ginger hair. I look over. Molly is in another chain of prisoners, being led the same direction as us. She's gritting her teeth and limping. I let out the breath I'd been holding as I see that a few people behind her stands Ben. I'm relieved to discover that he's completely unscathed from the crash, though there's blood on his clothes. I scan the rest of the line but Stephan and Zeke are nowhere to be seen. I can't help but fear the worst.

We're led past a stack of cages filled with animals. I see that crammed inside one of the cages are Penelope and Jack. They look terrified, huddled together, shaking. My only comfort is that they have each other.

As we trudge through the wasteland, I manage to catch Molly's eye. Silently, we try to communicate with one another. She's looking at the bikes, same as me. We're both thinking that they're our only chance of escape. If we want to live to see tomorrow, we're going to have to steal them somehow.

I gesture to the chains around my wrists. The way that we're all connected together means that if I yank hard enough, I could get the whole line to fall. Then, in the confusion, we might be able to find a way to break free.

I look back at Ryan and hold up my chained hands, trying to communicate to him what I intend to do. I mime tugging them down and he nods in understanding. But my attempt to communicate with him doesn't go unnoticed by the guards. A slaver zooms over on his bike and cracks his whip against my chest before roaring away. I cry out in pain and fall to my knees. Blood appears on my top.

Despite the pain making black stars flash in my vision, I know I can't let this opportunity go to waste. I pretend to be struggling to stand up, knowing that the slaver will return and whip me again. As I slowly struggle to my knees, I quickly glance over at Molly and nod, as if to say: now. We tug on our chains simultaneously. I see her line begin to tumble, and can hear the prisoners behind me begin to fall as well. At the same time, the slaver circles back around on his bike, his whip raised high, ready to discipline me for my rebellion. I reach out and grab the whip as he cracks it down. I grip with all my strength, not letting go, then yank it toward me. The slaver goes spinning off his bike, smacking to the ground with a crunch. The bike heads straight toward a crowd of people, making them scatter in all directions.

Chaos breaks out in that moment. Slavers start whizzing toward us on their bikes, attempting to quell the pandemonium with their whips. But the rest of my group understands what is happening—they know instinctively that I'm trying to free us all—and the other prisoners catch on too. The slavers may have weapons and bikes, but we have more people and an unbreakable will to live. If I can just get my chains off, I'll be a formidable opponent.

There's a bike screaming toward me, and I know I have only one shot to do what I'm planning to do. It's a crazy idea but I have no other options.

As the bike flies toward me, its rider ready to strike me with the whip, I throw my chained hands out directly in front of its tires. As the whip lashes against my back, making me scream with pain, the bike roars directly over the rusty chains, snapping them clean in half. I'm free.

I rise to my feet immediately and leap, like a cat, onto the back of the motorbike. The slaver is not expecting me to move so quickly and doesn't get his defenses up in time. After a short grapple, I manage to shove him off the bike. He hits the ground hard and goes rolling across the desert earth.

I take control of the bike and double back on myself, heading straight for Ryan.

"Chains!" I shout. "I'm going to cut your chains!"

I see him crouch and lay his arms out, closing his eyes, unable to look. But I steer perfectly over the chains, and they snap beneath my wheels. He's free. Now there are two of us able to fight.

The prisoners in Molly and Ben's chain are being surrounded by bikes, penned in like sheep, with nowhere to go. It's up to me and Ryan to liberate them.

I slow the bike, allowing him to leap on the back.

"You're bleeding," he says, leaping on.

"I'll be fine."

He encircles my waist with his good arm, the other hanging limply by his side, and I rev the bike again. Together we race forward, plowing straight toward the group. I'm trying to call their bluff, to get them to scatter, but they're holding their positions.

"WE'RE GOING TO CRASH!" Ryan screams in my ear.

I can see the terrified faces of the prisoners behind the line of captors on bikes. Everyone knows what is about to happen, and I'm the only one who can stop it. But I won't. This is our one chance. I gun the bike, gaining more and more speed.

"JUMP WHEN I SAY!" I shout back to Ryan, praying he can hear me over the roaring wind.

His grip on me gets tighter and tighter.

"NOW!" I scream.

We both jump to the side, letting our bike carry on forward without us, and hit the ground hard. I roll across the parched earth, one, two, three times, then manage to stop myself. I glance over my shoulder just in time to see the bike slam into the others at full speed. The gas tank explodes and I duck down, covering my head with my arms as flames and bits of twisted metal fly into the air and rain down over me.

This is the chance the other group needed. In the chaos and under the cover of thick, billowing smoke, they're able to scurry away from their captors, many of whom are now lying groaning on the ground or rolling around in an attempt to put out the fires ravaging them.

"THIS WAY!" I scream, leaping to my feet, ignoring the aches and pains in my body from hitting the ground.

A little way ahead, Ryan manages to drag himself up. His bad arm dangles uselessly at his side.

All the prisoners begin to follow me. For the first time since being chained to the front of my group, I catch sight of Bree, way, way back. She and Charlie are attempting to liberate Jack and Penelope from their cages. I'm about to scream at them that there's no time when they manage to get the cage open. The dogs leap down and start running toward me and Ryan. Bree and Charlie clasp their hands together and run at full speed through the fire and smoke, jumping over smoldering body parts and hunks of metal. I want to run to Bree, to sweep her into my arms, but I know I have to keep going forward. I have to trust that she'll follow.

Ryan is right beside me as I run. Out of all the prisoners, we're the only two completely free from our shackles. The others are still bound together. They're all running at different speeds and attempting to maneuver in different directions around debris. It's slowing us down, giving the slavers a chance to regroup. There's no way we'll be able to get all the prisoners free. But then I have an idea. Maybe we can use this to our advantage.

I tell Ryan my plan and he looks at me like I'm crazy. But when he looks back and sees the bikes racing toward us in a line, he knows this is the only chance we have of defeating our captors. We pass the message back to the prisoners and one by one they nod their agreement.

The bikes are gaining on us, and the slavers riding them swing their whips over their heads, ready to strike us down.

"NOW!" I shout.

All at once, the prisoners fan out in a long line, stretching the chains that connect them so they're just level with the necks of the approaching riders. One by one the slavers are caught in the trap, the chains pinging them from their bikes and throwing them to the ground.

Some of the bikes keep rushing forward before crashing and exploding, while others skid to their sides and halt. Ryan and I rush forward and grab the spare bikes. Now it's up to us to keep the remaining slavers at bay while the prisoners escape. Molly's using a dropped axe to start smashing apart the chains and freeing the prisoners. Once they have their arms freed they'll be in much better positions to steal bikes.

Ryan and I also grab discarded tools, brandishing them as weapons as we start circling back and forth on our bikes, facing off with the remaining slavers. We're trying to keep them at bay long enough for the rest of our group to be freed.

The scene behind us is one of utter chaos. Prisoners are cowering as the slavers attempt to whip them into submission. Other robed men are running around on fire, screaming, trying to fan out the flames. More still lie dead on the ground, their limbs twisted and jutting out at painful angles. There's thick smoke everywhere, obscuring my vision. Then, through the smoke, a figure emerges.

Despite being fully robed, I recognize him straightaway as the man who'd first spoken to us in the prison cell. He's standing at the front of a group of slavers, leading them to battle. A red mist descends over my vision. I rev the bike, brandish the crowbar in my hand, and race toward him. I swing the crowbar back and, as I pass, bring it down with all my strength. I hear the crack of his skull, see him fall, dead, to the ground, and a sick satisfaction washes over me.

I loop back and see that Molly and the others have managed to get hold of bikes. As much as I wish we could liberate all the prisoners here, I have to be selfish and look after my own. I drive up to my group.

"Bree, get on the back," I say to my sister, who is cuddling Penelope in her arms. "Molly, you take Charlie and Jack. Ryan, Ben, take a bike each. We'll need the spare spaces for Zeke and Stephan once we find them. Come on, let's go."

Everyone gets into position and I lead the way through the compound, racing past burning structures and groups of slavers and prisoners, trying to find Zeke and Stephan amongst them. But they're nowhere to be seen.

"We have to get out of here!" Molly cries from behind.

"NO!" I shout back. "We need to find Zeke and Stephan first."

"There's no time," she barks.

She's right. The slavers have noticed our little gang and they're starting to follow. But the thought of leaving my friends behind makes my blood run cold.

"We can't leave them!" I scream. "We have to rescue them."

Molly locks her eyes with mine. "We can't rescue them, Brooke. They're not here. They're dead."

CHAPTER SIXTEEN

We're still tearing along the road on the bikes, but it feels like the ground has fallen away beneath my feet. I can hardly breathe.

"I'm sorry," Molly cries over the wind as we race across the parched earth. "They didn't survive the crash. We have to go."

Stephan and Zeke are dead? I can't believe it. I don't want to believe it.

I look back over my shoulder. They others look as depressed as me. None of us wants to accept the reality of having lost two of our group, and I can't help but feel like their deaths are on my shoulders. I look at Ben, hoping that the only other person in the car who may have been witness to their tragic demise will be able to refute the bombshell Molly has just dropped on me.

"Ben was passed out," Molly shouts. "He didn't see. But I did. They're gone, Brooke. We have to save ourselves."

Emotions threaten to choke me. I feel like I could easily give in to the blackness, to give up the fight.

"Brooke!" Bree cries from the back of the bike. "Listen to Molly. We have to save ourselves."

The sound of her voice grounds me, brings me back to the moment. We may have lost our friends but we haven't lost our hope. Now isn't the time to break down. Like my dad would always say, crying won't keep you alive. No matter how terrible I feel, I have to do what needs to be done to survive.

I grip the handlebars of the bike hard in my fists and grit my teeth, more determined than ever.

"Let's go!" I cry.

Without another word, we rev the bikes, driving even faster through the thick smoke. We're searching for a road, a way out. The slavers got into the crater somehow, and we'll be able to get out if we find it. But driving through the crater city is dangerous. There are still slavers milling around, not to mention prisoners who are desperate to be liberated. The whole time I'm on a knife edge, feeling like my world could end any second. Bree must feel it too; her clutch on me is so tight it's painful.

Finally I see a steep incline leading out of the crater. It's been carved like a road, winding up the crater edge. I pray our bikes can handle such a difficult climb.

"THERE!" I cry to the others.

One by one we start to race up the steep road. I'm gunning the bike, knowing the only thing that will carry me up is speed. As we burst through the cloud of smoke, I know we're now in plain view of all the slavers below. There's no hiding on the crater's edge. We're completely exposed.

It's then that I hear someone cry out. Instantly, I recognize the voice as belonging to Ben.

I look back and see that his battered bike is struggling to get up the incline. It has clearly been damaged in all the fighting and is starting to give out. It's getting slower and slower. Behind him, racing along on their own bikes, are a group of slavers.

"Ryan!" I shout. "You have to go back for Ben."

Ryan grits his teeth. "No way. If I go back, the slavers will get me."

I stare at him, horrified. "We can't leave him!"

"We left Zeke," he spits back. "We left Stephan."

"They died, Ryan. You heard Molly. We have to let them go. But Ben is still alive and he needs our help!"

Behind me, clinging on with dear life, Bree starts to cry.

"Please," she begs Ryan. "You're the only one with a spare space. Don't leave Ben to die."

The motorbikes are getting so close to Ben now it's almost too much to watch. I feel like every muscle in my body has tensed as I wait for Ryan's decision.

Finally, he lets out a deep sigh and turns his bike around, heading for Ben. The rest of us keep gunning it along the narrow pathway, racing up and up, higher and higher. I can't look back, terrified that I've sent Ryan to his death. I can't lose them both.

"BREE!" I shout over the roaring wind and revving engine. "What's happening?"

I can feel her cheek pressed into my back. The vibrations from the bike are making the wounds from being whipped sting.

"They're okay," she says. "Ryan's got Ben."

I let out my breath. They've made it. For now.

Just then, there's an almighty explosion. I can't look back, too scared that if I do so I'll veer off the narrow road and plunge into the crater beneath. Bree fills me in.

"Ryan and Ben blew up the bike," she cries. "The rest of the slavers are gone."

They did it. We're free. We made it.

What's left of us, anyway.

CHAPTER SEVENTEEN

We travel south, following the dried up riverbed of the Mississippi, riding without stopping. I know it only takes about eight hours from Memphis to Houston, and I'm desperate not to stop. But everyone's weary, battered, and exhausted, and eventually, after traveling for two hours, even I have to concede that we need to rest.

The devastation here is absolute. Everything has been completely flattened, reduced to a desert. The bombs that caused craters as big as towns in the north have completely flattened cities in the south. What were once bustling metropolises have been completely eradicated. All around, as far as the eye can see, there is nothing. Which means nowhere to hide, nowhere to shelter, and nowhere to hunt.

Finally, we draw to a halt. I get off the bike and help Bree down. Her face is streaked with tears and I realize she must have been crying about Zeke's and Stephan's deaths the whole way. I can't say I blame her. If my dad hadn't drilled it into me not to cry, I would have broken down too.

I want to comfort Bree but the guilt I feel over causing her so much pain holds me back. Luckily, Charlie comes over and hugs Bree close. She cries into his shoulder. Penelope goes over to her as well. I leave the three of them to it and walk over to the rest of the gang.

Ryan is slumped in a sitting position against a rock, cradling his dislocated arm.

"Want me to pop it back into place?" I say.

"Want is a strong word," he says, wryly. "But yeah."

I position myself, holding him by the top of the arm with one hand and holding the shoulder with the other. Then I yank. There's a huge crunching noise as the bone pops back into its socket. Ryan cries out, causing Jack to run over and start licking him.

"It's okay," he says through gritted teeth as he pats the dog's head. "I'm okay, boy."

Ben comes over to my side.

"Remember when you did that to my broken nose?" he says.

I do. It feels like a million years ago, in a whole different world. Up north, the effects of nuclear war have turned the place to ice, making the winters harsh and unforgiving. But down here in the south, there's been a different effect. Winters have been all but

120

banished. There is perpetual, blistering sunshine. And we're all suffering because of it. Dehydrated, sunburned, sweating.

Despite my grossness, I can't help but throw my arms around Ben. The last time we spoke properly we were arguing. Now we're both still here. Both still alive. We hold each other for a long time.

"Brooke?" Ryan says, breaking up my and Ben's moment.

I let my arms fall from Ben and turn to look at him. I can't help but feel angry. Ryan almost left Ben to die. It will take me a while before I can forgive him.

"I think we'd better try hunting," he says. "The kids are starving."

I move away from Ben and look around. "Hunt where?" I say. "There's nowhere around for miles."

"There are birds," he says. Then he tips his eyes down. "Vultures."

I know what that means. That somewhere nearby, the vultures are picking on the bones of dead people, other survivors who've lost their battle to the harsh desert landscape. As much as it revolts me, Ryan's right to bring them up as a source of food.

"Okay," I say. "Let's go."

We leave Molly and Ben to set up a fire so we can roast whatever we come back with, and Ryan and I trudge out into the desert together.

All of our belongings were taken back in the prisons in Memphis, so the only weapons we have now are the crowbars, axes, and spades we managed to grab as we were leaving. It's going to make hunting even more difficult, but we have no other choice. We take Jack with us too, hoping that he may be able to sniff out an easier catch for us.

We're silent as we go, but after a while, Ryan begins to speak.

"I'm sorry about what happened back there," he says.

"You mean about you almost leaving Ben to die?" I challenge him.

He looks away, ashamed. "Yeah."

I shake my head, fuming. "How could you?"

"I thought it was a suicide mission. I didn't think I'd make it."

I realize then what Ryan did for me. He thought going back to get Ben would mean certain death, yet he still did it. I should be thanking him, not berating him. Feeling ashamed, I finally mumble an apology, and we carry on in silence.

After a good twenty minutes walking, Ryan freezes. "Look," he says, pointing into the distance.

I can just make out a patch of trees. The sight is completely out of place in the harsh desert landscape. As we draw closer I realize the trees aren't growing out of the ground at all, but leaning against something. A fence? My heart stops as I realize it's a dwelling that's been covered in branches to conceal it. Through the trunks I can make out signs of life: a shack, a tin roof, something that looks like a well.

Ryan and I exchange a look. Neither of us can handle more fighting and whoever lives inside could be dangerous. But we also can't give up on the chance that we may have found shelter. Our group could seriously do with some shade.

"Shall we?" he says.

I nod my agreement and tighten my grip on the crowbar I'm carrying.

Carefully we approach the dwelling, which consists of little more than a wooden hut. It looks so out of place amongst the desolation. It must have been erected after the bombs. There's no way it would have survived them if all the other buildings around here were eradicated. Someone, some survivor, decided to make this empty wasteland his home.

We get to the hut and Ryan opens the door, crowbar raised over his head. Inside, everything is in darkness. It smells of dust.

I go in first. Jack races in after me, sniffing all the corners and crevices.

Whoever lived here was as much a survival nut as my dad. There are weapons and medical supplies, matches, flashlights, bandages, thread and needle, and, even more importantly, a small, wind-up radio. There's also enough food for us to eat well for at least a couple more days, though we're too close to our destination to slow down now. Still, it would be a great place to rest up for the night.

While Ryan seems overjoyed by the feast we'll be able to eat, I'm happier about the discovery of the radio. I grip it in my hands, feeling like I've just witnessed a miracle.

"We can use this to try to get in radio contact with the military base in Texas!" I cry, clutching it to my chest. "Tell them we're coming. Get their exact coordinates."

Ryan seems happy for me and my discovery and smiles encouragingly.

"Here, look," Ryan says, as Jack becomes excited by something on the other side.

I walk over and see that there's a trap door in the floor. Whoever built this was clever enough to also dig underground for some protection.

"What if there's someone down there?" I say.

"I guess now's the time to find out," Ryan replies.

He heaves open the trapdoor and we descend into the darkness. The underground bunker is a small room with bedding and pillows. It looks a bit like a nest. Certainly big enough and cozy enough for us.

"Let's get the others," I tell Ryan. "I think this would be a great place to rest up."

We head back toward the camp to fetch the others, relieved that we won't have to dine on fire-roasted vulture tonight.

But as we draw up toward the spot where we left the others, something unusual catches my attention. I recognize the silhouettes of my friends milling around, but there is someone else there, someone unfamiliar.

I catch Ryan's arm. "Who's that?" I say.

He squints, trying to make it out. "A stranger."

We give each other a wary look. We've been lucky so far with the survivors we've run into but I'm always on edge, always on the lookout for danger. That the stranger seems to be amongst the group calms my nerves a little; they've clearly deemed him safe.

We start to draw toward the gang. The stranger who has joined them is an older man, rake thin, with long white hair. He has a rasping laugh that I can hear even from this far away. Jack sprints up, yapping away, and runs in circles round the man's ankles, making him let out another one of his thick, mucusy laughs.

"Well, well, well, who's this then?" I hear him say as he crouches down and pets Jack. Then he looks up and sees Ryan and me approaching. "Well, howdy," he says, straightening up and extending one of his grubby hands.

I take it and shake. Ryan, cautiously, does the same.

"I'm Brooke," I say. "Who are you?"

"Craig," he replies, squinting against the sunshine. "Craig Merryweather. Your friends here told me you've traveled all the way from Quebec."

I nod. "And you? Where are you from?"

He shrugs. "Here and there. But mostly here." He grins, showing off a row of rotten teeth.

Bree looks up at me. "Did you find something for dinner?" she asks. "I'm hungry."

I look at Ryan, trying to judge whether to reveal our find or not in front of the stranger. He gives me a slight nod, as if to say he thinks it's safe.

"We did," I say. "There's a shack up there with supplies in it."

Craig suddenly lets out one of his croaking laughs. "That's my shack!" he cries, slapping his knee like I've just said the punch line of a joke. "But you can all come along. Stay the night. Get some rest." He eyes the collar round my neck. "Looks like you've been through the wars."

I catch Ryan's eye, silently asking him whether we ought to go or not. But really, we have no other choice. We're too exposed here and we have nothing to eat. We can eat and sleep in the bunker. Plus, there's more of us than him. He's far too outnumbered to try anything.

"Okay," I say finally. "Let's go."

*

Everyone takes it in turns to eat a pickle out of a jar. Then we use the medical supplies to patch ourselves up. I hadn't realized how badly wounded I was by the whip. There's a huge gash across my chest and another across my back. Molly cleans them both and sews them up, but I'm probably going to have scars. The adrenaline must have stopped me from feeling any pain. I'm also covered in bruises from the car crash. I look like a state.

"How did you guys all meet then?" Craig asks as he offers around some canned peaches for dessert.

"It's a long story," I say, scooping one up with my fingers and plopping it in my mouth. It's sweet and sticky, and so delicious.

"It's nice you've got each other," Craig replies. "I've been alone for years."

I feel sorry for him. At least on Catskills Mountain we had trees around, and animals. The desert is completely barren. It's the sort of landscape that could drive you mad.

"Why did you settle here?" I ask.

Craig shrugs. "Good a place as any." Then he laughs again, wheezing as he does. "I mean there's nothing around for miles and miles."

For someone who has been alone for so long, he seems strangely jovial. I can't help but think of Emmanuel in the castle on the Thousand Islands. Being alone has driven him crazy, but maybe that's the point. Maybe because being crazy has made it possible for him to survive.

There's ample space in the bunker part for everyone to get a place to sleep, though we leave our stuff upstairs in order not to crowd the room. We all huddle up together, full after eating jar after jar of provisions. Knowing we're so close to Houston—just an eight-hour drive—has made us throw caution to the wind. We all know that once we wake up tomorrow morning, we'll head out on the open road and reach our destination. With the radio to help guide us, there's no way we can fail. That doesn't stop me whispering a prayer under my breath. This world is brutal and unpredictable and I know that between now and tomorrow evening, anything could happen.

For the first time in a long time, we feel like we can relax, let our guards down just a little bit. The bunker feels so secure, not to mention being in the middle of literally nowhere. But feeling secure gives our minds the chance to process what's happened. One by one, our emotions creep up on us. Zeke and Stephan are dead. So are Rose, Flo, and Logan. We've all lost so much, seen so much, fought for so long.

"Hey, Molly," I say when I realize sleep won't come to me. "What did you mean when you said we all had pasts?"

I hear her sigh in the darkness. "I meant that I was a bit of trouble when I was a kid. The hotwiring cars kind. My parents were going crazy because of me. I was always in trouble. Then the war came and they died. There's nothing like being orphaned to make you clean up your act."

Her words hang in the air. Silence falls in the cabin as we all process what she said.

"I lost my parents too," Ryan says. "During one of the first airstrikes."

I roll onto my side and look over at where his disembodied voice is coming from. It's so dark that I can't even make out his silhouette. I wonder if that's the reason for his sudden candidness. In all the six months we were together in Fort Noix, Ryan never spoke about anything personal like his family or life before the war. I never asked because I figured he had a reason not to.

"But it was when my sister died that it was the worst," he finishes.

"What happened to her?" Bree asks softly.

"She had an asthma attack. Can you believe it? With the war and the slaverunners and nuclear destruction it was her own body that killed her. She'd run out of medication and that was that. She was six years old."

Six years old. The same age as Trixie.

"My brother was killed by slaverunners," Ben says.

His voice is as clear as a bell. It's the first time I've heard him truly admit his brother is dead. For a long time, he was clinging onto the hope that he was alive, but it seems that he's finally accepted reality.

"You had a brother?" Ryan asked.

I think it's the first time I've heard Ryan and Ben behave cordially to one another since they first met back at Fort Noix. Finally, they have something in common, something that can make them realize they're not so different from one another, that they're both on the same team.

"I did," Ben says. "It's how Brooke and I met. We were chasing the car that had Bree and my brother in it."

"He was brave," Bree said. "Right up to the end. He didn't let the slaverunners hurt me. And he loved you. He said you would come for him."

There's a long silence.

"Thank you," Ben finally says. I can hear the emotion thick in his voice.

"Flo wasn't my only sister," Charlie says suddenly. "I had two other ones, Daisy and Rebecca. Flo was the oldest. I was the youngest."

"I didn't know that," I say into the darkness.

I can hardly believe we've all been beside each other so long without getting to know the fundamentals. It's just another thing the war stole from us: socialization, communication, friendship. When your life is reduced to fighting and surviving, there's never really a good time for a chat.

"That's why Flo wanted me to be stronger," Charlie adds. "She didn't want me to get taken like they were."

"Was it slaverunners?" Molly asks.

"Yes," Charlie says. "Slaverunners."

No one asks anymore. The very fact that we've even spoken feels like the beginning of a healing process has begun. It's like we've stepped over some invisible line, broken down one of our guarded barriers. In this awful, terrifying world, opening up to each other about our pasts has been one of the scariest things we've done.

Despite our exhaustion, no one sleeps well that night. Bree wakes several times, sweating and screaming. She used to have night terrors all the time when we lived alone on the mountains but they stopped when we were at Fort Noix. I feel terrible for putting her in a position where she is so scared again. The only difference now is she has Charlie to comfort her. I can't help but feel a little pang of jealousy as I realize she leans on him more readily now than she does on me. It's partly her growing up and becoming independent—she's starting to realize she can't rely on me forever—but it's also partly because of me, because of how I've had to shut down my emotions to get through it all. I've been through so much, I don't have anything left in me to give.

As I lie there in the darkness, my mind mulling over everything we've been through, it dawns on me that I've become the soldier my dad always wanted me to be, the practical, tough, emotionless son he never had. But I also know that my emotionless exterior will only last so long. I won't be able to keep it up forever. One day, all the heartache will hit me at once, and when it does, I'll cry enough tears to refill the Mississippi.

CHAPTER EIGHTEEN

I'm almost surprised when I wake the next morning, still alive and in one piece. No disaster befell us during the night like I've come to expect. I even slept at some point.

I still have the heavy metal neck brace on that the slavers put on me and have no idea how I'm going to get it off; I can't exactly get Molly to take her axe to it. It's irritating and cumbersome, but it's just another niggling pain I'm going to have to endure.

My wounds are sore as I start to climb the ladder. When I reach the trap door, I push up with my hands and discover that it's stuck. I push again, putting more strength into it. But it doesn't budge.

I start to panic. The darkness down in the bunker seems to suddenly envelop me, and the stagnant air seems to grow even hotter. I can't help but think of the prison cell Ben and I were locked in back in Arena 1 in all those months ago.

Finally, I jam my shoulder in the trapdoor hard enough for it to give. The hinges ping off as I slam my palms into it.

Quickly, I ascend the ladder, and the sight that meets me makes me cry out in despair.

Everything is gone.

From the floorboards beneath me, I can hear people jerking awake, scrabbling to get to the ladder and find out what's making me wail. Ryan's the first to emerge out of the hole. He looks at where I sit crumpled on the floor with an alarmed expression on his face.

"He took everything!" I cry. "Craig. He stole everything."

The others begin filing out of the underground bunker, and look around at the empty room with dismay. The food, the weapons, our backpacks, everything has gone. Then I realize, with an even greater despair, that our map has been taken as well.

Ryan comes over and drags me back up to my feet.

"We can't stay here, Brooke. We don't know who he will have alerted to our presence. We have to leave."

I know he's right but I can hardly stand. The shock of losing our possessions is too great for me to bear. All that food, gone, and the means with which to hunt stolen from us too. What are we going to do?

Finally, I manage to stand and stagger out of the shack and into the bright daylight. At the very least, our bikes remain. Craig must have left them knowing the engine noise would wake us up.

Without the map to guide us to Houston, we have no choice but to follow the Mississippi south. The roads are so destroyed here that there aren't even any signs we can follow, and the bombs have flattened everything, meaning there aren't even any distinguishable landmarks. It may add some more hours onto our journey but at least we'll end up in Louisiana eventually, and then it's just a case of heading west until we hit Houston.

We mount the bikes and go, my heart falling as I lose a bit more faith in the kindness of mankind.

*

After several hours driving, our gas gauges start to get low. It worries me to think we might have to make the last leg of the journey on foot.

We're in a town built on the banks of the river that hasn't been completely flattened. It's called Baton Rouge and the road here is still intact. There's a road sign informing us that Route 10 heads all the way west right to Houston. I can hardly believe our luck. The road sign tells us it's 271 miles, which will take about six hours if the road holds out the whole way. As long as we don't have to detour or run out of gas we should be there by nightfall.

It seems like everything is finally looking up. But a feeling inside of me says it won't last for long.

We've been riding for another four hours when something up ahead gets my attention. I can't quite tell what it is I'm looking at yet, but something about the view ahead of me isn't quite right.

The closer we get, the better my view becomes, and it dawns on me that we're approaching a series of massive craters that have completely obliterated the road.

We drive up to the precipice and stop. One by one, we dismount from our bikes and stand side by side in a row staring at the chasm before us, the latest hurdle blocking our way.

"It looks like the Grand Canyon," Bree says.

I don't know how she can find beauty in it at all. To me, it looks like a scar in the earth. A war-inflicted wound. A gash that will never heal, violently blighting the world.

I can't help the disappointment that bites at me. We're less than two hours from Houston and now we're facing another massive detour that might add who knows how many hours onto our journey. We're so low on gas, I don't even know if our bikes can handle going off course again. The last thing we need is to be stranded and have to proceed on foot. It would be a cruel trick for fate to play on us when we're so close to the Texas border.

"What are we going to do?" Molly says. "We can't go around it. It looks like it stretches on for miles."

She's right. The crater goes on and on, as far as the eye can see.

"We'll have to find a way down," I say.

"You want to drive through it?" Ryan questions me, an eyebrow raised.

"What about the radiation?" Ben adds. "It will be worse down there. We can't risk exposure."

As much as it frustrated me when the two were arguing, having them team up against me is even more annoying.

"Do either of you have a better plan? You know how to make a bridge?" I say sarcastically in response. When I'm met by a wall of silence, I add, "Didn't think so."

And with that, we get back on the bikes and begin driving slowly along the edge, looking for a place we might be able to drive down. But this crater isn't home to a slaver community. No one's chiseled a path for bikes into the crater's edge. It's just a sharp, jagged hole, blasted into the earth by a nuclear bomb.

"If we had some rope, we could try shooting it across with an arrow," Molly says.

"I'm pretty sure that only works in cartoons," I say. "Plus, there's the whole not having any rope situation."

"What if we abandon the bikes?" Bree says from behind me. "Maybe we'd be able to scramble down?"

It's one of the more sensible suggestions, but it's still too risky. Not having the bikes could mean the difference between life and death. We need to keep hold of them as long as we possibly can.

"Hey, look!" Charlie suddenly cries, pointing ahead.

We ride over to where he was pointing and see animal tracks leading down into crater. If we follow in their footsteps, we're bound to find a safe way down. It looks like a pack of them walk this route regularly, at least enough to have worn a wide groove into the mountainside. But I look at the others, unsure.

"They might be predators," I say.

Molly raises a cocksure eyebrow. "Last time I checked, we were the predators," she says.

I can't help but smile at her fighting spirit. She's right. Whatever animals made those tracks, we're stronger, better, and fiercer than them.

"Okay," I say. "Let's do this."

I lead the way down the perilous path. We don't use the motors, instead letting gravity do the work. Any way we can save gas now we'll have to take. Plus, if we're quiet enough, we won't draw attention to ourselves to whatever predators are lurking in the bottom of the crater.

Bree holds onto me tightly, tense as I maneuver down the steep incline. Bits of rock tumble from beneath my tires, making my heart fly into my mouth. She's gripping so hard it's starting to irritate the wounds on my chest and back.

After a tense ten minutes, we finally make it into the crater. As soon as I get on level land, an eerie feeling comes over me. My spine tingles as I get that undeniable sensation that we're being watched.

We race across the trough of the crater then reach the steep wall at the other side. There's no sign of a path back up. I curse under my breath.

"We need to search on foot," I say. "There's not enough gas to keep riding back and forth."

As I start scanning the crater's edge, it occurs to me that the only way we're getting the bikes back up is by pushing. Even if we do find a path we can follow, it's going to be back-breaking work getting back out of here.

"I think I've found something!" Molly calls.

We all go over and see her peering into a hole, five feet in diameter, dug into the side of the crater. It's clearly been made by an animal of some sort.

"Do you think it's a burrow?" I ask.

"I guess so," Molly says. "Pretty big burrow."

I don't want to even imagine the type of creature that's living inside. At the basin of the crater, the radiation will be high, meaning whatever lives down here will have taken a huge dose over the years. Just like the crazies in the lakes in the north, the creatures living down here will have evolved into something unrecognizable and formidable.

We all agree it's too risky to venture into the burrow, even if it does eventually lead out of the crater. If there is something sleeping inside, it's probably best to let it rest.

"I think I see something," Ben says, peering into the distance.

Sure enough, there's another path leading up the crater, made by the same prints as the one we took down. The animals that made these tracks have shown us down into the crater and are now offering us a way back out. They're like guardian angels.

We go back to get the bikes and head toward the path. But as we go, a new noise joins the thrumming of our engines.

Jack and Penelope are suddenly alert, their ears pricking up, their teeth bared.

"What's that noise?" I call out to the others.

We draw to a halt and cut off the engines. As soon as we do, the noise becomes perceptible. There's no mistaking it. It's the howling of wolves. And it's close. Too close for comfort.

Penelope and Jack immediately join in with the howling. Bree tries to quiet Penelope down but it's no use. The tiny Chihuahua is trying to make herself look fierce.

"Quick," I say. "We have to go."

But it's too late. All at once, we're surrounded by the most disgusting creatures I've ever seen. They look like wild dogs, but the radiation they've absorbed from having lived in the crater has made their bodies mangled. Their spines are curved upward, making them look more like hyenas than dogs. Their fur is balding in places, sticking up coarsely in others. Tumors grow out of their skin. Saliva drips from their jaws in thick strings, and their teeth, like their claws, are enormous.

I gun the engine of my bike, hoping that the noise will scare them off, and start whizzing around and around in circles, trying to tire the creatures out so that they're slow enough to take a hit. The others do the same. The wolves chase our bikes, their eager jaws snapping, treating it like a game, as though they're nothing but puppies. It reminds me of Sasha, our old pet dog, and the way she would lumber around play fighting with me. I'm almost relieved that she was killed by slaverunners; they saved her from this fate, of being turned into a grotesque, cancerous, murderous creature.

We're burning through our remaining gas fast, and the dogs are showing no signs of slowing. If only there was somewhere to ride the bikes up and out of the crater, but it's too steep.

Suddenly, I hear a scream. I look back and see Molly's bike careening away as she and Charlie tumble to the ground.

"Charlie!" Bree screams.

The wolf-dogs pounce on them straightaway. I turn my bike around and race straight at them. Thankfully, they're scared off and run away.

I leap off the bike and run over to where Molly and Charlie are sprawled on the ground, Molly cowering over him, protecting him with her whole body. I grab her by the shoulders and roll her back. There's a huge pool of blood there.

Charlie wriggles out and flies right into Bree's arms. Molly lies there panting, gritting her teeth in agony.

The dogs have torn a hole in her calf so deep I can see the bone. The sight turns my stomach. Ryan removes his shirt and bandages her up, but it soaks up with blood within a matter of moments. He looks back at me gravely.

"We can't stay here," I say. "There could be more packs waiting to get us. Can you walk, Molly?"

She tries to stand on her bitten leg but the second she puts weight on it she cries out in pain. I look up at the sheer face of the crater. Not only are we going to have to climb, but we're going to have to carry Molly. There's no way we'll be able to push the bikes up while carrying her at the same time. We're going to have to abandon them. From here on out, we're going by foot.

CHAPTER NINETEEN

My feet are blistered and swollen. My mouth is parched. I have no idea how long we've been walking. It feels like days. In fact, I think it has been days. The sun has set and risen several times.

With one hand, I cling onto Bree. She's so weak it reminds me of the time back in the mountain cabin when she had a fever. If she had been well enough to travel with me to the cabin I'd found, where would we be now? Would we still be safe in the mountains, hiding from the slaverunners? Would I have avoided fighting in the arenas and being forced to become a murderer? Or would we have perished in the mountains? There would always have been something waiting to finish us off. Death seems to lurk around every corner.

I don't even know if we're heading in the right direction, but I pretend that we are to the others. I don't want them to lose hope.

The metal collar around my neck is causing me sores. It weighs down heavily on my shoulders, making every step more painful than it needs to be.

Behind me, Molly stumbles along, propped up in the middle of Ryan and Ben. Her leg has become infected. There's nothing we can do. Just like Rose's arm back on the boat when we were floating in the Hudson, Molly's leg will turn gangrenous and eventually kill her. I haven't given up hope yet, but it's certainly starting to wane. Sometimes when I look back at her, I can't even tell if she's still alive, and I start to wonder if it's her ghost limping through the desert with us. Maybe we're all dead. We're all ghosts walking through purgatory.

Charlie stumbles to his knees for what must be the hundredth time. I pick him up, silently, and set him on his feet again. He doesn't say a word, just whimpers his distress. Then once more, we trudge onward.

Watching Penelope and Jack deteriorate is just as painful as watching the children struggle. The dehydration has hit them both hard. Ryan's taken to carrying Jack in a pouch across his chest, like he's a newborn baby. For the first few days he whined, but he's been quiet for a while now.

Penelope is still walking, but only just. Bree doesn't have enough strength left in her to carry the dog, even though she's small. Penelope seems to understand; she doesn't complain, but I can tell she's suffering and would love to be carried. We all would. Losing the bikes was the worst thing for all of us.

Charlie stumbles again. This time, when I go to pick him up, I find my arm muscles aren't strong enough. I fall forward too and land in a heap on the ground.

Bree falls to her knees beside me. "Brooke," she pleads, nudging me. "Get up. You have to get up. We have to carry on."

But something about my stumbling seems to spread to the others, as though it's an invitation that they too can give up. Ben unlinks Molly's arm from round his shoulders and together, he and Ryan set her on the ground. Then they both slump down themselves, their tired eyes barely able to stay open.

"No," Bree cries, her voice choked. "We can't give up. We can't."

My tongue is swollen it's been so long since I last spoke. "Let's just have a quick nap," I say.

"NO!" Bree screams. But her own voice is faltering. She can only just about croak out the word.

Realizing it's futile to protest, she lies down next to me, resting her head against my splayed out arm. Penelope lies down too, and finally lets out the pained whimper she's been holding in for days.

"Are we going to die?" Bree whispers in my ear, stammering on her tears.

I try to shush her, to calm her down. I want to tell her that we won't die but I know it's a lie. We can't go on any farther. My legs won't support my weight. The best I'd be able to do is crawl, but my arms are too weak as well. The only thing that could save us now is a rainstorm. Maybe with a bit of hydration we'd be able to make it another mile or so. Maybe Houston is just over the horizon. But we'll never know, because the rain will never come.

I stare up at the unforgiving sky. It is a beautiful blue, the sun a blazing yellow, but between them they signify death. I find myself secretly praying someone dies and draws the attention of vultures. Then we'd be able to shoot one and feast on it. But I feel ashamed almost as soon as I think it. It's better that we die together rather than live with that guilt.

"Do you really think Dad is still alive?" Bree says.

Her voice is floaty and sing-songy, as though she's becoming delirious.

"Yes," I reply.

"Do you think he still loves us?"

I let my heavy eyelids close, the scorching sun burning the tender skin. My mind has gone back to another place, to the time when my dad left for the army. I'd come home to find him and Mom arguing about it. He'd hit her and I'd been so filled with revulsion I wouldn't say goodbye to him. He'd told me through the door that he would always love me, no matter what.

"Of course," I say to Bree.

She doesn't respond. When I look over, I see that her eyes are closed.

"Brooke," I hear Molly say.

I manage to heave myself to my elbows and look back at her. She's holding her bad leg and breathing rapidly. Despite the heat, her face has completely drained of color. She looks like she's at death's door.

"I need to tell you something," she stammers through the pain.

"What?" I say, squinting against the glare of harsh sunlight.

"The crash," she gasps. "Zeke and Stephan… survived."

My heart hammers in my chest. "What do you mean?"

Tears streak down Molly's cheeks. "I'm sorry. I lied. I knew you'd never leave if you thought there was a chance we could save them."

She's shaking her head so frantically, making her matted ginger hair fly all over the place. She licks her parched lips. I can't help thinking that she's using the last ounce of strength left in her to make this confession. It's as though she's trying to atone before she dies, to rid herself of sin just in case she's about to meet her maker.

My grief is all consuming. It hurts so much my stomach aches. It's more painful than the blisters, than the gnawing starvation. It's more painful than the car crashes and the arena fights, than the snake bite and the slavers' whips.

I fall back against the hard, cracked desert ground, feeling completely defeated, and let my eyes close.

CHAPTER TWENTY

"Brooke. Brooke, wake up."

My eyelids flutter open. I'm flat on my back on the parched earth. I can't feel any pain at all; my whole body is comfortably numb.

There's a blanket of stars above me. I squint, trying to work out who it is standing before me. But it's impossible. The person is nothing more than a silhouette.

"Who are you?" I manage to say.

My voice is no longer parched. My tongue isn't swollen, nor are my lips dry and cracked. But it's still hard to get my words out. It's like I can't move, like I'm more than just numb, but paralyzed.

"It's me," the voice replies.

But I can't place it. It sounds like a hundred different voices in one. I can't even tell whether it's a man or a woman.

I don't know whether I'm dead or alive, awake or dreaming. All I know is that the pain has gone. I'm filled with peace and tranquility. My eyelids are so heavy, I could easily just fall back to sleep.

The person reaches out and touches my cheek with their fingers.

"Don't fall asleep, Brooke. Not now. Not yet."

As I finally place the voice, my heart clenches. Because it belongs to Rose. I can't make out her features in the darkness, I can only conjure a memory of what she looks like.

"How did you get here?" I stammer, confused by her presence.

"You brought me with you," she replies, touching my heart gently. "I'm in here."

As her hand presses into my chest, I realize that it's not Rose sitting beside me anymore. It's Flo.

"Thank you for looking after him," she says. "For taking care of Charlie all this time."

"Flo?" I stammer.

"I don't blame you, Brooke," she says. "You did everything you could for me."

She reaches down and presses a kiss to my forehead. But as she straightens up, it's no longer Flo. It's my mom looking down at me.

Disorientated and slightly panicked, I try to shake my head. My heart is fluttering, my breath coming in short, anxious gasps.

"Mom, I didn't want to leave you."

"I know," she whispers. Then she repeats the words Flo said a moment ago. "I don't blame you, Brooke. You did everything you could for me."

Emotion begins to well inside of me. All these people, all my dead friends, my mom; it's like they're saying goodbye.

I try to reach out for my mom, to touch her and feel her hand in mine, but I can't move at all. Even as I struggle against whatever invisible force is keeping me paralyzed, I can sense that the person has transformed again, that it's no longer my mom sitting beside me.

"We would have made a good team, you and me," the voice says.

It's instantly recognizable as Logan's. I gasp, but I can't see his face. How I wish I could look into his eyes one last time.

"You can let me go now, Brooke," Logan says. "You can be with him."

"With who?" I stammer.

"With whomever you choose."

I try to reach out for Logan but my arm feels like it's pinned to my side. I can't move at all.

"I don't want to choose," I say. "I can't. I don't want to hurt anyone."

"Then let fate decide," he says. "Like it did with us."

I don't know what to make of his words, but it's too late to try and decipher their meaning. His silhouette is moving, standing up and leaving an empty, yawning space beside me. Starlight illuminates the figure but doesn't show me any of his features. I don't want him to leave but I can't stop him. I watch helplessly as he paces across the desert ground, leans down, and picks up Molly in his arms.

"No!" I shout. "Don't take her! Please!"

But Logan doesn't listen. He holds Molly's limp body in his arms. Her hair splays over and swings in the breeze as he starts to walk away. Jack the dog trots along beside him.

I watch helplessly as they disappear into the distance. My heart aches. I can't tell what's real and what's not, but wherever my mind is right now, I know my body is giving up. This is what dying feels like. Like floating and falling all at once. Like a horrible, dark chasm opening up inside of you. I don't want to give up. I don't want to die here. But I don't think I get a choice. The fight is leaving me.

As I lie there, my weak arm gesturing in the direction Logan went, I see something else coming toward me. Another ghost? Another person from my past come to haunt me?

The person is drawing closer and closer. When they reach me, I notice that they're wearing army fatigues. They bend at the knees, and shadows judder against their face, obscuring their features.

"You can do better than this, soldier," the voice says.

It's my dad's voice. I recognize it instantly.

"I can't go on," I say. "I'm dying, aren't I?"

"Not on my watch, soldier."

In a split second, he disappears, taking the blanket of stars and the dark, empty sky with him. Suddenly, everything is replaced by the blistering heat, the bright, white daylight, and the searing pain of dehydration and starvation. There's a noise in my ear like a roaring sound. It takes me a long time to realize it's the sound of an engine.

I'm in a vehicle, moving forward, bumping along. Is this another dream? I don't know what's real and what's not anymore.

"She's waking up, sir!" someone shouts.

A woman's face appears above me. She's a soldier, dressed in a US military uniform. Her face is harsh and lined, but she's looking at me in a kind way.

"Can you tell me your name?" she says.

I try to speak, but my mouth feels like it's filled with cotton wool. The soldier helps scoop my head up in her hand. She tips water from a canteen into my mouth. It's tepid, but I don't care. It tastes delicious. I still can't tell whether I'm dead or alive—but if I did pass away during the night, this is surely heaven.

"Brooke," I finally say. "Brooke Moore."

The soldier's features change right away. She looks over at someone out of my sight line.

"Did you hear that?" she says to the other person. "She says her name is Brooke Moore. You'd better call the Commander."

I reach out and grab the soldier's arm, relieved to discover I'm no longer paralyzed.

"Where's my sister?" I stammer. "My friends? Did they make it?"

The woman smiles. "They made it," she says. "And so did you. Brooke, we're taking you to your father."

PART FOUR

CHAPTER TWENTY ONE

The road is bumpy, making the journey tough going. Every part of my body is aflame with pain. I slip in and out of consciousness, and each time I come around, I'm expecting to discover that it has all been a dream, that there is no US military vehicle taking us to Dad. But each time I am rewarded by the jolting sensation of the truck, by the sounds of its tires racing across the parched earth, and by the sight of the US marine as she tends to me, giving me water to sip and chewy protein bars for energy. Not long ago I was certain we were facing death, that my dead friends were appearing before my eyes in order to take me to the afterlife. Now, it is as though I've been given a second chance.

I can't believe what is happening. My dad is alive, and we have been rescued, right when it looked like the end had arrived. In my wildest dreams, I never imagined it would happen this way.

The truck I'm traveling in is part of a convoy. For reasons I don't fully understand yet, we're all traveling separately. I think of Bree and pray that she is being cared for as well as I am. I wonder if she's been told that our dad is alive yet, or whether she knows we're on our way to be reunited with him. I try to picture her reaction; I know she won't have held back her tears in the way I did. At the very least, I hope she's with Charlie, that the two of them are together, perhaps even with Penelope beside them. I don't dare let myself consider that the dog may not have survived, though I know it's a possibility.

I hear the sound of brakes and start to feel the truck slowing down.

"What's happening?" I say to the soldier who has been caring for me.

I try to sit up but she guides me back down.

"We're at the compound," she explains. "There are checkpoints to go through. Don't worry. We'll be there very soon."

I try to relax but it's almost impossible. I feel like I did when I was a little child waiting for my dad to come home after being stationed abroad for months. Only the sensation inside of me is a thousand times stronger than it was when I was younger, because it hasn't been months, it has been years. And while the concept of my dad dying while he was away was scary when I was younger, it still seemed abstract and unimaginable. But I've spent the last four years assuming I will never ever see him again. The sensation inside of me is more akin to discovering that someone has come back from the dead.

I can hear the sound of a chain-link fence being opened. Then the truck picks up speed and we're bobbing along once again. The jolting movement smooths out and I know that means we're riding on asphalt, that we're on a proper road again. I wonder if it's a new road, built after the war, or if the people of the compound managed to protect one that was already there. Nothing else in the south seemed to have survived the bombs, so I presume that means they've been rebuilding.

There are many more checkpoints to pass through, and row after row of fencing. If I'd thought Fort Noix was heavy-handed with its layers of guards and outposts, it was nothing compared to this. The fences are tall and topped with barbed wire. Guards are positioned all along them, though from where I am lying prone in the truck I can only see the tops of their heads. But I recognize their uniforms and the insignia of the marines. It gives me a sense of enormous familiarity and nostalgia.

"This is the last checkpoint," the soldier informs me. "Then we're heading straight to the Commander. Your dad, I mean."

My dad, a commander. I shouldn't be so surprised. If anyone was going to survive the war and find a way to thrive in spite of it, it was going to be my dad.

I'm surprised to see the tips of trees above me as the truck crawls past the final fence. I'd become so accustomed to the barren desert landscape that the sight of green leaves is shocking. Then, I'm certain in the distance I can hear the sound of running water.

"How do you have trees?" I say. "And water?"

The soldier smiles. "The Commander has turned this place into Eden," she explains. "We're completely self-sufficient."

As I absorb her words, my first feeling is relief. If they're self-sufficient here then there's no need for scavenging, no dangerous hunting trips out into the wild.

"Do you take in survivors?" I ask.

The soldier looks at me kindly. "Brooke, I know you have a lot of questions. But I don't want you to tire yourself out. Why don't you rest and gather your strength for when you see your dad?"

I know she's right but I can't help myself. The sensations inside of me are too great. They all vie for my attention, mixing around in my stomach and making me nauseous. My exhausted body is telling me to rest and recuperate, but my frantic mind is racing through a million thoughts. I'm filled with excitement, but at the same time I'm nervous. I haven't forgotten the sound of my dad's hand as he slapped my mom's cheek the night he left us, voluntarily, to join a war that went on to obliterate everything. Is he even still the same man I remember?

Just then, the truck jolts to a halt.

"We're here," the soldier says.

She stands and starts unlatching the flap at the back of the truck. I'm suddenly overcome with fear. What if my dad isn't the person I want him to be? What if he's been traumatized by the last four and a half years? He said he would always love me no matter what, but that was before the slaverunners and the arenas and the crazies. That was before the nuclear bombs and the fighter jets.

"Are you having trouble standing?" the soldier asks.

I am, but not in the way she thinks. She thinks I've been weakened by my ordeal out in the desert. In reality, my legs seem to have turned to jelly beneath me. My whole body trembles as she helps me to my feet, guiding me by my elbow down onto a step, then down again onto the ground.

I'm standing on paving slabs with moss growing up between them. I can smell grass and vegetation, and hear the sound of running water in the distance. The air is cool, not like the painful, sweltering heat of the Texan desert I've just come from.

I feel the soldier put gentle pressure on my shoulder, and I can feel that she's urging me on. Another truck has pulled up beside me, and Bree is being led down to the ground, trembling in much the same way as me. When she sees me, her eyes brim with tears. I know Dad always told me not to cry, but the sight of her alive makes me well up. I can still hear her screams in my head as she begged me not to give up back in the desert, to keep moving. I couldn't do it for her. I'm only here by a miracle. But if she holds any resentment toward me because of it, she doesn't show it. She rushes over and throws herself into my arms. She's been patched up well by the soldier she rode with, and is no longer as feeble as she was back in the desert.

"Did they tell you?" she says through her sobs. "Dad is alive."

"They told me," I gasp, stroking her hair beneath my fingers.

"You were right, Brooke. You were right all along."

I was. But people still died because of me. I will have to live with that guilt for the rest of my life.

Finally, Bree lets me go. I can see the other trucks pulling up behind us, and see Ben emerge from one. He looks as frail as he did when we first got to know each other back in the prisons of Arena 1. But he has transformed since then. He is leaner, more muscular, and the sensitivity I could always see in his eyes seems to have hardened. Like me, survival has taken its toll on him.

Bree slips her hand in mine, pulling me back to the moment. I turn away from the trucks. As much as I want to see each of our friends arrive safely, I know my dad is waiting for me. I can't prolong this anymore. It's time to face him.

The soldier who'd been riding with me gestures past some palm trees.

"He's over there," she says.

Bree and I squeeze one another's hands as we take small steps along the paving slabs. The vegetation grows thicker and lusher as we go, forming a thick canopy above that plunges us into cooling shadows. Then all at once, I see a figure.

We stop dead. There is a man down the path. He's wearing a military uniform. His hair is completely gray. He stands with his hands resting just lightly behind his back. I know the stance. "At ease." It is my dad.

I can't get the words out. I try to call to him but the only noise that comes from my throat is a croak.

It's enough for him to hear. He spins to face us. There is no denying it; though time has aged him considerably, the man standing before me is my dad.

"Brooke," he gasps, staring at me like he can't believe what he is seeing. "Bree."

And then we're running, both of us, full speed, finding reserves of energy from deep within our weakened bodies. Dad spreads his arms wide and we run into them. He sweeps us tightly into him. He feels so solid, so real. This is not the man in my dreams; this is my real dad, alive and strong.

I don't want to show my weakness in front of him, but Bree is sobbing uncontrollably, and I just cannot hold back anymore. My tears begin to fall.

We're all shaking with emotion. I clutch onto Bree and nestle my head into the crook of my dad's neck, letting my tears drop onto his uniform one by one. It is then that I realize, for the first time in my entire life, my dad is crying too.

CHAPTER TWENTY TWO

We stay like that for a long time, holding one another and weeping. It is like we never want to let go.

"You've both grown so much," Dad says finally, drawing back to look at us. He looks Bree up and down. "Eleven years old," he says, shaking his head as though in disbelief. She was seven last time he saw her. Then he looks at me. "Seventeen."

I nod. I wish he could have seen us back when we were in Fort Noix. We were healthy then, our muscles stronger, our hair and bodies clean. He would have been able to see firsthand how well I've looked after Bree. Instead, she looks more like a mangy cat.

"You've changed too," I say.

He laughs, sadly, and points to his gray hair. "I look older."

It's been four years since we last saw each other, but Dad seems to have aged so much more. The stress of war has taken its toll on him.

He reaches up to wipe a strand of hair tenderly from off my face. "I didn't think I'd ever see you again, Brooke," he says. "But I never gave up hope. I thought of you, both of you, every single day."

Tears blur my vision.

"How long has the camp been here?" I ask. "Is it yours? Did you build it?"

I know I sound like an eager child, but I want to know everything that has happened to him over the last four and a half years. How he came to defect from the army and create this place.

But Dad puts a finger to his lips to quiet me, and smiles. "We can talk about everything later. But first I think you should go to the hospital for health checks."

He eyes the metal collar around my neck, which has given me sores and rashes.

Bree slides her hand into his and holds on tight. "Will you come with us?" she asks.

"Of course," he says, kindly, smiling down at her.

While in the medical ward, I finally have the metal collar removed from around my neck. It feels like a huge weight has been lifted from my shoulders. The doctor gives me an ointment to help the wounds heal.

"Can we see our friends?" I ask the doctor as I take another gulp of the sugar and saltwater solution she's given me.

"Please," Bree adds.

The doctor looks at Dad for his approval. I can't help but swell with pride, seeing the way everyone looks up to him. He is clearly well respected.

Dad nods, and the doctor leads us through the ward to where Charlie is sleeping, with Penelope sitting on the end of his bed.

"That's Charlie," Bree tells Dad with an air of pride. "Brooke rescued him from an arena. And this is Penelope."

She strokes the Chihuahua behind the ear. Despite the ordeal we've been through, Penelope is looking well. If it weren't for her missing eye, she would look the picture of perfect health.

"You do have pets here, don't you?" Bree asks Dad, wide-eyed.

"Of course," he replies.

"Phew," she says, clearly relieved to know we won't have to fight to keep Penelope like we did with the Commander in Fort Noix.

Charlie murmurs and opens his eyes. As soon as he sees Bree, he breaks into a huge grin. Bree hugs him tightly and Penelope snuggles in. The three of them stay like that for a long, long time.

"It was touch and go," the doctor informs me. "His dehydration was so severe he had a seizure."

I press my hand to my mouth, alarmed at the thought of poor, sweet Charlie fitting.

"Will he be okay?" I ask.

The doctor nods. "He's had the same fluid solution as you and Bree. He's on the mend."

I'm so relieved to know Charlie will be okay. I don't know what Bree would do without him.

In the next bed along is Ben. His usually pale skin has been badly sunburned, making him a very sore-looking red color. Parts of his skin have been bandaged to stop the blisters from becoming infected.

"Ben," I say, taking his hand. "This is my dad, Laurence."

My dad would never shake hands with someone. Instead, he salutes Ben.

"Ben was living on Catskills Mountain, too," I tell Dad. "He helped me rescue Bree from the slaverunners."

Despite his sunburn, I can see Ben blush. "Only because Brooke helped save me from Arena One," he says shyly.

I can see my dad's eyebrows rise. He's not usually one for outward emotion, but I can practically see the questions in his eyes asking me how, exactly, we escaped from an arena. I'm almost excited at the prospect of telling him that we didn't just escape, but that I killed three of their most prized fighters *and* then killed their leader, all while snake venom swirled in my bloodstream.

"I look forward to getting to know you, Ben," Dad says.

"You too, sir," Ben replies, looking as awkward as a boy meeting his prom date's parents. Then he tips his eyes to me. "You did it, Brooke," he whispers, squeezing my hand tightly in his. I can see tears glittering in the corners of his soft, blue eyes. "I always believed in you."

I squeeze his hand back, overcome with emotion.

Next I take my dad over to Ryan's bed. It's only now in this clean hospital setting that I realize how disheveled Ryan has become since we left Fort Noix. His hair has grown a little longer, softening his look. Normally, he'd be the sort of clean-shaven, buzz-cut kind of guy my dad would immediately respect. But with his unkempt appearance he looks much more boylike. His arm is in a sling, his dislocated shoulder having been injured further by supporting the weight of Molly and having to carry Jack.

"Where is Jack?" I ask, expecting to see him sleeping on the end of the bed like Penelope was with Charlie.

Ryan looks at me sadly. "He didn't make it," he says.

Bree lets out a sob. Grief washes over me. Jack had been a trusted ally, fighting side by side with us since day one. He even saved our lives back in the tunnels in Toledo. To have lost him now seems so unfair.

"I'm so sorry," I say to Ryan, squeezing his good arm.

He nods, but I can tell he's not ready to talk about it. Jack was his best friend. When others died around him, Ryan always had Jack. The loss will take a long time to heal.

"Where's Molly?" I say, realizing that the bed beside Ryan's is empty.

But before he has a chance to answer, I look up and see a shock of ginger hair peeking through a gap in a curtain around a bed a few down from where we stand. I'm in two minds about seeing Molly again. Because of her, Stephan and Zeke were left behind in Memphis. If Molly hadn't lied, perhaps I'd have been able to save them. But despite the feelings of anger inside of me, I'm glad that she's here. Molly had it worse than any of us back in the desert. She is my friend, after all, and no matter how disappointed I am in the decision she made back in Memphis, I still love her.

I prepare myself for the sight that awaits me, knowing full well her leg will have been amputated because of the bite she sustained from the radiated wild dogs. But as I approach her bed, the doctor quickly rushes over and blocks me from proceeding.

"Brooke, maybe it's time for another saline solution," she says.

"In a minute," I reply, trying to move past her. "I need to see Molly first."

The doctor becomes more insistent. "I really think you should have another drink now. Please, this way."

Bree can tell something's up. She ducks past the doctor quick as a flash and hauls open the curtain surrounding Molly. As I look over the doctor's shoulder, I see Bree suddenly halt and gasp.

"Bree," I say, feeling my heart begin to thump. "What is it?"

The doctor finally drops her arms and sighs loudly. "Your friend didn't survive," she tells me.

The words hit me like a punch in the gut. "What?" I cry, barging past her. My stomach churns as I hobble over to Molly's bedside.

She's covered in a white sheet, and her skin is so pale it makes her ginger hair even more strikingly red. She looks peaceful in death in a way she never did in life. It's like her fight is finally over.

"The bite on her leg was too infected," the doctor explains, coming up beside me. "Even amputation couldn't have saved her. We gave her pain relief and then she slipped away. I didn't want you to know in case it caused too much shock to your system. I'm sorry."

Bree and I stand side by side, looking over Molly's lifeless body.

Dad grips my shoulder. "I'm so sorry," he says. "We will give her a proper funeral."

Bree leans down and kisses Molly's cold cheek.

"Come on," Dad says, guiding us gently away from Molly. "I think it's time to go home."

Home. The word echoes in my mind, feeling unreal to me. I can hardly believe we have a home again. A real home. That for the first time in four years, we will be a family again.

Dad leads us out of the hospital and through the compound. Everyone we pass salutes him. He is so well respected and it fills me with pride to be his daughter.

"So you were living in the mountain cabin?" Dad asks as we walk.

"Yes," I say. "Bree and me. Sasha too. She was killed by slaverunners."

He looks downcast. "I didn't think to look for you there," he says.

"What do you mean?" I say, frowning.

"I came back for you," he says.

A pit opens up in my stomach. I made us leave home. I told Mom there was no point waiting for him anymore, that he'd left us for good. I'd been wrong.

"It was my fault we left," I stammer. "I thought you would never come back for us."

Dad squeezes my shoulder. "You did the right thing, Brooke," he tells me. "When I got back, the place was bombed. The whole street. If you'd stayed, you would have died." His voice becomes quieter. "I thought that maybe you had."

I shake my head. "We were in the mountains all that time. For four years. We only left about six or seven months ago."

"I'm impressed with how well you coped," he says.

I shrug. "I didn't have much choice."

Dad falls silent. I hadn't meant the comment to be pointed, but my anger at him abandoning us is evident in my tone.

"Here's the house," Dad says, gesturing to a brick bungalow. "Let's get inside. You can wash while I make something to eat."

I raise an eyebrow. "You cook?"

It sounds so domestic. So unlike my father.

"Badly," he replies. "But yes, I cook."

He opens up the door to the bungalow and we all go inside. When we'd entered Neena's house back at Fort Noix, I'd been overwhelmed by the smallest of things—the real pillow and duvet, the chest of drawers, clean clothes. But entering Dad's house is even more surreal. It looks like a completely normal house, like the ones that existed before the war blew them to smithereens. He shows us the living room, the bathroom, the bedrooms, each one furnished and decorated.

"I can't believe this place," I say, awestruck by the fact that this will actually get to be our home, that we can live in this place together as a family.

We follow Dad into the kitchen.

"Do you girls like bread?" he says. "Jam?"

"I love jam!" Bree exclaims. "Brooke once found a house in the mountains full of provisions. She brought me back a jar of jam. It was delicious."

Dad smiles. He seems proud of me, of my resourcefulness and the way I took care of my sister. It's the best feeling in the world.

We sit down and tuck into the jam sandwiches, relaying stories about the time I managed to get sap from the tree, how I drove his old motorbike and sidecar down the mountainside at 100 miles an hour without crashing, and how I hunted a deer. But the more we speak, the harder it becomes for me to ignore the dark cloud hanging over us. The unspoken words seem to be swelling around us, crushing down on us. None of us wants to talk about it, to rip the scab off that old wound. But I can't help myself. I need answers. I need to know why he abandoned us all those years ago.

"Why did you leave us, Dad?" I finally blurt out.

Bree stiffens, immediately awkward. Dad sits silently for a long, long time, his hands laced together on the table. He looks so much older than I remember. Not only is his face more lined and his hair completely gray, but there's a stoop in his posture that was never there when I was younger. It's a vulnerability he would once have never allowed me to see.

"I was barely fourteen," I continue. "Bree was seven. How could you abandon us like that? Why did you choose the war over us?"

Dad doesn't look at me when he finally speaks. "It's complicated, Brooke. I know you think I chose the war, but I didn't. I chose you two, I always did. I chose to give you a future, and that meant leaving you in the present and fighting in the war."

"But it hadn't even begun yet," I shoot back, anger making the volume of my voice rise. "You *volunteered*. You left before you even needed to."

"I had to put myself in the best strategic position," he says, sighing heavily. "I don't expect you to understand. But know that I'm sorry for the hurt I caused you two—"

"And Mom," I interrupt. "Or did you forget about how you slapped her the night before you left?"

He looks away, ashamed. "I haven't forgotten. And I've regretted it every day that's passed."

"You know she waited for you," I say, and I can hear the bitterness in my voice. "Even after the mushroom cloud. She said we couldn't leave, in case you came back. You hit her and she still died for you."

Bree begins to weep softly beside me. I know she wants me to stop but I can't help myself. All the rage and anger I've felt over the last few years is spilling out of me. There's no amount of apologies Dad can say to atone for the death of our mom, or make up for the fact that I had to leave her to her certain death and look after Bree alone. Because of him I had to grow up overnight, make adult decisions, and live with the consequences. I was just a kid and his actions robbed me of my childhood.

"I understand if you never forgive me," Dad says. "But I had to be right in the thick of it in order to fight it from the inside out."

I pause and frown. I'm confused, not able to comprehend what he's saying.

"What do you mean, 'fight it from the inside out'?" I say.

"The compound," he explains. "What we're doing here. We're building an army. A resistance to both sides of the war. We're working to take the system down from the inside out. It's a long, slow process. Once we're strong enough, we'll take control of all the cities, destroy all the arenas, and bring the slaverunners to justice. But first we need to unite all the other pockets of resistance across the country. We've been trying to communicate with all the other resistance groups that we know of. It's only when we're together that we can fight and win."

My heart begins to thud. "The radio message to Fort Noix. That *was* you?"

He nods. "We're making contact with every base we can. There are resistors all over the country. We created compounds because we knew the war would mean mutually assured destruction. We knew it was the only chance we'd have of restoring civilization once it was all over."

My mind swirls with emotions. "You mean, you left… you volunteered for the army because…"

"Because it was inevitable and I knew it couldn't be stopped," he says, sternly. "Because I knew the only way the human race would survive was by making sure there were still people alive after it was all over. And now we're almost ready to reclaim the country."

I can't believe it. It really is a dream come true. All I've wanted, ever since meeting Trixie in the forest, is to create a safe world for everyone; a world free from slaverunners and crazies. A world free from arenas.

"When is it happening?" I say, slamming my fists onto the table. "When are you reclaiming the country?"

Dad looks at me. "It's a strategic military operation, Brooke. I can't reveal that to you."

"I want to help," I say, determined.

"I'm glad to hear it. There's plenty to do around here and—"

"No," I say, cutting him off. "I want to fight."

"Brooke," he begins.

"I've survived two arenas, Dad," I say. "I'm a fighter now, the fighter you always wanted me to be. I can do this. Whatever it takes to get justice, I want to do it."

He looks at me hesitantly. But he can tell I'm not backing down. I'm not the fourteen-year-old girl he abandoned all those years ago. I'm a young woman now, one who can hold her own, one who's taken all the lessons he taught me and used them again and again and again to survive. I'm stronger than he ever thought possible.

"Well, all right," he says, finally. "If you really want to fight, I won't stop you. We need all the help we can get."

"Good," I say, standing.

"Where are you going?" Dad asks.

"To join the rest of the soldiers," I say. "There's a meeting about to happen, isn't there?"

I raise an eyebrow. Dad gives me a look of disbelief, but he doesn't challenge me. Instead, he stands from the table.

"Lead the way, Moore."

CHAPTER TWENTY THREE

The meeting is taking place in one of the vast underground rooms of the compound. When my dad enters, all the soldiers stop talking and rise to their feet and salute. Then Dad steps aside and lets me into the room. Though they try not to react, I can almost feel the ripple of confusion as it passes down the line. Everyone's wondering who this beat-up girl is and what she's doing here.

"This is my eldest daughter, Brooke," Dad says. "She's joining us."

I hobble into the room and take a seat. I am by far the youngest person here. Though there are plenty of women, most are like the soldier I met in the back of the truck; hardened, bulky, emotionless. I stick out like a sore thumb. I'll be relieved once I'm given a US Marine Corps uniform to replace the strange, stiff, homemade uniform of Fort Noix that I am still wearing. For the first time, I wish I hadn't been so hasty in demanding to join in the meeting. I could have really done with a hot bath, a hair brush, a proper sleep, and a change of clothes. But just like when I was a kid, I find myself wanting to please my dad, to do everything right and be the daughter he always wanted me to be. I know, now, after my ordeal and everything I've survived, I am so close to making that a reality.

I can tell that the atmosphere in the room has changed. Everyone is a little wary of me. I'm not surprised, to be honest. Just like the Commander at Fort Noix, the people here have learned to be suspicious of everyone. There's probably more than just a flicker of doubt in the back of each of their minds, questioning whether I really am who I say I am or if their grief-stricken Commander has let in some kind of slaverunner spy. I will just have to prove myself to them and earn their trust and respect.

"Please," my dad says. "Resume your meeting."

The General nods obediently and walks over to a map of Texas hanging up on a board.

"This is Arena Three," he says. "Our target."

I can feel a coldness spread through my body at the thought of another arena. There must be so many all across America now, filled with kids like me forced to fight to the death.

"We've been in strategic communication with the compound up in Massachusetts," the General continues. "We're preparing to coordinate a large-scale attack on Arena One and Arena Two in New York, while at the same time taking down Arena Three, here in Texas. We have only one shot to get it right. We've amassed enough bombs and weapons to eradicate all three. Once the first three arenas fall, it won't take long to break the stranglehold of the other, smaller ones across the country. A coordinated attack on the major arenas is step one in the liberation of the people of America."

I hadn't fully understood the arenas and how they came about before now, but as I listen in on the meeting, I start to comprehend the logistics behind the war. The first two arenas weren't for bloodsport at all, but mass public executions. Different sides of the civil war had different strongholds in the north and south. Anyone who opposed the dominant group in the north were taken to the arenas and killed. In retaliation for their people's slaughter, Arena 3 in the south turned the public execution of rebels into a vicious game. It was a form of retaliation for what was happening to their sympathizers in the north. The north responded with more bloodshed, turning the arenas into perverse battlegrounds. This all had the effect of making the arena places for survivors to congregate. As more and more people died and the different sides slowly obliterated one another, the arenas became the central hub of the remaining cities, and the survivors who'd gone there had a choice: join the brutal new societies or die.

I remember the moment back in Arena 1 when I'd been offered the opportunity to join them. I'd chosen to face death instead. I wish others had been as strong when the moment counted. Perhaps if they had, the cities wouldn't have gotten such a strong hold over what remained of civilization.

The General moves over to another board, this one showing a picture of a small electronic device.

"This is the GPS tracker which needs to be placed in each of the arenas in order to guide the bombs. Once detonated, they will completely eradicate the arena and the city around it entirely. Over a hundred thousand people will die in each attack."

The thought of all those deaths makes my stomach turn. But I also know it's a necessary evil. Fighting war with war doesn't sound like it makes much sense but I understand why it has to be this way.

As the conversation turns to strategy and how, exactly, we can get the GPS devices inside, I am hit by a sudden moment of clarity.

"Send me into the arena," I say, before my brain has even had time to catch up to my mouth.

Silence falls. Everyone looks at me. I can feel their eyes burning into me.

"I'm sorry?" the General says. I can almost hear the derision in his voice. He's wondering what a seventeen-year-old girl can do in an arena built for slaughter.

"I've fought in them before," I add. "They'll all know my name, all recognize my face. I'll be able to walk right in there. Everyone will want to see me fight. I'll be able to draw every single person in the city into one place. Once I'm there, I can activate your GPS device."

It's my dad who speaks first. "How will you get back out again?" he says.

I can feel my hands trembling. I don't want them to. This is my moment, I have to be brave so that everyone knows I can do this.

"I've done it before," I say.

I can tell Dad is growing tenser. "That doesn't mean you can do it again," he says.

"I know. And if I can't, you'll just have to blow the place up with me still inside."

There's a perceptible change in the atmosphere as everyone realizes what it is I'm offering. Instead of sending a group of soldiers into the city and risking all their lives, I'm offering to infiltrate, to allow myself to be caught. I'm offering to return to the worst place I've ever had the misfortune of entering in my entire life, without the guarantee of coming out the other end, just for their cause. I can feel the respect of the soldiers in the room begin to build.

"You don't have to do this just to prove a point, Brooke," my dad is saying.

I shake my head. "I'm not," I say. "I'm doing it because I can. Because I'm the best person to do it. You said we get one chance, that we only have enough weapons for one attack. So let me draw everyone to one place. It will increase our chances of success, won't it?"

My dad can't argue against me. He knows I'm right.

"Let me do this," I say again, firmly. "It's the right thing to do. If we don't take these cities down, if we don't eradicate the arenas and the slaverunners, then survivors will keep being tortured and enslaved. Children will keep being taken for the mines, for the sex trade."

My voice falters as I think of Ben's brother whisked away on a train for the mines beneath Grand Central. I have to do this for him, and for everyone else who died because of this stupid, brutal war.

I can tell I have the support of the rest of the soldiers. But I've put my dad in a difficult position, because now he has to fight between his heart and his head. He has to decide whether to listen to the father in him who is inevitably telling him not to let his daughter do this, or the commander in him who knows this is the best chance they're ever going to get.

Eventually, he stands, having made his decision.

"Brooke's right," he says. "She's in by far the best position to infiltrate Arena Three."

And with that, I have sealed my fate. For the third time in my short life, I am heading back into the arena.

CHAPTER TWENTY FOUR

I'm raring to go, but the doctor tells me I have to wait a week until I can go on any missions at all. My body was so badly damaged from the time I spent in the desert, I will need to give it time to recuperate. I spend the days in the hospital with my friends, sharing memories of those we lost along the way. I know none of them want me to leave, to do what I have to do, but they know better than to argue with me. If I die on this mission, it's a sacrifice I am willing to make.

Finally, the day comes when I am to leave. Dad has been in communication with the other compound in Massachusetts in order to coordinate our efforts. The time is now. Today is the day the world will be reborn.

I stand in the meeting room deep beneath the compound, the walls lined with blueprints and strategic maps. For the first time, I am wearing my US Marine Corps uniform. I feel a surge of pride to be standing before my dad in this uniform. Though he doesn't show it on his face, I know he is proud of me too.

"There's no need for you to take weapons," Dad says. "Anything you take will be stolen by the slaverunners as soon as you're captured. It's better for them not to get their hands on any weaponry. But I want you to have this, just in case you run into any crazies along the way."

He holds out a knife. It is the same one I used back on Catskills Mountain, the one that helped keep me and Bree alive and fed for four long years. It was taken from me back in Arena 1. I hadn't realized how much symbolic value I'd placed on that knife until now, as I hold its replica in my hands.

I stash the knife away and swallow down the emotion in my throat.

"This is your GPS chip," Dad says, placing a small device securely in my pocket. "Once you're inside the vicinity of the arena, activate it. It will be our signal to launch the bombs and the tracker inside will guide them to the right spot. Then you'll have five minutes to get out. So as soon as it's activated you need to get the hell out of there. Do you understand me, Brooke? No matter what happens, don't let them take you into the arena to fight."

I understand what he's saying. If I end up fighting in the arena, there's no way I'll make it out in five minutes. I'll be at the mercy of whatever fighters they decide to throw at me. It would be a suicide mission. I pray it doesn't come to that, but I also know I'm willing to give myself up if it does.

It's time to go. I begin the long walk through the underground corridors, then I'm up into the compound, surrounded by trees and vegetation. It feels so strange standing in this beautiful Eden in a military uniform. That war must exist for peace to prevail is a concept I can hardly wrap my head around.

Up in the compound, my friends have been allowed out of the hospital to see me off. Ryan has shaved his head again, and he gives me his confident, cocky smile. For the first time in a long time, he looks like the Ryan I first met at Fort Noix, the only difference being the sling around his arm and the absence of Jack.

Charlie has bounced back to full strength remarkably. I hug him goodbye, knowing that Flo is watching down on us, grateful that I have gotten him this far.

Ben is still weak from our ordeal. He was always the gentler, more sensitive of us, and it stands to reason that the toll the desert took on his body would be greater than the toll it took on mine. I feel bad for leaving him when he's still vulnerable, but I know Ben can look after himself, even if his mournful blue eyes are silently pleading with me not to go. Like always, the words we want to speak to each other seem bound up, tied in our throats. Ben and I always struggled to talk about the shared experiences we'd been through, and I vow in that moment that if I make it out of the arena alive, I will open up to him about everything. But for now, I take his hand in mine, noting how the skin has become soft again thanks to a week resting in the hospital, and press a kiss onto the back of it, just like he did with me when we first parted ways all those months ago. Back then he went off searching for his brother, while I went after Bree. Now we're parting ways again, united in our goal, knowing that the whole future of the world is resting on my shoulders.

Then it's only Bree and Dad left to say goodbye to. Bree is holding onto Penelope, clutching her against her chest. She looks like a little girl again, like the seven-year-old I raised on the mountainside, the girl who relied on me for everything. It's as though being back in our dad's presence has allowed her to regress. She can claim back those childhood years she lost again. I wish I could do the same.

I bend down so my eyes are level with her and Penelope. I address the one-eyed dog first, rubbing her behind the ear.

"Take care of Bree while I'm gone," I say.

Penelope tips her head to the side as though she's taking in everything I'm saying. Then she licks Bree's face, lapping up the salty tears that are rolling down her cheeks.

"I wish you didn't have to go," Bree stammers. "I wish there was another way."

"I know," I say. "So do I. But this is the last fight, Bree. After this, the world will begin to heal again. I'll be able to heal again."

She doesn't say what we are both thinking; that there is a chance I might not make it back at all.

I pull her into me, hugging her tightly. Over my shoulder, I catch sight of Charlie watching me. I know he'll take care of Bree if I don't return. She'll have Charlie and Penelope and Dad. If there was any time for me to disappear from her life, it would be now.

I let go of her and straighten up before my own tears have a chance to fall. I can hardly bear to look into her sorrowful eyes, and so I don't. I move along, pain swirling in my gut, and come face to face with my dad.

In unison, we salute.

"Commander," I say.

"Good luck, soldier," he says.

Then he reaches forward and pulls me into a tight embrace. "You can do this, Brooke," he says into my ear. "I believe in you."

"Thank you, Dad," I whisper back.

And then there's nothing left to do but to mount my motorcycle and head off into the desert, alone. I kick the engine to life and rev, making fumes spew out behind me. Then I'm off, heading away from the compound, away from the Eden my dad has created. I am leaving behind everything I care about.

I decide not to look back.

*

The Texas sunshine is blistering hot. It's the height of midday and the sun's rays are burning into me. Being back in the desert makes me uncomfortable. It brings back all those horrible memories, of the wild dog attack, of the slave city in the crater of Memphis. I try not to think about all that I've endured because it just serves to remind me that what I'm about to do is only the first step in reclaiming the planet. Ridding the world of slaver cities and crazies and mutated creatures will take far, far longer to do. Eradicating the arenas is just the catalyst needed to start that process.

I head west toward San Antonio, where Arena 3 is located. Remarkably, the road is still intact. It will barely take me three hours to reach the city. Which means that in three hours' time, I'll be heading back into an arena, back into the place of my nightmares. But for now, everything is peaceful. The road stretches on forever, seemingly into oblivion. There is nothing left of the civilization that once used this route. No gas stations at the side of the road, no fields growing crops. There's just desert as far as the eye can see, and above it a cloudless blue sky. If there was anything that could make me feel insignificant, it would be driving along this road alone.

I have to remind myself that I am not insignificant at all. Right now, I am a very important cog in a machine that will change the course of the world forever. I know that elsewhere in the country, there are other soldiers like me, riding motorcycles alone down endless, straight roads, heading toward other cities and other arenas.

As time passes, I feel my anxiety growing. It's forming a knot in my stomach. There is so much resting on my shoulders, the pressure is almost too great to handle. But then, all at once, I see San Antonio appearing on the horizon and a strange sense of calm settles over me. I feel like I was always meant to be here. I was always meant to do this. Every road I have traveled, every decision I have made, every person, crazy, and creature I have fought, every friend I have lost, it was all to take me to this exact place, this exact moment. I am about to face my destiny.

Then I see it, appearing out of the distance. Arena 3. It is enormous, rising up from the ashes of the city that once thrived here, casting a shadow over everyone who still lives here. Light glitters off its metallic surfaces. It is by far the most imposing arena I have seen yet.

But my time to dwell has come to an end, because all at once, as though appearing from nowhere, several motorcycles appear and surround me. Their riders are dressed all in black and they each have gun trained on me. Slaverunners.

I kill the engine of my bike and slowly get off, my hands raised into a truce position. I'm surprised by how completely calm I am. My heartbeat has hardly increased at all.

The slaverunners approach me cautiously, as though expecting me to pull a weapon out. But when they frisk me, all they find is the knife. Once again, my Marine Corps branded weapon is stolen from me. This time, I know I will get it back again. I will survive. Because I'm not doing this alone; I have a whole army behind me.

Somewhere back in Houston a red light on a machine is relaying my GPS's coordinates back to a room full of soldiers.

"What have we got here then?" one of the slaverunners says to me.

"My name is Brooke," I say. "I'm a fighter. The only person to have survived Arena One."

The slaverunner raises his eyebrows as though in disbelief. "Is that so? A slight little thing like you?" His face is so close to mine I can smell his breath.

I set my jaw firm. "You could've asked their leader if I hadn't killed him."

There's a murmur around the rest of the slaverunners. News of my victory over the leader in Arena 1 must have filtered down south. The man questioning me frowns, studying my face.

"What are you doing here?" he says. "How'd you make it all the way to Texas if you were fighting in Manhattan?"

"I've been touring the arenas," I lie. "Giving the spectators what they want to see: the famous Brooke Moore."

He looks at me skeptically, as though not sure whether to buy my story. But since I'm not packing any weapons, I'm not exactly a threat. They have no reason not to cuff me.

I don't resist as my hands are wrenched behind my back, nor when I'm marched toward a bike. In fact, as I'm sat on the back, heading down the road toward the arena, I smile to myself.

Game on.

CHAPTER TWENTY FIVE

It is like déjà vu, like stepping into a nightmare. The sounds of the arena, the metallic smell of blood in the air, it all brings back such horrible memories. Since it's midday, there are no fights taking place yet and so no crowds to satisfy. It means I don't need to worry about accidentally being thrust into an arena anytime soon. It also means I have plenty of time to plant my device and plot my escape. We need everyone in the arena before I set off the device because we only have one chance to destroy the city and the people within it.

But it also means the place is more or less silent. The only noises I can hear, other than our boots as we march along, are the crazed screams of the prisoners deep in the bowels of the arena.

The slaverunners lead me far underground, along winding corridor after winding corridor. They seem thrilled to have found me and keep grinning to one another, rubbing their hands with glee. I despise every single one of them. The farther I go underground, the stuffier it becomes. The prisoners kept down here aren't afforded any kind of ventilation system, and the air is thick with the smell of sweat, urine, and terror. The cries become louder the closer I get to the cells. I try to keep my emotions deep inside, but my heart breaks for them.

As I go, I mentally map out the whole route, every corner we turn, every staircase we descend, committing everything to memory. I'll need to know the exact route to take to get back to the surface when the time comes. Five minutes is all I'll have to escape the arena before the bombs obliterate it. So the whole time I walk, I take mental pictures of every single twist and turn, every little chink in the brickwork, anything that will help me find my way to the surface.

It grows darker and darker with each new corridor I'm led down. The place is lit only with emergency lights which bathe everything in a grimy dark yellow light. It's hard to believe how harsh the light is on the surface down here.

My captors don't speak to me. They just prod me along, like an animal, like I'm less than human. I keep my chin high, not about to give them any kind of satisfaction for their bad treatment of me. Then they draw to a halt outside of a large steel door. One of the guards takes out a key and unlocks the door. It swings open and I'm kicked in the small of my back. I stumble inside and fall to my knees, colliding with the hard cement ground. Before the door is slammed harshly behind me, just enough light streams in from outside for me to see the gaunt, hollow faces of the prisoners locked up inside. Then the doors are locked behind me, and we are plunged back into darkness.

The smell in here is horrendous. There must be at least a hundred prisoners in here all crammed together, chained, sitting in their own dirt and filth. I wouldn't be surprised to learn that no one inside here has washed since being locked up. Being so close to them brings awful memories flooding back to me, of the gnawing hunger I felt when I was locked up in Arena 1, and of the heavy cuffs around my wrists. I feel nothing but empathy for them all. But I don't speak to anyone. I'm not here to make friends. If I so much as let myself care for anyone inside here, I could jeopardize the whole mission. Everyone here is going to die. They're collateral damage to a grander plan.

It shocks me to hear myself thinking this way. I really have turned into Flo. She didn't care who she hurt as long as she survived. At the time, I hated her for it. But now I understand. And I understand, too, why my dad did what he did. Sometimes small acts of evil build up to greater acts of kindness. Not that anyone could call blowing up a stadium filled with slaverunners and spectators small...

My mission doesn't leave my thoughts for even a second. Straightaway, I fumble in my pocket, searching for the red LED light of my GPS tracker. It's hard to reach with the cuffs on and in the pitch blackness, but I find it nevertheless. I know once I activate it I'll only have five minutes to escape before the bombs are dropped, so it's absolutely critical that I secure myself an escape route before I do. I wish I had just the smallest amount of light to see by, so I could work out how many steps it will take me to reach the door. Every detail matters now. My plan is to activate the device when the guards arrive to take me to my fight, then attack them. I'll be up and out of the arena before the bombs fall.

"What have you got there?" a disembodied voice says to me. It sounds like the voice of an old woman. The cruelty of the slaverunners for putting an elderly woman in an arena for entertainment is unimaginable.

"It's nothing," I say, not knowing whether I can trust her.

"Looks like something to me," comes her reply.

I deliberate whether to tell her more. But then I remind myself that I'm not here to be polite or friendly. I have a mission and nothing should be distracting me from it, even if that something is just a light-hearted conversation with an old woman.

As I'm feeling my way in the gloom along the perimeter wall, I pray the other survivors don't suss out what I'm doing, or haven't been drawn to my movements by the nosy old woman. I can't trust anyone, not even people who in other circumstances would be on the same team as me. I feel guilty knowing that my actions will be causing their deaths, but I have to remind myself that they'd all be dead anyway. At least this way, other people elsewhere will get to live. I shouldn't have to turn them into martyrs, but I have no choice.

As I'm searching for a strategic place to prepare for my attack, I start to hear something that piques my suspicion. It sounds a lot like the distant shouts of a crowd. I listen intently, straining to hear over the sounds of the other prisoners shuffling around in the cell. It is unmistakable. I can hear the sound of an approaching crowd, their cries for blood growing louder and louder and louder.

The old woman who'd spoken to me before must hear it too.

"Must be a special event," she says. "There ain't usually fights this early in the day."

I want to ask her how she can even tell what time of day it is, since we're in a completely dark cell without any way of seeing outside, but I have more important things to think about. A special event could only mean one thing: the slaverunners have announced my arrival. I knew I'd be a draw for the crowds but I didn't realize I'd be such a draw that they would move the games forward to the middle of the day. I won't get the evening to prepare at all. They're holding a special fight, right here, right now.

A jolt of panic races through me. I've barely been here twenty minutes and already the plan is diverging off course. My escape route hasn't been planned. I haven't had time to figure out what I'm doing.

Suddenly I hear the sound of footsteps approaching from outside. They're coming for me. The lock screeches as someone opens it from the other side of the door, then a slaverunner appears, a silhouette against the dim light coming from outside.

"Brooke Moore," he says. I recognize his voice as the slaverunner who first captured me back out in the city. "You were right about you being a crowd pleaser. The second we said we had you, our leader called a fight. A special fight. You're coming to the arena."

I try to keep calm. Everything's happening more quickly than I was expecting—it's barely been four hours since I left Ryan, Ben, Charlie, Dad, Bree, and Penelope at the gates of the compound—

but I have to keep my wits about me. I'm a soldier, a fighter, I can do what I have to do. The time is now. The moment has arrived.

The old woman begins to chuckle. "Oh, *you're* the special event. Well, good luck to you."

I turn and glare at her, at her wizened face. She's missing all her teeth and her hands are gnarled.

But I don't have time for anger, I have work to do. I reach into my pocket for the GPS device. But before my thumb hits the button, the woman screams.

"She's got something in her pocket!"

Chaos breaks out in the cell as prisoners start panicking. I quickly press my thumb into the button, but in my trembling haste I can't tell whether it fully activated or not. I don't get a chance to double check; the guard is there in one second flat, wrenching my hand and the device out of it. I can't see whether the red blinking light has been activated because the guard drops it on the ground and slams his heavy boot into it.

My insides drop like a ten-ton weight. If I didn't manage to activate it before he destroyed it, the rest of the army won't have seen my signal. They won't know that the moment has arrived much sooner than anyone was anticipating. Even if they did pick up the signal, it would only have been for a split second. They could easily have blinked and missed it. And there won't be anything to guide their missiles. They have one shot to hit their target and now they're going to have to do it blind.

I'm so taken aback by the speed with which everything has changed, I don't even have time to attack. The guard has already grabbed me roughly by the arms and is dragging me from the prison cell. Meanwhile, the sounds of the crowds above intensifies. I can hear their footsteps as they march above my head and take their seats. I'm being taken to the arena and there's nothing I can do about it.

As I'm pulled from the cell, I narrow my eyes at the old woman who turned on me at the very last minute. I know she probably just wanted to survive another day, to not be the one called to fight today, but her callousness has ruined everything. That one decision to call me out might even have changed the course of the future of the world.

The cell door is slammed shut and I'm dragged, stunned, along the corridor. As I go, my calmness completely disappears. In its place comes a frantic, racing heartbeat, a whirring mind, and palms slick with sweat. It's all gone wrong. My worst nightmare has been realized. I'm heading for Arena 3.

CHAPTER TWENTY SIX

Each one of my footsteps echoes as I am prodded along the corridor by the guard. My mind is a frantic blur. It is so dark down here with only the emergency lights to illuminate the path I can hardly see my hand in front of my face. It makes everything stark. I feel like I am walking into hell.

Slaverunners walk ahead of me and behind me. They must have gotten the lowdown on me. They know what I did in Arena 1, how I killed the leader there, and they're not taking any chances.

The corridor bends, taking me away from the path that leads to freedom, steering me in the opposite direction, toward the jaws of death. I can hear the crowd above stamping their feet, chanting my name. Everyone wants to see me fight, but no one wants to see me survive. They all want to bear witness to my death.

I dig my heels in, my body not letting me move. A slaverunner comes up behind me and kicks me in the small of my back, making me take a stumble forward. I almost lose my footing. Because my hands are bound so tightly, if I fall, there will be nothing I can do to stop myself hitting the floor. I have no choice but to let myself be shoved onward.

Finally, the corridor opens out into a circular room.

"Stand there," one of the slaverunner says, pointing at the ground.

I can just about make out a metal shape on the floor in the middle of the room. It looks like some kind of trap door.

As I step on it, metal cuffs wrap around each of my boots, sticking me to the ground steadfast.

"What is this?" I ask, frustrated to hear my voice trembling. "What's happening?"

The slaverunners don't get a chance to respond, because in that moment a circular panel opens up directly above my head. Stark daylight pours in through the hole above me, blinding me. I turn my head to protect my eyes from the glare. Along with the light, a blast of sound comes down the hole, so loud it's deafening. It's the chanting, screaming, braying crowd. At the same time, I feel someone fiddling with the cuffs around my wrists. They're unlocking me. And that can only mean one thing.

All at once, the ground moves beneath my feet. The metal thing I'm standing on is beginning to rise. My hands are free but my feet are locked into the ground, making sure I don't go anywhere. I rise slowly, the light blinding me. I want to cover my eyes but I know that within a matter of seconds I'll be in an arena where anything could happen to me. I have to be alert, ready for anything they might throw at me.

A voice booms over the loudspeakers as I rise.

"Ladies and gentlemen, please put your hands together for Brooke Moore!"

The crowd roars, the noise so loud it is deafening.

My head tips through the hole, just enough for me to be able to see the arena before me. It's circular, built in an old sports stadium. The arena is like a desert, with dusty yellow sand covering every inch of the ground. It is completely open to the elements and the blue sky up above me.

The crowds stretch up in the bleachers as far as my eyes can see. I'm shocked to discover that none of them are biovictims. Whereas the spectators in the other cities had been deformed and mutated by radiation, their nuclear fried brains turning them into savage beasts, the people here have no such excuse. They're humans, just like me, ordinary people who survived the war. But every single citizen of the city must be here—the elderly, the young, everyone's turned out to watch my death. I wish I could find a way to empathize with them, to remind myself that they're victims of a brutal society as well. But I just can't do it. They had the same choice I was confronted with back in Arena 1: join them or fight them. They've chosen the path of least resistance and for that, I can never forgive them.

Any residue of shame I felt about blowing this place to smithereens dissipates. These people deserve to die. Now I just hope that I activated the GPS device, that the bombs are on their way. But it's already been five minutes and nothing has happened yet. Whether something's alerted them to my being in danger or not, there's no way of knowing. All I know is that I'm still here, the arena is still standing, and there's no sign of my dad's army. I'm alone.

The platform finishes rising and clunks into place. But my metal cuffs keep me frozen to the spot. I look around, trying to work out what is happening and what I am supposed to do. I'm on high alert, my senses listening out for the smallest sound, my body feeling out for the smallest tremor. Anything that will tell me where my foe is coming from. I don't know what to expect. Arena 1 was like a wrestling ring. Sumo, Shira, Malcolm—all my opponents were celebrity fighters in their own right. But Arena 2 was more like a sport or a game. All the competitors were children my age. They wanted us to die but they wanted to be creative with it. They wanted their crowds to be entertained. I wonder what Arena 3 will be like. It's not giving away any of its secrets yet.

All the while I stand there, I look around at every crevice and cranny in the whole building, praying that somewhere I'll see a way out, an escape hatch. Other than the disc I stand on, I cannot see a single entryway. But my competitors will have to get in here somehow. Just as soon as they do, I'll make a beeline for it and take my chance at escape.

That's when I see movement from opposite me. Another person is coming out of the ground, rising on their own metal disc. I expect them to be my competitor, but once the disc clicks in place and the dust settles, I realize I am facing a child. She can't be more than twelve years old. She stares at me, terrified, her face completely white.

Suddenly, all around me, children start rising up on discs, clicking into place, until we're in a circle. There are ten in total.

I can feel my stomach roiling at the realization that they're expecting us to fight each other to the death.

The announcer speaks.

"There can only be one survivor. Whoever is left standing will be crowned the winner. Let the games begin."

Suddenly there's a loud honking noise and the metal cuffs across my feet snap open. I'm free to move. To fight.

The crowd begins to cheer. I can feel the anticipation buzzing in the air.

No one moves. None of my fellow competitors prepared to fight one another. But that's when the ground begins to rumble. I wobble on my platform, trying to keep my footing, but the shaking is too great. We begin to stumble from our discs, landing on the desert ground.

The second we do, the desert sand suddenly sifts away through a million pinprick holes in the ground. As it disappears, it reveals a huge metal framework on the floor, like a lattice. Then, out of each gap, a red laser beam bursts out, making a crisscross pattern above my head. The arena has been transformed in a matter of seconds from a barren desert into a strange, futuristic stadium. The crowd goes wild, delighted by what is unfolding before their eyes.

I crouch down, certain that the laser beams mean danger. I know that the electricity in the laser beams won't be strong enough to kill us because that would make the game a huge disappointment. But they're certainly designed to hurt and I don't want to risk touching any of them. I have no idea what they're for when I suddenly see a bright red light coming from one end of the stadium.

I look over and see that a huge doorway has been illuminated. It's the exit. They're trying to tempt us toward it. But I'm not about to play their game. It's like a magician, always trying to get you to look in a certain place so they can distract you from the real trick. I won't fall for it. That exit is probably fake anyway. They just want to see my desperation.

Two of the kids race for the exit. The second they do, the laser beams begin moving, chasing them across the desert ground. They scream in pain and collapse to the floor, writhing around as though shocked by electricity.

The crowd is momentarily entertained by the sight, but they quickly grow frustrated at the lack of fighting. As though in response, the laser beams begin to move, rotating so that we have no choice but to move. They're forcing us together. I duck and weave through them, like I'm dancing a horrible dance. I step and leap, crouch and spin, trying to get out of the path of the moving laser beams. I'm hit and the pain is excruciating, like barbed wire all over my body. At last the crowd begins to cheer, pleased to see some suffering for their entertainment. But I know this isn't it. There is more to come. This is just the beginning. This is like the warm-up act, trying to pump up the crowd for the main show.

All at once, the ground begins to vibrate. I can hear the sound of grinding metal coming from somewhere beneath the floor of the stadium. Then two slits open up in the ground and rising from them are giant, twisting blades. The crowd simultaneously oohs, and I feel sick to my stomach.

At the same time, a platform like the one I rose into the arena on appears at the far end, opposite the neon, flashing exit. I can only just about see the silhouette of whatever it is being raised into the arena. All I can tell is that it isn't human. It is some kind of beast, a disgusting, huge, spiny creature. A spotlight appears on the creature. It looks like a giant, spiky earwig covered in mucus. Its pincers click together.

So that's how they're going to play it. If we won't fight each other, then they'll pit man against beast, humans against the deformed creatures our radioactive world has produced. I swallow hard and try to psych myself up. If I can fight crazies and kill radiated wild dogs, I can do this. But none of my dad's training has prepared me for this, and the creature is so revolting it takes every ounce of resolve in my body not to run away.

The crowd goes crazy, cheering and shouting.

There's a split-second pause as the creature takes in the sight of its prey standing defenselessly in front of it, then it launches itself forward, racing toward me and the other children at a frighteningly fast pace.

My heart flies into my throat. The adrenaline pumping through me sharpens my faculties and helps me make sense of what I have to do. I understand how this arena is set up. I have opponents, obstacles, but no weapons, but they didn't go to all this effort just to see us die in five seconds flat. They want to be entertained and that means watching us fight, having us die one by one. I'm supposed to want the other kids to get killed before me.

I spring forward, racing right at the creature. The crowd gasps, clearly not expecting me to make such a bold move. As though following my movements, the rotating saws crash down. I only just manage to leap out of the way. I fall on my side and go rolling across the hard metal grid floor.

But the creature manages to avoid the blades as well, and remains completely unscathed. It rears up like a centipede, showing off a thousand spindly teeth, then roars. Huge strings of spit hang between its teeth, and a fine mist of hot spit sprays the crowd. They squeal like children at Sea World. Don't they realize they're watching humans fighting for their lives? Have they become so desensitized to violence?

The creature zooms toward me again. I'm up on my feet quick as a flash, racing toward the spinning saws. It was too easy for the creature to duck out of the way of the last blade, so I get a different idea this time. Instead of trying to get one to crash down on it, I'm going to run straight through the middle.

It's a risky maneuver and the crowd knows it. They start bouncing up and down in their seats as I make a beeline straight down the center of the groaning, rotating saws. As I go, they start crashing down, just inches from the place where I last stood. They're so close, I can feel the rush of wind created by each slam.

The creature is right behind me, right on my tail. Just as its pincers reach out to snap me up, one of the blades crashes down. I'm thrown forward by the force and land chest down on the hard ground. The wind is knocked out of me and I wince. Then I look back and see that barely a foot behind me, the creature is twitching against the metal ground, a saw rammed right through its head and black, sticky, gooey blood oozing out of it.

Across the other side of the arena, a group of about five of the children are huddled together, staring at me wide-eyed as though in terror. I just have time to spin onto my back when a boy barrels into me.

"Don't fight me, you idiot!" I scream as we roll across the ground.

He pins me down, grappling with me.

"I'm trying to keep you all alive!" I shout back.

As the boy wrestles with me, the ground begins to rumble and the saws start to disappear down into the slits in the grating, taking the disgusting earwig creature with them. The crowd chants my name but I know better than to fall for it. There will be another monster to fight. There always is. These games will only end when the humans die.

I managed to get my knee up and kick the boy in his stomach. He goes flying back and the ground starts to rumble and shake. I know something else is coming for us, that the arena is about to transform again, but I need a moment to catch my breath. As I take in a deep gasp, I'm suddenly aware of a pungent smell coming from behind me. Whatever is there, the crowd has already seen it, because they start to clap and squeal with excitement.

I flip onto my feet in a crouching stance and spin, coming face to face with three enormous rodent-like creatures. They're completely furless, covered in painful-looking sores and boils, and their eyes glow red. They're each at least six feet long, and the stench coming off them is unbearable. In the crowd, people cover their mouths, but it's all part of the spectacle for them, all part of the evening's entertainment.

The rats see the group of five children huddled in the corner. Within a second, they gobble them up. The boy next to me screams. I cover my mouth, trying to stop myself from retching, and glance around me desperately, searching for somewhere to run and hide. But all around me is nothing but the flat open arena ground.

Then the ground suddenly begins to shake and rumble. A series of walls burst up, so fast I'm knocked off my feet. The giant rats scurry to the far end of the stadium, seemingly afraid. I take my chance and run to the opposite side. Walls spring up all around me, blocking me in, forcing me to backtrack. At the very least, they provide a barrier between me and the boy who was trying to kill me. But when everything stops shaking, I realize what has happened. Surrounding me is a maze.

My heart pounds. I can hear the rats scurrying around at the other end of the stadium. The sound of their claws on the metal grating makes my stomach turn, as does the screaming of the children they are catching and eating. I can smell their odor as it wafts through the maze toward me, but the walls are so high there's no way I can see where they're approaching from. I'm completely blind.

I start running, disorientated and panicked. I've always been a fighter, not a runner. This is completely out of my comfort zone. And it's made worse by the way the ground suddenly rises and falls, by the way the walls suddenly grind and begin to move. I feel frantic, like I'm trapped in a nightmare.

I can hear the pounding feet of the rats from just the other side of the wall and smell their putrid flesh. They are so close. A wall is starting to move and I launch myself at it. It's just low enough for me to pull myself up on top. It springs back up to its full height, and I'm just a few yards above the rats. Their disgusting noses sniff me, but I'm just out of their reach. I run along the top of the wall away from them. While being able to see where they are is useful, it won't help me in any way if I don't find a way to kill them.

I race along the top of the wall, searching for anything that I might be able to use as a weapon. As I go, I wrack my brains, trying to think of a way to defeat them. It's when I see one of the rats nip the other that I get a brilliant idea. In the last fight, I used the obstacle against the opponent. What about if in this fight, I pit the opponents against one another?

I notice ahead a place where the walls move in and out, forming a block like a prison cell. I know then what I have to do.

"HEY!" I shout at the stinking creatures, trying to get their attention. "I'M UP HERE!"

All three of them turn their disgusting faces up to me, twitching their crusty noses. Revolted by the sight of them, I start to run. My feet slap against the hard wall. The rats are right behind me, chasing so fast, getting so close. I have to time this perfectly or it won't come off at all.

I take a running leap just as one of the walls is starting to rise and manage to grip it by my fingertips. I hang there, dangling helplessly as it continues its slow rise. I try to heave myself up but I can't quite get purchase on the wall. Gritting my teeth, I begin to scrabble and kick, searching for a nick in the wall where I can get my footing. The rats are racing toward me; I can hear them, smell them, can feel the crowd on the edge of their seats with anticipation. Finally, I get my foot onto a rough part of the wall and start to scramble, heaving with all my might. Then, in the nick of time, I'm crouching on the top of the wall.

The rats congregate beneath me, snarling, snapping their teeth. I stand there, trying to catch my breath. I need to time this perfectly.

I turn on top of the wall and watch the one opposite as it begins to lower. Then I jump, right into the enclosed space. It's a complete dead end. The audience has no idea what I'm doing and must think I've chosen suicide, because they all gasp in unison.

I back away, my heart hammering, prepared for the wall ahead of me to lower and my opponents to race in and devour me. The screeching, grinding noise of the walls begins to sound out, and it starts to lower. The rats are clambering over one another, trying to be the first into the small space. Then, just as I hoped, the wall my back is pressed against begins to rotate. I barely have a second to press myself through the gap before it slams shut with a humongous crunching noise. The rats are locked up inside the tiny room on the other side. Within a matter of seconds, I hear the sounds of them tearing one another to pieces. The crowd erupts with applause, thrilled by the spectacle I'm giving them.

But of course, it's not over. There will be more deformed creatures to fight. More races to run and hoops to leap through. I'm their entertainment for the evening. My only chance of survival is if I can draw the game out long into the evening, long enough for the troops back at the compound to realize I'm in trouble. Right now, I don't care if I die in their bomb blasts. Anything would be preferable to playing this disgusting death game. Right now, a bomb strike would feel like mercy.

As the ground shakes and the maze disappears, I get my first look at the other competitors. Only three of them remain. The boy who attacked me is gone, swallowed by one of the putrid rodents. The sight makes me feel hollow, but the crowd loves it. They roar their approval, loving the entertainment and the way we are being slowly tortured to death. Of all the arenas I've fought, of all the crowds I've faced, these are by far the worst because they know better but have adopted a "rather you than me" attitude. The hatred I feel for them is all consuming.

The ground begins to shake again and when I look down, I see hot, boiling water bubbling up through the grid at my feet. It's so hot, steam curls up with it, and bubbles pop on the surface. Then platforms rise up.

I have no choice. My instinct to survive is stronger than anything inside of me that wants to give up. I grab hold of a rope attached to a podium and start to swing across the burning water. I'm moving like a pendulum, back and forth, the whole time looking down to see what hybrid creature will be sent up to terrorize me. But instead of a creature, the water keeps on rising.

My muscles scream in protest as I force myself to climb up the rope, inching myself away from the water that just keeps on rising.

At the other end of the arena, one of the boys loses his grip on the rope. He slips into the boiling water and lets out a bloodcurdling scream. I climb even quicker and manage to pull myself, stomach first, onto the platform. When I look down, I realize that the water is filled with giant, wriggling maggots, at least fifty foot long and completely see-through. Clearly, these animals evolved in hot, radiated, toxic waters.

The crowd squeals as though they find the sight squeamish. I'm so angry with them, with the way they're treating us and the pleasure they're deriding from our fear and misery. But the fight is leaving me. I have no energy to spare to scream at them. All that's left in me will have to go into fighting the maggot-like creatures.

In the water beneath me, they writhe and wriggle around. More keep appearing, squirming, their disgusting transparent bodies making me feel sick. If the audience is expecting me to kill them, they're going to be sorely disappointed. There's no way I'll be able to fight all those disgusting creatures; there are literally hundreds of them.

But the waters are rising, bringing them closer and closer, and there's nowhere left to climb. I can't get any higher.

That's when I realize I'm not supposed to climb or fight. This is the end of the line. For the crowd, the enjoyment comes with the toe-curling anticipation of knowing one of us is about to die, of watching the terror on our faces. I have no choice but to delight them by cowering back from the platform edge.

The water begins lapping at the side of the platform. The maggoty worms are so close to me now I can see their bulbous eyes. They have rows of perforated teeth, like needles. The crowd squeals with delight as another quake begins to shake the podiums. I hear the shrill scream of a girl and know another one of the competitors has fallen into the deathly waters.

I cling on for dear life, praying that I make it out of here alive. But I know it's futile. The end has come.

All at once, the platform tips. My grip on it tightens but I can't hold on forever. My muscles fail me and I let go. I hit the boiling water and scream in time to the gasping crowd of thrill seekers. It feels more like fire than water. I thrash around, screaming at the top of my lungs. But something is changing in the crowd. No one wants to see me die this way; not because it's vicious and brutal, but because it's too cheap. Whoever is controlling the game gets the hint, because suddenly the water that had been filling the stadium suddenly begins to drain away, and before the worm creatures even have a chance to bite me, I'm plummeting down, swirling as the water is sucked away.

I hit the metal grid of the arena ground once more. The worm creatures lie all around me, flapping and gasping in the air, drowning in oxygen, no longer a threat.

The crowd bursts into applause.

I look over and see there's just one other competitor left alive. A boy of roughly eighteen. He's lying on the floor too, his skin red and scalded like mine.

I realize then that there will be no more creatures to fight. It's down to the final two. They want us to kill each other.

With a clunking noise, two swords are dropped into the arena. But I can't even move. I'm exhausted, completely spent. My body feels like it's on fire, the scalding water making every part of me hurt. It feels like I'm back in the desert again, when my body gave up and I just couldn't carry on. My limbs are heavy, and my mind whirring.

I can see the boy rising to his feet, picking up his sword, and, for the first time, I admit to myself that no one is coming to save me. My GPS device failed. The bombs weren't triggered and I will die before anyone realizes too much time has passed. No one was expecting me to be hauled into the arena so soon. As far as they know, I'm still a prisoner within the compound, plotting out my plan of escape. But in reality, I've failed in the one thing I had to do. I will die in this place and the world will keep on turning, just as brutal as before. Children will keep being stolen and survivors will keep fighting to the death in arenas until there's nothing left of the old human race, nothing to show for all our accomplishments. I will die and there will be hell on earth.

The boy's face appears above me, the sword glinting. He looks mournful, like he doesn't want to kill me but knows he has to. I lie there, unable to move. But something catches his eye. There's something coming toward us, floating as lightly as a feather on the wind. It's coming from the audience. Someone has thrown a piece of white cloth, or a feather, in our direction. We watch it float down. Is it some kind of peace offering? I look up and scan the crowd, trying to see the person who threw it. When I do, my heart stops beating.

There, in the crowd amongst the other spectators, are Ben and Ryan.

I don't think I've ever been more happy to see them in my life. They leap over the barriers and start running for me.

"Intruders!" the commentator cries.

I try to rise to my feet, finding my legs weak beneath me. Then suddenly their arms loop beneath mine and I'm wrenched to my feet.

"What are you doing here?" I cry to Ben and Ryan.

"We're your plan B," Ryan says.

"We're getting you out of here," Ben says, holding me close.

I wince, my scalded flesh sending bolts of pain through my body where he touches me. I notice Ryan is holding a GPS device and he hits it, turning the blinking red light into a solid one. The army has been mobilized. We have five minutes to get out of here before the whole place blows.

The crowd erupts into pandemonium. Half of them seem to be loving the abrupt change in course; the other half are angry to have been cheated out of seeing me and the boy fight to death.

But the boy doesn't seem to understand what's happening. He must think Ben and Ryan have been sent to help me kill him. He charges us, his sword raised.

Ryan snatches up the sword that was dropped for me and turns. Their swords clang together.

Ben gets to the metal disc that delivered me into the stadium and uses some kind of device in his hand, a tool of some sort, to ram the edge of the disc. It opens.

"RYAN!" I scream behind me. "COME ON!"

"GO!" he shouts. "While you still can!"

Ben tugs my arm and all at once we plummet downward, through the hole.

We hit the ground hard, winded. I feel one of my ribs crack on impact and take a sharp breath. The hole above closes over, plunging us into darkness. We're back underground, and Ryan is trapped up in the arena.

"NO!" I scream, my voice tearing from my lungs.

But Ben keeps on tugging me, pulling me, forcing me to move on. We only have a matter of minutes to get out of the arena before the whole thing blows.

I'm hardly in a fit enough state to run. Ben has to hold me close to him to keep me on my feet. Numb with grief, I'm somehow able to trace my steps back through the twisting, labyrinthine underground. From above, the audience is roaring, the commentator desperately trying to quell the chaos. It sounds like we've started a riot.

I'm hardly able to stand. I wince with every step. But we reach the very last corridor and race up the very last staircase. Then all at once, we burst out into the desert heat, into the abyss of nothing. We're free from the arena.

We start running full speed, knowing we only have a few minutes before the arena blows up. Even from outside we can hear the angry crowd. Shots start ringing out and it occurs to me that the slaverunners have opened fire on their own people.

As we race across the expanse, away from the arena, I hear the whining sound of bombs flying through the air.

The bombs hit and explode, the force so strong Ben and I are both flung forward. Heat blasts my face, singeing my hair. I land with a hard thud on my back and my head slams against the asphalt, making me bite down hard on my tongue.

I taste blood in my mouth. There's a ringing in my ears that's beyond painful. I'm completely dazed, unable to move or think or get my thoughts in any kind of order. Acrid smoke billows above me. I manage to roll over onto my chest. A little way behind me, I can see Ben lying face down on the ground. He's completely still and I pray that he's just been knocked unconscious. Behind him, I can see a scene of utter carnage. Enormous flames are leaping into the air, and bits of metal and body parts rain down. I duck as pieces of the arena grating thud just an inch to the side of my head.

I look back and see that where the arena stood is now nothing more than a smoldering crater. The bomb obliterated everything. It wiped out thousands of people in one blast.

There is no arena. There is no Ryan.

Then the world turns black.

EPILOGUE

They tell me this is what victory feels like. But I can't bring myself to celebrate. Not when I wake from my coma two days later in Dad's compound in Houston as a hero, nor when I'm reunited with Bree. I don't celebrate when my dad tells me how proud he is of me for what I've done.

We won. The plan to destroy the arenas simultaneously went off without a hitch. Or at least it did as far as everyone else is concerned. No one knows about the grueling hours I spent in Arena 3, fighting for my life against the vicious mutants the nuclear war created. Nor does anyone know what Ben and Ryan did for me, about how they both had a gut feeling that something was wrong, and how they put their differences aside to unite and help me with their secret plan B. No one realizes that if it weren't for them, I would have died in the arena, our whole plan would have fallen apart, and we'd all be under slaverunner control right now.

I know I'll never be able to tell them, that I will never be able to admit that I screwed up the most important thing I was ever going to do. I have to accept their praise even though I don't deserve it. I have to let them comfort me over Ryan mysteriously running away from the compound, knowing I will never be able to tell anyone that he is in fact dead because of me.

No one knows any of that. They all believe, when they found me unconscious in the desert, that my skin had been burned by the bomb's blast. They all needed me to be their hero and so I had no choice but to accept.

Only Ben seems to understand why I am so subdued. He knows why I don't dance and drink and celebrate like the rest of them. Like always, it's Ben who understands that what I have experienced has marked me, damaged me, possibly forever. The only good thing to come out of all of this is that I know we'll be by each other's side, silent, supporting, not needing to speak to understand where the other is coming from.

In the first week after the arenas are obliterated, we receive a message from a squad in the Midwest. Arena 4 has fallen, its prisoners liberated. They're all on buses heading south since we have the infrastructure in place and plenty of food to support them. But still I don't celebrate.

In the second week, we get an even bigger surprise when the Commander from Fort Noix arrives with his troops. He admits he was wrong to ignore my dad's appeal for help. He vows to do everything he can to help, and they strike up a bargain to take in a thousand orphans from the fallen cities and rescued from the sex trade. They'll be placed with families in the cabins in the woods.

But even this is not enough for me to celebrate. Nor is the moment when Charlie and Bree's friendship blossoms into first love, nor when Zeke and Stephan are rescued from Memphis, nor the moment when I am finally able to look Ben in the eye and tell him that I love him, that I finally can be with him in the way he wants me to be.

The point when I am finally able to smile for the first time comes a whole year later.

*

It is a week before the newly formed American army begins mobilizing into the deserts, and a month after the first full, reestablished communication device between the different compounds becomes fully operable. I'm sitting in my bedroom in my dad's house. Ben's asleep in my bed, his hair mussed up. Sunlight streams through the curtains, illuminating his pale torso, making him look more beautiful than ever. There's a faint knock at my door.

"Come in," I say.

Bree tips her head around the door. When she sees Ben asleep in my bed, she turns bright red.

"Yes?" I ask her, amused by her embarrassment.

"Dad wants to see you," she says.

Ben stirs and, realizing he is revealing a little more than he'd like, quickly pulls the cover up to his armpits.

"Hey," he says to Bree.

She just turns around and darts out the door.

I go over to Ben and bring my arms around his neck. Then I lean down and plant a slow, lingering kiss on his lips.

"Good morning, sleepyhead," I say. "Did you sleep well?"

"Perfectly," he replies. "What did Bree want?"

"She said Dad wanted to see me," I say, getting up from the bed. "Coming? I'll make you breakfast."

Ben grins and slips on his clothes.

We go through the corridor of the bungalow and find Dad in the kitchen. Bree is sitting at the table with him. He smiles when he sees the both of us.

"What is it?" I say. "Bree said you wanted to see me."

"I do," he replies. "I've got some news for you. Sit."

I exchange a glance with Ben, then we both take a seat.

"I received a call from a compound in California today," Dad begins. "They told us that the arena there has fallen. The city has been reclaimed."

I gasp.

"That was the last one?" I say, feeling my heart begin to thud.

Dad nods. "It was the last one."

I can hardly believe it. It's real. America has finally been rid of its arenas. No more fighting will ever take place in them again.

Dad steps forward and gives me a long hug. In that hug, I can feel all the years of grief, of agony, begin to melt. I can feel a new beginning forming.

I look from my sister, to my dad, to the boy I have finally let myself fall in love with. And then I smile.

Today, I realize, *life can begin again.*

Author Note

Thank you so much for reading all three Arena novels. I am so honored that you've read them all! I hope you'll continue on this journey with me. Although this is the final installment of my dystopian novels, you might enjoy one of my other series. You might especially enjoy RISE OF THE DRAGONS, which features another tough female protagonist who I am sure you will fall in love with! If you like Brooke, you will love Kyra! Read it for free and let me know what you think! I can't wait to hear!

Best wishes,
Morgan

RISE OF THE DRAGONS
(Kings and Sorcerers—Book 1)

"If you thought that there was no reason left for living after the end of the *Sorcerer's Ring* series, you were wrong. In RISE OF THE DRAGONS Morgan Rice has come up with what promises to be another brilliant series, immersing us in a fantasy of trolls and dragons, of valor, honor, courage, magic and faith in your destiny. Morgan has managed again to produce a strong set of characters that make us cheer for them on every page.…Recommended for the permanent library of all readers that love a well-written fantasy."
--Books and Movie Reviews, Roberto Mattos

The #1 Bestseller!

From #1 Bestselling author Morgan Rice comes a sweeping new epic fantasy series: RISE OF THE DRAGONS (KINGS AND SORCERERS—Book 1).

Kyra, 15, dreams of becoming a famed warrior, like her father, even though she is the only girl in a fort of boys. As she struggles to understand her special skills, her mysterious inner power, she realizes she is different than the others. But a secret is being kept from her about her birth and the prophecy surrounding her, leaving her to wonder who she really is.

When Kyra comes of age and the local lord comes to take her away, her father wants to wed her off to save her. Kyra, though, refuses, and she journeys out on her own, into a dangerous wood, where she encounters a wounded dragon—and ignites a series of events that will change the kingdom forever.

15 year old Alec, meanwhile, sacrifices for his brother, taking his place in the draft, and is carted off to The Flames, a wall of flames a hundred feet high that wards off the army of Trolls to the east. On the far side of the kingdom, Merk, a mercenary striving to leave behind his dark past, quests through the wood to become a Watcher of the Towers and help guard the Sword of Fire, the magical source of the kingdom's power. But the Trolls want the Sword, too—and they prepare for a massive invasion that could destroy the kingdoms forever.

With its strong atmosphere and complex characters, RISE OF THE DRAGONS is a sweeping saga of knights and warriors, of kings and lords, of honor and valor, of magic, destiny, monsters and dragons. It is a story of love and broken hearts, of deception, of ambition and betrayal. It is fantasy at its finest, inviting us into a world that will live with us forever, one that will appeal to all ages and genders.

Book #2 in KINGS AND SORCERERS is also now available!

"RISE OF THE DRAGONS succeeds—right from the start…. A superior fantasy…It begins, as it should, with one protagonist's struggles and moves neatly into a wider circle of knights, dragons, magic and monsters, and destiny….All the trappings of high fantasy are here, from soldiers and battles to confrontations with self….A recommended winner for any who enjoy epic fantasy writing fueled by powerful, believable young adult protagonists."
--*Midwest Book Review,* D. Donovan, eBook Reviewer

Books by Morgan Rice

THE WAY OF STEEL
ONLY THE WORTHY (BOOK #1)

VAMPIRE, FALLEN
BEFORE DAWN (BOOK #1)

OF CROWNS AND GLORY
SLAVE, WARRIOR, QUEEN (BOOK #1)

KINGS AND SORCERERS
RISE OF THE DRAGONS
RISE OF THE VALIANT
THE WEIGHT OF HONOR
A FORGE OF VALOR
A REALM OF SHADOWS
NIGHT OF THE BOLD

THE SORCERER'S RING
A QUEST OF HEROES
A MARCH OF KINGS
A FATE OF DRAGONS
A CRY OF HONOR
A VOW OF GLORY
A CHARGE OF VALOR
A RITE OF SWORDS
A GRANT OF ARMS
A SKY OF SPELLS
A SEA OF SHIELDS
A REIGN OF STEEL
A LAND OF FIRE
A RULE OF QUEENS
AN OATH OF BROTHERS
A DREAM OF MORTALS

THE SURVIVAL TRILOGY
ARENA ONE (Book #1)
ARENA TWO (Book #2)

the Vampire Journals
turned (book #1)
loved (book #2)
betrayed (book #3)
destined (book #4)
desired (book #5)
betrothed (book #6)

vowed (book #7)
found (book #8)
resurrected (book #9)
craved (book #10)
fated (book #11)
obsessed (book#12)

About Morgan Rice

Morgan Rice is the #1 bestselling and USA Today bestselling author of the epic fantasy series THE SORCERER'S RING, comprising seventeen books; of the #1 bestselling series THE VAMPIRE JOURNALS, comprising twelve books; of the #1 bestselling series THE SURVIVAL TRILOGY, a post-apocalyptic thriller comprising three books; of the epic fantasy series KINGS AND SORCERERS, comprising six books; and of the vampire paranormal series VAMPIRE, FALLEN, comprising one book (and counting). Morgan's books are available in audio and print editions, and translations are available in over 25 languages.

Morgan's new epic fantasy series, OF CROWNS AND GLORY, will publish in April, 2016, beginning with book #1, SLAVE, WARRIOR, QUEEN.

Morgan loves to hear from you, so please feel free to visit www.morganricebooks.com to join the email list, receive a free book, receive free giveaways, download the free app, get the latest exclusive news, connect on Facebook and Twitter, and stay in touch!

CPSIA information can be obtained
at www.ICGtesting.com
Printed in the USA
BVHW061940121121
621458BV00007B/141

9 781632 915696

UNDERTOW
OF
VENGEANCE

A HARRISON WEAVER MYSTERY

JOSEPH L.S. TERRELL

BellaRosaBooks

UNDERTOW OF VENGEANCE
ISBN 978-1-62268-096-2

First Printed: June 2014

Library of Congress Control Number: 2014941768

Also available as e-book: ISBN 978-1-62268-097-9

Printed in the United States of America on acid-free paper.

Cover photograph by Veronica Moschetti.
Author photograph by K. Wilkins.

Book design by Bella Rosa Books

BellaRosaBooks and logo are trademarks of Bella Rosa Books

10   9   8   7   6   5   4   3   2

This book is dedicated with happy appreciation
to Cathy Kelly and Gale Anne Friedel,
founders of the Harrison Weaver Fan Club.

Books by
Joseph L.S. Terrell

Harrison Weaver Mysteries

TIDE OF DARKNESS
OVERWASH OF EVIL
NOT OUR KIND OF KILLING
UNDERTOW OF VENGEANCE

Jonathan Clayton Novels

THE OTHER SIDE OF SILENCE
LEARNING TO SLOW DANCE

Stand Alones

A TIME OF MUSIC, A TIME OF MAGIC

A NEUROTIC'S GUIDE TO SANE LIVING

Acknowledgments

Thanks to former FBI agent and profiler Larry Likar for his most helpful insights into the minds of killers; to Lee Lofland, author and founder of the Writers Police Academy, an expert on police procedure and weapons; and to manuscript readers Veronica Moschetti and Gale Anne Friedel, whose suggested edits and keen eyes have made the story better. As always, too, a special thanks to my editor and publisher, Rod Hunter of Bella Rosa Books, for his support of me as a writer.

—*JLST*

Author's Note:

Once again I've chosen to compress time to use the historic courthouse in Manteo to house the sheriff's and other offices as it did years ago. The characters in this story, while real in my imagination, are purely fictional, with the exception of one or two local people who don't mind if I mention their names. Let me emphasize that the church that figures in the tale is completely made up, as are all of the people connected with the church. After all, that is what fiction is about—letting the imagination take one on a magical journey. I hope you enjoy the trip.

–JLST

UNDERTOW
OF
VENGEANCE

Chapter One

Her words tumbled together so rapidly, breathlessly, it sounded like she spoke in an unknown tongue.

I rolled over, sat on the edge of the bed, and planted my feet on the floor. I pressed the phone against my ear. "Slow down, Linda. I can't understand what you're saying."

I heard her take a controlled breath. She exhaled and tried again. "An arm," she said. "And a hand, too, right there in the picture."

"What picture, Linda? What are you talking about?"

"Picture I took yesterday at Nags Head Woods on one of the trails." She struggled with her voice again. "An arm and a hand. I didn't see it until this morning when I zoomed in on the picture." I could almost visualize her shudder. "It scares hell out of me, Weav. It's somebody's arm on the ground, just sticking out from the brush."

"Yeah?"

"There's got to be a body attached to it. I know there is," she gasped.

I stood, still clutching the phone to my ear, and rubbed the sleep from my face with my free hand. "Take another deep breath. Start at the beginning and tell me—slowly— what's up."

"I want you to go with me this morning," she said. "to make sure it's what I think it is."

"Wow. Hold on. I'm not going anywhere until you tell

me what's going on." There was a pause on her end of the line and I sensed she tried to calm herself, speak more slowly. She started again, her voice sounding more normal. "Yesterday, Weav, I got off early from the paper, took my camera and extra lenses. I wanted to practice, you know, nature shots like Jeff Lewis does that are always in the paper. I went over toward the beach to Nags Head Woods, to the Nature Conservancy. I wanted to go down some of the trails, look for birds, wildlife, and get some good shots."

"I understand, but didn't you see . . . see whatever it is you're talking about, see it then?"

"No. I took a few shots, just sort of location pictures with a regular lens, fifty millimeter, before I used my new long lens in case I saw some birds or something. But I didn't really look at the first shots, the location shots, until early this morning when I got up, and I saw something that didn't look right. I had downloaded all of the shots to my computer and I zoomed in on that one, and I'll tell you, Weav, it's an arm sticking out, mostly covered up with leaves and stuff."

I tried to lighten her mood a bit, make sure she wasn't trying to kid. "You PhotoShop that picture?"

She almost sobbed. "No, I swear, Weav. It's the real thing. I know it is."

"Anyone else had access to your computer, your pictures?"

"No. I'm right here at home, and no one goes near my stuff. Besides, just Mother here now and she doesn't even know how to turn on the computer."

I sat back on the edge of the bed, paused a moment, and then said, "Okay, Linda, so why are you calling me? Why not the authorities? Sheriff's office?"

"Aw, you know why, Weav. You're a crime writer and if I called the sheriff's office they probably wouldn't pay any attention to me, or laugh at me or something."

"But they know you're a reporter . . . and don't make stuff up." I permitted myself a soft chuckle, hoping to ease her back down: "At least most of the time."

Linda Shackleford had worked for *The Coastland Times*

for about four years, starting in classified ads, then managing to become a reporter, and now a reporter and steadily improving photo-journalist, with ambitions, obviously, of becoming a nature and wildlife photographer.

I glanced at my bedside clock. "You know what time it is, Linda?"

"Yeah, about eight o'clock. I figured you'd be up and be over jetlag by now."

"Jeeze, we just got back last evening. Long trip." We'd flown in from Paris to JFK in New York, then down to Norfolk, and picked up my car; drove down to North Carolina's Outer Banks, where I make my home.

"I know, I know, Weav. But this is important. I mean, hell, it's a body and I know it is."

"Now listen to me, damn it, Linda. Just listen to me . . ."

"Okay, okay."

"I'm not about to go down to Nags Head Woods with you, just the two of us—just in case it *is* a body. And I kind of doubt that, actually. But I don't want us to go down there by ourselves. Just in case."

"What're you saying?"

"I'll call Deputy Wright, see if he's on duty. I've gotten in enough trouble with DA Schweikert from stumbling across bodies. He accuses me of being a magnet for dead bodies."

"Think Odell will go with us?" She referred to Chief Deputy Odell Wright, who had become a friend of mine.

"Maybe. If he's on duty . . . and doesn't think this is too much of a wild goose chase."

"I tell you it's not, Weav. I could email you the picture but I'm not sure you could zoom in on it."

"Probably couldn't. I take your word for what you see." I knew Linda usually was not this excited and upset about anything. She was pretty levelheaded, and I was beginning to believe her. "Okay," I said, "I'll call Deputy Wright. Sound him out, if I can get hold of him. At any rate, I'll call you back in a few minutes."

When we hung up, I made a trip to the bathroom. I

splashed water on my face and looked at the bags under my eyes, muttering to myself. I went to the phone in the living room, uncovering my parakeet's cage as I passed it. She started chirping and doing her good-morning head-bobbing dance. "Yeah, in a minute, Janey," I mumbled.

I called the Dare County Sheriff's Office and asked the dispatcher for Deputy Wright's extension. "He's out," the dispatcher said.

I identified myself and told the dispatcher I had Wright's cell number, and I'd call him. The dispatcher hesitated, then said, "Okay," as if he wasn't sure I should be doing that. I punched in Odell Wright's cell number and he answered before the second ring completed.

"Wright," he said, his voice clipped and authoritative.

"Odell, this is Harrison Weaver . . . and I've got a strange request from our friend Linda Shackleford . . ." Then I outlined what Linda had said to me and told him I didn't want to go to check it out without him.

Odell was quiet for a moment or two. I was about to ask him if he was still there. Instead, I said, "I know this all sounds a little farfetched, Odell, but . . ."

He puffed out a sigh. "I hope it's farfetched," he said, sounding weary. "I've just been assigned a missing person search, getting started on it. I just hope . . ." His voice trailed off as if he mulled over options. Then, "Yeah, Weaver, maybe we better check it out. Linda's a straight-shooter."

We agreed to meet at the gravel parking area at the Nature Conservancy, Nags Head Woods, at nine-thirty. I told him I was sure Linda could be there by that time, with her camera and maybe a printout of the picture that sparked all of this. Then I immediately called Linda.

"I'll be there," she said. "I'm uneasy about going there. I don't want to see what I think I'm going to see, but I'll be there."

I drove south to Ocean Acres, the street beside Pigman's

Barbecue, turned right and kept going until the paved road became gravel. I passed the house that has all of the Christmas decorations each year—attracting hordes of visitors, and even national television—and continued to the small parking area at the Nature Conservancy. A pickup truck was parked close to the wood frame Conservancy office, and a Nissan Maxima was pulled in near to the vegetation on the opposite side from the office. I eased my Outback in behind the Nissan, but leaving room for the other driver to maneuver out. A couple of minutes later, Deputy Odell Wright pulled up in his cruiser and backed in next to me. I got out to greet him.

He gave a tight smile as we shook hands. There's now just a touch of gray in his hair, but it looks good against his chocolate-colored skin. His silver rectangular nametag reads "O. Wright," and with his usual wry humor he will tell someone he is one of the original Wright Brothers. But he wasn't joking today.

He looked around. "So Linda's not here yet?"

"Any minute, I'm sure."

Then he did a quick double-take of the Nissan. "Uh-oh," he said, staring at the vehicle, noting the license tag and dust-covered body of the car. As he took steps toward the Nissan the door to the Conservancy office opened and a young woman in khakis came forward.

"I was just thinking that maybe I should call the police about that car," she said. She smiled and approached Deputy Wright. "But I guess here you are." She nodded toward the Nissan. "It's been here a couple of days now, and I didn't know what to do about it. Call the police? Have Seto's tow it, or what?"

"We'll leave it right there for now," Odell said, frowning. He turned and opened the door to his cruiser, punching in something on his computer. I assumed it was the Nissan's license plate number. He stepped away from his cruiser. With a dead-serious expression, he shook his head. "It's Dwight Fairworth's vehicle all right," he said quietly. "The missing person . . ."

Now it was my turn to say "Uh-oh."

He sighed. "Linda say where this . . . this picture of hers was taken?"

"On one of the trails. She'll lead us there." I glanced around at the tall trees, both pine and hardwood. With such a thick truly maritime forest, it was hard to believe we were that close to the sound, less than a mile away and not much farther from the ocean. I turned back to Odell and cast a quick glance at the Nissan. "A missing person report?"

He nodded. "Janet Fairworth reported her husband didn't come home from a Wednesday church meeting. Just been thirty-six hours now. Usually wait forty-eight. Well, close to forty-eight now. The sheriff wanted us to get on it. The wife's very upset, and Sheriff Albright knows her." He compressed his lips. "At first I figured the husband's probably off with someone else—praying or something." He shook his head. "No, I shouldn't say that." He breathed in with a sigh. "But now, I've got a bad feeling . . ."

Linda drove up fast and pulled her older model Toyota into the parking area. Dust rose, hanging around her blue-jean clad legs as she got out of the car. She's sturdy, has short-cropped dark hair and big strong teeth she flashes as she smiles. But her smile today was quick and disappeared in an instant. She had a camera around her neck and a printout of some sort in her hand. She handed the printout to Odell. "Not a good quality, I know, but it's the best I could do."

I stood beside Odell as he studied the printout of a wooded area. There was something light-colored and elongated near the base of a tree and underbrush. It could be just about anything, including a broken limb minus its bark.

"This supposed to be an arm?" Odell asked, glancing at Linda and back at the printout.

"You can see it much better on my computer," she said defensively.

"Where's the spot? Where'd you take this?" Odell continued squinting at the eight-by-eleven printout, which was on regular copy paper.

"On the Roanoke Trail. Just down there. Fifty yards or so after the road comes to that other little road off to the right. Then I walked down the trail on the left, taking pictures."

Odell nodded. "We'll take my vehicle," he said.

"Not much of a place to park on that little road," Linda said.

Odell managed another of his tight smiles. "We'll make a parking place," he said. He opened the back door of his cruiser. I started to get in but Linda shook her head at me and slid into the back. I squeezed into the passenger seat, along with his computer and radio equipment that occupied much of the space.

He drove a short distance farther along the gravel road to the intersection with another dirt road. Over his shoulder, Linda pointed to the right, and he eased along the narrow road. We saw a short split-rail fence on the left, with a wooden sign that said "Roanoke Trail." I knew it led eventually all the way to the Roanoke Sound. Odell pulled his cruiser's left wheels up on the low embankment so that we were tilted at about a twenty-five degree angle. Linda and I exited easily, but Odell had to push hard against his door to struggle out.

"Down this way," Linda said. She took a deep breath, and exhaled audibly.

"Lead the way," Odell said. He walked beside her on the trail. I was close behind them.

We moved slowly along the path that was dappled every few feet with morning sunlight. The temperature, here in mid-September, was well into the seventies. A beautiful fall day at the Outer Banks. After about fifty yards, Linda stopped, studied the area. "I was thinking it was about here, but I guess it's farther along."

Odell didn't say anything and we started walking again.

"See, I stepped off the trail and went into the woods a little ways." Linda looked again at her printout, which was becoming wrinkled and sweat-stained in her hand.

We continued forward with measured steps. Linda

glanced repeatedly to her left and right. "It looks a little different," she said softly, and swallowed again as if she tried to get moisture into her mouth.

"Take your time, Linda," Odell said.

After a few yards, Linda said, "I think it was here. Right about here that I left the trail and walked into the woods a little . . ." We followed her in several yards, and she stopped suddenly. "No, no, this isn't it."

I watched her face. She appeared to be fighting back tears.

She looked up at Odell, almost pleading. "Can we go down the trail some more?"

"Of course," Odell said, and smiled kindly at her.

You had to like the man.

A short distance later, we were now more than a hundred yards down the curving trail, Linda stopped again, shook her head. "I'm really not sure I walked this far before I went into the woods more." She looked around at the vegetation on both sides of the trail, walled in by tall pines, sycamores, maples, and shorter fir trees. She smoothed the printout and appeared to be scrutinizing it, glancing up and looking around. She chewed on her lower lip. "I don't know," she said. "I guess I'm sort of confused now, or nervous or something."

"Take it easy," Odell said.

"It's got to be around here somewhere," she said, the trace of a sob in her voice. Her brow wrinkled, thinking hard. "I stepped off the trail to the right . . . It had to be about here, but I don't see where I might have . . . It was by a tall tree . . ." She gave a short, self-deprecating laugh. "Hell, nothing but tall trees around here."

The wind had shifted, coming now from the west off the sound.

Suddenly Odell stopped. He tilted his chin upward, and sniffed the air. He looked straight ahead. Very softly he said, "Bingo." He inclined his head toward an area ahead of us and to the left. Low brush gathered around three tall maples.

There was the barest hint of disturbed vegetation leading to the three trees. "There's something up there." His voice was quiet and level. "And it's not good," he said.

Chapter Two

I breathed in deeply. Yes, there was the faintest odor, an unmistakable smell, slightly sweet and nauseating at the same time. Linda looked frightened as she studied Odell's expression.

Odell nodded at the three maples. "Over there," he said, his voice barely above a whisper.

Linda held up her printout again. "But it was just one tree . . ."

Odell glanced to his right. "If you were standing over there on that side to take the picture, the trees line up like one tree."

She nodded, her lips drawn tight.

"Stay here," he said to Linda.

"I'll come with you," I said. I realized anew that we were all whispering.

He looked at me. "Okay," he said. "Walk where I walk, right behind me."

We'd gone maybe ten yards when I saw the arm. It lay bare and white, palm up like begging for alms. A bulk of leaves and brush covered what else might be visible from that angle.

Odell stopped and motioned with his hand, signaling for me to stop, also. "Stay here," he said "I'm going back to get Linda's camera."

"I'll go," I said. "I know how to use it."

He kept his eyes straight ahead, but nodded slightly, and I took careful steps back the way we had come. Linda stood in the middle of the trail. She trembled as if she might be cold.

"Let me borrow your camera," I said. "Odell wants it."

She slipped it from around her neck and mechanically started to show me how to turn it on.

"I know how," I said.

She looked up at me, moving closer. "You know, Weav, I'm a reporter—or supposed to be—I ought to go over there ."

"In a minute, Linda. There'll be time." I saw the tenseness in her face. "Stay here until Odell checks it out." Then I lied, "May be nothing at all."

Taking Linda's camera, I went back to Odell. He remained standing motionless, studying the scene from a few yards away. I saw him scrutinizing the ground leading up to the maples. When I came up behind him, he nodded, and we moved forward. I kept my eyes on the outstretched arm. As we got closer, I saw that part of a finger was missing and that there were animal bites along the forearm. I felt the breeze on my face and then the odor, stronger again. From under my shirt, perspiration trickled down the sides of my chest.

Odell stepped wide around the maples. I did the same, not waking too close to the base of the trees. He kept studying the ground. I couldn't see anything. Then he pointed to what might be a footprint; and I snapped a picture, zooming in close.

We moved carefully to the left. Then we saw them. It wasn't just the one body. There were two. A man and a woman, only partially obscured with a couple of broken bushes piled near them. They were seated together at the base of one of the trees, side by side. They were fully dressed, both in slacks, he in a golf shirt, and she in a light green cotton blouse. Brown dried blood had oozed from their chests. Blood had also pooled behind her back. His face was tilted downward. Her head was turned to the side, toward the man. Their eyes were partially closed and flies and other insects buzzed them. The odor was bad.

Odell keyed in a number on his cell phone. At the same time, he nodded his head at the camera slung around my neck. I began to take pictures of the bodies. Up close, back a few feet, and from different angles. Odell spoke to someone at the sheriff's office. I knew we would have a lot of activity here soon.

When Odell signed off, his gaze fell on the man's body: "This wraps up my missing person case." I realized he was speaking in almost a normal tone of voice, no longer whispering. "That's the husband the woman was calling about." He puffed out a sigh. "But who's this woman?" He peered more closely.

Then we saw what had been partially obscured by leaves: a beige plastic cord, like a piece of clothesline, tied the right wrist of the man to the left wrist of the woman.

I took more close-up pictures. Then I turned away from the bodies as I felt bile rise in my throat. Fighting back a flood of nausea, I looked up at the sky and tried to control my breathing, make it more even, and I wanted the breeze to shift so that I would no longer smell anything bad.

I looked back at Odell. Perspiration beaded his forehead and upper lip. He didn't look too well either. He took a breath and then bent forward slightly to peer more closely at the woman. "I may know her, or have seen her," he said. His voice was soft again. The flesh on her face had begun to discolor. He straightened up and turned to me. "I know I'm the senior deputy, but I don't want us to disturb anything at all until I've got backup here. Document everything." He shook his head wearily. "Looks like your buddy Agent Twiddy will be needed on this one."

He referred to my long-time friend State Bureau of Investigation Agent T. (for Thomas) Ballsford Twiddy. He worked this area of Eastern North Carolina out of Elizabeth City. I had known him since my newspaper reporter days and had earned his confidence and trust on a couple of cases he investigated and I had covered as a writer.

Then Odell appeared to have remembered Linda for the first time since we had left her on the trail. "Better go tell Linda to . . . to stay put. She doesn't need to see this. But tell her she was right. She led us to it. Her picture."

Back at the trail, Linda stood watching me approach, her eyes wide. She rolled her shoulders as if trying to loosen her muscles.

"Yeah?" she said. Her voice was uneven.

"It's not good, Linda. There're two bodies. A man and a woman. Been shot, looks like."

"Oh, God, that's awful. Really awful." Then, "You know them?"

"No, but Odell knows who the man is."

Tentatively, almost like a question, Linda said, "Maybe I know them."

"They're not in real good shape, Linda. You don't need to see them."

"Yeah, but I'm supposed to be a reporter, and I should be able to cover just about anything." She shook her head. "Shit, not sure I even want to be a reporter anymore."

"Odell wanted me to remind you it was your work— your photography—that led us to this. The fact that you saw something in one of your photographs."

We heard a vehicle approaching. We were far enough down the trail that we couldn't see back to the road. But it sounded as if the vehicle slowed to a crawl as it turned onto the narrow sandy road. I moved a few yards up the trail. I could see blue lights pulsating through the foliage. A vehicle apparently had stopped just behind Odell's cruiser. Linda stayed in place and I continued up the trail several more yards. Two uniform officers approached. They tensed when they saw me. I waved and said, "Down this way." They didn't smile, but watched me carefully. I saw that they were with the Kill Devil Hills police department. They must have been nearby when Odell made his call, and I'm sure it went out over all of the police radios in the area.

The two officers approached, eyeing me steadily. "Dare

County Chief Deputy Odell Wright is down at the scene," I said.

One of the officers, his nametag identified him as Jordan, said, "Has he secured the site?"

"Not yet. But he's there at it."

Kill Devil Hills Police Sergeant Midgette said, "Who are you?"

"Harrison Weaver."

The sergeant eyed me more closely. "Oh, yeah," he said.

"Linda Shackleford of *The Coastland Times* and I came with Deputy Wright. She had taken pictures and saw something . . . something like an arm."

Both officers looked puzzled, and I realized it didn't make much sense. The sergeant turned to Officer Jordan and said, "Go back to the vehicle and get some crime scene tape. We got to help Deputy Wright secure the area." As Jordan started to move swiftly back up the trail, Sergeant Midgette called, "And then maybe you'd better post yourself back up that way and don't let any unauthorized persons come down this way."

Sergeant Midgette and I went down the trail to where Linda stood. Midgette apparently recognized Linda and nodded his head at her. She still looked distraught. Then officer Jordan came scurrying back with a roll of yellow crime scene tape. He handed it to Midgette, turned and headed back up the trail.

"Over there," I said to Midgette.

Linda put her hand on my arm. "Want to give me my camera? I really need to get some shots . . ."

"No pictures," Sergeant Midgette barked.

"I've already taken a number of them, at Deputy Wright's request," I said.

Grudgingly, he said, "Okay."

Linda took her hand away from my arm. "Well, maybe you better keep it for just a while longer."

With me leading the way, Midgette and I walked off the trail to the maple trees. After a few yards we could see Odell standing stiff and straight like a sentinel. He turned to face us as we approached.

"Hello, Deputy Wright," Midgette said, but his gaze was on the two bodies there at the base of the tree.

"You got here quick," Odell said.

"We were in the area when your call came in. Others will be here shortly."

Odell glanced at the roll of yellow tape Midgette held. To me he said, "Weav, you mind stringing some of that tape wide around here . . . and out on the trail, too."

Midgette handed me the tape without looking at me, his eyes still on the dead man and woman. I set to work making a big circle with the tape. But I heard Midgette say, "How long you think they've been here?" Shaking his head, he pulled a handkerchief from his back pocket and held it to his nose.

"A little more than forty-eight hours, I'd guess," Odell said. "The man was subject of a missing person report I was looking into."

"The woman?"

"I don't know," Odell said. "She looks familiar, and I'd say they knew each other. Maybe too well."

"Looks like an execution, doesn't it?" Midgette said. I knew that was already what Odell was thinking. So was I.

After I had encircled the area with the crime scene tape, I looked back at Odell and Midgette standing there near the bodies. From where I stood, the bodies were not visible, so I snapped a quick picture. I knew it was one that Linda could use for the paper. Not graphic at all. She could use it if she could get the memory chip back from the sheriff's office when they were through printing out all of the other ones I'd taken.

I headed out to the trail to string more of the tape, get Linda to help me. That would make her feel better, I knew, to be doing something. Another cruiser from the sheriff's office had arrived. A young deputy, looking serious, spoke to Linda. He asked for Deputy Wright. I motioned for him to follow me. I couldn't remember his name but I knew I'd seen him around the courthouse.

The young deputy approached Odell. "Sheriff Albright is on his way, too," he said. I watched the expression on the deputy's face as he viewed the bodies. He turned his head away. To Odell he said, "Along with about half the county, I expect."

The young deputy looked at me, then back to Odell: "Civilians?"

Absently, Odell said, "He's okay. He and Linda Shackleford . . . It's okay."

I came up close to Odell. Softly I said, "Agent Twiddy?"

"I've already called him," Odell said. "Sheriff said to get in touch with him." He appeared lost in thought a moment or two, then said, "Sheriff Albright'll do the notification. He knows the wife . . . and that's her husband lying there."

"Yeah," I muttered, "and tied up to that woman . . . whoever she is."

Sergeant Midgette said to Odell, "I'll go out there and help make sure the area is secured."

"Good," Odell said, not looking at Midgette. Odell chewed on his lower lip. Perspiration had made a small circle of stain on the chest of his shirt and under his arms.

Quietly to me, almost whispering again, he said, "Somebody sure had it in for these two. Maybe didn't want them to be together."

"Or maybe whoever did it, wanted the whole county to know that they *were* together . . . and shouldn't have been," I said.

"Gonna need to talk with the spouses of each of these two victims," he mused. "I'd better go with Sheriff Albright when he notifies the wife." He looked toward the woman sprawled out before us. "Identify her, and talk to her husband or boyfriend right away, too."

I heard more activity out on the trail. Another deputy approached with a camera. He swallowed, breathed out, and then began taking pictures from angles that Odell indicated.

The deputy said to Odell, "Medics have come part of the way down the road with their ambulance."

Odell shook his head. "Don't want the bodies moved. Not yet."

I knew the acting coroner, Dr. Willis, would be one of those coming soon, and I was sure that Agent Twiddy would arrive within an hour or so.

Odell turned to me. "At some point, we'll need an official statement from you and Linda as to how all of this came about."

"I know," I said.

"Like for you to stay around a while," Odell said.

"Of course."

Just then, we heard Sheriff Albright speak to someone. He came up to the yellow tape, with young Deputy Dorsey at his side. I assumed Dorsey had been his driver. My presence didn't seem to cause him any curiosity, maybe because he'd seen me around his office so often. Sheriff Albright was a big bear of a man, with a kindly face that could quickly register the pains of the world. This was one of those times. "Oh, lordy," he said, looking at the two bodies. "That's Janet Fairworth's husband all right. Dwight." He shook his large shaggy head sadly, and pointed to the dead woman sprawled out at the base of the tree. "And I know her, too. It's Gladys Chaffey. She sings—or used to sing—in one of the church choirs."

Chapter Three

The first thing that popped into my head, and I'm sure it did in Odell's and the sheriff's mind, too, was why hadn't someone reported Gladys Chaffey as missing—unless perhaps the person who would have reported her missing knew exactly where she was.

Albright spoke to Odell. "You better go with me on the notifications. Lordy, I hate that job."

"Yes, sir. I was thinking it best I go with you." Then he said, "Want to wait for Agent Twiddy before we . . . before we do the notifications?"

Sheriff Albright rubbed his chin, appearing a bit undecided. "Maybe not to see Janet Fairworth. You and I'll do that." He stared at the bodies, sighed deeply, then turned away. "But it'd be best if he goes with us to see Gladys Chaffey's husband. Can't remember his name. Not sure they're still married. On again, off again."

There was something about the mention of the name Chaffey that nudged at the edge of my memory. But I couldn't pin it down; it was like a half-remembered dream.

During the next few minutes, Odell explained to the sheriff how the discovery of the bodies had come about. Shortly after that, one of the deputies—and the place was beginning to swarm with lawmen—reported to the sheriff that Dr. Willis had arrived.

As acting coroner (and I don't know why he was still

referred to as "acting" coroner; I'd never known of anyone else in that job in the almost three years I'd lived here). Dr. Willis had the unenviable job of inspecting bodies in various stages of death, mutilation, decay, violence, or just curious causes of end of life. Dr. Willis was a little out of breath as he trudged onto the scene. He wore a white shirt, a little wrinkled as usual and not tucked into his trousers very neatly. His tie was only slightly askew. To the sheriff he said, "I was at the hospital when I was beeped." I assumed this was his explanation for arriving as promptly as he had. He immediately knelt to look more closely at the bodies. The smell didn't seem to bother him. I realized I had become more used to it. Dr. Willis had donned latex gloves and he used one hand to tilt the man's shoulder forward so he could see his back. No exit wound. He did the same to the woman. A bloody hole the size of a baby's fist was in her back. Exit wound. "No other trauma," he mumbled. "Single gunshot wounds to the center of the chest. Right into the heart. Bullet's probably lodged in his spine." He cast his eyes toward the base of the maple tree behind the woman. "One's imbedded in there, I suspect," he said.

Then I saw him carefully examining the line binding the two wrists. "This is interesting," he said. "Not much of a knot tying this, fairly loose, and no indication of any abrasions on the wrists." He looked up at Sheriff Albright. "I'd say their wrists were tied together after they were already dead."

Sheriff Albright sighed. "This gets curiouser and curiouser." He turned to Odell. "Where's Agent Twiddy? Any word from him?"

Odell's cell phone chirped and he pulled it from his belt. He answered and held up his index finger at the sheriff. He mouthed the word "Twiddy." Into the phone he said, "Yes, on your right coming down the Bypass. Turn at Pigman's Barbecue . . . Yes, sir. You'll see all of the activity at the end of the road." He finished his call. Turning to the sheriff he said, "He's on his way. Be here shortly."

"Good," Sheriff Albright said. "I'd like us to get these bodies out of here, soon as he's satisfied viewing them." Then he looked at me, as if for the first time it registered on him that I was hanging around. "You don't need to be here any longer, Mr. Weaver. Neither does Ms. Shackleford."

I wasn't about to leave unless he ordered me to. "Deputy Odell wanted a statement from the two of us," I said.

Albright appeared to be directing his thoughts elsewhere. He came back to me with, "Okay, okay. That's fine." But I don't think he was really thinking about me or what I had said.

It wasn't long before I heard Agent Ballsford Twiddy speak to one of the deputies and then to Linda Shackleford, who I realized remained there on the trail, probably trying to look unobtrusive. He came up to the scene, stopping at the yellow tape momentarily, then ducking under it and getting closer to the bodies. He nodded at Sheriff Albright and Odell Wright. Glancing briefly at me, he shook his head a tiny bit and allowed himself the barest trace of a smile. As an aside to me he muttered quietly, "More bodies, and here you are once again."

"Balls," I acknowledged, as a manner of greeting, the aptly descriptive shortened version of his first name that he was known by to all of his friends.

He wore his customary beige cotton sports coat over dark slacks. He's a big man, thickened now in the middle but still looks solid as a brick shithouse. He's been sporting a Tom Selleck mustache for a couple of years. Pulling latex gloves from the side pocket of his jacket, he worked them on and knelt in front of the bodies. He held his breath as much as he could. He studied the bodies, their positions, clothing; he ran his hand along the left hip of the man, felt a wallet and removed it. There were several bills in the wallet, a couple of fives and ones that I could see. He knew, and I think all of us did, that robbery was certainly not the motive. He looked carefully at the line that bound their wrists together.

Sheriff Albright said, "Dr. Willis thinks that was tied

after they were dead."

Balls nodded, eased himself upright. "Sending a message, I'd say."

"What?" Albright asked.

"The killer was sending a message," Balls said.

"What do you think it was?" Albright said.

Balls shook his head. "I have no idea, yet. But it's a key. There's a reason for it, at least in the killer's mind." He glanced at the deputy standing nearby with his camera. "Got plenty of pictures? All well documented?"

"Yes, sir."

"I believe we can have the bodies removed now?" Sheriff Albright said.

Balls puffed out a sigh. "Yeah, in a minute," he said. He turned to Deputy Wright. "No shell casings?" Wright shook his head. More to himself than to those of us around him, Balls muttered, "Then either it was a revolver or the killer picked up the casings." He rubbed his chin, still staring at the bodies. "I'll wager it was a revolver." To Wright he said, "Can you carefully dig the slug out of that tree when they move the bodies? Bag it. Other slug's still in the man. M.E. will get that one." He stood there studying the bodies. He moved slightly to the right, then to the left, eyes still on the two corpses, the way they were placed. "Made to sit down, then shot." He shook his head, as if imagining the horror they faced in the last moment of their lives when they knew what was going to happen. He heaved out a sigh. "Okay, move 'em."

Albright spoke to the young deputy, who left to get the medics standing by at the trail. Then to Balls again, with a lift of his shoulders and a wry smile that played across his face for an instant, he said, "And welcome back from Paris." He shook his big head. "Some welcome back, huh? But hope you had a good vacation."

"We did, thanks. Still a little jetlagged." Balls glanced at me. "Guess you are, too."

"Yep," I said, "but Paris seems a long way off now"

Balls and his wife, Lorraine, and my—my sweetheart?—Elly
Pedersen and I had all four spent nine days in Paris. First
time the three of them had been there and I loved showing
them around my favorite places. But it did seem like our visit
was now really far in the past.

Chief Deputy Odell Wright, who had stood silently beside Balls, said, "I'm glad you're here."

Balls turned from the bodies and spoke to Odell. "We'll
work it together."

"Yes, sir," Odell said.

"You mentioned something on the phone about how the
bodies were found. Tell me in detail." Odell related it, beginning to end.

The medics, two husky men, moved in with a col-
lapsible gurney. They conferred quietly about the situation,
the trail path and narrow road they would have to navigate
removing the bodies. It was not going to be an easy task.
One body at a time.

I approached Balls and said, "I know you'll be busy on
this, but I thought maybe later, maybe this evening, we could
get together."

"Maybe," he said, but his attention was on the medics
going about their work. I didn't want to watch.

Sheriff Albright turned to face Balls. "Agent Twiddy,
I'd appreciate it if you'd go with us on the notifications."

"Yes, by all means," Balls said. "I definitely want to do
that . . . and I want to know why no one had reported this
woman as missing."

As a crime writer, I naturally wanted to hang with Balls
and the others as much as possible. It was a side of me I
wasn't too proud of; I really didn't savor being self-serving
and callus, but one thing I needed to do, of course, was call
my editor, Rose Mantelli, about these killings, alerting her to
the fact that we'd have a full article—heck, maybe even
another book—coming up once this thing unraveled. I was
assuming, of course, that it would unravel. Sometimes they
don't.

Out on the trail, I saw Linda standing there to one side, studying the activity that bustled around her. I came to her side, and handed her back her camera. "How you doing, Linda?"

"I gotta go to the bathroom," she said.

"Yeah, we been here a while. Maybe back at the Conservancy headquarters?"

"Hope so," she said. "If not, we'll scoot up to Pigman's Barbecue. But, God, I sure don't want anything to eat."

I shook my head. "Me either. Not for quite a while."

Linda and I walked up Roanoke Trail to the gravel road, now packed with official vehicles, and hiked up the main road to the Conservancy parking area. The closer we got to the Conservancy, the more I realized I needed to go to the bathroom as well, but we opted to take our cars back up Ocean Acres to the Bypass and duck into Pigman's. We drove a bit faster than we should have and didn't waste any time parking our cars and scurrying inside. I ordered two iced teas and took them to one of the small tables while Linda headed for the bathroom. I waited as long as I could for her to come out so she'd know where we were sitting. I was about to give up and go into the men's room when she came out and I pointed to our table.

A few minutes later when we were both seated, I said, "Hell of a morning."

"I've never been around anything like this before," she said, "and don't care if I never do again."

"But you got a heck of a good newspaper story on how this whole thing developed. First person account. It was your photography that launched the discovery. Tell it that way, how it came about. Great story."

She warmed to the idea. "I've been thinking about that." She managed a smile. Then she added, "I'm surprised they gave you back my camera. I thought they'd want the pictures you took."

"A deputy came up and started taking pictures, too. But I tell you what, there's at least one shot you could use for the paper. No bodies visible. Then if you print out the pictures, or turn over the memory chip to Sheriff Albright, I know they'd appreciate it. Earn you some brownie points, too."

"Not sure I want to see any of the other pictures," she said, and took a noisy sip of her iced tea. The place was beginning to bustle with lunch hour traffic. "We'd better leave," she said.

As we went outside, I said, "The shot you want is the last one I took, I believe. Print it out. You don't need to look at any of the others."

She nodded. We went to our cars. "I'm heading on back to Manteo," she said.

I suddenly felt very tired. "I'm going home, too."

As I drove north on the Bypass, which is what we call Highway 158 even though it doesn't bypass anything, I realized I probably needed to eat something. I was washed out. I tried to think of what I could eat, what I felt like I could eat. Maybe a hotdog at Capt'n Frank's. Get one of the "snap dogs" that actually make a snapping sound as you bite into the wiener. The dogs are produced locally up the road toward Grandy at the Weeping Radish. I continued driving past my turnoff at Wright Shores, and pulled into the parking area at Capt'n Frank's. Inside I ordered a snap dog with light chili and mustard, a small order of cheese fries, and a Diet Coke —my usual. Might as well mainline some cholesterol. Bring me around.

I sat at one of the booths and started to eat. I tried not to think of what I had been witness to this morning. Vainly, I tried to erase the images. I took a sip of the Diet Coke. It helped some.

Young Harvey came by the booth. "Everything okay?" he asked, eyeing my snap dog, which I'd barely touched.

"Fine, fine," I said.

"You feeling okay?"

"Oh, you know, maybe a little queasy. But fine. Not as hungry as I thought I was."

I managed to eat most of the hotdog and three or four of

the cheese-laden French fries. My head hurt. I drove down the Bypass to my turnoff and pulled into the cul-de-sac and parked under my carport. I sat there in my car for a minute or so before I trudged up the outside stairs into my little house. I wanted to call Elly, chat with her, get to feeling normal again. Try to forget about murder and mayhem. I spoke to my parakeet, glanced to make sure she had water and seeds. Thought again about calling Elly, but decided to wait. Instead I went into the bedroom, kicked off my shoes, and flopped on the unmade bed. I lay there on my back. I closed my eyes, but the image of the man and woman propped against the maple tree with bullet holes in their chests, their bodies deteriorating, projected itself on my brain.

I opened my eyes and stared at the ceiling.

Chapter Four

Surely I dozed because later I looked at my watch and saw that it was after three. I got up and splashed water on my face and went to the telephone, called Elly's home number. She didn't have to go back to work at the Register of Deeds office until Monday. Had the weekend to get over jetlag.

She answered on the second ring. "Well, Harrison, I thought maybe you'd forgotten all about me—now that I'd gone off to Paris with you and . . ." She lowered her voice, but there was a trace of humor in it. ". . . and lived in sin."

"'Twas no sin," I said.

Still quietly, she said, "Mother doesn't really believe that Lorraine served as a chaperon, you know."

"Oh, Balls and Lorraine were excellent chaperons." I chuckled. "That's our story and we're sticking to it."

"Okay, Harrison, enough idle chit-chat." Her voice got serious. "I'm sure you heard about what was discovered at Nags Head Woods, those two people. It's just awful." She added, "Mabel called me before lunch." Mabel, with her swollen ankles and unsuccessful diets, was a veteran of the sheriff's office and had been around the courthouse for decades.

I was silent a moment. It was obvious Elly didn't know about how the two bodies were discovered, the role played by her long-time friend Linda Shackleford and me. I didn't know what to say, so I mumbled, "Mabel called you, huh?"

She paused. "Yes . . ." Her voice trailed. Then, "Harrison, you know something I don't? I can tell it in your voice." Elly was one of the few people who called me by my full first name, and she retained a bit of that fast-disappearing Outer Banks "hoigh toide" accent that I loved.

"Well, yes, I guess maybe I do. What did Mabel tell you?"

"She didn't have much of the details except that a man and woman were found in the woods and they'd been shot." She puffed out a sigh. "Okay, speak up, Mr. Crime Writer. Are you involved again? That the reason you haven't called?"

"Well, I'm not involved exactly, but this is what happened." And then I related to her the details about Linda's excited early morning call, our meeting at Nags Head Woods with Deputy Wright, and what we discovered.

"So you *are* involved."

"No, not really. Agent Twiddy and Odell Wright are working it."

There was another sigh. "You'll be involved. I know you."

"Well, it is a hell of a story, Elly."

Her voice came across harshly. "It's not a *story*, Harrison. It's the murder of two people. We're talking about human beings . . . not one of your crime stories."

Lamely I said, "That didn't come out the way I intended." Jeeze, I thought, maybe I am getting too callus, unfeeling. I smoothed things over the best I could, and then tried to change the subject. "What about tonight? Can we get together? Go over some of the Paris pictures? Relive those glorious days?"

"You're a charmer, aren't you?" She chuckled. "Why don't you come over here about suppertime? Mother'll fix something. We've eaten out enough to last us awhile. Besides, I need to be here with Martin." Elly, a young widow, lived in Manteo near the airport with her mother and son Martin, now almost five and finally getting so he will speak to me, usually.

"Sounds great," I said. "I'll see you just before six." I met Elly shortly after I moved to the Outer Banks from Washington three years ago. When I moved here, really seeking peace and quiet, I was nurturing the grief over the loss of my wife, Keely. Okay, I still have a difficult time saying it, but Keely committed suicide. She was a vocalist with a number of small bands, some of which I played upright bass with; I could never understand what caused her to sink deeper and deeper into depression, into places within her soul where no one could reach. She did her death with pills, and I found her there in the bed one golden afternoon, curled up like she was asleep, which she was—forever. Since then I'd felt I never wanted to play with a jazz or swing band again. I turned to classical music, when I played at all.

Dusk was coming on late that afternoon as I drove south on the Bypass to Whalebone Junction and swung to the right toward Roanoke Sound and the bridge over to Roanoke Island and Manteo. As I crested high on the bridge I could see the trees on Roanoke Island silhouetted black against the western sky. The weather was mild and the surface of the sound dimpled with waves. A beautiful Indian summer evening. Paris was wonderful, but it was good to be back home on the Outer Banks, and I always felt good making the drive over to Elly's. She had given new purpose to my life, and I'm sure I was falling more and more in love with her. Happily, she professed to feel the same way. And our stay together in Paris had been magical. It may sound old fashioned, but it was a very big step for her to agree to come to Paris with me—and Balls and Lorraine as our "chaperons"—without the benefit of matrimony. After all, she had a young son and she lived in a small town and those were things that did give her pause, but thankfully only momentary pause. She was enough of a tough Outer Banks gal, to use her own description of herself, to do whatever she damn well pleased, once she had made her mind up.

Traffic slowed a bit into Manteo and past the Christmas Shop and grocery stores. I continued out the western part of town toward the airport and Fort Raleigh. I made my left turn off the highway and then a short distance farther made another left onto the lane where Elly and her mother and son lived. It was a comfortable house, one of the early Sears houses that had been modified and enlarged a bit. It sat white and inviting, flanked by two ancient live oaks, the branches of which hung down and made canopied play areas for young Martin and his friend Lauren, who lived next door, a door that was only fifty yards away.

Except for brief intrusions into my consciousness, the horror of this morning seemed as far away as if it had all been a bad dream. But every now and then, despite my efforts to push it into the background, the image of the deteriorating bodies, and the smell, came back and pressed damply and heavily against my chest. I would take a deep breath and exhale slowly to make it go away.

I had just vanquished one of those images when I pulled into Elly's gravel driveway beside her eight-year-old white Pontiac. As I expected she would be, there stood Elly on the low front porch to greet me, her right hand raised, wiggling her fingers hello.

Stepping on the porch, we hugged each other. She whispered, "Love you." With her arms still around me she chuckled and said, "Still respect me after Paris?"

"More so," I said.

We went into the living room, which always looked comfortable and lived in. As usual, there was today's mostly finished crossword puzzle from *The Virginian-Pilot* lying under the warm glow of the lamp on the end table. A history book on the Middle Ages, with a bookmark about a third of the way in it, lay on the coffee table. Martin came into the room and eyed me without smiling.

"Hello, Martin."

"Show him your new drawing, Martin," Elly said.

He left the room and returned with a piece of paper on which he had drawn an amazingly detailed rendering of the Eiffel Tower. "This is excellent, Martin." I was truly impressed. "Really good. You're quite an artist."

"He did it freehand from the postcard I brought back," Elly said.

Mrs. Pedersen appeared from the kitchen, drying her hands with a limp dishtowel. "Welcome back," she said. With a twinkle in her eyes, she added, "Elly said it was a wonderful trip."

"It was indeed."

Mrs. Pedersen is taller than Elly, and has short, gray hair she keeps cut rather severely. She's a no-nonsense Outer Banks native, and I like her. Elly's late father met his future wife when he was stationed nearby with the Coast Guard, and never went back to his native Minnesota. From pictures of him I have seen, Elly took after him, and even when she was married to a young classical cellist, she kept her maiden name. The cellist, whom Elly had met at Meredith College in Raleigh, died of a virulent flu-like virus shortly after Martin was born. His ghost, I know, is one of the reasons Elly draws back from time to time from a full commitment to the two of us.

"We'll have supper very shortly," Mrs. Pedersen said. "Hope you like country ham and sweet potatoes."

"Oh, my goodness yes."

As she turned to go back into the kitchen, Mrs. Pedersen stopped and said, "Wasn't that a terrible thing about that man and woman they found in Nags Head Woods?" She shook her head. "Just terrible. You wonder sometimes what the world is coming to."

Her hands on her hips, head held to one side toward me, Elly said, "It wasn't some anonymous *they* who found the bodies, Mother. It was Mr. Crime Writer here and my dear friend Linda Shackleford, who still hasn't bothered to call me and tell me all about it."

"It was you and Linda?" Mrs. Pedersen said, her voice

rising in pitch. "Who found that man and woman?"

"Well, actually Chief Deputy Wright found the bodies." Then I told her about Linda's call and what happened afterward.

"Awful. Really awful." Then she asked, "How's Linda? I know that upset her." To Elly, she said, "That's probably the reason she hasn't called you. Still upset." She twisted the dishtowel in her hands. "So why don't you just call her? Hearing from you would make her feel better."

"She's probably busy writing her story. I promise I'll call her later."

After we ate, and it was delicious and filling as always, Elly and I sat in the living room awhile and Martin sat on the floor, coloring. I couldn't understand how Elly and Mrs. Pedersen both stayed so trim. I had to work at it. Elly could eat anything it seemed and never gain an ounce. I felt comfortable and at home. I could get used to this, I knew. Before I left, Elly and I walked together onto the front porch. It was fully dark now but still mildly warm. September days at the Outer Banks were some of the best. The weather generally held into beautiful October and November days as well. I remembered one warm Thanksgiving I went surfcasting down on Hatteras Island at the Boiler and caught the largest bluefish I'd ever caught. When I picked it up by the tail its nose dragged in the sand of the beach.

Elly and I stood close together on the porch. I took her hand. "I like being with you, Elly."

She looked up at me, her eyes soft, a trace of smile on her lips. "I like being with you, Harrison." She squeezed my hand. "And wasn't Paris wonderful, not just the city, but being together, all the way together."

She glanced back at the living room. Martin concentrated on his coloring, and she gave me a quick kiss goodnight.

As I started to my car, Elly stood on the edge of the porch, and said, "Just let Agent Twiddy and Deputy Wright do their jobs—without any help from you."

"No problem," I said and waved.

"Yeah, right," she said.

I felt good on the ride home. Traffic was light, the stars were out, and all seemed really great with the world. Just on the edge of Manteo, before swinging left over Roanoke Sound, my cell phone chirped. It lay on the passenger seat. "Yes?"

"Don't you carry that cell phone with you?" It was Balls.

"I left it in the car when I went over to Elly's. What's up?"

"Thought maybe you'd go to church with me Sunday."

"Huh?"

"New church. True Gospel of Jesus Christ, or some such name. In Kitty Hawk."

"What are you up to, Balls?"

"Seems our two victims were active in that church. Minister's going to talk about them this Sunday. Since you live nearby, just thought you'd take in this new church . . . and invite me to go with you."

"Uh-huh, and just happen to look around for a suspect. Right?"

He chuckled. "Well, that thought might occur to you."

I didn't like driving and talking on the phone. "I'll be home in about fifteen more minutes. Let me call you back then."

"Sure."

"Where are you?"

"Staying here in Manteo. Been rather busy today . . . and tomorrow morning."

As soon as I got home and went upstairs, I called Balls on my landline. "Okay," I said, "can you tell me what happened today?"

"Notification, at least to the wife, Janet Fairworth, who reported her husband, Dwight, missing. That was him, of course, there in the woods." He paused a moment, sighed, sounding weary. "Wanted to see her reaction."

"And?"

"She just about collapsed. Really, really distraught. Unless she's one heck of an actor, then . . . well, you know what I mean. A friend of hers next door came over to sit with her and take care of the two small children."

"What about the woman there in the woods?"

Again he hesitated, as if deciding how much to tell me. "That's what took most of the afternoon. Gladys Chaffey. We couldn't find her husband. Neighbors say they've split— at least from time to time. Seek him out again tomorrow."

At the mention of the woman's name, that half-remembered dream suddenly became more vivid. I mumbled the last name repeatedly, Chaffey, Chaffey. The brain cells began to click. Then it came to me. I blurted out, "His name Charles? Goes by Chaz? Chaz Chaffey?"

"Yeah. You know him?" Balls sounded suddenly animated, no longer tired.

"No, not know him. But I think I know who he is. I've seen him and he made himself known—to me and half the people in the restaurant. He's not real good news." Then I smiled to myself, "And I'll bet I know where you can find him."

Chapter Five

Balls wanted to know the details of my chance encounter with one Chaz Chaffey, husband of the woman found murdered in Nags Head Woods.

"I was eating a very late lunch or early dinner alone at the Outer Banks Brewery Station before any of the crowd was there, except near the bar it seemed like a crowd because of one guy who'd apparently been there for some time drinking beer. He was getting louder and louder. A woman was with him. He kept calling her Molly, honey. She was drinking, too, but she wasn't quite as loud as he was. She looked a bit older than him, and sort of sexy in a way. One of the managers, I guess it was, said something to the man about maybe it was time for him to go home, take a nap. The guy got even louder. Said, 'I'm free, white, and twenty-one.' I remember that because that's a phrase I haven't heard in years. Didn't know anyone ever said anything like that any longer. Anyway, the manager knew the guy because he called him Chaz. Then another employee came up and said, 'Come on Mr. Chaffey, I think it's time you went home.'"

Balls interrupted me. "How come you remembered his name?"

"I'm a reporter, Balls. Still a reporter, and I make it my business to remember names." I chuckled. "Besides, there was not much else to watch that afternoon in the restaurant. He was sort of entertainment. And as he was leaving, he

stumbled over to my table and wanted to shake hands, intro-
duce himself."

"Yeah, I'm impressed. But where is he?"

"Molly had hold of his arm when he came over to my
table, and she led him out of there, being a little huffy with
the manager. As she was leaving with him, she said, 'Come
on Chaz. Hell with this. We'll go back to my place in
Moshoes.' I remember that because it was one of the few
times I've heard anyone mentioning going home to
Moshoes."

Puzzlement in his voice, Balls said, "Where?"

"Moshoes. Right across Croatan Sound. Manns Harbor
area."

"But you don't know where this Molly-honey lives. And
that was—what?—more than two or three weeks ago?"

"Yes, but I'll be willing to bet that anyone over there in
that community will know where Molly-honey lives. And if
Chaz Chaffey had split again with his wife, I've got a feeling
he's hanging out with Molly."

Balls breathed out a sigh. "Well, you've been my lucky
charm in the past, and I sure don't have anything else to go
on right now. It will be worth taking a ride over there
tomorrow, ask around, see if we can't find this Chaz Chaffey
and his Molly-honey." He added, "You'd recognize him or
his girlfriend?"

"Yes."

"I'll keep Deputy Wright in the loop. He may want to go
with us." Before we hung up, Balls said, "And Chaz Chaffey
is the only person of interest we've zeroed in on at the
moment."

Saturday morning before I drove to Manteo to meet
Balls at the courthouse, I swung into the Kangaroo service
station to pick up a copy of *The Virginian-Pilot*. Wanted to
see how they had treated discovery of the bodies, and assumed they'd have a story on it. The story was prominently
played but not that full. Names of the victims were withheld
"pending notification of next of kin." I scanned quickly

through the article. Mention was made of Deputy Wright discovering the bodies while he was involved in a missing person investigation. Good. No mention of Linda or me. I laid the paper aside on the passenger seat, and continued on to Manteo.

When I got to Manteo, I parked in a lot off Sir Walter Raleigh Street, across from the courthouse. Balls stood on the front porch of the red brick courthouse, built in 1904. He chatted with one of the deputies. Plans were underway for a new Dare County Center, with courthouse and administration buildings near the intersection of business 64 and 64-264. Conceding that a county center was needed, I still hated to see the old courthouse become a thing of the past. Well, it'd be a while yet.

The deputy went inside the courthouse and Balls watched me approach and then made a show of looking at his wristwatch.

"Don't want to be too early," I said. "Give our person of interest a chance to bring himself around with a couple of beers."

"Spoke with Deputy Wright. He thinks it best if he doesn't go. That if we just mosey over there in my Thunderbird, not looking too official, have a better chance of having some of the folks talk to us."

As we started to Balls' car, he said, "Well, I see that you made the papers, your name, Linda Shackleford's, too."

"What do you mean, made the papers? I just picked up *The Virginian-Pilot.* Nothing in there."

Balls unlocked the doors to his Thunderbird, but stood there a moment. "Maybe not in the newspaper yet, but it's online. That *Outer Banks Voice* thing. Got the lowdown there, how photo-journalist Linda Shackleford—she'll love the term—and crime writer Harrison Weaver alerted Deputy Wright about the possible location of bodies in Nags Head Woods."

"Jeeze," I said. Then, "I didn't even know you knew how to go online, Balls."

"Man, I know all sorts of things." He chuckled as he
folded himself to slide into the driver's seat of the Thunderbird. "And I know this: Your friend Schweikert is gonna be
all over you once again because you found a body—attracting bodies like a magnet."

He referred to District Attorney Rick Schweikert, whose
dislike of me was well known around the courthouse. It all
dated to a magazine article I'd written three years ago that
described Schweikert in very unflattering terms—actually
like the pompous ass that he is.

I shook my head, knowing that Schweikert would want
to hassle me concerning how I came to be involved in, once
again, finding a body, or in this case, two bodies.

Balls' Thunderbird is an older model—must be fifteen
or twenty years old, but in pristine condition. His pride and
joy. I squeezed into the passenger seat. Balls grinned and
revved the engine a couple of times. "Yeah, I know, I know,"
I said. "You got you a classic car that'll really shit-n-go."

"Come on, it's show time," he said.

He pulled away from the curb on Budleigh Street,
swung around to the left, and headed down toward Highway
64. We turned west toward Fort Raleigh, which is believed
to be the site of the ill-fated "Lost Colony." In 1587, Sir
Walter Raleigh sent 117 men and women over to the New
World in an effort to establish the first permanent English
settlement. It was three years before help with supplies could
return to Roanoke Island, and there was no trace of the
settlers, only the word "Croatoan," the name of an Indian
tribe, carved on a tree.

We took the older Manns Harbor Bridge across Croatan
Sound, the sun behind us, sparkling the low, undulating
waves of the shallow water. I said, "Let's stop in at White's
Market, get a coffee, Coke, or something and ask about
someone named Molly who lives in Moshoes."

Balls nodded. "Sounds good."

As we crossed the bridge onto the mainland, I inclined
my head to the right. "We'll come back this way because

Moshoes is that way."

We drove the narrow road over to White's Market and parked. "Now we start to mosey," Balls said. He was having fun. Following a puzzle always pleased him. But just as quickly, when things didn't go right, he got testy, grouchy and depressed. He was like a relentless bulldog as an investigator; he grabbed onto a case and wouldn't let go, alternating between buoyancy and scowling frustration, but never giving up.

Only one other customer happened to be in White's when we strolled in. I went to the soft drink cooler and picked up a canned Diet Coke. Balls studied the selection of beef jerky, picked up one, and then approached the man behind the counter. I joined him and set my Coke on the counter. "I'll get it," Balls said and he pulled out a five to give to the clerk. "How you doing?" Balls said to the man.

"Okay, thanks," the man said. "Got good weather and the fish are running. What could be better?" The man, dressed in khaki slacks and sweatshirt, had a couple of days growth of gray whiskers adorning his cheeks and chin, and down his wattled throat.

Balls leaned an elbow on the counter and worked at tearing open the package of beef jerky. He popped a piece in his mouth, and while chewing said, "I hope you can help me. We're looking for a woman named Molly who lives over in Moshoes." Balls smiled. "Sorry I don't know her last name." He continued chewing the beef jerky.

The man eyed both of us, then shook his head. "Don't believe I know any Molly around here."

Balls feigned a casual lack of interest. "Yeah, a friend of ours wanted to give her a message, and since we were over this way anyway . . . Oh, well, probably not important she gets the message." Balls put the change in his pocket.

The clerk studied Balls. He appeared to be weighing his thoughts as to whether say anything else.

The other sole customer, a man well into his seventies, wearing faded, loose-fitting jeans and a denim shirt buttoned

at the neck, came close to the counter, standing slightly behind and to the right of Balls. The older man had a package
of Little Debbie oatmeal cookies in his hand. To the clerk he
said, "Bet he's talking about Molly Suptkins. She lives over
in Moshoes, that little gray house with the old station wagon
out front. That car ain't been moved since Jesus was wearing
short pants." And he chuckled, displaying a sparsely toothed
mouth. "I hear tell she's got friends here and there who enjoy
delivering messages to her." And he winked.

Balls turned to the man. "Yeah, maybe that's her.
Where's this little gray house of hers?"

The clerk turned away from the counter, straightening
items on the shelf behind him, acting as if he wanted no part
of the conversation.

The elderly customer said, "Well, you go back down
that way . . ." and he pointed with a long, boney finger, "then
when you come to the second road I think it is, you turn left,
go just a little ways and do a dogleg to the right. Little house
sets off by itself a bit, and that old station wagon's out front,
'bout to rust away."

"Thanks," Balls said. "I think we can find it."

I wasn't at all sure we could.

As we started to leave, I heard the clerk say rather testily
to the man, "Hugh, you want them Little Debbies or not?"

I deposited my mostly finished Diet Coke in a trashcan
outside the market.

We drove slowly into the Moshoes community. Several
of the houses were much more upscale than years ago when I
visited the Outer Banks and explored various areas. But as
we turned onto scrawny little roads, the houses were more
like I remembered. Balls slowed to a stop, then shrugged and
on a hunch, chose the road to the right. It was more like
traversing along an ill-kept, sandy driveway. Then when the
road appeared it was about to peter out completely, we spied
a little gray house, sagging front porch, and with an ancient
Chevrolet station wagon squatting on rotted tires in the
grassless front yard. Beside the station wagon there was a

Dodge pickup, reasonably new, and an older mostly white Toyota parked beside the house. Balls eased his Thunderbird into the front yard. There was no driveway. He looked over at me, winked, and said, "Let's see if we can't manage to speak to Molly-honey."

We walked carefully up the three askew steps to the porch. As he prepared to knock, Balls said, "You think you'll recognize them?"

"Yes."

He knocked loudly on the torn screen door. We waited. No movement was heard. He knocked again, and then we heard a woman irritably calling out, "Hold on a minute." In a moment the inside front door opened and a woman stood in the semi-darkness behind the screen door. "Yeah?" she said, a scowl on her face. It was Molly, all right. She clutched a faded blue robe around her middle. He hair was sleep-deranged, her eyes puffy.

"We're looking for Mr. Chaz Chaffey," Balls said.

"Who're you?"

"Is he in?"

"Who wants to know?"

"We have a message for him. Ma'am, can you please ask him to come to the door?"

She stared from one of us to the other, turned her head to shout, "Chaz, somebody here to see you."

We heard a muffled response from the rear of the house.

"I don't know who they are. They won't say," she called.

Balls said, "Tell him it's about his wife."

"Humpf," she snorted. Then over her shoulder again: "You best come on up and see what they want." She stepped back from the screen door and in the dimness we saw Chaz Chaffey slouching toward us, hitching his trousers up over tatty boxer shorts.

He stood behind the screen door. He had a wrinkled shirt in his hand and worked his arms in it as Molly glared at us. He pulled the shirt over his scrawny chest. "Yeah? What a you want?" Even through the screen I could smell him, a mixture of old sweat and older beer. "And who the hell are you?"

Balls flipped out his wallet, displaying his badge. "I'm SBI Agent T. Ballsford Twiddy, and this is Harrison Weaver. May we come in a speak to you?"

Chaffey eyed me. "I've seen you before," he said.

I nodded. "We met briefly at the Outer Banks Brewery the other week."

He turned back to Balls. "What a you want to talk about?"

"May we come in? Be easier to talk without this screen door between us."

He paused, then shrugged and pushed open the screen. "Come on in."

Four or five empty beer cans were on the coffee table. The place smelled like cigarettes and beer. A sofa with sagging cushions and two equally sad upholstered chairs essentially completed the living room's furnishings.

Chaffey glanced around the room. With what probably passed as a smile, he said somewhat sheepishly, "We hadn't had time to straighten up yet. Wasn't exactly expecting company." Molly, who stood near the front door, made another of her snorting "humpf" sounds. The trace of a smile on Chaffey's face disappeared and he cocked his head toward Balls, a hint of aggression in his tone, "And what brings the SBI here?"

"Mr. Chaffey, when was the last time you saw your wife?"

"I don't know exactly. Why?"

"Try to think. Was it yesterday, last week? When?"

Chaffey narrowed his eyes, his face pinched. "What's this about?"

"Mr. Chaffey, just asking when was the last time you saw your wife."

"It's been a few days. I dunno know. First of the week, I guess. She's always at that damn church. I don't see her that much around the house." With more of a smirk than a smile, he said, "What she file a complaint or something?"

"Mr. Chaffey, I'm afraid I've got some very bad news."

His face softened and his shoulders sagged. He fumbled with the buttons on his shirt. "What are you saying?"

"I'm sorry to have to tell you, but your wife is dead, Mr. Chaffey."

Chaffey sat down abruptly in one of the chairs. He sat on the edge of the chair, staring up at Balls. Molly made a noise with her throat. It wasn't a "humpf" but more of a gasp. Chaffey shook his head. "Dead? Dead? You gotta be kidding. Why would she be dead?"

"She was killed, Mr. Chaffey. Someone shot her."

He grabbed his knees with both hands and I thought for a moment he would leap out of the chair. "Shot her? Who the fuck would shoot her?"

Softly, Balls said, "That's what we are trying to determine."

Chaffey glared at the floor, then up at Balls, anger in his eyes, his lips curled back in a snarl. "You mean you come here asking me questions about when I seen my wife and all the time you know she's dead and been shot and . . . and shit, you think I know something about it? That's why you asking when I seen her. And who the hell shot her?"

Keeping his tone level and quiet, Balls said, "I'd like to know where you were on Wednesday night, Mr. Chaffey."

"Wednesday? What's Wednesday got to do with it? Today's Saturday. What you been waiting all this time for?"

"We didn't know where you were, Mr. Chaffey." Balls nodded toward me. "Mr. Weaver here had an idea where you might be. That's how we found you."

Chaffey finished buttoning his shirt, but he had it wrong; the first button was in the second buttonhole. He looked down at his shirt and began unbuttoning it again. His chest was white except for tan around his throat. He took quick gulps of air as if fighting back sobs. Molly had come up and stood beside him. She put a hand on his shoulder. He shuddered slightly and she removed her hand.

Molly raised her chin and spoke to Balls, her eyes steady, defiant. "Wednesday he was here with me. All day Wednesday and Wednesday night, too."

Balls looked down at Chaffey. "Is that correct, Mr. Chaffey? You were here in Moshoes all day Wednesday and Wednesday night?"

"Huh? Wednesday? Yeah, I guess." His hands drooped away from his shirt and he rubbed his palms together. "Yeah, Molly would remember. More than me."

"Where do you work, Mr. Chaffey? Didn't you have to work?"

"I've been laid off for a few weeks now."

"Months," Molly said.

"Yeah, it's been a while."

"What sort of work did you do?"

"Heating and air conditioning . . . but where was Gladys when she was shot? And don't you know who the sonofabitch did it?" For the first time, a sob escaped him. "Why would anybody shoot Gladys? She never did anything but go to church, sing in the choir."

"We'll find out who shot her, Mr. Chaffey. That's our job, my job, and believe me, I'm good at it."

Chaffey's expression had softened and his tone had a pleading quality to it as he asked, "Where was she when she was shot, detective? Was she at the church? At home? And where is she now?"

"Her body's at Twiford's Funeral Home in Manteo."

Chaffey shook his head. "We don't have any kids, not together, we don't. I'm glad we don't." He stood and made an effort at tucking in his shirt. "But you ain't told me where she was shot."

"Her body was found in Nags Head Woods, off one of the trails."

"Nags Head Woods! What the hell was she doing in the woods? She didn't like the woods. She was scared of spiders and snakes and things."

"We're in the midst of a full investigation, Mr. Chaffey,

and of course there are things we don't know, and things that are best kept confidential until we know more. But it is our initial belief that Gladys Chaffey did not go voluntarily into the woods." Balls cleared his throat and appeared to relax his stance ever so slightly. "Now, what I'd like you to do—you and, and Molly—is come down to the sheriff's office in Manteo and give a formal statement, all written down and everything."

Molly stepped toward Balls. "Statement about what?"

"Yeah," Chaffey said, but he said it weakly.

To the two of them, looking from one to the other, Balls said, "About when was the last time you saw Mrs. Chaffey alive, and about Wednesday and Wednesday night. We need it for the record."

Molly said, "What you need me for? It's *his* wife."

"I need your statement—formal statement, written down —that Mr. Chaffey was here with you Wednesday and Wednesday night."

"What about my reputation?" Molly said. "I mean, me saying he was here all night and everything."

"It will be kept confidential," Balls said, knowing I'm sure, that it might not be.

"Wednesday? That's when she was killed, huh?" Chaffey said.

"Best we have determined at this stage," Balls said.

Again, Chaffey stared at the floor and mumbled, "And here it is Saturday." He canted his head toward Balls. "What about a funeral?"

"You can work that out at Twiford's," Balls said.

To Molly, Chaffey said, "I guess we better go like he says." With open palms, he tried to smooth out his shirt. "We gotta get dressed."

"We'll meet you there," Molly said.

"If you don't mind," Balls said, "we'll just wait for you to get dressed. We can wait out there in my car." He tried to look pleasant. "We'll all go to the sheriff's office together. I'll follow you."

Chapter Six

Balls and I sat in his car. He lowered the windows and a soft breeze blew through. The sun was warm. It was very pleasant sitting there. Balls was quiet.

I waited as long as I could before saying anything. "What do you think?"

Balls puffed out a sigh. "I wish we had a better suspect."

"You don't think . . ."

"She's giving him an alibi . . . so far. But I don't believe either one of them know for sure where they were Wednesday." Then he said, "Even though they were split up much of the time, he didn't seem all that broken up about his wife getting herself killed." He drummed his fingers on the steering wheel. "But something about that whole set up at the scene, though—the man and woman, wrists linked together." He shook his head. "Not the kind of posing I can picture our Mr. Chaffey taking the pains to do." He glanced at his watch. "Guarantee you they're both in there now fortifying themselves with a couple of beers before going to the sheriff's office."

"If they've got any left over from last night."

"When we get back to Manteo, I'll drop you off. You don't need to go into the sheriff's office."

"I know," I said.

"You were helpful this morning, but . . ."

"I understand." I knew I was fortunate that Balls let me

tag along with him as much as he did. I certainly didn't want to do anything to jeopardize that.

The screen door opened and Chaffey and Molly stepped out on the little sagging porch, squinting at the brightness of the day. They both wore faded jeans, his baggy and low on his waist; hers tight and hitched up to her waist. He had tucked his shirt in and it was buttoned properly. She wore a red short-sleeve sweater, open enough at the neck to display her cleavage. Her lipstick was bright red, also. Molly paused before taking a couple of careful steps off the porch, heading to the passenger side of the pickup truck.

Balls started the engine, let it idle with its deep-throated yet soft and even rumble that you could feel in your legs and hips.

Chaffey pasted a half-grin on his face and slouched over to Balls' Thunderbird. He eyed the car, sitting there idling. He came to my side of the car, leaning his elbows on the door at the open window. "Don't look much like a cop car," he said. I could smell his breath. He nodded toward the console and the packed radio equipment, small computer. "Except inside."

Balls leaned forward to peer at Chaffey without responding to Chaffey's comments. "Let's get going, Mr. Chaffey. I'll follow you to the sheriff's office. Park on Budleigh Street right by the courthouse. One of the reserved spaces."

Chaffey took one last appraising look at the Thunderbird's interior, shrugged, and said, "Okay."

We drove a couple of car lengths behind Chaffey's pickup out of Moshoes and headed for the old Manns Harbor bridge. Balls was quiet. As we started across the bridge he surprised me by saying, "You ever see the purple martins swarming in here to roost at dusk? Thousands of them."

"Couple of years ago, yes. Impressive. They fatten up on insects before making the fall trip all the way to South America."

We were on the middle of the bridge span before Balls

spoke again. "It's been about four years since I've seen them. Tell you the truth, Weav, I miss that sort of thing. You know, being able to just do normal things. Not always chasing after some scumbag." He shook his head.

I watched him closely. There was a sadness in his face and in his tone that was usually not there at all. I tried to lighten the mood that had descended upon him. "Oh, hell, Balls, you'll feel better after you've captured a crook or two."

He glanced at me, and then that old grin of his came back.

As we exited the end of the Manns Harbor bridge, the road noise changed, got quieter, more sustained and even. Chaffey had kept to the speed limit and slowed even more on Roanoke Island. A quarter of a mile or so beyond Fort Raleigh was the entrance to the late Andy Griffith's home, a compound actually.

At Budleigh Street, Chaffey made a slow, careful left turn and we followed him to the end of the street at the courthouse. He slid into one of the reserved spaces, leaving one behind him for Balls' Thunderbird.

I put my hand on the door latch. "I'm just right around the corner." Then I said, "Church tomorrow? You want to do that, huh?"

"Absolutely," Balls said. He nodded toward Chaffey and Molly who stood awkwardly beside the pickup truck. "I'm not all that hopeful about these two." He added, "But you never can tell."

I walked around the front of the courthouse to Sir Walter Raleigh Street and unlocked my Subaru. It was warm inside the car and smelled pleasantly of leather. I lowered the windows and sat there thinking. I agreed with Balls. Chaffey might not be a very savory character, but whoever executed that couple did it with precision—and methodically, with a purpose in mind. I couldn't see Chaffey pulling off something like that. I realized I sighed. I started the engine and pulled away from the curb, heading back across the sound to Kill Devil Hills.

Close to lunchtime. Choice: Either stop in one of the restaurants along the way, grab something quick, or swing by Food Lion and stock up on a few groceries, something I needed to do anyway, although I was not much in the mood for it. Just the same, light grocery shopping won out. Stocks at home were lowered considerably before we took off for Paris. A few miles farther north I turned left into the Dare Centre and ducked into Food Lion. Got one of their smaller pushcarts and zipped along, throwing in a head of lettuce, tomato, packaged Smithfield ham slices, sandwich rounds instead of a loaf of bread, orange juice, and a few other odds and ends, and I was through, checking out—in twelve minutes, max.

At my little blue house, I carried the groceries up the side stairs and flung open the door to the kitchen area. Janey started chirping happily as soon as I came bustling in, bobbing around in her cage. Amidst the chirps she said, "Shit," then chirped some more. That was one of two words she said perfectly. The other was "bitch." Although female parakeets are not supposed to mimic words, she had picked those two up from me over a two-year period as I practiced an especially difficult Mozart piece on my bass, bowing away at the musical score and obviously repeatedly muttering those two expletives—aimed at Mozart and my frustration with mastering the passage, one that required crossing over the strings time after time.

I put my finger in her cage and let her nibble at it a moment, at the same time casting my glance over to the answering machine's blinking red light. I checked the messages. There were two. The first one was from Linda Shackleford, thanking me for going with her yesterday, and mentioning that her first-person article—a long one—would run in Tuesday's paper, the next edition of the thrice-weekly paper, starting on the first page, the lead story. She was excited, and asked if I'd call her if I had time.

The second call was from Jim Watson, a trumpet player who wanted to get a jazz combo started. "Hello, Weav," his recorded voice said, "I guess you're getting over some of the jetlag now, so time to start thinking again about playing some tunes, and see how we're sounding. We got a drummer all set, of course, and the good news is that now we've got a keyboard guy lined up, too. And he's good. Has a real light touch and a feel for jazz—even though his day job has mostly been playing organ or piano at churches." He chuckled. "But we won't hold that against him. Just please give me a ring when you can, and keep that fiddle tuned up and ready to move."

The messages ended, and I erased them. Didn't need to save them. I had both numbers and I would return the calls. Just not now. I sat in the rattan chair by the phone. Sunlight came in through the sliding panel door to the deck, and was warm on my shoulders. Janey cocked her head, looking at me.

I had real mixed feelings about playing with a group again. Too many memories. Yet, at the same time, maybe it would be good for me to force myself back into something that haunted me, maybe help get rid of ghosts. I don't know. I have a tendency to want to test myself, rid myself of things that are uncomfortable. Part of a built-in sense of discipline, I suppose.

I got up and moved to the kitchen. Actually, the entire inside front of the little house is one open space—the kitchen melding into a dining area that I use as an office and for writing, with one corner of the table that can accommodate a place setting if I choose, instead of the coffee table at the sofa. A Formica-topped counter extends from the wall, providing something of a divider between the living room and kitchen. I try to keep the counter as uncluttered as possible, but it's a handy place to put stuff, and right now the bag of groceries sat there, waiting to be put away.

Lunchtime, too. Needed to eat something. Okay, a ham

and tomato sandwich with a bit of lettuce thrown in. As I prepared the sandwich, I cleaned up as I went. Countertop looking pretty good. Sandwich on a paper plate, a glass of instant iced tea. I went outside on the deck to eat in the sunshine I carried Janey's cage out, too. Let her enjoy the day. She's used to having her cage moved around. While we were in Paris, Janey was tended to by my neighbor Misty, who lives alone, and who said she'd be delighted to look after her. When we returned—now three days ago—one of the first things I did was to retrieve Janey. Misty met me at her door, brushing back a strand of gray hair that always appeared to be falling across one of her eyes, and, with a chuckle, said she didn't realize Janey could say a couple of words. I shrugged and said female parakeets are not supposed to talk.

When I finished eating, I sat there and enjoyed the day. Couldn't help but wonder what Balls was up to, and whether he was making any progress. Rather reluctantly, I broke my reverie, went in and brought the phone out to call Jim Watson. He answered right away with a hearty greeting. I suggested that we get together maybe midweek. He said that would be great because the piano player could meet with us Wednesday about three o'clock, and then he'd have to leave after an hour or so for a gig at one of the churches. I wasn't all that eager about it, but was determined to give it a try.

Then I called Linda's cell phone. She said she was at the paper and doing a bit of final polishing on her story. Her tone was animated. She sounded like she actually squirmed with pleasure at having a scoop on the story. "And, Weav," she gushed, "tomorrow I'm going to the church where Gladys Chaffey sang in the choir, and Dwight Fairworth was an elder or something because the editor wants me to do a sidebar about what the preacher says about them. Isn't that great?"

"Well, Linda, I'll be there, too. Agent Twiddy, also."

"Wonderful. Maybe I can get quote from him or you."

"Kind of doubt it, Linda. Try to ignore us. You'll have enough with color and comments from the minister."

"Yeah, yeah. Maybe so."

"Probably be a big crowd there."

"Lots of singing and stuff." Her excitement and enthusiasm radiated over the phone. "Okay," she said, "I'll let you go . . . and try to ignore you at the church." She gave a short, husky laugh, and hung up.

I sat there on the deck, still holding the phone in my hand when it rang less than a minute after I had talked with Linda. I figured she'd thought of something and was calling me right back. "Yes?" I said.

The slightest pause, then a deep voice that was obviously disguised, muttered: "Deaths. There'll be others."

The phone clicked off. I checked caller ID, which I almost always do before answering. It was blocked: "Unknown Caller." My pulse had speeded up. I realized I gripped the phone hard, squeezing it. A prank? Someone I knew? I didn't think so. But why call me? Then I thought about what Balls had said about my name being mentioned on the electronic *Outer Banks Voice*. I was identified as a crime writer, something I had gained a bit of notoriety for here on the Outer Banks. The killer, himself, getting his jollies by taunting, teasing, sending messages . . . like the couple's wrists tied together?

Okay, now it was time to call Balls.

Chapter Seven

Balls was still around the courthouse and had finished getting statements from Chaffey and Molly. He sounded weary, the way he always sounded when he felt he wasn't making progress. He perked up a bit when I told him about the call I had received. I told him the caller's ID had been blocked.

"You're right," he said. "Probably a disposable cell. Just the same, I'll see if there is some way we can get a line on the call." He made a dismissive sound in his throat. "Don't really think so." Then he said, "Whoever it was figures that you'll get the word out. Surprised he didn't call Linda Shackleford at the paper. He wants to send messages, obviously." There was a pause at his end. "And he ain't through, that's pretty sure, too."

Balls puffed out a sigh. "I'm heading back toward Elizabeth City and home. That service in the morning is at ten. I'll pick you up at nine-thirty. In the meantime, keep your eyes open—and doors locked. You don't know who the killer might be thinking of targeting."

We ended with that chilling thought.

I went back inside, stepped over the neck of my bass that lay on its side in the middle of the living room, went to the kitchen and got another glass of iced tea. I stood at the sink drinking it, looking out the window at the pine trees, thinking, wondering what was behind the telephone message.

Saturday night coming on in just a few hours. I would

like to see Elly and I wanted to tell her to be careful . . . but of what? I didn't want to alarm her and I decided not to tell her about the telephone call. She had already indicated she wanted to spend the time with her son Martin at home. I could understand that. And then early tomorrow morning she and her mother and Martin were going to Greenville to visit one of Mrs. Pedersen's sisters. They wouldn't be back until almost dark Sunday evening. Surely Monday we'd get together.

So, a Saturday night and I'd spend it here at my little house with my parakeet and bass fiddle. Maybe this would be a good time to practice jazz riffs on the bass, playing pizzicato, forsaking the bowing of classical pieces. See how I did with swing and jazz once again. I thought about Jim Watson's urging me to play with his combo, and tried to decide whether it would be fun.

Sunday morning sparkled with sunshine. I stepped out on the deck and breathed in deeply, smelling the pine trees and the sun-warmed wood of the deck. Turning my face to the east, I breathed in fully again and was sure I could detect the refreshing salt air coming off the ocean. I was already showered and dressed, wearing reasonably fresh khakis, button-down oxford-weave shirt, boat shoes, and even with socks. About as dressed up as I ever got here at the Outer Banks. Fit for church. And shortly before nine-thirty, here came Balls in his Thunderbird. He backed in on the side of my carport.

When he got out, he looked up at me and said, "Let's go in your vehicle. Attract less attention at the church than my classy, classic T-Bird."

"Coffee?" I called down to him.

He glanced at his watch. "Okay." He lumbered up the stairs on the side of the house. He came in while I quickly fixed fresh coffee. Looking at the bass lying across the living room floor, he shook his head and made an exaggerated effort of stepping over the neck of the bass. "Can't you ever pick up that cello?"

"It's a bass, Balls," I said, my back to him as I got the coffee going. He knows damn well it's a bass and not a cello; a bit of banter that continues. He sat on the sofa and awaited his coffee, taking another quick peek at his watch. He wore his cotton beige coat and even had on a tie, slightly loosened around his thick neck. "Got some prelims," he said, "from the M.E. Both slugs from the same weapon, of course, .38s, and I'll bet from an old revolver. Slugs are in good enough shape for accurate ballistic tests . . . if we ever get something to test them, like the murder weapon." He took a loud sip of his coffee, looked up at me as I stood near the divider counter. "Okay, Sherlock, what kind of killing?"

I stood there and looked at him. "Not a professional hit. Would have been smaller caliber, a couple to each head."

Balls pursed his lips and nodded. "And . . . ?"

"I'd say the two of them came to Nags Head Woods in Dwight Fairworth's car, planning to do a little strolling along the paths, holding hands. Got to believe there was something between them. Somebody followed them, came up on them . . . and that was it. The person who did it was planning to do it. Knew they'd be there or followed them. It wasn't random. The tied wrists tell us that."

Balls finished his coffee, set the mug on the table, and stood. "Pretty good, Weav, you're coming along." That quick time-check again. "Okay, it's off to church for us."

As we got into my Outback, Balls moved the passenger seat back as far as it would go. He rolled his shoulders, getting comfortable fastening his seatbelt. "This ain't too bad," he said, "for an old settled guy like you."

I started the engine. "Room in the back, too. Carry stuff. My cello fits back there quite nicely."

"It's a bass," Balls said, and we pulled out of my cul-de-sac.

On the way over to the church, Balls informed me that closed-casket services for both Dwight Fairworth and Gladys Chaffey were scheduled for Monday, at two different funeral homes.

"Who's paying?" I asked.

"Huh?"

"For the funerals."

"Oh. I'm checking. I expect the Fairworth family but for Gladys Chaffey, don't know. Old Chaz ain't got it. Bet the church is handling it."

We drove north on the Bypass to Kitty Hawk Road and turned left. Balls extracted a small slip of paper from his inside coat pocket and referred to it. A short distance up Kitty Hawk Road he said, "Turn here," and pointed to his left. Three blocks later we came to a white frame and cinder-block building that had probably been something of a ware-house at one time. Dozens of cars were parked in the gravel and crumbled concrete driveway. A six- or eight-foot white cross adorned the roof above what appeared to be a new shiny brown wooden door. A sign in black letters on a white background proclaimed "True Gospel Church of Jesus Christ."

After I parked, Balls got out, looked around at the other vehicles. He nodded toward a pickup truck. "Looks like our friend Chaz Chaffey is here to listen to the preacher eulogize the wife he pretty much abandoned."

I didn't say anything.

Three women and an elderly man approached the front door. We stepped back and smiled pleasantly to them and then followed them into a small vestibule that may have been an office at one time. In an aside to me, Balls whispered, "We'll sit at the back."

I nodded and thanked a woman with tinted reddish hair who handed us a single-sheet bulletin, folded to make four pages.

When we took our seats on the aisle in the back row, I was mildly surprised to find that the chairs were almost pew-like in that they were attached in rows and had places on the backs of them for hymnals. The church was almost full. Another cross was on the wall in the front of the church. A

simple podium was on the platform that held chairs for the
choir. A full-size piano was on the left, near the choir chairs.
One of the chairs, the second one in from the right, had wide
black ribbon woven across the back.

We had just gotten settled and perused the bulletin,
which Balls appeared to be reading in full detail, when the
choir filed in from a door on the right. The women were in
dark blue choir robes. The men were in suit coats, no robes.
Along with the choir came a young man who headed for the
piano. Immediately he began playing a hymnal I didn't recognize, but it provided nice background as the choir members arranged themselves, leaving the black ribbon chair
pointedly empty. We knew, of course, it had to be the chair
that the late Gladys Chaffey had occupied.

Then the minister came in. He wore a vestment that
reached down to mid-shins. He was tall and angular, and
looked young to be a minister. He smiled brightly at the congregation, then sat behind the podium and the woman who
served as choir director stood and led the choir in a hymn,
accompanied by the piano player—and I'll confess I kept
wondering if he might be the jazz piano player Jim Watson
had mentioned. He appeared to be in his early thirties. He
was short, maybe five-six at most; a full head of dark brown
hair that was long, spilling a bit over the collar of his white
shirt. I listened to see if he'd sneak in a little jazz lick or two.
He didn't. He played straight and somber.

When the young minister came back to the podium and
began to speak, I was surprised at the deep resonance of his
voice. It didn't seem to go with the rest of him. I knew Balls
was looking around at members of the congregation, studying them, and paying more attention to the people than to
what the minister was saying. I realized I was doing the same
thing. Balls nudged me and directed my gaze to the far right
near the back. Chaz Chaffey sat there, stiff and straight, his
unruly hair mostly combed. He wore a long-sleeve checkered
shirt, buttoned at the neck. Empty seats were on both sides of
him.

When he got into the sermon, the Rev. Kermit Kessler, used a theme of when bad things happen to good people—and he quickly referred, of course, to what he described as "the tragic loss of two beloved members of the family congregation." He pointed dramatically with his right hand at the black-draped empty choir chair and spoke with a catch in his throat of the "silencing of an angelic soprano voice." He had praise, too, for our "beloved building committee chairman and stalwart supporter of our founding church, Mr. Dwight Fairworth." Rev. Kessler paused and let his words hang there as he fixed his eyes on the front row where Janet Fairworth sat with slumped shoulders between a couple that were probably her parents or in-laws.

As he continued his homily, I used the time to concentrate on the people there in the church. I guess I had assumed that many would be older, post-retirement age, the demographics I'd observed at the few church services I'd attended at the Outer Banks. This congregation was younger—not young, but younger—with most in their late thirties and forties, I would guess. Never good to try to catalogue groups, but if I had to, I would surmise that the church was filled with people who were seeking solace, support, a path that maybe had been denied them for one reason or another. Directly in front of us, a youngish mother with thin shoulders underneath a cotton blouse, sat with two children, one on each side. The girl was about eight years old, the boy about seven. He squirmed a bit in his chair as if he couldn't get comfortable but the little girl sat as still as her mother, and seemed just as dejected.

We stood a couple of times for the singing of hymns. When it came time for collection, three men and one woman came to the front and were handed silver-colored plates by the minister. The woman was the one with the tinted reddish hair who had greeted us at the door. One of the men was much shorter than the other two, somewhat pear shaped, late fifties or maybe sixty. The other two were ten or fifteen years younger. One had close-cropped hair, mostly gray on the sides, face tanned and a bit lined; the other deacon, very tall, had not been in the sun often. His hair was longer, lighter, and combed back neatly. All of them, including the woman, had pleasant expressions, almost smiles. They began the process of passing the collection plates. On the back of the bulletin, names of church officers were listed. I assumed the four were something like deacons or elders. And, yes, four deacons were listed, along with the reverend and a couple of church committee chairmen, including the now-vacant post of building committee chairman. The collection plates were beginning to be passed along by the deacons. As the tall deacon came up our aisle, I couldn't help but notice that the young mother in front of us didn't put anything in the collection plate but the little girl did. The tall deacon had leaned over and spoken softly to the mother. His eyes were the brightest blue I'd seen in some time; reminded me of young Prince Philip's eyes, the Queen's husband. The woman nodded solemnly and tried to smile. He lightly patted her shoulder and moved on. Both Balls and I put in bills folded neatly

When the service ended, a couple of minutes after eleven, and Rev. Kessler had pronounced the benediction, which I always like to hear, the piano player started a rendition of "The Old Rugged Cross." He played it straight, but there was an indefinable bounce to it that wasn't present during any of the other hymns. I decided I wanted to speak to the piano player, so I delayed leaving the sanctuary. To Balls I whispered, "Zero in on anything?"

He shook his head. "I want to speak to the good reverend. You go ahead."

"I'm going to meet the piano player." I moved against the people coming up the aisle, nodding pleasantly and shaking hands with one or two of the men. A small young man continued to sit on the front row, closest to the piano. The seated young man smiled at the piano player as he finished "The Old Rugged Cross" with just a touch of flourish. The younger man made a show of applauding silently.

The piano player closed the lid on the piano, stood and stepped off the raised platform just as I approached. He was even shorter than he appeared sitting at the piano, pale, and with one hand he brushed the hair away from his ear. He looked at me, and smiled.

"Enjoyed your playing," I said. "I'm Harrison Weaver, and I wonder if you happen to know a trumpet player named Jim Watson."

"Oh, my goodness, yes, I know Jim." He extended his hand. "I'm Maurice Beckham, but everyone calls me Mouse." The younger man had stood. He was shorter than Mouse, rather wispy blond hair and frail looking. "And this is my friend Billy. Billy Overton." Mouse stared at me a moment, his brow wrinkled a bit in thought. "Weaver, Weaver . . . You're the bass player, right?"

"Yep."

"Oh, yes, and writer, too. Murder and that sort of thing." He cocked his head to one side, mentally making a connection; the hint of a sly smile played across his face. "Oh, and that's why you're here today. Is that right? It is, isn't it?"

I shrugged. "I'm here with a friend of mine."

"Yeah, right," Mouse said. He reached behind him and gathered up music that rested on the piano bench. "Even though I don't play here every Sunday, I'd met the woman who was killed. She was very nice. I didn't know the man, but I'd seen him around. Sort of an official type, you know what I mean."

"I won't keep you," I said. "Maybe see you soon if Jim Watson gets us all together. He's rather determined to get a group going."

"Oh, my goodness, yes he is." He turned to leave, his friend Billy with him. "Be fun, though." He gave a half-crooked smile out of the corner of his mouth and whispered with exaggerated confidentiality, "Beat some of these boring hymns."

I headed back up the aisle and saw Balls talking with Rev. Kessler. Balls tried to look pleasant but the minister's expression registered concern; he compressed his lips and leaned forward into whatever it was that Balls was saying. In a flicker of an instant, though, Rev. Kessler would acknowledge the greeting of one of his congregation with a bright smile, then get back to the conversation with Balls. The crowd had thinned considerably, even though there was a coffee urn and cookies on a small table against the far wall. Off in an alcove of an office, two of the deacons tallied the donations for the day.

I stood a few feet away and waited for Balls. He shook hands with the minister, and took his leave. The woman with the reddish hair appeared to be waiting to speak to Kessler. She smiled at Balls and me again and said, "Please come back to worship with us again."

When we stepped outside into the bright sunshine, Balls said, "I got a feeling we just may be coming back to this church again."

Chapter Eight

We sat in my car and waited for one of the members to back out in front of us. Balls stared at the church's sign. Softly, he said, "I believe the 'true gospel' is that these murders are somehow tied to the church."

I wanted to ask how, aside from the fact that both victims were active in the church. Instead I said, "Saw you talking with Rev. Kessler. Seemed quite serious." I eased out of the parking area and onto the little street that led back to Kitty Hawk Road.

Balls said, "I've got an appointment with him tomorrow. He was not all that happy about it. Says Monday is his day off. Told him I just wanted him to give me something of a rundown on his members." Balls rubbed his chin, and then used his thumb and index finger to stroke his mustache. "He was defensive, of course, but I tried to assure him we certainly didn't want anymore of his congregation in danger."

"He buy that?" I turned south on the Bypass at the light, heading back toward my place.

Balls didn't answer me. He stared straight ahead but didn't seem to be focusing his sight on anything. Lost in thought. Finally he said, "Worried about that phone call you got. Don't believe that was just some crank call." He raised his left hand and checked his watch. "Almost lunch time," he mused. Then, "You get any them cookies?"

I shook my head. "Henry's?" We were approaching the

restaurant, still crowded with a number of cars, more coming in after church.

"Sure."

I was already pulling into the parking area, and found a place on the south side of the restaurant and left empty spaces on both sides of me.

Balls grunted: "Why didn't you just park back in the south forty?"

"Little walk be good for you, Balls."

"We walked enough in Paris to last me quite a while."

"Not many fat people there." I chuckled, remembering. "And you got in a bit of running, too." I shook my head. "I had no idea you could run that fast, Balls."

"Wasn't about to let that sumbitch get away."

We got out of the car and strolled toward Henry's porch. "You nailed him, all right," I said. We waited as an elderly couple stepped carefully onto the porch. "Had to admire you, Balls. That was beautiful."

In Paris a week earlier, the four of us—Balls, his wife Lorraine, Elly and me—had made the expected tour of the Eiffel Tower. We had taken the No. 87 bus from our neighborhood in the Fifth Arrondissement to the end of the line at Champ de Mars and the Eiffel Tower. Their reaction, like everyone who sees it for the first time, was that it was much larger and more impressive than they had even imagined. We didn't try to go up the tower, either walking part way or waiting in line for the lift. It was enough to stand under it, gaze up in wonder at the massive structure. After about an hour walking about—enjoying the fresh air, and plantings, taking pictures, people watching—we headed back to the far side of the park to catch the return bus to our area.

As we started to get on our bus, along with several other people, someone bumped me. I thought it was Elly, just cutting up. But then I heard Balls yell out, "No you don't!" There was a bit of scuffling behind me and a young guy in a bulky black jacket took off running, with Balls right behind him. Within twenty yards Balls had caught up with the guy, tackled him, and was on top of him in the dusty gravel. The pickpocket wasn't about to go anywhere; Balls had the young man's arm twisted behind his back, his face forced down in the dirt. Almost simultaneously, two police officers, who patrol the area regularly, pulled up in their cruiser and ran over to assist Balls—and take the guy in custody. He had lifted my wallet expertly when he bumped me and still had it in his hand when Balls caught him. From then on I kept my wallet in a side pocket of my pants.

I smiled to myself remembering it. "You were impressive," I said.

A quick, puzzled glance. Then he realized what I referred to, and the grin appeared. "Yeah, Lorraine was impressed, too."

"First time she'd ever seen you in action?"

An even bigger grin: "Well, in that kind of action."

Inside Henry's we were guided to a booth that had just been cleared. Balls asked the waitress, a young woman who'd served us before, what the specials were. She recited the lunch specials. Balls asked if he could still get breakfast. She hesitated. Then agreed he could. We both ordered the three-egg omelets with hash-browned potatoes, toast.

I said, "Okay, Balls, tell me what you're thinking. I know you're pondering something, and have some ideas."

He loaded his coffee with sugar, sipped at it. Made a production of that before he responded to me. "I asked the reverend if Mr. Fairworth and Mrs. Chaffey were having an affair."

"Right off the bat, you asked that?"

"Well, first I told him who I was."

"Uh-huh."

"That took him aback. Flustered him, but then he admitted he had heard rumors to that effect. He said some counseling was warranted, and considered. That's when he agreed he would meet with me tomorrow and talk confidentially."

The waitress brought our omelets. As she left, Balls said, "People kept coming up. Wasn't good to try to talk to him too much then."

"Jilted spouses taking revenge?"

"You would think so. Normally yes, but I don't see Janet Fairworth pulling off this type of killing, an execution really. And I've already said that about Chaz Chaffey." He forked a chunk of omelet, and while chewing, said, "But ol' Chaz ain't completely out of my gun sights." He swallowed a mouthful of omelet, washed down with a loud sip of coffee. "He was there this morning, which surprised me."

I had continued eating. "Yeah, I saw him. I kept looking around at the people. Trying to imagine . . . well, you know, who would be capable."

"Don't want to assume it's someone from the church did these two. Could be from anywhere, but these two were connected heavily with the church. Can't overlook that. So . . . crap, I don't know what I think." He pushed in hash browns behind another bite of omelet. Frowning.

When we finished eating and settled the bill with Linda, who with her husband owns the restaurant, we stood for a moment or two on the front porch. Balls had picked up a toothpick and went through his ritual of poking vigorously at his teeth. It hurt me to watch him. In between jabs and probes with the toothpick, he said, "Just can't help but flirt with the pretty ladies, can you?"

"Linda is pretty, Balls, but just being friendly."

"Uh-huh." Then, "Drop me off at your place. I'm heading back to Manteo, spend a little time talking things over with Deputy Wright. He said he'd be on duty today."

"Going back to Elizabeth City this evening?"

"Yeah, want a be home. Sunday night and all. Back here in the morning to visit with the Rev. Kessler."

After Balls left, I went up the side stairs and into the kitchen area. Janey did her head-bobbing dance to welcome me back.

She even did a sort of back flip from the side of the cage. I spoke to her and told her she was showing off. She made her chirping noises and then quite clearly said, "Shit."

"Watch you language, Janey."

I decided to call Jim Watson, tell him about meeting Mouse Beckham, the piano player he'd talked about.

"Great," Jim said. "I've already spoken to Mouse today. He's clear to rehearse on Wednesday afternoon, three o'clock, at my place. Drummer Bert Campert can make it, too. The fact is, he keeps his traps at my house most of the time. How about it?"

I agreed. Maybe agreed a bit reluctantly but agreed nonetheless. Couldn't help the mixed feelings about playing again with a jazz group. I told myself, though, it was just a rehearsal and if I didn't feel good about it afterward, I'd bow out.

A pretty, sunny, fall day and here I was at loose ends. I went out on the deck, surveyed the sky and the pine trees and thought about the ocean. By myself on an early Sunday afternoon. I put seeds in the birdfeeder on the deck railing. Sat for a moment or two in one of the webbed lawn chairs there on the deck. Stood again, took a deep breath and sighed. Be nice if Elly were back but I wouldn't see her until tomorrow at the earliest. I missed her, and it had been so nice living together in Paris, and now Paris seemed like a long, long time ago.

Okay, I told myself. I would not be a member of the PLOM club—the Poor Little Ol' Me club. Get your ass in gear. Do something.

And I decided to go fishing. Surfcasting. Wasn't actually in the mood for it, but knew that forcing myself to do something would put me in better spirits, and I made myself face the fact that there was no reason for me to feel out of sorts. Just one of those moods you have to fight against, and I was determined to fight against it. So I changed into scruffy shorts, baggy T-shirt, sandals and I was set. I got bait shrimp out of the freezer, told Janey I'd see her later, and went down to the utility room and retrieved my surfcasting rod, which was already rigged for bottom fishing, a plastic bucket, sand spike, a small plastic pouch that contained hooks, a couple of lures, and two-ounce weights.

Although certainly not the greatest fishing spot on the Outer Banks, the ocean off Ocean Bay Boulevard would do for today. Only three other cars were parked there, which surprised me since the day was so pleasant, with a warm breeze out of the west, Carolina Blue skies, and temperature in the mid- to high-seventies. The ocean would be warmer here in September than it was in June. I would wade out a bit, cast and try not to think about anything other than fishing and the possibility of a good, healthy strike on my line.

I carried my gear south of the beach house walkway, away from a couple ensconced in beach chairs straight ahead. Three or four other people were to the north. The ocean rolled in nicely, behaving rather calmly today. I knew, however, how quickly the ocean could change here on the Outer Banks. I guess you get used to it, but the sound of the surf is so prevalent, that it doesn't seem like something apart from the air we breathe. It is just there. And breathe in deeply, I did. I was already feeling better.

I realized—and not for the first time—that I felt more reverent, more spiritually lifted, here at the ocean than I ever did in church, and over the years I had tried in church, really tried. I had concentrated on making myself more reverent, struggled to have more faith, to have the kind of acceptance I believed others had. But it just didn't seem to work, not for me. Not something I was necessarily sad about; I'd just come to accept it. And I didn't talk about it with others, not even Elly, who went to church regularly with her mother and Martin. I knew that one day I would ask Elly about her beliefs. I would be careful about it. I never wanted to say anything negative about another's faith. Maybe I was a little envious of them.

All the while I was mulling over my spiritual wellbeing, or lack thereof, I was baiting my rig with shrimp and casting out, using a side-arm cast rather than overhead. The bottom rig plopped nicely a goodly distance out. It had hardly settled before I suddenly felt a sharp tug on my line. A definite strike. I pulled back and set the hook. Yep, I had one, and while it was certainly not a monster, the fish was putting up a nice tug-of-war. I kept reeling in. As the rig got close to the breaking surf, the fish rolled near the surface, its skin glistening in the sun. I got him in. It was a gray trout, a good size, maybe eighteen inches. I decided to keep him, have him tonight.

I definitely felt better.

And I continued to feel good all afternoon and into the evening. The trout fillet was good, and along with a small boiled potato and salad, the meal was nice. I turned on the television, surfed about a bit, and went to bed early. Slept well and didn't wake again until after seven when the phone rang. I jumped at the sound of the phone and reached over to answer it.

It was Balls.

Then I didn't feel good anymore.

Chapter Nine

"Been another killing," he said. "I'm on my way to Kill Devil Hills. Meet Deputy Wright and others there." He paused a moment, probably concentrating on his driving, and I knew he was driving fast. "Guess maybe that phone call you got was the real thing."

I sat on the edge of the bed. "Jeeze. A killing?" I shook my head. "Who? Give me some details . . . and what makes you think it's connected to that phone call. Not necessarily . . ."

"True, but a dollar to a doughnut it is. One shot apparently. To the center of the chest, just like the other ones."

"Victim at Nags Head Woods?"

"Nope. But not far away. Guy still in his vehicle in the parking lot—far side, near that beer place a mile or so south of Dare Centre shopping."

"Okay if I show up?"

Another pause, apparently while he pondered my request. "Since you got that phone call, guess so. Just stay out of the way, especially if Rick Schweikert shows up wanting to know what you're doing there."

"See you shortly," I said. I rushed into the kitchen, started the coffee, then uncovered Janey, and got dressed quickly. I strode toward the door to the outside with a half a mug of coffee when the phone rang again. It was Linda Shackleford. She blurted out about the killing, which one of her sources with the sheriff's department had tipped her off about, but I cut her short. Told her I was heading out the door to go to the scene, also. Knew she'd be there. I put the phone down hurriedly, and had taken only a couple of steps toward the door when the phone rang again. I muttered an expletive, and snatched up the phone. "Yes?"

The disguised and muffled voice said, "I told you there would be others. More to come." As the caller clicked off, it sounded as though he was laughing. Nothing joyful about it. I glanced at caller ID. Blocked, which I knew it would be.

I rushed out the door, trying not to spill my coffee, set the mug in the cup holder, started the Outback, wheeled around and headed out of the cul-de-sac. As I came up to the Bypass and waited a moment for a break in traffic, I saw Balls' Thunderbird streaking by, a blue light flashing on his dashboard. I pulled onto the Bypass and headed south, also.

A short distance down the Bypass I saw the police and rescue squad activity off to the right at the far end of a parking area. There were two Dare County Sheriff's Department cruisers, two Kill Devil Hills police cars, a bulky rescue squad ambulance, Balls' Thunderbird and a couple of civilian cars, all scattered about outside a large circle of yellow crime scene tape that made a loop around a fairly new Dodge pickup truck. Balls and Deputy Wright and another officer I didn't recognize were inside the yellow tape, peering into the driver's side of the pickup truck.

I parked several yards behind the civilian cars and started toward the yellow crime scene tape. A Kill Devil Hills uniformed officer stopped me as I approached.

"Sir, you can't go in there," he said.

"I know," I said, "but I've got a message for Agent Twiddy when he gets a chance."

The officer studied me, then nodded.

And here came Linda Shackleford, her short hair bunched up a bit in the back like she hadn't bothered too much with a comb or brush, her Canon camera, adorned with a medium range zoom lens, at the ready. The officers went through the same routine with Linda. She said she understood. She raised her camera and focused in on Balls and the others at the pickup truck. The officer appeared ready to tell her she couldn't take pictures, but hesitated, not sure whether she could or not, and then turned his back and pretended not to notice her. The camera clicked five or six times.

Another civilian car came in and stopped near my Outback. A young man of about thirty or so got out and stared at the activity and the pickup truck. He looked bewildered and as if he'd been roused out of bed. He approached the officer and identified himself as the manager of the café. He didn't call it bar or beer hall. He told the officer, "A deputy called me and told me I'd better come down here." He kept staring at the pickup. Balls and Deputy Wright remained standing like sentinels.

The officer said, "Stay here. I'll go tell them you're here." He started to duck under the tape.

"Excuse me, officer," I said, "but when you go to the scene would you please tell Agent Twiddy that Weaver—Harrison Weaver—got another phone call this morning."

The officer frowned at me.

"Just tell him. He'll understand."

"Weaver? Phone call?"

"Yes. That's all." I wasn't sure he would do it, but apparently he did because after the officer approached Balls and Wright and spoke to them, Balls glanced quickly at me and nodded slightly.

The officer pointed to the young café manager, and motioned for him to come inside the tape to the scene. The young man inhaled deeply, flexed his shoulders, and ducked under the tape. With jerky steps he advanced to the pickup. At Balls' prompting, the young man peered briefly inside the truck's window, turned his head and nodded affirmatively.

I wanted to go up to the scene . . . as if I had any real business doing so. But maybe I did. After all, I was the one who'd received those cryptic and unsettling phone messages. Stepping closer to the tape, I tried to get Balls' attention. He talked with the young manager. Then a few seconds later, he took notice of me, and motioned me forward. The uniformed officer saw this and permitted me to duck under the tape and approach the scene.

Pausing at the truck, I studied the dead man. I was aware I didn't know him, and couldn't remember ever having seen him. He was slumped away from the window, a bloody wound on his chest and blood behind him on the back of the seat. I assumed the bullet had gone through him.

Balls stood close to me. He leaned forward and spoke softly. "You got another phone call?"

"Yes, just a few minutes after you called. Disguised voice. Same as before. He said, 'I told you there would be others. More to come.' Then he sounded like he chuckled or laughed as he hung up. No caller ID, of course."

Balls didn't say anything.

With a nod at the cab of the truck, I said, "When did this happen?"

"Don't know for sure. Sometime shortly after closing last night. The manager over there says the man was about the last to leave the place. When the manager came out in the parking lot after locking up, he thought there was another man leaning in the truck's window and talking to the guy. Manager was several yards away, though, and said he didn't pay any attention, except that best he recalled the man doing the talking was white and sort of tall. Manager got in his own car and left, went back to his place . . . until Deputy Wright called him this morning."

"One shot to the chest?"

"That's what it looks like. Don't want him moved until Dr. Willis gets here. Wright has called for a tech to try for fingerprints on the door frame, but glancing at it, looks like it's been wiped clean."

"Who is the guy?"

Balls consulted the small spiral notebook he had in his left hand. "Earl Ray Willard. Truck's registered to him. Haven't checked his wallet yet, but I can see it's still in his hip pocket."

Three emergency medical technicians stood back several yards but inside the tape, waiting. I had seen one of them approach the truck earlier; he had done a quick check and then had gone back to join his two coworkers.

Balls said, "You better go back outside the tape. Be enough folks in here in a few minutes." I didn't say anything. "But hang around," Balls added. Then he remembered his appointment with Rev. Kessler because he said, "Got to postpone my meeting with the good reverend." He checked his watch. "Try to remember to call him a little later."

"I'll remind you," I said.

He acknowledged that with a quick jerk of his head.

When I left the immediate scene, I went over and stood beside Linda. "Who is it?" she asked, her voice shaky.

"A guy named Earl Ray Willard. Looked to be about in his early forties. Shot in the chest."

Linda frowned, repeated his name a couple of times, her newly acquired reporter's memory for names clicking in. "I think he was in court last week. I'm sure he was. Not the first time. Child support. What they'd call a deadbeat dad. I'm sure that was his name. Going to be sentenced on the road if he didn't pay up."

"Doesn't have to worry about going on the road now."

"Yeah, but what about his kids, his wife?"

I shook my head. "Life's a bitch."

A short while later, while we stood around, watching from a distance, Dr. Willis arrived, shaking his head sadly as he ducked under the yellow tape and shuffled toward the pickup truck, a black medical bag in his right hand. Don't know what was in the bag, but certainly nothing that could do Earl Ray Willard any good.

Wearing latex gloves, Balls carefully opened the driver's door so Dr. Willis could get a better look. He rolled Willard's body to the right, presumably so he could see the exit wound in his back. Balls squeezed partly in and probed in the seatback with what appeared to be a penknife. He extracted something I guessed was the slug and dropped it into a small plastic evidence bag.

I tried to imagine the scene as the shooting had taken place. Willard had to have been facing the killer, or at least turned somewhat toward him, to have been shot in the center of his chest. And probably the shooter held the gun in his left hand? True, the probing that Balls did for the slug was on the far right side of the seatback. So the bullet went in at an angle. I'll bet that exit wound is underneath Willard's right shoulder blade.

Linda gazed hard at my face. "What are you thinking?"

"Huh?" Her voice brought me back to the here and now. "Oh, just trying to imagine how the shot was fired, where the shooter was. Trying to picture it." I shrugged my shoulders. "I have a tendency to do that."

She wrinkled her nose a bit. "It's enough for me that he's shot. I don't need to picture it any more than that." She shook her head. "I tell you the truth, Weav, I think I've seen more and mentally pictured more in a couple of days than I really want to."

Wanting to make her feel better, I said, "You're becoming *The Coastland Times* chief crime writer." Then I recalled that the next edition—Tuesday's paper—would carry her first-person account of the killing at Nags Head Woods. "You'll have a story about this one, too."

She did a quick take at her bulky, mannish wristwatch. "If I can get enough here to squeeze something in for tomorrow. I'm going to have to hustle, though, 'cause deadline is practically on me." She turned her head toward the scene and the activity there. "You think Agent Twiddy will give me a statement?"

"Maybe," I said, "if you can catch him. Deputy Wright might be more likely. He sort of owes you."

A radio reporter had shown up in his van, emblazoned with the call letters of the station, and right behind him came the woman reporter from *The Virginian-Pilot*, one of the few reporters still left from the trimmed-down staff. The radio reporter called out to Deputy Wright, as the uniformed officer kept the reporter outside of the crime scene tape. The other reporter also tried to get Deputy Wright's attention.

As Deputy Wright conferred with Balls, I told Linda, "You better join them. I think Odell Wright will be over to give a statement—or no comment—in just a moment."

"Right," Linda said. She didn't have the aggressiveness that is frequently associated with reporters—at least she didn't have it yet, thankfully.

Balls gave an affirmative bob of his head, and Deputy Odell Wright strode briskly to the reporters and stood just on his side of the yellow tape. I moved toward the group, also, standing at the back. I didn't need to compete with the dailies.

Wright told them that the only thing he was authorized to say at this point was that a Caucasian male, of about forty years of age, had been shot once in the chest and was pronounced dead at the scene, and that apparently it happened at some point the night before shortly after the—the—establishment closed. No, he couldn't give them the identity of the victim until the next of kin was notified. Robbery did not appear to be the motive. The investigation is just getting underway and no arrests have been made. And, no, there are no persons of interest that he can discuss at this time. Sorry, he said, but that's about all he could give at this time.

There were more questions, rapid fire from the radio guy and the woman, that got nowhere. Linda stood there mute. She knew the victim's identity, but she wasn't about to say anything. Deputy Wright courteously excused himself, saying he needed to get back to the scene.

Linda and I moved away. "By the time you're going to press, the man's identity will be out to the public," I said.

"I better get back and start writing," she said.

Balls was on his cell phone. Calling to cancel with the Rev. Kessler, perhaps. He finished the call and slowly attached the phone to his belt. I felt I could practically hear him sigh from that distance. He motioned me forward. I got the attention of the uniformed officer and pointed at Balls, who repeated his beckoning.

Ducking under the tape, I met Balls about halfway to the pickup truck. "I don't need to call Rev. Kessler to break the appointment. He just called to cancel on me. Says he has emergency grief counseling." Balls took a deep breath, and this time I actually could hear him sigh. "A woman in his congregation has just received word that her estranged husband has been found shot to death."

Balls stared hard at me. "The distraught woman in his congregation at the True Gospel Church of Jesus Christ is none other than Mrs. Earl Ray Willard, mother of two young children, and the legal wife of that man lying dead in his pickup truck."

Chapter Ten

I stood there with my mouth open. "Jeeze," I muttered, for about the third time that morning.

Balls shook his head, as if in disbelief. "Looks like everything leads back to a connection of some sort with that church."

"Yes, but what?"

He rubbed his face with the palm of one hand. "I have no idea . . . at least not yet."

Deputy Wright approached us, his face creased with fatigue or worry. "Okay if they take the body away?"

"Dr. Willis finished?"

"Yes, sir. Says victim has been dead about six hours or so. Single shot through to sternum, exiting lower on the right side."

Balls nodded.

Wright continued. "It looks like the shooter was there at the window of the vehicle, aimed from slightly higher up. Bang! Right through the chest. And that was it. No struggle. Wallet still there with a few bills, so is his watch, some change in his right pocket. No robbery."

"Naw," Balls said. "This wasn't about robbery, or even an argument." He did that moustache-smoothing motion with his thumb and index finger before he spoke again. "This was more personal," he said.

Wright consulted the small notebook he held in his left

hand, flipped a page. "Our victim was employed by J.L. Roy Heating and Air Conditioning. Separated but not divorced from his wife, Delores Willard. They have two children."

"Good job, Odell," Balls said.

"Notification?" Wright asked.

"Someone has already notified her," Balls said. "Can't say that I miss that part. Minister is meeting with her." He turned his head toward the pickup truck where the medical technicians were removing the body, a gurney and body bag at the ready. Then he spoke softly, as if talking to himself, "And I want to spend time with the minister and Mrs. Willard, too." He straightened his shoulders. "In fact I'm going to get with them right now." He punched in a number on his cell. Someone answered at the church, and gave him directions as to where the minister would be meeting with Mrs. Willard.

Balls told Wright that by noon he could certainly release the name of the victim. He extracted the evidence bag from his pocket that contained the slug he'd dug out of the seatback, handed it to Wright. "This is a .38, I'm sure, and in fairly good shape. Want to know, of course, what ballistics says about this one compared with the other two slugs."

"Yes, sir."

Balls took a long stride away, stopped and turned back to Deputy Wright. "Odell, cut out that 'yes sir' crap with me."

"Yes . . . okay." Odell Wright smiled for the first time that morning.

By the time I got to my house, it was almost noon. After speaking to Janey, checking to see whether she needed more seeds or water, I stepped over the neck of the bass, went to the phone and called Elly at work. She sounded professional as she said, "Register of Deeds Office, Elly Pedersen speaking."

"Harrison," I said.

"So, another one," she said, her voice flat.

"Word gets around."

"So do you." Her voice still flat. "Linda called."

"I see."

"Tell me, Mr. Weaver, just how it is that you show up at these . . . these scenes."

"You sound like Rick Schweikert."

"I'm beginning to understand why he says that."

"Okay, Elly. Balls called me on his way there."

Her voice softened a bit. "Any connection with the other two?"

"Have no idea," I lied, even though I thought, as Balls did I'm sure, that there was indeed a connection, just didn't know what.

I tried to change the subject. "How does it feel to be back at work?"

She must have stepped away from her desk because her tone became more intimate. "Both Becky and Judy want to know all about it." She referred to her two coworkers, who teased Elly about our relationship, and I suspect knew that it was considerably more than platonic. But they kept digging, smirking, and giggling. "They keep asking to see pictures. I've printed out some. You know, Eiffel Tower, Notre Dame, and so forth. But they want to see pictures of the apartment." She laughed softly. "It's the sleeping arrangements that they're really interested in, I know."

"Insist that Lorraine was a tough chaperone. That's our story, and we're sticking to it."

She spoke to either Becky or Judy. "Be right there." Then to me, "See you tonight?"

"Why don't we go out to eat? Regular dinner date, like Paris."

"Okay," she said. "Sounds good."

We were about to sign off when I told her briefly about Jim Watson and rehearsing Wednesday afternoon.

"Oh, I wish I could hear you."

"We may be at it until close to five. Maybe you can slip away from work a few minutes early."

"We'll see."

And we left it at that. I was to pick her up at six.

For a few minutes I sat there in the little chair by the phone, staring alternately off at nothing or watching Janey, who kept her head cocked at me, awaiting some attention. "Okay, Janey, you over being mad at me about leaving you to go to Paris?" She chirped and bobbed her head a couple of times. "I've got to go to the grocery store, but I'll be back very shortly."

Janey chirped again and then said, "Shit."

Back at the house after a quick trip to Food Lion, I absently put away groceries, the whole time thinking about the murders. Knew I needed to call Rose Mantelli, my editor, but decided I'd wait until I knew a bit more. Tomorrow at the latest. She would be excited about the story possibilities. Heck, why wouldn't she? Three slain people, all directly or indirectly connected to the same church.

With the groceries put away, I stepped into the living room and picked up the bass. I started to pluck at it and then just as suddenly laid it back down. Not into it. Sighed again, and loudly, felt for my car keys and headed out the door. On a whim, and I guess that was about the best word for it, I decided to take a ride up to Kitty Hawk Road, turn left, and at least drive by the True Gospel Church of Jesus Christ. Why? I couldn't, or wouldn't, try to explain it to myself. Just wanted to see if maybe something was going on. That's the best explanation I could give myself.

When I drove slowly up the side road to the church, I spotted Balls' Thunderbird parked in the lot, close to the side door of the church. An older model Chevrolet sedan was there, also. I pulled in beside Balls' car and sat still. Of course I wanted to go in, but I forced myself to stay put, at least for a few minutes. I knew I had no real business being there. After a while I came to my senses enough to know I should leave. I started the engine just as the side door of the church opened, and Balls emerged, saying goodbye to someone as he exited.

I cut the engine and got out of the car.

If Balls was surprised to see me, he made no sign of it. I approached him as he stood by the driver's side of his car. He looked tired. His shirt was wilted, maybe a little sweat-stained. No greeting from either of us. He leaned his hips against the car door. "We did the notification. Well, not notification exactly, since Mrs. Willard already knew. One of the other members of the congregation—a Miss Busybody, whose nephew is on the Kill Devil Hills police force—called her when the body was found, and in turn . . . well, you know. But Rev. Kessler and I went to see Delores Willard, the new widow." For the first time, Balls actually looked at me, as if just now registering that I was standing there. "She was the woman with the two kids sitting in front of us in church . . . yesterday, Sunday . . . or whenever it was."

"Yesterday," I said softly.

"Yeah . . ." His voice trailed off. "Then I came back here to talk with the reverend about his congregation. Trying to get a rundown on some of them."

I waited for him to say more, but he just stared down at his feet. He straightened up, flexed his back, and said, "I'm going to head on back to Manteo, sheriff's office, meet with Odell Wright. Check ballistics and anything else."

"You had lunch?"

"Huh? Oh, Kessler and I had some of those cookies left over from the other day."

"Yesterday," I said.

"Right." He opened the door to his Thunderbird. "Staying in Manteo tonight. Heck, maybe most of the day tomorrow, too."

"Be in touch," I said.

He nodded. Folded himself into the driver's seat, and looked up at me, a trace of his grin there for an instant. "And you and me are coming back here for Wednesday night prayer meeting." He started the engine, with its low, smooth, and powerful sound. "Have no idea—yet—but somehow . . . I'm convinced the 'true gospel' is right here," and he inclined his head toward the church.

Chapter Eleven

Getting in my car, I more or less followed Balls out to the Bypass. I stayed in the slower right hand lane and Balls was soon out of sight. I mulled over Balls' words. What could possibly be the connection with the church? I agreed with Balls, but was just as much at a loss as I thought he was as to what that connection could be. Go back to the church again day after tomorrow? Wednesday night prayer meeting? Shook my head. Didn't know what time that started, but I assumed it would be after rehearsing with Jim Watson and the group. So much for having Elly join me there at Jim's, not if I had to "go to meeting" as soon as the rehearsal was over. Well, I'd check the time and where to meet Balls.

These thoughts and others bounced around in my head as I turned into my cul-de-sac and parked under the carport. I sat there a moment or two. A dull headache began to develop. Realized I'd only snacked a bit. No real lunch. I needed to eat something. I took a deep breath, got out of the car and trudged up the stairway on the side of the house.

Then I heard my phone ringing and I quickened my steps up the stairs. But the phone quit ringing as I opened the door. I expected the voice mail to kick in, but nothing. I glanced at the phone's caller ID. Blocked. That guy again, or just a telemarketer. No, that guy again. Well, the sonofabitch would call back, I was sure.

Now, damnit, maybe it was time to go ahead and call my

editor. Quit putting it off. I guess I was just a bit weary with everything that was happening and dreaded having to try to explain it all to Rose.

But explain it I did. She barked and coughed and said in that heavy Brooklyn accent of hers, "Damn, Weaver sounds like you got Civil War all over again down there. What the hell's happened to all the magnolias and mint juleps we hear about?" She cackled out a laugh, followed abruptly by a mild fit of coughing. Then she got serious again. "Tell the truth though, Weaver, it does sound like the germ of a heck of a story, especially if that church angle plays out."

"Now wait a minute, Rose. I'm not saying there's what you call a 'church angle.' So far there's just the fact that the victims—that is the first two—were members of the church. This third victim is not a member—his estranged wife is."

Rose made a dismissive sound in her throat. "Sounds like a church connection to me."

"Last thing I want to do down here, Rose, is somehow get crosswise with the good church members. Not just at this church, but all the churches . . . and there're a lot of them."

"I unnerstand, I unnerstand," she said rapidly. But I don't think she did understand. "Keep me posted. I believe you've got quite a story going there."

A bit more and we ended the call. I know she is removed from the scene, and I know it is her job to think in terms of articles, stories, books even, but I felt a little—what?—soiled by the conversation. These were human beings who had been alive, had lives going, whether good or bad, and I never wanted to lose sight of that. I'm a crime writer, sure; but a human being first of all, and I wanted to guard against viewing everything as meat for a story. The nagging headache was gaining ground.

I stood a couple of steps away from the phone, looked at Janey cocking her head. "Shit," I said, beating her to it.

By five-thirty, after resting a bit and with the aid of a Tylenol, and a shower, I was dressed and ready to go get Elly. Feeling much better. Heading to her house in Manteo, driving the familiar route, murder and mayhem always took a back seat. The late afternoon sun made pinpoints of light on the Roanoke Sound as I crested the bridge. The days were getting shorter, but there was still plenty of light, and the weather was good and clear. There was an item on the weather channel about a tropical depression possibly developing east of Africa beyond Cape Verde in the Atlantic, but that was a long way off and it might not develop at all.

The time was five after six when I pulled into the Pedersen's driveway, my tires crunching on the gravel. As I expected she would, Elly came out on the porch to greet me as I got out of the car. She raised her right hand and wiggled her fingers and smiled, and I loved her. I realized, too, I was happy about loving her.

After brief hellos in the living room with Mrs. Pedersen and Martin, we prepared to go. Martin, who had eyed me suspiciously, began to tear up, and Elly got down on her knees in front of him and assured him we'd be back probably before he was asleep. "We're just going to get something to eat," she said, "and we'll be right back." Elly told her mother where we would be. Elly slipped on a lightweight white cotton cardigan. She wore trim beige slacks that showed off her hips quite nicely, without being too revealing.

The Blue Moon Café in South Nags Head was crowded early but the hostess showed us to a table for two along the window side. Perfect. The server, who said her name was Megan, greeted us with a big smile and asked about our drink orders. We both wanted sweetened iced tea.

When Megan left to get our drinks, I said, "Hard to believe, but just a week ago you would have opted for a glass of wine with dinner in Paris."

"In a way it does seem like a long time ago, doesn't it? Well in some ways." She beamed and reached across the table and touched my hand. "It was wonderful. Really wonderful." She glanced around, and withdrew her hand, but kept the smile. "I know I've said it before, but I never thought I'd get to Paris. And it was . . . was so special, seeing the places you knew. Showing us around."

Megan brought out iced tea. "Give us another minute or so," I said, picking up the menu for the first time.

When Megan left, I said, "Loved the part, too, of living together in the little apartment." The four of us had rented a small two bedroom apartment on Rue des Grands Degres, across Quay Montebello from the Seine and Notre Dame. My favorite neighborhood in the Fifth Arrondissement, Left Bank.

"It's a good thing we had Lorraine and Ballsford for chaperones," she said, a sly smile playing across her lips. "No telling what might have happened in the apartment without them."

"Very considerate of them to occasionally go shopping or sightseeing without us."

"Very considerate indeed." Then, "Okay, enough of that. I know how wicked your mind can work." She pretended to study the menu. "What shall we have?"

"Not on the menu tonight, but I wonder if they'll fix us a couple of those 'Shrimp Not a Burger' that they have at lunch?"

"We'll ask," Elly said brightly.

Megan reappeared and I asked her about the Shrimp Not a Burger. She got the hint of a conspiratorial smile, nodded her head, and whispered, "I think I can talk 'em into it."

The Shrimp Not a Burgers arrived shortly, open faced, garnishments, some fries and grilled shrimp piled high on top. Delicious.

We concentrated on our food for a few minutes. "Got to keep eating as slowly as they do in Paris," Elly said. But she was having a difficult time slowing down.

Swallowing a nice hunk of food, I said, "What did you really like most about Paris?"

"As I've said, Harrison, of course it was a thrill to see all the places you've heard about—Notre Dame, the Eiffel

Tower, the Seine—but I think I liked best just looking at the people, sitting in the cafés and sipping on some coffee and watching the Parisians with their little dogs. Café du Metro was great for that, right there on the corner."

I nodded in agreement.

She went on: "All the people on bicycles and motor-cycles, the traffic without all of the horn-honking." She smiled at me again, resting her fork on the side of her plate. "And I liked that you showed me the places you'd been to— Hemingway and Hadley's first apartment up near Place de la Contrescarpe . . . on . . ."

"Number 74, Rue de Cardinal Lemoine."

"Yes, and naturally Shakespeare and Company . . . such a quaint place, always so crowded with people, most of them young, or looking like the tortured poet you read about, and thousands of books stacked around . . . books and people, books and people."

We went back to eating, trying to be slow at it like the French.

"The bakeries, too," she said suddenly, a big smile light-ing her face. "I loved the little boulangeries." She added. "Good thing we walked as much as we did." She cast her eyes toward my wristwatch. "I promised Martin we'd be home before he went to sleep."

"Eat faster," I said.

She laughed.

And then to our surprise Linda Shackleford bustled into the Blue Moon, camera slung around her neck. She took a quick look around, spotted us and hurried to our small table. To Elly she said, "Called your mom. She said where you two were." Reaching behind her, Linda snagged an empty chair and pulled it up, trying her best not to block the path. She waved Megan away, saying she'd be here just a minute or two.

Leaning into the table, she spoke softly, in great secret confidence, and I swear out of the corner of her mouth like a mobster in a movie: "Been to J. L. Roy's Heating and Air

Conditioning, doing a bit more checking on our latest victim, Earl Ray Willard. Martha, the office manager, is a friend of mine. Earl Ray may have been charged with being a deadbeat dad, not paying child support half the time, but looks like he's left his widow better fixed than when he was alive." Hardly missing a beat, Linda eyed Elly's iced tea, reached a hand out and picked up the glass; a quick sip and she set the glass back down in front of Elly. "Thanks," Linda said. Elly rolled her eyes at me, but with a half-smile on her lips.

"Anyway," Linda said, "Mr. Roy is certainly generous with his employees, even the half-ass ones like Earl Ray. Get this: Every one of them has a life insurance policy worth two years' salary. And of course the spouse is beneficiary in practically all cases."

"Well, that's good, Linda," I said. "Looks like Mrs. Willard may have an easier time for a while than she did when he was alive."

Linda eyed our food. "That good?"

"Very good," Elly said. "But, Harrison, you know we'd better . . ."

"Yes, I know. We're going to have to go."

Linda grabbed another sip of Elly's tea. "But the main thing, Weav." She leaned in even closer. "I wasn't the first one to ask about Earl Ray Willard's insurance policy."

I cocked my head. "He was just found this morning . . . not wasting any time."

"Yeah, Weav, but Martha said somebody asked Mr. Roy about the insurance policies, and specifically about Willard's, a week ago."

Elly stared at the expression on my face.

"Uh-oh." I said. "I need to talk with Balls."

Chapter Twelve

Linda had very little more to add about J. L. Roy's insurance policies for his employees. She said her friend Martha didn't know who it was who spoke to Mr. Roy last week about the policies. He had simply mentioned it to her in passing, and apparently the inquiry came when she was out to lunch. Martha had not queried as to the identity of the questioner. Linda said she decided not to pursue it with Mr. Roy. Leave that to me or to Agent Twiddy. Linda added, "But I thought that was mighty interesting. You know, just before Earl Ray Willard gets himself killed."

"Yes, it is," I said. I signaled Megan for the check. To Elly I said, "I know we've got to go."

"Lemme get another sip of that tea," Linda said, reaching for Elly's glass as Elly began gathering herself to leave.

After paying the check and tip, I thanked Linda for the information. The three of us left together. Linda got in her Toyota and waved a vigorous goodbye.

"Do you need to call Agent Twiddy?" Elly asked as we maneuvered out of the strip shopping area.

"Sorry?" I was lost in thought.

"Agent Twiddy. You said you needed to call him."

"Yes, that's what I was just thinking about." Glancing at the clock on the dash, I said, "Still early. I'll call him when . . . when we get to your house."

Elly gave a short little laugh. "You mean you'll call him

after you drop me off."

"Aw, come on, that's not exactly what I meant."

She patted my forearm, and smiled at me. "I understand," she said.

I shot a quick look at her as we drove along the Bypass toward Whalebone Junction. "You getting sort of used to me?"

She settled back in the seat. "I figure I might as well." She chuckled rather contentedly. "Especially now that we've lived together in sin in Paris."

"No, no, remember we had chaperones."

"Yeah, right," she said.

We got to her house a few minutes past eight-thirty. Martin had his pajamas on but was not in bed. We said our goodnights; I gave Elly a discreet kiss.

As I left her driveway and headed out to the main road, I was already calling Balls. He answered his cell before the second ring had ended. He greeted my call with a gruff: "This better be good. I'm here at the Elizabethan Inn and ready for bed."

"And a good evening to you, too, Balls."

"Okay, Weav, what's up?" He sounded a little less gruff, and his gruffness I knew was frequently something of an act.

I related to him what Linda Shackleford had learned from the office manager at J. L. Roy's Heating and Air Conditioning.

Balls digested the information in silence for a beat or two. "But Linda doesn't know who was asking about the policies—and Willard's policy in particular?"

"No, she doesn't know. Most interesting, though, that a query about his policy, and I'm sure the beneficiary, is made a week before he's killed. Might mean nothing, but does seem awfully curious to me."

"Yeah, me, too," Balls said.

I was past the Elizabethan Inn and Budleigh Street and getting toward the eastern edge of Manteo. I waited for Balls to say something else. "You still there?"

"Just thinking," he said. "I've got a couple of appointments first thing tomorrow, but I think I'll postpone them—and instead see if I can't meet with Mr. J. L. Roy to chat with him about insurance policies."

I waked Tuesday morning wondering what Balls might find out in talking with Mr. J. L. Roy. Couldn't help but wish I could go along. I wanted to query Balls and see what he thought about that. But it was still early, only a little after seven. Uncovered Janey's cage and fixed coffee. Going to be another pretty day. Clicked on my handheld maritime radio to listen to NOAA weather. That depression, now well out into the Atlantic, was gaining strength. Still questionable whether it would develop into a tropical storm. I took my coffee out on the deck and sat in one of the webbed lawn chairs. I really ought to get nicer chairs for out there, but, heck, I thought, maybe these are good enough. As I sat there, I couldn't help but debate with myself about calling Balls and try to tag along with him. Kept thinking of reasons I could give him as to why it would be a good idea. Didn't have much luck, but didn't give up.

Finished my coffee, poured another cup and started back out on the deck. As I passed my phone, I said to myself, why not? So I punched in Balls' cell number.

"Trying to have breakfast in peace," he said. "You don't have any more hot tips do you? Or are you just content to bug me?"

"You know I was thinking, Balls . . ."

"Yeah, here it comes."

"Well, I was thinking, Balls, that since I've sort of been involved in this thing from the beginning, what with Linda Shackleford and all, and since she knows Martha, the office manager there at Roy's and that Linda could call her and alert her to the fact that a friend of hers—*moi*—and my friend Ballsford Twiddy would like to come by this morning and chat with her a bit, and—"

"You're pushing it, aren't you?" Balls said, interrupting me. But he didn't sound angry. In fact, I could tell he mulled over the idea. I could almost sense that he shrugged. "All right. Why not? It'll be just a friendly little chat. Want to know who was asking, and why."

"Great," I said. "After all, we've been together at church and going to prayer meeting tomorrow night . . ."

"That's enough," he said, the faux gruff tone back again. "I'll be at your place at nine." He signed off.

I was pleased. Finished my coffee in quick gulps and picked up the bass and ran through a couple of jazz riffs. Janey chirped and bobbed her head at the activity and the sound. She even did a little flip along the side of her cage.

When I called Linda, she promised to call Martha at J. L. Roy's. Then she asked, "Have you seen today's *Coastland Times* yet? It's got my full article in there. I mentioned your name, too."

"Uh-oh. How come my name's mentioned?"

"Because you went with me. First-person account of finding the bodies. All that stuff. Used that scene picture you took. The last one. Not of the bodies."

She was proud of her story, and I was happy for her. "I'll pick up a copy this morning. Congratulations, Scoop."

"Oh, that's my name for you."

"Yes, but you deserve it now."

At five minutes until nine, Balls drove into my cul-de-sac. I went downstairs to meet him.

He got out of the Thunderbird. "Don't I even get offered a cup of coffee?"

"Thought you'd be ready to roll. Coffee? Sure. Come on up."

Took only a few minutes to make fresh coffee. Balls tried poking a big finger in Janey's cage. She treated him with frank indifference, stayed on the far side of her cage. Balls gave up on Janey and plopped down on the sofa. I brought him coffee.

"Don't have any cream and sugar?"

"I've got sugar, yes, and one percent milk."

"Crap. I'll take it black."

Then he looked up at me. I leaned my elbows on the counter. It was easy to see he was busting to tell me something. "Okay," I said, "what is it?"

"Got the ballistics on those three slugs—the two from the couple and the one from Earl Ray Willard."

"That was fast."

"Put a rush on it. Priority." Then, the grin appearing, but something else behind it: a serious determination, an air of I'm-zeroing-in-on-it, and things, by golly, are going to begin to fall into place soon. "Wanna guess what the ballistics show?"

"Tell me."

"All three slugs came from the same weapon, a .38, and I'll wager a revolver, probably an old Smith & Wesson."

I left my coffee on the counter and sat quickly in the chair opposite him. "The same killer." It wasn't a question. "Same killer did all three people."

He nodded slowly and solemnly. A sip of his coffee and then set it on the glass-topped table.

We were quiet a moment or two and then I said, "So there's a connection. But what? These aren't random."

"No, they're not random. And as far as a connection, I don't know what it is yet, but I know that somehow or other the key that unlocks this is right there in the church." He shook his head and frowned. "Don't know how, or why, and I got nothing really to pin it on specifically, but I know in my gut that the church is going to lead to the killer."

I shrugged my shoulders in mild show of disbelief. "The church?"

"Oh, I don't mean the church per se. Or necessarily somebody there in the church. But there's a common thread that leads back to the True Gospel Church of Jesus Christ, or whatever the name is."

"That's the name," I said.

He glanced at his watch. "Let's call on J. L. Roy." He

stood, started to pick up his coffee cup, but left it there on the table. "Thanks for the coffee." He grinned. "Next time how about getting something besides that wimpy one percent milk crap. Get some real cream." He took an exaggerated step over the neck of my bass, and we left.

J.L. Roy's Heating and Air Conditioning is on the By-pass north of my place, beyond Eckner Street. We arrived in Balls' Thunderbird. He backed around in the parking area, nose out. Balls said, "You speak to Martha, or whatever her name is, real pleasant, and then keep quiet."

I nodded.

We went in. Martha's desk, a gray metal one, heavy duty, was inside to the left. She was ready to take her seat, a folder of some sort in her hand. She appeared to be in her mid-fifties, little if any makeup; her face lined a bit from the sun. She gave us a quick, nervous smile. "Mr. Weaver? Mr. Twiddy?"

Balls and I both tried for friendly, reassuring and disarming smiles. Maybe they worked.

After I'd spoken to her, she said, "Yes, Linda Shackleford called this morning." She pursed her lips severely. "I've spoken to Mr. Roy. He's not very pleased that I'd said anything about one of his employees—now, a deceased employee—to Linda, or anything about his business—"

"Well, we're certainly sorry about that," Balls said, "but we needed to chat with Mr. Roy informally for a couple of quick minutes." He donned his most sincere expression. "And we don't mean to pry into his personal business."

She gave a quick, jerky nod of her head. "He's said you could come on in." She led us a few paces down a hall to an office. The door was open. Mr. Roy, a heavyset man in shirt-sleeves, stood up from his desk and extended his hand. No smile. But his expression was not unkind. We shook hands and he motioned to two metal chairs facing his desk. His desk was the same heavy-duty metal as Martha's.

Balls introduced us, and handed Mr. Roy one of his SBI cards. "We apologize, Mr. Roy, for taking any of your time, but as you know there's an investigation into the death of Earl Ray Willard, who was employed by you, so I'm obliged to check every detail I can. I do hope you understand, and that in no way do I want to, or intend to, delve unnecessarily into matters that don't in some way have a bearing on the late Earl Ray."

It was one of the longest and most eloquent spiels I'd ever heard from Balls.

Mr. Roy said, "Yes? And you want to know . . . ?"

"I understand, Mr. Roy, that your employees are very fortunate in that they have life insurance policies that you've made available to them."

"Correct." His eyes met Balls and stared at him unblinking.

"That's very kind of you, Mr. Roy."

"Straight term policies. I believe in them," he said. "They're really not that expensive, all things considered."

"Let me get right to it, Mr. Roy, so we don't waste any more of your time. What I'd like to know is the name of the person who came in to see you last week asking about Earl Ray Willard, and whether that person did, in fact, ask you about an insurance policy for Mr. Willard, with his wife as beneficiary."

Mr. Roy leaned back in his chair, folded his hands across his stomach. "I'm not sure, Mr. Twiddy . . ." He referred to the card Balls had given him. ". . . Agent Twiddy, whether that's any of your business."

Balls smiled. But I'd seen that smile before. It didn't really mean anything. "I understand. It's not any of my business, personally, but it *is* the business of the State Bureau of Investigation that is examining the untimely death of your employee." The smile vanished. "If you don't mind, sir."

Mr. Roy appeared to roll that around in his mind before he answered. He puffed out a breath of air. "You make the case, Agent Twiddy. The person who came to see me is a man I've known for some years. A good Christian gentleman who is a deacon at this new church—the True Gospel—and he came to see me because he is concerned about the welfare of a member of his church, a woman who happens to be the wife, now widow, of Earl Ray, and the mother of two small children. Earl and his wife have been separated for some time and it seems that Earl Ray, while a good worker and very skilled, wasn't too good at making child support payments. This friend of mine wanted to know if there was anything I could do to prompt Earl Ray to be better about the child support payments." He leaned forward and put his big forearms on the desk. "During the conversation the business of life insurance came up, but that was not the sole purpose of his visit."

"Thank you very much, Mr. Roy, for that explanation." This time it was Balls who leaned forward in his chair. "Now if you could just give me the name of that good Christian friend of yours."

Mr. Roy hesitated so long that I didn't think he would answer. He stared at his desk and moved a ballpoint pen back and forth across the top. He looked up at Balls. "His name is Dewey Womble. He's a man about my age. When you see him and talk with him, you'll be like me—that is, you'll realize there's no way Dewey could be involved in anything . . . anything like Earl Ray's death."

"Would like to talk to him, though," Balls said.

I watched both of them. Balls kept his eyes on Mr. Roy, who met Balls' gaze, then looked back at his desktop again, touching the pen, thinking.

Mr. Roy raised his head, moving his mouth slowly like he chewed on a palatable thought. "Dewey did say something that was sort of ironic, the way things turned out. It was just as he was leaving, and in an offhand way, he said that he guessed Mrs. Willard would be better off if Earl Ray was dead."

Chapter Thirteen

Outside of J. L. Roy's Heating and Air Conditioning, we settled into Balls' car and he started the engine, easing out of the parking area before he said anything. "That went better than I thought it would," Balls said, keeping his sight on the road ahead.

"Dewey Womble a 'person of interest'?" I asked.

"Dunno. Certainly want to have a little sit-down chat with him." Balls chuckled. "Wonder if the good Christian gentleman has a .38 caliber Smith & Wesson revolver."

"Yes, but what about the other two killings? The couple at Nags Head Woods?"

Balls made that "humpf" sound of his. "I'm taking you home."

But as we came to the light at Kitty Hawk Road, Balls maneuvered over to the far right and turned. "Up this way, might as well swing by the church, see if anyone's there."

Two midsize sedans, not new, sat side-by-side near the side door of the church. One of the sedans, a Chevrolet, I assumed was Rev. Kessler's. It was the same one that was parked there yesterday.

"Wanna go in with me?" Balls said. "Just be quiet, like you were with Mr. Roy." As we moved toward the church, he conceded with a trace of smile, "Matter of fact, you did good."

We went in the side door and were met by the church

secretary, a woman probably close to thirty but with no makeup, mousey hair, slumped shoulders, so she appeared more like forty-five. Balls told her we'd like to see Rev. Kessler. She looked over her shoulder toward the open door to an office behind her. "Rev. Kessler, there's someone here to see you." She went back to her computer. "Excuse me," she said to us. "I'm in the midst of the church bulletin."

I heard stirring in the other office, and Rev. Kessler e-merged. He wore khakis and an open-neck short sleeve sport shirt.

Balls introduced me, and Rev. Kessler commented that he had seen me on Sunday. He asked us to come into his office. Balls said, "Don't want to take up much of your time, Reverend. Actually I was just wondering if I could talk to one of your members, a deacon I believe . . ." and Balls pretended to be looking up a name in his little spiral notebook. "Oh, yes, Dewey Womble."

"Well, I'm afraid you'll have to wait until Wednesday evening. Mr. Womble left Sunday after church to go to Rocky Mount in order to spend a couple of days with his brother." Rev. Kessler shook his head sadly. "His brother has cancer, real bad. But Mr. Womble will be back for our service tomorrow night." He smiled at Balls and then me. "I would like to have both of you back here for Wednesday night service."

Balls nodded his head, returned the smile, and said, "You can count on that, Reverend. We'll definitely be here."

Outside, I said to Balls, "If Dewey Womble left after church for Rocky Mount, he wasn't around to kill Earl Ray Sunday night."

Balls opened the door to his car. Looking over the low roof of the Thunderbird, he made that sound of doubt he makes in his throat. "Yeah, *if* he went to Rocky Mount after church. Big if." We got in the car. "Now I'm going to drop you off, head on back to Manteo." He sighed wearily. "I don't know," he said. "Nothing so far to get my hands on." He shook his head. "Three people dead. Two directly involved in the church. The other one's wife is having the deacons looking out for her . . ." He shook his head again. "And maybe I'm putting too much emphasis on the church. Maybe has no bearing at all. Gotta look at it from a different angle, take a different track." He obviously was talking more to himself than to me.

He slowed as the stoplight at Fifth Street went from amber to red. I raised an index finger. "About at my turnoff," I said.

"Huh? Oh, yeah."

He could swing that Thunderbird around expertly.

When he dropped me off at my house, I said, "Stay in touch."

"Yeah, sure," he said, but he wasn't focused on me.

I spent the remainder of Tuesday catching up on correspondence, updating records of my writing business. But every so often I would stop and daydream a bit about our time in Paris. It was my fifth visit there, and I loved it. Sitting quietly at my writing table at the Outer Banks, and staring out the windows at the blue sky, I could conjure up sounds and sights and smells of Paris. I could almost feel myself sitting at one of the little tables on the sidewalk outside the bakery on rue Lagrange, sipping on an espresso and smelling the yeasty odor of fresh-baked bread and pastries from inside the café. I could hear the determined, no-nonsense click-clack of young women in boots or high heels striding up the sidewalk, off to work or some place of great importance and urgency. There would be the rumble of motorcycles and motorbikes on the street, and the whisper of bicycle tires on the pavement. And occasionally I would hear the "ooo-eee, ooo-eee" of police vehicles racing down Lagrange or up on Boulevard St. Germain, sounding every bit like they do in the movies.

Our apartment on rue des Grands Degres had double windows that faced the Seine and Notre Dame, and at night, like some giant illuminated sea creatures, the cruise boats would come along the Seine, their powerful lights turning the leaves of the trees along the Seine to shimmering gold. In just a few minutes the boats would be gone, moving upriver, and the leaves would drift back to a rich green there in the night. Elly and I had watched the light show and listened to the sounds and we made love in Paris.

Yes, Paris was magical.

But to me, too, so were the Outer Banks. And it was the here and now I had to concentrate on. Late afternoon I called Elly at work. One of her colleagues—I think it was Becky—answered on the first ring, and in a sing-song, teasing voice told Elly she had a phone call.

As soon as she came on the line, Elly said, "About tomorrow afternoon, your rehearsal, I'm not going to be able to be there. We've got a meeting for all the staff at four-thirty, and it'll probably last at least an hour. Something about the plans for the new county administrative headquarters."

So, I didn't have to tell her that it might be awkward for me, also, since there would be a service at the church that I wanted to go to with Balls.

"Sorry," she said. "I'd really like to hear you play." There was that trace of the hoigh-toid accent in her words "like" and "play."

"That's all right," I said. "There'll be plenty of other times if I decide to go with it. Still not sure about that." Then I said, "Tonight?" although I was pretty sure what her answer would be.

"Oh, Harrison, it would be nice, but I really need to stay home with Martin. He hasn't completely forgiven me for leaving him for Paris."

"Thursday, definitely," I said. "But call me tonight, tell me goodnight."

"Absolutely," she said. "On both counts."

Late Wednesday morning, I picked up the bass and tuned it using harmonics. Then I tested my tuning-by-ear against the electronic tuner. Pretty close. The low E was only a tad flat, so I felt good about my tuning-by-ear. Then I played a series of scales using the bow, no vibrato. Did a couple of exercises with the bow. Put the bow down and began pizzicato, playing traditional twelve-measure blues in various keys. Felt fairly comfortable about playing. So I got out the canvass case from the closet in the second bedroom and my bass was ready for traveling. Lying there on the floor in its black case, it made me think for a moment of a body bag and what I'd seen over the past few days. But I erased that image and spoke to Janey. She had enjoyed the activity and the sound of the bass and had chirped and head-bobbed along with some of the jazz. Well, she didn't have the rhythms down. I had to smile to myself thinking that she was about like Steve Martin, all off-rhythm with his black "family" in *The Jerk*.

Shortly after two, I took the bass down the outside stairs to my car. I'd folded the back seats forward earlier so the bass fit perfectly from the rear. Checked my watch. Started the drive to Manteo and Jim Watson's house on the west side of town.

When I arrived at Jim's, there were two cars parked near the rear. I figured one of them was Jim's or his wife's and the other maybe the drummer's. As I was getting my bass out of the rear of the Outback, another vehicle, an older model Suzuki, eased in beside me. A grinning Mouse Beckham waved from behind the steering wheel. His friend Billy, sitting low in the passenger seat, smiled and waved, also.

"Can I help you with that?" Mouse called.

"I got it okay," I said, and we three proceeded into the house, the neck of the bass pressed against my neck, right hand tugging up on the shoulder of the bass. Heavy. But I'd carried it many a mile.

Inside Jim's "studio," the drums were set up and Bert Campert, the drummer, sat at the traps, adjusting the high-hat cymbal. He appeared to be in his late forties, a droopy mustache and bald and shiny pate. We shook hands. I repeated his name. "Like the German bandleader after World War

Two?" I said.

"Sounds the same," he grinned, "but not spelled the same way."

"A good legacy," I said.

Mouse sat at the piano and ran his long, tapered fingers over the keys, lightly. He frowned, apparently deep in thought. Then he looked up at me. "That was horrible. You and that lady reporter finding those bodies at Nags Head Woods. I love Nags Head Woods. Billy and I take walks back there." He made a face, "Now I'm not sure how I feel about going there."

"Got to always go back, force yourself," I said. "Chase the spooks away." I think I said it more for my sake than for his.

Mouse did a quick nod. "Know what you mean. You're right. Always got to chase the spooks."

Jim said, "Let's get started right away. Mouse has to leave by four-thirty. He's got another gig. At the church."

"Full-time, now," Mouse added, with a grin.

I had the cover off my bass, and tossed it aside. Mouse looked at me and hit a low G on the piano. I tuned to it, and the rest of my strings. Transporting the bass, different temperatures and humidity, two of the strings had gone slightly sharp, or either the piano was a little flat.

Jim was already tuned. He stood at a stand with a binder on it, working the valves on his trumpet with his fingers, like a nervous habit. The valves made a soft, fat clicking sound. I'd met Jim a couple of times briefly before. He was in his mid-fifties, tending toward portly now; a round, pleasant face, with the trace of a perpetual, open and friendly smile playing across his face. His expression and whole demeanor drew you to him, made you like him from the start. He had played with bands up in Richmond, where he had lived for many years before moving to the Outer Banks. Jim said, "The binders have a playlist and fake book." By the so-called fake book, we knew he referred to sheets of music that contained only the melody lines and chord symbols. Mouse nodded and so did I. All we would need.

Mouse's friend Billy had taken a seat not far from the piano and appeared to try to make himself look as inconspicuous as possible. He shrunk into himself, shoulders hunched, but with the trace of a smile on his lips.

The first tune in the book was "A Foggy Day," a nice medium bounce number. "Give us a four-bar intro, Mouse," Jim said, and counted off a beat. I came in on the first and third beat of the intro, then played it four-four as we started into the chorus, with Jim taking the lead. Bert played softly using sticks instead of brushes.

We went through a number of tunes, including a few slow ballads. Bert kept a good steady beat, not rushing on the fast ones or dragging on the slow ones. I was surprised, I guess, at how good we sounded. Really damn good. I was beginning to get into it, and enjoy it. It was like a new experience, a different environment, a beginning all over again. On even a couple of the songs, like "Dancing Cheek to Cheek" (and I love the chord progressions on that one; fun to play) that I'd performed with Keely before she became fatally depressed, I was somewhat detached and not bothered by the old ghost of a few years back. Maybe, just maybe, I was getting over that feeling of never wanting to play again.

After an hour, we took a short break. I saw Mouse check his watch. I said to him, "Congratulations on the church job."

"Thanks, Weaver. Not that much of a job, but if we pick up a few gigs with this little group . . ." He gave a brief self-deprecating smile. "Then maybe I can make it financially without having to depend on my parents as patron saints. That's rather embarrassing for a guy almost thirty, still depending on his parents." He glanced at Billy, who had stepped over to a cooler of bottled water that Jim had supplied. "And friends," he added.

I wasn't sure what to say. I didn't expect Mouse to be quite so frank about his financial situation, but I should have known better, and I did. That's because there exists a quick bonding among artists, writers, and musicians, I've learned.

It's like we're all in it together and understand how tough it can be.

"Well, they surely must be impressed with you at the church," I said, somewhat lamely. And I assumed, without having been told, that we talked about the True Gospel Church, where I'd seen him on Sunday.

"Most of them seem very nice," he said.

"Most of them?"

"Yes, most of them. There was one member . . ." He lowered his voice and leaned closer to me, ". . . wanted to know about my bringing Billy to church. I told him I thought everyone was welcome. He said, 'Yes, it's God's house,' or something like that. And I said, 'Well?' He didn't know what to say. But I know what he was thinking, that we seemed like a couple and that bothered him."

Without thinking about how it sounded, I said, "Screw him."

Mouse chuckled and gave an exaggerated toss of his head, rolled his eyes. "He's really not that attractive," and then we both laughed.

"Okay," Jim said, "we've just got a few more minutes. Flip to 'How High the Moon,' and let's knock it out."

And we did, and we played a couple of Latin tunes, having trouble getting the rhythm just right, and called it quits.

Jim said, "Okay, guys, we're good. I'll be calling in a day or two because I'm pretty sure I've got a couple of gigs lined up, and nice paying ones, too."

Outside, as I was putting my bass in the rear of the Subaru, I looked over my shoulder at Mouse, who stood nearby offering to help if I needed it, which I didn't. Billy was already in the passenger seat. Somewhat quietly, I asked Mouse, "Was that church member's name—the one you mentioned—was it Dewey Womble?"

Mouse shook his head. "No, Mr. Womble was very nice. It was another one. I didn't catch his name. Doesn't matter. I expect he'll be there this evening—and so will Billy, with me."

Chapter Fourteen

Barely had time to swing by the house and carry my bass up the stairs, something of a chore. I either had to bend backward at an uncomfortable angle or go up the stairs in reverse. I compromised and went up half at an angle, half sideways. Bumped the bass lightly once. Decided I had to do the backbend next time.

Inside, I told Janey I'd see her later. Didn't bother to take the cover off the bass. A quick trip to the bathroom and I was off again, headed to the True Gospel Church of Jesus Christ. When I got there, several cars were already in the parking area, including Balls' Thunderbird, nose out as always.

Mouse was at the piano, awaiting cue, I supposed. Billy sat quietly on the chair closest to the piano. He had that rather angelic half-smile on his face. If he suspected that he and Mouse made anyone uncomfortable, he gave no indication of being aware of it. Mouse had probably not said anything to him about what the church member had said.

I looked around, watching the people, deciding where to sit. I saw Balls at the back, an empty seat beside him. I moved over there and sat beside him.

"Glad you could make it," he muttered. "You could use some salvation."

Rev. Kessler came in from a side door. He wore a tie and suit coat, gray slacks. He was followed by the four deacons: three men and the woman with reddish hair. The men wore jackets but no ties.

To Balls I whispered, "Which one's Dewey Womble?"

"Don't know yet," he said under his breath. "What's your guess?"

I studied the three men, gave a slight shrug. They were the three I had seen on Sunday. If I had to guess, based on what Mr. Roy said, I'd pick the oldest one, the pear-shaped deacon. All of them, including the woman, had pleasant expressions, almost smiles.

With a nod from Rev. Kessler, Mouse began playing a processional piece. Lots of heavy chords, more lugubrious than uplifting. The deacons sat in front. Rev. Kessler took his place at the podium. When Mouse finished playing, Kessler said, "Thank you, for the music, Mr. Beckham. And I'm pleased to announce that Mr. Beckham is now with us full-time as our music director."

Mouse smiled and nodded a thanks to Kessler and to the congregation.

I watched the deacons. They turned toward Mouse and smiled quickly. Billy started to applaud the announcement but when no one else did, he folded his hands back in his lap.

To Balls I whispered, "The short one's Dewey Womble, I bet."

"Probably," he said in a soft aside.

I wasn't at all familiar with what was supposed to take place during a Wednesday night prayer meeting, and to be honest I didn't pay that much attention to what was going on. I was too busy looking around at everyone, trying to fathom what, if truly any, connection there was with anyone here with the murders of three people. We stood and sang a hymn, which wasn't very pretty, no more so than most of them. Then Rev. Kessler talked about Paul's letter to the Corinthians. His sermon—or lesson—was more like a Bible study session than a sermon. I did gather that much.

The collection plates were passed and Balls and I put in bills when one of the taller deacons came our way. It was the one with fair skin and combed-back hair. He nodded pleasantly at us. His eyes were a very pale blue. We all stood and sang something else, something I remembered from childhood that was always sung when the collections were made and taken up front. In a short while, the service was over. It had lasted an hour.

Balls moved toward the front and I followed him, going against the traffic. The deacon with the tanned and lined face had stepped up to the piano and spoke with Mouse, who stood solemnly and listened. Billy sat hunched in his seat.

I continued forward, smiling, and muttering an apology to a couple as I squeezed by them.

Balls had approached Rev. Kessler, who chatted with the woman deacon and the short, pear-shaped man we had guessed was Dewey Womble.

The deacon who had spoken to Mouse came over and stood beside Rev. Kessler. The other deacon had taken the collection plates to the office. He stacked them on the desk, and paused as if he couldn't decide whether to join Rev. Kessler, Balls, and the others.

I caught up with Balls just as Rev. Kessler introduced Balls to the woman and the short man. Kessler said, ". . . and Dewey Womble."

"Glad to meet you both," Balls said. Then he introduced me. The woman's name was Carol something. Dewey Womble shook hands. His palm was damp. I wanted to dry my hand off against the leg of my khakis, but I refrained. Kessler introduced the deacon with the tanned face. "This is Deacon Hunter Richardson, and . . ." He looked around and smiled at the other deacon who had come up beside him. ". . . and this is Deacon Darien Brody."

We all stood there rather awkwardly, smiling at one another.

Then Balls bobbed his head smartly and addressed Dewey Womble. "I wonder if we could step over to the office there and chat just a minute or two."

"Rev. Kessler told me you wanted to talk to me." He

gave a short, nervous laugh. "Hope I'm not in any trouble with the FBI."

The others gave polite chuckles and shifted on their feet as if they didn't know what else to do.

Balls tried a reassuring smile. "It's SBI. State Bureau of Investigation. No, sir, in no trouble at all. Just wanted to see if maybe you could help me."

"Do my best," Dewey said, bobbing his head and trying for a smile himself.

We stepped away from Kessler, Carol-something, and the other two deacons. We didn't go into the office but stood just outside of it. Deacon Darien Brody went back into the office to tally the night's offerings.

"I understand, Mr. Womble, that you had a conversation with J. L. Roy about one of your congregation, a Mrs. Delores Willard, widow of Earl Ray Willard."

Dewey's face clouded in what appeared to be concern, whether because he was being asked about his conversation or whether Mr. Roy had divulged it. "Well, yes," he stammered. "It was about a week before that tragic thing happened to Mr. Willard." He cocked his head to one side, looking up at Balls. "What did J.L. say about our conversation?" He straightened his shoulders. "Which frankly I thought was confidential."

"Oh, it was confidential," Balls said. "And it will remain so. It just seems . . . seems fortuitous that you're asking Mr. Roy about Earl Ray . . . well, and asking about his insurance and all, and then Mr. Willard ends up dead a few days later."

"Hey, wait a minute," Dewey said loud enough that the deacon in the office looked our way. Dewey put his hand on Balls' arm, and shook his head sternly. "Now you're not suggesting—my Lord!—that I had anything to do with . . ."

"No, sir," Balls said. "But I would like to know why you asked about the insurance."

Dewey appeared to run a memory through his mind. "I didn't go to see J.L. about the insurance. That came up later." He lowered his voice and leaned toward Balls. "We—

that's those of us who have some responsibility, and rightly so, to be concerned about the welfare of our congregation— we were concerned that Earl Ray wasn't making his child support payments to Mrs. Willard. She is needy, and so are those children. I knew Earl Ray worked for J.L. and I've known J.L. for years, so it seemed natural that I would be the one from our church leadership to . . . to see what could be done."

"I agree," Balls said, attempting to be his most understanding. "And you say the insurance matter . . . just came up later."

"Yes, about the time I was leaving. The insurance policies J.L. has for his employees are most generous." He gave a wry, half-smile. "I know," he said. "I know, I made one of those stupid statements one should never make, and one that really haunts me, because when the insurance policy was mentioned, I said something like Mrs. Willard could be better fixed financially if Earl Ray was dead." He shook his head and stared hard at Balls. "But I certainly didn't mean anything by it . . . and I wish I hadn't said it."

"I understand, Mr. Womble." Balls tucked his chin down, stared kindly back at Dewey, put out his hand and said, "I really appreciate your taking the time to talk with me."

"Any time," Dewey mumbled, but I don't believe he meant it. He appeared relieved and somewhat surprised that the conversation with Balls was ending.

But then Balls did one of the classic Colombo routines as we turned to leave. "Oh, just one other thing. Did you happen to relay your conversation with Mr. Roy to anyone else?"

"Well, sure," Dewey said, a trace of annoyance in his tone. "We had a meeting of the deacons and Rev. Kessler when I returned. And I told them what J.L. and I talked about and the fact that he'd see what he could do."

"And you mentioned the insurance?"

He pursed his lips in thought. "Yes, I guess I did."

Before we left, Rev. Kessler cast his eyes in our direction, and then put a quieting hand on Carol-something's forearm, who had been talking to him non-stop, and excused himself to approach us.

To Balls he said, "I hope you got the information you wanted." Then Kessler paused as if he wanted to say something else.

Balls filled the gap: "Tell you the truth, Reverend, I'd really like to sit down with you and have you tell me as much as you can about various members you have here. Doesn't have to be tonight, of course, but tomorrow or the next day—you name the time—would be helpful."

"Well, I really don't know what I could possibly tell you, but of course I want to be helpful." A flicker of concern clouded his face.

"And I appreciate it, Reverend."

Rev. Kessler nodded and managed a weak smile.

The church was almost empty. Mouse remained standing near the piano. Slowly he gathered up his music; Billy waited near him watching. Balls and I went outside into the twilight and stood for a few minutes silently beside Balls' car. He puffed out a breath of air, rubbed his mustache and stared toward the ocean.

I couldn't wait any longer. "Okay, what do you think?" I said softly.

He shook his head. Didn't want to talk. Then he said, "Dewey Womble?" He gave a dismissive shrug. "Dunno." That was it. Balls got in his car. "I'm going home tonight. Try to think things through." He started the engine. "Be back tomorrow, all probability." He drove away.

I had started to my Subaru when Mouse and Billy came out the side door. Mouse had his head down, one hand on Billy's shoulder speaking to him. I waited for them. As they came up, Billy glanced at me. Even in the gathering darkness I could see his eyes were red and tears sparkled.

Mouse noted the concern on my face. He said, "Not sure I want this gig at all."

"What happened?"

"Somebody said something to me and especially to Billy."

"Who was it?"

He shook his head. "No matter who. Doesn't bother me that much anymore. You get used to it." He opened the passenger door to his Suzuki and Billy got in without saying anything. "But it was unkind." He turned to me, his jaw set firmly. "And it hurt Billy." He shook his head again, went around and opened the driver's door, sat down quickly, jabbed his key in the ignition. He raised one eyebrow. "So much for this True Gospel bullshit."

Chapter Fifteen

When I got home, the voice mail message light was blinking. I punched the button and listened. Jim Watson's voice said, "Got great news, Weaver. Friday night we got a gig at the Hilton Garden, a benefit for one of the charities. Doesn't pay much, but gets our foot in the door. A buffet of some sort. So we'll just be playing from six-thirty to eight-thirty." He paused, caught his breath. "You're in, aren't you? Call me."

I sat in the chair by the phone and thought about it. "Okay," I said to myself. "I'll give it a shot." And I returned Jim's call and said I'd be there. I asked about bringing Elly, if she was interested. He said he didn't think there'd be any problem. He chuckled, "You know the old ruse, she just has to say, 'I'm with the band.'"

Glanced at the time. Not even eight. I called Elly at home. When she answered, I said, "You want to be a groupie Friday night?"

I told her what was up. She laughed and said she thought it would be fun. "It's a date, then," I said. "I'll pick you up about five-thirty, at your house, right after work. Get back up to Hilton Garden about six."

"Tight schedule," she said, "but we can make it."

I felt good, and I spoke to Janey. Checked her seeds and water, gave her a sprig of millet seed as a treat.

Knew I needed to get something to eat. Suppertime, and beyond. Fruit and cheese, with a small piece of ham, a bit of mustard. Enough to suffice. As I sat on sofa, food on the coffee table, I surfed television without really watching. I clicked off the TV. The image of Billy with tears in his eyes, Mouse's anger, came back to me. I felt some of the anger, too. I couldn't ignore it. They weren't hurting anything. Two gentle souls, trying to be together.

Then suddenly, and I don't know why it hadn't hit me before, a connection of dots linked together in my mind. I left my food on the coffee table and went to the phone, dialed Balls. He answered with a gruff, "Now what is it?"

"I got a theory, Balls," and then I told him about how Mouse and Billy were upset as they left the church.

"Yeah? That's small-minded and mean, but what's your theory?"

"Look, Balls," I said, "first there's this couple who apparently were having an extramarital affair, and they're members of the church. Then there's the business of Earl Ray Willard not paying his child support to a member of the church. Now someone in the church—don't know who yet—is coming down hard on Mouse and Billy because . . . because of their partnership, or something."

"Yeah, well, we know there is some . . ." His voice trailed off, thinking.

I filled the void, my words tumbling out: "Suppose, just suppose, there's someone at the church who—I don't know who—wants to take vengeance in his own hands, wants to rid the world of couples who are playing footsie when they shouldn't be, rid the world of deadbeat dads, especially when they have an insurance policy that helps a destitute family, and just suppose, too, this whacko would like to rid the world of people who . . . who have a different lifestyle?"

"Aw, come on, Weav. That's a pretty big leap you're making."

"I know it is." I realized how fast I had been talking and I tried to slow down. "Just the same, we see a link. There's no doubt about that."

He made one of those "humpf" sounds in his throat.

"Who? Dewey Womble? Rev. Kessler? Who?"

"It's possible," I said, "or someone else. One of the other deacons, or someone we haven't even noticed yet."

"Yeah," he said, "and we can interview everyone in the church and ask them how they feel about adultery, deadbeat dads, and gays."

"Okay," I said. "I know it sounds like a pretty wild theory but—"

He interrupted me, and said rather softly, "Actually, Weav, it's not all that wild a theory, I don't think." He gave a short, mirthless laugh, "Because that's what I've been chasing around in my head, too. Same time, I didn't know about the thing with Mouse and his friend." There was a pause. "I'd like to know who it was who said something to them." I could almost see him shaking his head. "Of course it's a long, long leap from being—what do you call it?— homophobic to taking a gun to people."

"Maybe," I said.

Before we signed off, Balls said he was going to be talking to people there at the church, the deacons and others, including Rev. Kessler. "Meantime, Weav, check with Mouse and find out who it was said something to them."

I sat again at the sofa. Knew I needed to finish eating. But I kept thinking that there was someone out there who thought they were God.

All day Thursday I didn't hear anything further from Balls. I refrained from calling him; knew he was talking to officials at the church and elsewhere probably, and figured he'd call me if there was some real break, or if he just needed to sound off to someone. I was good at being a sounding board for him. Also, I'd had a call on Thursday from my editor Rose Mantelli. She wanted me to do an update on an unsolved murder near Franklin, Virginia, that we'd written about earlier. Okay, another assignment, and I promised her I get on it the first of the week. Of course, she wanted to know what was going on with the "slaughter there in Magnolia-ville." Told her I'd certainly keep her posted, just as soon as I finished my mint julep. She cackled and coughed.

By Friday morning I still hadn't been able to get in touch with Mouse. I'd left him a couple of voice mail messages, asking him to call me. Then in mid-afternoon, shortly before getting ready to load up the bass and go pickup Elly, I did get a call from Balls. He wanted to know if I'd talked with Mouse about who had said something to him and to Billy on Wednesday evening. Told him no, but that I would see Mouse tonight and find out for sure. "Mind filling me in on what's going on?" I asked.

"Not a whole lot, unfortunately," he said. "Been spending some time in church. Not praying, maybe, but sort of asking for guidance." Then in a semi-serious aside, "Forgive me, Lord." He chuckled. "Did have a nice long talk with our good reverend. He was working on his sermon. Thought of you. Kind of irony you'd appreciate. His sermon this week is on 'Vengeance Is Mine, Sayeth the Lord.'"

"You're serious."

"Yeah." He puffed out one of his sighs. "I'll tell you, Weav, there're some real hardnosed religious types there at that church. Now nothing wrong with that. And I consider myself something of a religious, or spiritual, person, but man, not as devout as some of them I've talked to." I could visualize him shaking his big, shaggy head. "I did get the feeling that the good Rev. Kessler has some thoughts he'd like to share. But so far, he's not sharing with me."

"Yes, but any suspects?"

"I don't need to tell you everything. This is an ongoing investigation." He chuckled again. He was in better spirits than I expected at this stage of an investigation—one that obviously wasn't going all that well. And, then, just as quickly he got serious. "We don't need any more killings. Not sure whether our guy is ready to stop."

That wasn't at all comforting. Not a good thought.

I told him it would be late when I got back tonight from playing at Hilton Garden, and he said to call him first thing in the morning with the name of the person at the church who had said something to Mouse. "I've got a feeling I know who it was. Like it confirmed." He hung up.

Shortly before five, I'd showered, dressed in black slacks and black T-shirt like Jim wanted us to wear, and had loaded the bass in the rear of the Outback. I was on my way. When I pulled into Elly's driveway, she came out on the porch to greet me with, "Your groupie is all ready to go." She looked at me, giving me an up-and-down appraisal, a smile on her lips. She shook her head. "I feel like maybe I'm going out with someone who's playing backup band for Simon and Garfunkle."

"At least I don't have to wear sparkling sequins or a cowboy hat."

"True," she laughed.

"Well, you look great," I said, and she did: in a loose-fitting top of cotton, which bared her shoulders just a hint, and trim slacks and low-heel shoes. Plenty dressed up for the Outer Banks.

As Jim had instructed, I parked on the south side of the Hilton Garden. A side door was propped open. Bert was in the process of unloading a drum case from his SUV. I slid my bass out and cradled it against my neck and shoulder. "It's show time," I said to Elly, who stood by me offering to help but trying at the same time to stay out of the way as I hoisted the bass.

Jim was already inside on a low-rise bandstand, and Mouse was fishing for an extension cord plug-in for his electric piano. A good Yamaha with a full keyboard, eighty-eight keys. With my bass, I squeezed between the piano and the set of drums that Bert assembled. I judged the space. Just enough room to lay the bass on its side when I wasn't playing. A woman who apparently was in charge of the event, spoke with Jim. Elly came around close to the bandstand. Mouse's friend Billy stood a pace or two behind her. In a mock stage whisper, Elly said, "Where do the groupies group?"

Jim heard her and laughed. "Grab a Perrier from the cooler and you and Billy can take that little table there," and he nodded toward two chairs at a small utility table, just off the bandstand. Jim's trumpet case and empty drum cases, plus a case for Mouse's piano, were stacked behind the table, which was certainly out of the mainline of traffic. A few people began to come in through the double doors on the other side of the hall.

After removing my bass cover, passing it over by way of Bert to Elly for storing with the other gear, I turned to Mouse. "Want to check my tuning?"

"Oh, heavens," Mouse said, "Wasn't that thing tuned at the factory?"

It was an old, old joke on the bandstand. I grinned.

We started with the low E, went up to the G. Pretty close all the way.

"Factory did a good job," he said.

Black music stands fronted Jim, me, and Bert. Mouse's playbook was on the piano in front of him. Jim called up three tunes for the first set, leading off with "A Foggy Day." He checked his watch. "About three minutes, and we'll kick it off." He checked his tuning again with Mouse, and he stood there rapidly fingering the valves on his horn.

I saw that Elly and Billy chatted. He seemed relaxed with her, and she was animated and used her hands as she talked. Billy smiled at her and nodded, but his face went back to sad as soon as the smile faded.

I leaned closer to Mouse, who remained seated at the piano bench, and spoke softly: "Agent Twiddy would like to know who it was at the church who said something to you and Billy."

Mouse pretended to be studying his music score, which I knew he didn't need to do. "I got your messages," he said. "Apologize for not getting back. But I really would rather not talk about it."

"I understand," I said, "and I wouldn't be prying if we . . . if Agent Twiddy . . . didn't think it was important."

Mouse shrugged. "It was just one of those things. It happens. People say things. If you wanted me to start listing folks who say things, or snicker, or exchange knowing glances at each other, or give us a dirty look, well, I don't think you have enough paper and pencil to list them all." There was a bitterness in his voice that set me back.

"But something is going on there at that church, or with someone maybe connected with the church."

Mouse played a soft chord, delaying a moment. Without looking at me, he said, "Weav, it really doesn't make any difference." Mouse turned his face toward me. "But please don't say anything about it around Billy, or ask him. He's really depressed." He looked back at the keyboard and said softly, "I'm worried about him."

I was too well acquainted with those suffering deep depression to say anything further. I decided to let it drop.

Jim spoke out, "Okay, let's hit it," and he kicked off the tempo for "A Foggy Day." We hit it, and hit it well. Sounded good. Bert and I played just a hair ahead of the beat, giving the combo a light lift, moved us along. There was a scattering of applause. Elly and Billy were enthusiastic. Jim winked at Bert and me. Then he quickly counted off a slower beat and we went into "Talk of the Town," a real oldie.

The job went well. Crowds arrived. They appeared appreciative of the way we sounded. I realized I was actually enjoying it. An hour into playing—and the first two fingers on my right hand were getting a bit tender—we took a short break and I went over to the table where Elly and Billy sat.

"Oh, you sound wonderful," Elly beamed. "I like being a groupie," she laughed.

Billy started to get up. "Take this seat," he said.

"Oh, no. Keep your seat." I snagged a nearby chair and pulled it over. As I sat, I glanced at Billy's face, which had gone sad again.

Mouse came over to the table, stood behind Billy and

lightly put a hand on his shoulder. To Elly he said, "How we sounding? Marvelous, right?"

"Absolutely," Elly said. "You all are really good."

"That's because we practice together so much," Mouse said with a wry smile. He looked at me, grinned, "Well, one rehearsal anyway."

Elly had managed to get a couple of plates, loaded with hors d'oeuvres and tiny finger sandwiches. Plenty to eat. And we made short order of it.

When we went back, we did a bouncing rendition of "How High the Moon." Jim did a nice solo and so did Mouse. Mouse really had a great jazz touch and feel, light, simple, and then intricate enough that you weren't sure he'd work his way back in, but he always did. I shook my head in admiration. And I was pleased and surprised at the easy jazz style that Jim played. He didn't try to strain himself on the upper registers, played medium range, relaxed. Reminded me in a way of Bobby Hackett, and that's saying a lot. Then a little later we played a medium blues in B-flat and I took a twelve-measure chorus, with Mouse doing chord fill-ins but leaving it mostly to me. I was pleased with it, and so were Jim and Mouse. They both grinned. Elly applauded from her table.

When we played the last tune, the woman in charge came to the microphone and thanked us, and there was a good round of applause. In fact the people kept it up so the woman asked if we'd play one more piece. Jim called up "Jumpin' at the Woodside," a rollicking jazz number that's really for a big band, but we did all right. The audience seemed to love it. When we finished, we grinned at each other. I nodded over toward Elly who stood, applauding and smiling. We began to pack up.

Outside afterward, and after Jim had paid us fifty dollars each, I slid the bass in the rear of the Outback. Elly kept saying how much she enjoyed it. And I enjoyed it, too. It was a new experience here at the Outer Banks and for some reason the old memories of playing with groups along with

Keely didn't come back to haunt me like I was afraid they would do. Now, maybe, just maybe, it would be different.

I opened the passenger door for Elly. "How are your hands?" she asked.

Rubbing my thumb against the first two fingers of my right hand, I said, "Not bad. They'll get tougher." I realized, too, that a finger on my left hand was a bit tender. Not a blister, but not far from it.

As we settled in the car, I turned to Elly and said, "You and Billy appeared to get along well."

She said, "Oh, yes. He's sweet." She compressed her lips a bit, slight frown playing across her face. "But he seemed really depressed when he wasn't talking, answering something I'd asked."

I nodded, and started the car.

She spoke again. "He knows who you are, of course, and that you and Linda found those bodies in Nags Head Woods. He said he and Mouse loved to walk there but he didn't know whether now he ever wanted to go back." She brightened into a smile. "But I played Harrison Weaver and said sometimes it's best to go ahead and face our spooks—I think that's what you call it—and not let them get the best of us."

"Glad to know my wisdom is being passed around," I said, and I could tell that Elly grinned at me.

Pulling out of the parking area at the Hilton Garden, we headed south on the Beach Road. I said, "Okay to swing by my house and drop off the bass? Still early."

"I thought you'd never ask," Elly said and reached her hand over and put it on my arm.

As I struggled the bass up the stairs at my house, Elly quipped, "You need an elevator just for this thing."

Janey chirped when we came in. I'd left one lamp on. Never liked to enter a dark house. I got both of us glasses of iced tea. She sat on the sofa and I came over and sat beside her. We didn't say anything. We were both thinking, I know, about being together, alone, and the first time since Paris. A virtual palpable tension enveloped. Simultaneously, we put our iced teas down and went into an embrace like we were starved for each other.

When our lips parted, our faces still close, Elly gave the tiniest nod to her head, not much more than a tremor, and said, "Now."

I stood and took her hand and led her into the bedroom. She quickly kicked her shoes off, slid the slacks down, and removed her top. I undressed, too, but watched her the whole time. She unhooked her bra and stepped out of her little cotton panties. She was lovely.

She looked at me, smiled, and said, "Oh, my . . . just like Paris." Then she actually giggled, a girlish sound, but still managed to say, "I keep thinking Eiffel Tower."

I chuckled, too, and said, "And I think Paris, also, when I look at you. I'm reminded of those lovely, delicious French pastries . . . Come here."

Afterward, we lay there holding hands. Elly raised her head to check the clock on my bedside table. "I know," I said. "We've got to take you home."

She lightly kissed my lips. "Well, it is like Paris, the being with you."

At almost the same time we both said, "I love you." And we laughed.

We got dressed and went back into the living room. Janey eyed us. She didn't chirp and didn't bob her head. I said, "She knows that we've been up to something."

"None of your business, Janey," Elly said, leaning toward her cage.

Then the phone rang. It startled me, broke the serenity of the moment. I went to it. The ID was blocked. I picked it up and before I could say anything, that disguised, muffled voice said, "There'll be another." The phone went dead.

Elly stared at my face.

"I need to call Balls," I said.

She nodded. "No, it's not like Paris, after all, Harrison."

There was a sadness in her voice. "We're back with this . . . this evilness."

Yes, the magic of the evening had ended. Just like that.

Chapter Sixteen

After I called Balls and he said "Damnit," we got in the car to take Elly home. We rode in silence. I thought about what might happen next. I don't know what Elly thought about but I knew she was not at all happy about the murder business intruding into our lives.

So I said, "Elly, you know I'm a crime writer, and I write about this stuff, and . . ."

"I don't have to like it," she said when my voice trailed off.

I didn't say anything. There was nothing to say. I was a little pissed.

I took her home and we somewhat awkwardly kissed goodnight. It wasn't the same as it had been a short while earlier. Before I turned to leave, she said, "I'm sorry, Harrison, but every now and then . . . I don't know. I guess I just get tired of there being—what?—evil lurking just so nearby to us."

"I understand," I said. It was the best I could do.

"And I worry about you. You've been in real danger at least twice since I've known you. And you've been hurt, and could have been killed, and . . ." Tears welled in her eyes and began to spill over onto her cheeks. She rubbed them away with the back of one hand.

I held her again as we stood near the front door. This time it wasn't so awkward. She relaxed into me more. She eased her head back and looked up at me; a smile appeared despite the tear-glistened eyes. "Sorry," she said again. "It really was a wonderful evening, being a groupie and . . . and everything."

"We'll keep it that way. I promise." I knew there was no way I could possibly make such a promise, but I did it anyway. Not real proud of that, but I know I have a tendency to want to ease things, when I really don't believe they're going to be eased. A failing, sure. But I tell myself that I want things to be happier for those I love. So I go ahead and do it, time after time.

"Sure," she said, and I knew she saw right through me. As I opened the door to leave, she chuckled softly and said, with that trace of Outer Bank accent, "Might give some thought to being a romance writer, instead of crime. Or even erotica." A sly smile tugged at her lips. "You'd be good at it."

Driving back to my house in Kill Devil Hills, Elly was on my mind of course, but the thing that kept coming back to me was the sound of that muffled and disguised voice saying, "There'll be another." And why call me? It was obvious, Balls believed and so did I. The person making the calls knew who I was, knew I was involved in the discovery of the first two bodies, and knew I was in a position to spread the word. A game he played. He enjoyed the fact that he could stir things up without being caught. A thrill of some sort for him. He liked the danger of it, the excitement it gave him. Being in control, calling the shots. Gave him a feeling of omnipotence, of being God. I became more convinced than ever that we were looking for someone who, in his twisted psyche, believes his actions are somehow settling scores, setting the world aright. More thoughts tumbled in my head. Who would be next? Who was targeted? It would be someone in the killer's twisted mind needed to die. Playing God, he would make the world a better place by killing those he saw as undesirable and deserving of death.

Jeeze, it was a scary thought.

I realized I'd almost zipped through a stoplight at the Outer Banks Mall. Had to brake hard. Better pay attention to my driving; let the theories rest a bit. Then, for the umpteenth time, I tried to remind myself, as Elly did with me, that it was SBI Agent Twiddy's investigation; not mine. But I couldn't help it.

When I parked under my carport, I still mulled over the type of person who would do the three murders, and threaten that there would be another. Has to be someone who has flipped, a real psycho. And, without playing amateur shrink, the term "messiah complex" certainly came to mind.

Inside my house, I sank into the semi-comfortable chair that faced Janey's cage and stand. She watched me silently. I sighed, and realized I was tired. "Let's go to bed, Janey." She gave one half-hearted chirp. I checked her water and seeds and covered her cage, and I went into the bedroom, stripped my clothes off, and flopped in the bed.

It was already a bright sunny day when I waked just before seven. I went to the bathroom and then out into the living room. Sun cleared the scrubby pine trees on the southeast front of the house. I uncovered Janey's cage; she acted more lively than she did last night. I didn't. I shuffled to the kitchen to make coffee.

Leaning on the kitchen sink while the coffee brewed, I watched the pine trees and the canopy-like live oak through the window over the sink. No leaves stirred on the oak. Strangely calm for the Outer Banks. Something about the weather stirred an uneasy a feeling inside me. It didn't seem right. I poured a cup of coffee and took it out onto the deck. The sky sparkled blue; the sun shone golden. Yet . . . yet just the same in my bones the weather didn't seem natural. Almost too perfect. I went back inside and brought my maritime radio out, clicked on NOAA weather.

Sure enough, that tropical depression had developed into a cyclone, or category one hurricane, and it had a name, Nannette; it had picked up westward speed and intensity. NOAA gave the latitude and longitude as of 4:06 a.m. I repeated the numbers in my mind and retrieved one of my charts from behind the bookcase. Tracing the latitude and longitude with my finger, I pinpointed where the storm was earlier today. Over the past couple of days or so, it had moved beyond midway across the Atlantic and was headed toward the Caribbean islands. If it continued on this course it could slam into Florida, or it could take one of the customary northerly swings and rake the Carolina coasts.

Knowing that television in the area would be on this weather news—always a big event here on the Outer Banks —there would be extensive coverage. True to form, as soon as I clicked on one of the Norfolk stations, the screen was lit up with projected models of possible courses Nannette could take—and the Outer Banks was smack-dab in the middle of those computer-generated lines.

Here it was Saturday morning and I knew that for the next few days—at least—Nannette would be a prime topic of conversation and speculation. I realized how interest waxes and wanes, and the triple homicides here would likely fade from the number one topic. Balls, however, would dog the case unrelentingly. This would be true even though he got stretched thin at times and always seemed to be juggling more than one investigation simultaneously.

Time to eat a bite. So I moved mechanically in the kitchen. I toasted half a bagel slathered a light coating of honey-nut cheese on it, poured a small glass of orange juice; decided, too, to nuke one of the precooked sausage patties to go with my little repast, which I realized had become an increasingly routine breakfast for me. Needed to consciously vary it. Don't want to get into too much of a rut like they say people have a tendency to do who live alone.

When I finished, I decided it wasn't too early to call Elly, check with her, and just chat.

On the first ring at her house, the phone receiver clattered as if being dropped, and then a tiny voice said, "Hello."

Oh, boy, I thought. Here we go again. "Lauren? Is that you?" The little girl next door, Martin's friend.

The tiny voice again: "Yes."

"Is Martin's mother there?"

"Yes." Then silence.

"Would you get her to the phone, please?"

A pause, then, "Yes."

I waited. No movement could be detected. "Lauren, are you still there?"

"Yes."

Elly's voice was in the background, a laughing lilt to her voice. "Thank you, Lauren. I'll take it now."

I chuckled as Elly came on. "I know, I know," I said. "Lauren is good at answering but hasn't got the follow-up perfected yet."

The humor was still in Elly's voice. "And how are you, Harrison?"

In a tiny falsetto, I said, "Yes."

She laughed aloud.

"You been watching the weather, Elly?"

"Oh, yes. The weather folks are getting all excited. They love it."

"Looks like we might get something."

"Oh, Harrison, we may get a bit of a blow, but it may not be too bad. We've certainly had them before."

"Better rush to the grocery store and buy lots of toilet paper, candles, flashlights, and water."

She laughed again. "You mean try to beat the tourists and get stocked up?"

"Isn't that what you're supposed to do?"

She was having fun. "And don't forget the plywood. Got to get lots of plywood, board up the windows. Oh, gasoline-powered generators, too."

"Don't forget the liquor stores, getting in the long lines."

"Any excuse for a party."

Then more serious, I said, "Actually, we could get some of it, you know."

She responded in kind: "We're high enough here that we don't get flooding. Only thing I worry about is a couple of the pine trees. That big old live oak isn't going anywhere."

I said, "My house is on stilts, except for the utility room."

"Probably sound-side flooding if anything. But it's still too early to tell." A pause and then she asked, "Heard anything more from Agent Twiddy?"

"No, but I expect I will shortly. I'm sure he's busy." I knew I'd promised Balls I'd call him, let him know whether Mouse had given me the name of someone at the church who had spoken to them.

"Well, after all, it is *his* investigation," Elly said.

"I know, I know."

We talked a bit more and decided that I'd come over in the early afternoon and we'd take Martin and maybe Lauren to play miniature golf. Heck, a regular family outing for us. With the beautiful weather on a Saturday in early fall, it would be lovely—and so normal.

When we hung up I called Balls on his cell phone. "Yeah?" he said. "I'm my way up to Norfolk. Whatcha got?"

"Nothing."

"What are you calling me for?" That faux gruffness there.

"To tell you I got nothing. Mouse didn't want to say who at the church had said something to them. He said the list of folks would be too long."

"Yeah, probably so." Silence for a moment. "I got a couple of ideas." Another pause, maybe concentrating on his driving, or thinking. "Meeting with some federal types in Norfolk. Something of a joint operation. Gonna have to put the Outer Banks thing on the back burner for a day or two. But Rev. Kessler has promised to meet with me again." He puffed out a sigh that was audible even over the cell phone. "Not much more to go on but nosing around the church, and that's pretty slim. Maybe take another look at Chaz Caffey." His frustration with an investigation that appeared going nowhere hung there heavily in his voice.

I changed the subject. "We may be getting a blow in a

couple of days."

"Yeah, yeah. That's all we need. Stay in touch if anybody else gets done in there at the peaceful Outer Banks." He snorted and hung up.

Shortly after noon I drove over to Elly's. She met me on the porch when I pulled into the driveway. Standing beside her were Martin and his little friend Lauren. All three of them were dressed in shorts, and Martin had on his T-shirt with an imprint of the Eiffel Tower on it that we had brought him from Paris.

As I got out of the car and they came toward me, Lauren scowled as she spoke to Martin: "You never been to France. You never been anywhere."

"Have, too. Been lots of places."

Lauren tossed her head dismissively.

"Okay, you two," Elly said, "hush up and get in the back seat and buckle up."

She gave me a quick hug and peck on the cheek. I looked at her hips and rear as she held the back door open for Martin and Lauren, and then slid into the front seat. "Nice," I muttered.

"What?"

"Nothing."

"Why are you grinning?"

"Just happy."

"It's not just happy. I know that grin."

We drove through Manteo and headed toward the bridge over Roanoke Sound. The sun was high in the bright blue sky; the wind was calm; water in the sound sparkled from the sun.

"Beautiful day," Elly said.

"Couple of days from now, I expect it'll look a lot different."

"Maybe. I've got a feeling Nannette will veer off and head up the coast north of here."

"Even if it does, we'll get some of the backlash."

"Oh, well, no worse than a strong northeaster." I'd no-

ticed the Outer Banks natives referred to those weather phe-
nomena as a "northeaster," and not a "nor'easter." Also, they
didn't get as excited about a coming storm as did those of us
who were relatively recent "come-heres."

In the back seat, Lauren and Martin continued light
bickering about where he had been in his travels. Actually, I
knew that Greenville, North Carolina, a couple or three hours
away, was about it.

Elly turned to me. "They've requested we play at the
miniature course with the dinosaurs."

"It's right up here. They've had lunch?"

"Oh, yes."

"After we play, kids, maybe we can go to Sweet Frogs
for some frozen yogurt."

"Oh, boy," Martin said.

"With all that googy stuff on top," Lauren added.

"Winner buys," I said.

We parked and approached the kiosk to pay, where Elly
and I haggled happily with each other over who was paying.
She insisted that she at least pay part of the fare. Okay, I
agreed.

As we came to the fourth hole I looked across the course
to the sixth hole and did a double-take. There was Rev.
Kessler in shirtsleeves and shorts, concentrating mightily on
his next shot. He was playing alone, completely absorbed.

Elly caught my look. "What?" she said.

"The minister from the church. You know, the True
Gospel Church."

She glanced toward Kessler. "Oh," she said, her brow
wrinkled a tiny bit. She shrugged. "Well, I guess ministers
can play mini-golf same as anyone else." She went back to
helping Martin and Lauren make their shots.

Of course Martin and Lauren struggled making their—
multiple—shots. But to everyone's joy (well, maybe except
Lauren's) Martin made a hole-in-one on the 16th hole. He
whooped and hollered, and so did we. Then on the 18th,
when the hole was made, the balls disappeared. Lauren was

upset about that but we explained it was the end of the game.

"Okay," she said, "so now we get frozen yogurt with that googy stuff on top?"

"Absolutely," I said. "My treat."

We turned in the clubs and started out, and I saw Rev. Kessler. He sat slightly hunched at a bench, nursing a soft drink, lost in thought. I touched Elly's arm. "I need to speak to him," I said.

She nodded and began herding Martin and Lauren toward my Outback.

I approached Rev. Kessler. As I stood close he looked up, shaken from his reverie. Then he smiled quickly and extended his hand as be rose. "Please, stay seated," I said.

"I'm Harrison Weaver," I said, "we met the other . . ."

"Oh, yes, I remember quite well."

I don't think he did, but he covered it nicely.

"Getting in a little miniature golf, huh? We did, too," and I indicated Elly and the children, who were several yards away.

Kessler shrugged, a somewhat sheepish smile playing at his lips. "I find it best," he said, "if I get away from time to time and vent any frustrations at something like miniature golf." Then he looked up at me, his face dead serious. "Your friend, Agent Twiddy, wants to talk further." He shook his head. "I don't know . . ." He let his voice trail. He tried his smile again. "I hope you'll both come back to worship with us again."

"Plan to be there tomorrow morning," I said, although until that moment I hadn't given it any thought.

"Wonderful," he said softly, and then he opened his mouth and I was sure he was going to say something else, but no words came, just a very troubled and melancholy cast behind his eyes.

I took my leave. He remained sitting on the bench; his shoulders sagged.

Chapter Seventeen

Elly secured Martin and Lauren in the back seat of the Outback as I approached. I came around to the passenger side and opened the front door for Elly. She said, "Thank you, kind sir," and she gave me a questioning look concerning Rev. Kessler.

"Just passed pleasantries," I said. "But may go to his church tomorrow."

"I figured," she said as she slid into the seat.

I couldn't help but admire her thighs in those shorts. Nice.

When I got under the wheel and started the engine, I said, "He seemed very dejected about something."

"The way he sat there," Elly said. "And he's still sitting there."

Yes, something troubled Rev. Kessler. Of course I had no idea what it might be but my natural instinct centered his concerns on what most concerned me—certainly a typical human reaction, I knew. And my focus was on the murder of two people from his church and a third person with a destitute wife and children in the church. No way around it. That had to be burdening him. And maybe something else, too. But what?

We pulled out on to the Bypass. "Oh, boy," Martin said. "Sweet Toads."

"Sweet *Frogs*," Lauren scolded.

"Same thing," Martin said.

"Is not!"

"Okay, you two," Elly said, "be good back there . . . or . . . or . . ."

"You'll get warts on your hands," I said.

Elly laughed. "You're awful."

"We won't get warts, will we Mother?"

"Mr. Weaver's just teasing," she said.

"What are thwarts?" Lauren wanted to know.

"It's warts, dummy."

"Don't be calling anyone dummy, Martin," Elly said.

We parked at Sweet Frogs and Martin and Lauren raced in as soon as I opened the store's door.

We got cups of different flavored frozen yogurt, and each of us put ample amounts of "googy stuff" on top. At a table, with plenty of napkins, we began to dive in.

I looked out the window at the blue sky. "Hard to believe there's a storm churning away out there," I said, nodding toward the ocean.

"Almost always this way before, and really nice afterward," Elly said. "Be a couple more days."

"Your plans tomorrow?"

Elly took a good size bite of yogurt, which was too cold for comfort, wrinkled her nose as she moved the frozen glob around in her mouth, and then spoke. "Mother wants to go back to Greenville to see Aunt Gretchen. She's worried about her. Just for the day, but it makes for a long day."

Martin turned to Lauren. "See, we're going on a trip tomorrow. I go plenty of places."

"That's not Paris, France, Martin."

"Part way," he mumbled into his half-finished yogurt, the top layer of candy bits and other googy stuff was long gone.

I said, "With a storm coming, maybe you should stay there in Greenville until it's over."

Elly gave a short, dismissive chuckle. "No way. A couple of storms ago, friends of ours evacuated the Outer

Banks to go inland—Greenville, matter of fact—and there was more flooding there than here. They got marooned in a motel." She dabbed at her spoon with the tip of her tongue. "We'll ride it out here, if it even comes here."

"We'll get some of it, at least, according to all predictions."

"Probably right," she said. "Okay, children, finish up and thank Mr. Weaver."

Which they did, very dutifully.

When we got back to Elly's, it was close to three o'clock. She said she wanted to try to get Martin down for a short nap, which of course Martin objected to. To placate him somewhat, we all walked next door to take Lauren home. Her mother, a young woman with another child on the way, met us at her front door and thanked us for taking Lauren with us. "Always a pleasure," Elly said.

Back at Elly's, I said, "I guess I'd better head on to Kill Devil Hills."

"It has been wonderful," Elly said. "A very nice family outing."

"It did seem that way, didn't it?" We stared at each other, smiling. "I could get used to it."

She nodded. "Me, too."

It was the closest we'd come to broaching the subject of what the future for us might bring.

I drove back toward the beach and my house and felt good about the day. I marveled at the blue skies and the gentle water of the Roanoke Sound as I crested the bridge. The fact that a storm was out there somewhere over the ocean seemed unreal. Had to double-check. My Outback has the NOAA weather channel on it and I punched it in. Following some tide reports from Duck on down to Ocracoke Island, the reporting began on Nannette. Yes, it was getting closer and might develop into a category two hurricane by tomorrow.

When I got home I flipped on the television to track the weather further. The latest projections did show Nannette might, indeed, come ashore within in the next couple of days anywhere from south of here at Wilmington to the north toward New Jersey. It appeared Florida and South Carolina would be spared, except for some high surfs, wind and rain from the backside of the storm. Of course, I knew the paths of hurricanes can be erratic, and maybe it would swing more northeast and blow itself out over the cooler waters of the Atlantic's Labrador Current.

Janey chirped, trying for my attention. "Okay, gal, I've been ignoring you today. We might as well take you out on the deck to enjoy the sunshine—while it lasts." I put her cage outside and went back in and made a cup of coffee to take on the deck. I had just settled in one of my chairs when the phone rang. Glanced automatically at my watch. Five after four.

Caller ID displayed M. Beckham.

"Hello, Mouse."

"Ah . . . Weav, how you doing? Hope I'm not bothering you."

"Oh, no, just taking it easy, enjoying the weather while it lasts."

"Yes, it's very nice . . ." His voice trailed off.

I filled the void. "Really enjoyed playing last night. It was great."

"Yes. So did I. Hope we can do it again soon."

Again there was a pause, as if there was something else Mouse wanted to talk about but was having difficulty getting to it. So I took the initiative and said, "What's up, Mouse?"

I heard him take in a breath. "Well, it may seem—"

Then I heard Billy in the background say, "There he goes again."

"What's that, Mouse? What did Billy say?"

Mouse forced a short laugh. "Well, it may seem foolish to even mention it, but my goodness, it does make us nervous. There's a pickup truck that keeps coming by our house real slow . . ."

"You know who it is? Maybe the driver's just looking

for an address."

"I guess it spooks me with, you know, everything that's been going on."

"Where do you live, Mouse? Other houses around?"

He told me his address, just off Bay Drive.

"Heck, we're practically neighbors."

"I know," he said. "We've got one of the little beach boxes up on stilts, and there are vacant lots on each side of us. And that pickup truck, an older one, has come by here four or five times. Real slow."

I was at something of a loss as to what to say next. I did the best I could. "Mouse, I'm glad you felt like calling me, but I guess I wonder . . ."

"I know, I know." I heard him swallow. "But I figured that with your experience as a crime writer and all if you thought, I don't know, if maybe there was something we should do." He gave a short, embarrassed laugh. "I guess we're just upset and I wanted to talk with someone."

"Can you see who is driving? Get a license number if you can. I've got friends who can track that real quick."

"No, we're up high you know and we can't see inside the truck, or make out the license."

I heard Billy. "Here he comes again."

Mouse called out, "Billy, don't step out there . . ."

Billy's voice came through loudly and I sensed he was just outside the door. He was yelling something at the driver of the truck that I couldn't quite make out. Then Billy's rather breathless voice as he spoke to Mouse: "He took off. Gunned it out of here."

I tried a chuckle. "Sounds like Billy scared him off."

"I hope so," Mouse said. I could hear him breathing. "But it does seem strange. Unsettling."

"Yes, I can understand."

"I apologize for calling you. I'm being silly."

"No, it was fine for you to call. What friends are for. I have a feeling he won't be back, but if he does, call me right away and we'll have some officers from Kill Devil Hills cruise over there and scare him off for good." I chuckled again. "But I believe Billy's done that."

After a pause, I said, "Mouse have you ever seen that pickup truck before?"

"No, not that I recall. I don't know much about cars, especially trucks. I don't even know what kind it was, except that it looked old. It was definitely not a new one."

I hesitated a moment before asking him, but I did it anyway: "You haven't by chance seen that truck in the parking lot at the church, have you?"

"No, but I don't think I would have noticed." He gave another of those jabs at a forced laugh. "But I'll know it if I ever see it again."

When we hung up, with a promise from him he would telephone me if the truck came back, I went out on the porch to my now-cold coffee. I stared at the cup but didn't pick it up. The sun had moved to the west, casting shadows from the pines and live oak across my driveway.

The truck's repeated presence, almost as if stalking, was probably nothing, yet it did bother me, and it obviously had shaken both Mouse and Billy. I was haunted, I know, by the muffled and disguised voice: "There will be others."

Chapter Eighteen

By Sunday morning, the wind had picked up noticeably. Not strong yet, but it was coming off the ocean briskly, moving the tops of the pine trees and I could feel it when I stepped onto the deck. Smelled the ocean, too. Salt in the air, vaguely fragrant. The sun was out. Puffy bits of clouds scuttled in the south. I went back inside to shower and get ready to attend the ten o'clock service at the True Gospel Church of Jesus Christ. Playing observer again, taking on Balls' roll.

When I pulled into the parking area at the church, I checked out the vehicles there. Just on a hunch looking for an older pickup truck. There were two pickup trucks already there, but they were new, shiny and freshly washed. A number of sedans and several SUVs, large and small. Mouse's Suzuki occupied a space near the back. Glanced at my watch. Had a few minutes more to sit there and wait, watch some of the late arrivals. No older pickup. Silly to be doing this, I mused. The older model pickup driver was probably just lost or looking for an address, maybe hunting for his girl friend. Don't want to succumb to being paranoid, thinking every action points to a murderer.

At the door of the church I was greeted by the deacons Carol-something and the tall, tanned Hunter Richardson. Carol handed me a folded, single-sheet bulletin and said, "Welcome again. Glad you are joining us." Hunter smiled and shook my hand. I sat near the back so I could look around, studying everyone, playing a good imitation of Balls.

Mouse sat hunched at the piano, staring toward the door through which the choir and Rev. Kessler would enter. I didn't see Billy. I looked around. Billy wasn't in the church. The row of chairs closest to the piano was empty. Softly, Mouse began to play, and the door at the far side opened; the small choir filed in, the women in those choir robes, the men in suits again and most of them had on ties as well, a rarity at the Outer Banks, even in church. Rev. Kessler, dressed in his dark vestment and tie, entered behind the choir and sat on the raised area to the right of the choir and piano. The pulpit, standing unoccupied in the center, appeared to be equipped now with a microphone. Wasn't there the other Sunday. Church coming along, I figured.

On the front row, Deacon Dewey Womble rose and stepped haltingly onto the raised area, obviously favoring his left leg. He approached the pulpit and tapped the microphone; no response. He fumbled with a switch on its side, tapped again. The microphone squealed and screeched loudly. Dewey jumped back as if he had received an electrical shock. A man at a console in the rear of the church twisted a dial and the volume went down. Dewey leaned forward into the microphone. "Good morning everyone." He chuckled self-consciously, as his voice came through loud and clear. "We've just gotten this new speaker system, and I guess I'm not quite used to it yet." Murmurs of suppressed chuckles came from the congregation. "I want to welcome each and everyone of you, members and visitors, and we hope that all of you will come back to worship with us again at the True Gospel Church of Jesus Christ. We have just a few announcements about coming events here at the church, including an effort to have a stronger youth group . . ."

I stopped listening to the announcements and continued to look around. Earl Ray Willard's widow was present with her two children, sitting closer to the front. She held her head up. After the congregation stood for the singing of a hymn, Rev. Kessler rose to begin his sermon, but first making a pleasant remark about the weather, and cautioning that the weather would change in a day or two. The changeability of the weather was his segue into his sermon, and how we must all expect adversities, which can often be followed by blue skies, or something of the sort. I lost him part way through and wondered why Billy wasn't present, and I thought I knew. A shame. I was somewhat surprised that Mouse continued, but I was sure he needed the job. Then it occurred to me, also, when the collection was sent around, that one of the deacons—the tall, pale one—was not present. Darien Brody. That was his name.

The collection plate came to me by way of Dewey Womble, who stood at the end of my row as it was passed along until it reached me. Dewey smiled, nodded, and took the plate.

As the service ended, I made my usual trek against traffic to approach Mouse at the piano as he concentrated on gathering his sheets of music. He did not look at the scattering choir or congregation, and he didn't see me until I stood below him, and he turned to leave.

"Oh," he said, "my goodness I didn't expect to see you here again, Weav."

I extended my hand. "Where's Billy?"

A frown clouded Mouse's face. "He's not feeling well . . ." He stacked the sheets of music together, buying some time. "You know, Weav, and no sense skirting around it, Billy's really depressed. Not at just what was said here—and he swears he never wants to come back to this, this church— but, I don't know, I'm really worried about him."

I nodded. I knew how he felt. Helpless.

He smiled, shrugged his shoulders. "At least we haven't seen that truck anymore." He tossed his head, a touch of embarrassment. "I still feel foolish for having bothered you yesterday."

"Certainly no bother," I said. "And I checked the parking area here. No old pickup trucks."

"Probably nothing. It's just with, you know, everything

that's been going on . . ."

"I understand," I said. I thought about the muffled voice, with its warning of others.

"I'm going to hurry on back home," Mouse said, adding, "and, oh, Jim Watson called that we may have another gig this coming Saturday. Depends on the weather and what happens with the storm."

As Mouse left through the side door of the sanctuary, I headed toward the main entrance where Rev. Kessler spoke to one of the last couples. I waited my turn to speak to him.

"Enjoyed the sermon," I said, "and I hope you enjoyed the miniature golf yesterday."

He smiled as he took my hand, and then darted his eyes around sheepishly as if concerned that someone else might have heard the remark about miniature golf. "Does help me relax," he said. He didn't look all that relaxed at the time, or now either.

"I noticed one of the deacons wasn't here today. Darien Brody, I believe?"

I swear that for a flicker of an instant, Rev. Kessler had an expression of alarm on his face. He recovered quickly. A weak smile making an attempt of a return. "Oh, yes. Yes, indeed." He licked his lips. "Deacon Brody's sick today." The smile back bravely now. "First Sunday he's ever missed." He bobbed his head. "Yes, first Sunday ever. I'll check on him today."

"Hope he's better," I said. We shook hands again, and I started to turn to take my leave.

He held onto my hand an instant longer. "Interesting you'd note he wasn't here."

I shrugged and smiled. I mumbled something like, "I just notice things. Part of my training, I guess."

He nodded, and I thought he might say something else. But he didn't. The man who had controlled the newly in-stalled speaker system approached Rev. Kessler and I left.

Outside, the first thing I noticed was that clouds had moved in completely. The sky wasn't pretty any longer. The

wind had picked up more. It wasn't strong, but it was definitely present. I got in my car. There were only three other
cars left; one was that older Chevrolet that I had presumed
was Kessler's. I thought about him. He was uncomfortable
about something. I couldn't figure out what. He had certainly
appeared, if just for an instant, to be especially uneasy when
I mentioned Darien Brody's name. I hadn't meant anything
by it. I had just made that mental note from the beginning of
who were the major players in the church, and one was missing this morning. It had been more of a thrown-out remark
as a conversation filler. But it sparked something.

Instead of going straight home, I drove up the Bypass
toward Southern Shores and took Fonck Street off to the
right to the Beach Road and parked in the space designed for
unloading, just south of Hilton Garden Inn. I wanted to take
a look at the ocean. Mine was the only car there in the small
parking area, in front of a sign that said parking was limited
to five minutes. Figured I wouldn't be a whole lot longer
than that.

Strolling up the slanting wooden walkway to the obser-
vation deck, I could hear the roar of the ocean. It had started
kicking up and changed from a light green at the shoreline to
a dark metallic out at sea. White foam crested waves out
three hundred yards, and surf pounded on the beach, smacking the sand. A few birds, gulls and stiff-legged sandpipers,
searched the beach just out of reach of the water as it rushed
in. Some of the sea foam was beginning to blow inshore. I
thought about my car and wanted to move it before the salty
foam blew against it and clung like residue of glue. I could
feel the growing wind on my face and it got inside at my
neck and billowed out my shirt. I could smell the ocean, and
I breathed deeply, and turned and walked back to my car.

When I got home, my message light was blinking. Balls'
voice, the reception crackling over the hands-free speaker in
his Thunderbird, boomed out: "On my way to Norfolk.
Might as well live there these past few days. But hopefully
we'll end it tonight. Pretty big operation should go down."

He paused and muttered a few words about another driver. "Wanted to let you know won't be down there—probably until this storm blows away. Get on that case. Give me a ring on my cell if you get this before two o'clock."

Not quite one o'clock. I punched in his cell number. He answered on the second ring. "Yeah?" The line sounded clear and static-free. Figured he was out of his car.

"Got your voice mail. Anything happening? You know, on the case down here?"

"Hoping you'd have it all wrapped up by now." He chuckled. "You been over at your sweetie's already today?"

"Actually, Balls, I went to *our* church. Just looking a-round, seeing what I could see." I told him about running into Rev. Kessler at miniature golf the day before.

"Well, I guess preachers gotta relax time to time, also." He spoke more softly. "But you figure he appeared worried about something." Another pause and he said, "Yeah, there's something bugging him. Aside from the obvious. Soon as this blow's over, I'm gonna have another serious sit-down with him." He snorted out a short laugh. "Have a come to Jesus meeting." Then, "Forgive me, Lord."

"We're going to get blasted a bit by Hurricane Nannette," I said. "It's already beginning to feel like it—and smell like it."

"Yeah, the air's charged, even up here. Smells like electricity. But maybe the eye'll stay off shore mostly."

"Still get wind, rain and flooding," I said.

The frustration and determination returned to his voice. "When this storm's over, and I get through with the feds up here in Norfolk, I'm damn well going to solve that case down there."

We ended the call and I sat there a while, thinking. I ignored Janey's chirping and her half-hearted head-bobbing.

There'd be enough drama the next few days, certainly, without a fulfillment of that muffled voice's promise: "There'll be another."

Chapter Nineteen

I spent much of the rest of Sunday alternately stepping out on the deck to marvel at the sky, the clouds, feel the wind, or to surf the weather reports on television.

At nine o'clock that night Elly called. "You just get in?" I asked.

"No, but we didn't get here until almost eight. Martin was worn out, and fussy going to bed because he slept off and on in the car on the way from Greenville."

"We're going to get a visit from Nannette," I said.

"Hatten down the batches, or something like that," she laughed.

"Yes, I've brought in my chairs from the deck. About all I can do."

"You mean those fashionable, state-of-the art lawn chairs from K-mart you have out there." She laughed again. In good spirits.

"Okay, smarty. They're good enough."

She got more serious. "You'll be all right," she said. "If you're worried, you can always come over here."

"I'll be fine," I said. "Actually, I'm interested in watching, see what happens."

"We'll have plenty of wind, rain, and ocean overwash. Probably from the sound, too, if the storm goes inland and we get the backside of the wind."

And that's exactly what the eleven o'clock news predicted: that the eye of Nannette would come ashore by Monday night or Tuesday north of Wilmington but south of us. I had to almost chuckle because it looked like it was heading right toward the Greenville area, where Elly's friends had fled in a previous storm.

But on Monday, weather reports said the storm had stalled offshore, although gaining strength. Now predictions centered on reaching the coast Tuesday night south of the Outer Banks as a category two storm. Later that day it was downgraded to a category one hurricane, still plenty powerful enough to do damage from wind and flooding. Sustained winds were just above hurricane force at seventy-five miles an hour and gusting closer to one hundred miles an hour.

By Tuesday morning my little house shuddered as powerful gusts of wind smacked it. Rain came down in horizontal sheets. At times it rained so hard I could hardly see out to the end of my cul-de-sac. Twice the lights flickered but didn't go out. County offices closed early on Monday and were not open at all on Tuesday. Elly was home. She and I chatted on the phone several times. She was fixing popcorn for Martin. Little Lauren wanted to come over but her mother wouldn't let her because small limbs and twigs were blowing around her house.

I knew traffic had been heavy on Sunday and Monday leaving the Outer Banks. A mandatory evacuation of tourists and non-residents had been ordered for Ocracoke Island and Hatteras. "I hope they haven't headed for Greenville," I said to Elly. She laughed.

As I became more and more absorbed in tracking the storm and watching shots of TV reporters standing out near the pounding surf and rain, dramatically bending from the force of the wind, I realized that the ongoing murder investigation had not been entering my mind.

Surely, this wasn't the time for the killer to make good on his promise.

On Tuesday night the storm came ashore south of the Outer Banks, as predicted. By Wednesday morning the wind was ferocious, coming now strongly from the northeast. A counter-clockwise spiral of wind spun out from the eye of Nannette. I called a friend of mine at one of the bookstores in Duck. Paige reported that she had looked out at the Currituck Sound near her shop and the water was very low indeed. The northeast wind had blown the water back up into the Pasquotank, Perquimans and Chowan rivers. I knew they would be flooding low-lying areas in Edenton and Elizabeth City.

But I knew, too, that as the eye of the storm moved on northward, and as the wind's counter-clockwise movement passed over us, that just the reverse would occur—that the backed up water in the rivers would come racing full-force into the sound. A wall of water would surge back into the Currituck and Shallow Bag Bay at Manteo, flooding streets and doing damage.

Reports earlier said that Highway 12 down at Rodanthe on Hatteras Island had been washed out. Much of Highway 12, or the Beach Road, as far north as Kitty Hawk was closed because of ocean overwash.

All day Wednesday wind and sheets of rain pounded us. The shifting wind did bring water surging back into the sounds. I called Paige again. She said she stood outside and watched what looked like a four or five foot wall of water racing into Currituck Sound. Low-lying streets in Manteo and Duck flooded. The water in Manteo came up to the steps to the courthouse, but didn't get beyond that. Over the inland counties, the storm, though still fierce, got downgraded to a tropical storm. I saw a shot on TV of the Bypass near Capt'n Frank's that looked like a shallow lake.

Late Wednesday afternoon as the storm began to subside, I put on rain gear with a hood, and ventured outside. Plenty of debris of small branches, pinecones and leaves, littered my driveway. Walking out toward the end of the cul-de-sac, I saw a neighbor's big plastic trashcan that had blown from three doors away. I righted it and left it beside the road. Gusts of wind and rain whipped at my face. On the main road, about two blocks from the Bypass, I gazed up and down the street. No one else was around. Pools of water skittered and danced. Small pieces of debris banged against my jeans. My sneakers were soaked. It was foolish to be out in it, I knew, but my curiosity couldn't be curbed. I looked at the sky and watched plum-colored clouds forming and re-forming and moving fast.

I walked up to the Bypass, still not seeing any other fools out, and looked both ways up the highway. Deserted. The blinking red lights of a police car or rescue squad vehicle were visible in the distance toward Dare Centre. After a while I came back to my place, took one last look around at the yard and the sky, and went inside and peeled off my wet clothes, got in a hot shower, and vowed to stay in the rest of the evening.

A couple of tries were necessary before I could get a dial tone on the phone. Then I called Elly. "You doing all right?" I said.

"Fine here. Tired of popcorn . . . and we had hotdogs, too. Regular hurricane party. Oh, and ice cream." Then, "And you?"

"Fine, too. Did go out a little while ago and look around. Weird with no one around."

"I assumed as much—that you'd be nosey enough to go outside." She chuckled softly and I could imagine her shaking her head. "No paper was delivered today, so I finally finished Sunday's crossword."

"I believe it is really dying down now."

"I've checked about the courthouse offices. No damage there. The water didn't get in although the streets are still flooded."

"Water'll go down by tomorrow."

"That's one of the advantages of living on a sandbar," she said. Then, "Excuse me a sec. No, Martin don't put the popcorn in the ice cream."

She came back, a lilt to her voice. "Maybe since you've been concentrating on the storm, your first real one since moving here, it at least should have kept you from thinking about murder and mayhem for awhile."

"Farthest thing from my mind," I said.

And it stayed that way long until almost seven o'clock the next morning.

It was Balls on his cell: "Been another one down your way. Woman found washed up on the beach. North of you."

"Drowned? In the storm?"

"You'd think. 'Cept she's got eight or nine stab wounds, report I'm getting. So drowning wouldn't count for much."

Sitting on the edge of the bed, I looked out the side window at the sky. It was a vivid blue. With the phone in my hand, I moved to the living room area. Mostly bright sunshine, typical and most welcome after a storm. A few puffs of white clouds moved fast across the southern sky from winds aloft. "You coming down this way? With roads . . ."

"I know about the roads. But I'm in my four-wheel-drive big ol' Dodge. Ain't taking that sweet Thunderbird out in this."

"How was she found in this storm?"

"One of the managers at a beach front motel called 911 when he saw a body out on the beach, washing around in the surf."

"This the one the killer promised?"

"Don't know yet, but I kinda doubt it. Expect you do, too."

"Not his style." It wasn't a question.

"Hasn't been—not yet, anyway."

"Where's the body?"

"Still out on the beach. Kitty Hawk. Right there south of Hilton Garden."

I thought about how I could get there.

He must have read my thoughts. "You don't need to show up," Balls said.

"Aw, come on, Balls. I'm the one been getting the calls . . ."

He was quiet a moment. I could hear road noise over his hands-free cell. "Okay. Just stay out of the way. If you can even get there."

"I can get there." It might be touch-and-go, but I was sure I could get up the Bypass, even through that flooded area near Capt'n Frank's, in my Outback. Just hose it down good later. Then I said, "How far away are you?"

"Only about twenty minutes or so. Roads not too bad. Crap, like limbs and stuff, every so often. Couple of telephone poles leaning sort of crazy. Roof off one or two houses just before Grandy. Flooding back toward Elizabeth City and Edenton. My place okay." A pause again, probably as he maneuvered around some debris: "Yours?"

"Fine. No problem at all. I didn't lose power. There's water on the streets in Manteo, up at Duck. Little lake near Capt'n Frank's."

He made a sound that I took to mean "Good."

"I'll see you there," I said. I was already headed back to the bedroom to get dressed.

"Stay out of the way." He clicked off.

Several leaves and pine needles were on my car. I peeled leaves off the windshield and a couple of small twigs. The others would blow off as I drove, and I was already planning a good washing for the car.

Traffic was almost nonexistent on the Bypass. I turned left and started up toward Kitty Hawk. That small lake or pond had subsided somewhat from how it appeared yesterday on TV, but it still covered the five-lane road from curb to curb. Ahead of me a big 18-wheeler slowed as it approached the water. It was the only other vehicle near me. I slowed even more, staying well behind the big semi. I watched his wheels. The water was not deep but there was plenty of it, and fountains of water sprayed out from his wheels as he made his way through the pond that stretched close to fifty yards along the highway. Sunlight caught the spray from the wheels on the east side of the truck and made rainbows in the water.

I drove slowly into the water. The Outback moved smoothly. I could feel the water against the car and hear it, but it was no problem and when I got on the other side onto pavement not covered by water I realized I was smiling. I looked down side streets to the east and saw that barricades were up. At Eckner Street, the stoplight blinked caution. Maybe it had shorted out. Near the ocean, a police vehicle was parked, its red and blue lights flashing, blocking any possible access to the Beach Road, which I knew was closed with overwash and lots of sand.

I already knew where I would try to park to get down to the scene where the woman's body lay. Just as I approached the intersection of the Bypass and Highway 12—the traffic light was blinking there, also—I swung to the right in behind Rite Aid drugstore, and parked as close as I could to the Beach Road. As I got out of the car and started walking to the south side of Hilton Garden, I could see flashing lights of police and emergency vehicles. Trying not to step in pools of water too deep, I made my way to the Beach Road and the flashing lights. I wore a rather scruffy pair of shorts, my still-wet sneakers, no socks, and a faded blue golf shirt. The wind gusted, but it was sunny and mild.

Plenty of sand and water covered the Beach Road, making it virtually impassable in most places. Crews would be out today beginning the clean up process, pushing sand off the roadway. Most of the water would soak into the sandy soil by tomorrow.

Four police vehicles were parked haphazardly near the unloading area a short distance south of the Hilton where I had stopped briefly before the storm to look at the ocean. Two of the police cruisers were from Kitty Hawk, two were from the Dare County Sheriff's Department. Then I saw a fifth one, from Southern Shores, on the other side of the Beach Road near Fonck Street. Balls' Dodge 4X4 squatted partly on the Beach Road. A Dare County emergency vehicle had squeezed in between two of the cruisers. Someone yelled instructions to a fellow officer, and I heard crackling radio static as I made my way past the police cruisers onto the beach itself. I stood there surveying the scene. A long ribbon of yellow crime scene tape, mostly blown down, looped close to the surf. Several people, many in uniforms, were down that way. I saw Balls, his big hulk in a windbreaker with SBI emblazoned on the back, and wearing a baseball cap that I'm sure had SBI embroidered on its front.

A body, shrouded in a dark, rubberized covering, lay on the sand near where the group stood. A Kitty Hawk officer stopped me as I approached the crime scene tape. I pointed at Balls and said, "SBI Agent Twiddy authorized me." The officer called down to the group. Balls turned and motioned me forward, nodding an okay to the officer.

Balls was busy talking with a person I assumed was one of the officials from the motel, maybe the person who had called 911. The woman's body had obviously been pulled up from the surf after she was found. Not much of a crime scene to protect with the yellow tape. One of her hands, poked out from the covering, was all that was visible of her. The hand was of a young person. I realized I was shaking my head. A sad ending.

Balls finished talking with the civilian, then glanced at his watch and spoke to one of the uniforms. The officers nodded and spoke into his handheld radio. He held up three fingers to Balls, and clicked off the radio. In less than three minutes, a Dare County deputy approached from the parking area. With him was a young woman in shorts, flip-flops, and a baggy shirt. The young woman's eyes were wide with distress, and her mouth was half open. She saw the covering for the body and she stopped and shuddered. The deputy stood beside her. She took a deep breath, squared her shoulders, and gave a short nod. They approached the body. I stood to one side, behind Balls, who had barely acknowledged my presence. Balls spoke to her. From what I could hear, she had reported last night that her roommate was missing.

Balls knelt beside the body, and put his hand on the edge of the rubberized covering, all the while looking up and studying the face of the young woman standing there. She gave the briefest nod of her head and Balls pulled the covering back, exposing the face of the dead woman. The face was gray; specks of sand clung to her cheeks and forehead; her short, light brown hair was matted and wet.

The roommate gasped out, "Oh, God!" She brought the palms of her hands to her eyes and shuddered and turned away. To something Balls said, she nodded and said, "Yes, yes . . ." He put the covering back in place and stood, rather wearily. The Dare County deputy spoke softly to the young woman. He tentatively patted her shoulder, very lightly. He acted as though he didn't know whether he should do that.

Balls lumbered over to the young woman. He had his small spiral notebook and a pen in his hand. I moved in closer while trying to stay out of the way. I wanted to hear the exchange. While I couldn't catch every word, I did get the gist of the conversation. She told Balls that she and her roommate and another girlfriend had holed up in a motel down the beach a short distance, refusing to evacuate, thinking it would be fun to ride out the storm. Balls moved his chin up and down and muttered, "A little hurricane party."

"Yes," she said. "We were partying and, yes, drinking some beer and wine and snacking and everything. Having a good time. We had met three young men—"

"Their names?" Balls said.

She appeared on the verge of crying again. "Oh, I don't know. We'd just met them . . . you know, Bob and Larry and something. I'm sorry, I don't know . . . I don't know."

Balls waited. His pen poised.

She continued, "But it wasn't them, I know. They stayed there with us for, well, for some time. Then they left and it was late. We'd been partying, you know, drinking, and we were all three ready to go to bed when Cecile's boyfriend from Suffolk . . ." Her voice trailed off as she gulped in breaths of air, fighting tears. "When Cecile's boyfriend, Keith Saliavo, started banging on the door, calling for Cecile. And he grabbed her and took her outside with him. Almost dragged her outside." Then her tears won out. Sobbing, she said, "That was the last we saw of Cecile."

Balls waited for her to stop crying, then he started asking for Cecile's full name, her address, next of kin, and how to spell Keith Saliavo's name.

While that information was being requested and noted, my attention shifted to the sight of a man, a young man, approaching our gathering from the south. I stared at the figure. He walked unsteadily, jerkily, almost stumbling as he approached. None of the others in the group appeared to take notice of him. He wore shorts and a shirt hanging loosely on him, and there were dark stains on one side of his shirt. He began to move faster, his gait unsteady and wobbly. His arms flopped at his sides.

Then I saw what he carried.

In his left hand he had a piece of clothing by one end. It appeared to be a bra or a woman's colorful halter top.

His right fingers clutched a long knife by the handle, its wicked blade reaching to his knee.

Chapter Twenty

Softly, I said, "Balls?"

He turned and glared at me.

I nodded toward the figure, now only about twenty yards from us. Two of the officers had also noticed him. The young man's hair was long and windblown. His eyes were wild and didn't appear to focus properly. I could see now that his shirt appeared bloody, whether from his own blood —or someone else's.

Balls muttered, "Oh boy." Without facing her, he said to the woman he'd been interviewing. "Stick around."

She gasped out, "It's him. It's Keith Saliavo." She shrank back a step or two.

Balls spoke to one of the nearby deputies and a uniformed officer. "Go get him," he said levelly.

Keith Saliavo, his jaw slack and his mouth open, fixed his wild-eyed stare at the shrouded body. Before the officers reached him, he sank to his knees, his upper body more or less upright. With officers on each side of him, hands on Saliavo's arms, they brought him to his feet.

"The knife," Balls said. "Handle it carefully."

The uniform removed a handkerchief from his pocket and eased the knife from Saliavo. He gave up the knife as if in a trance. He wobbled and the officers steadied him. That *was* a woman's halter in his other hand. The deputy, copying the uniform, took a handkerchief and grasped the clothing item with his fingertips.

With the officers on both sides of him, they walked him to Balls and the shrouded body.

Saliavo, his voice croaky and hoarse, nodded at the shroud and said, "Is that her?"

"Who?" Balls asked.

"Cecile . . . oh, Jesus, no."

Balls knelt beside the body and eased the covering back, exposing the woman's face. Balls kept his gaze on Saliavo.

"Oh, Jesus . . . Jesus . . . it is." He began shaking his head, making sobbing sounds, and the officers had to support him to keep him from sinking to the ground again.

Balls covered the woman's face and straightened up slowly. He lumbered to Saliavo, and stood there silently face-to-face. I eased a few steps closer. I could see that the left shoulder of his shirt was soaked with blood, and there was a long gash, red and open, on his forearm. There were other cuts on the hand and forearm that had carried the knife.

"Okay, son, tell me all about this. Why'd you stab her to death?"

Saliavo couldn't tear his gaze from the shroud. He barely acknowledged Balls' presence. "I didn't stab her. I was trying to protect her. I told her to run . . . and she started to run but he'd already stabbed her once or more, and I was trying to fight him."

"Uh-huh," Balls said. "And who was this?"

"I don't know," he said. "He just came up on us out on the beach . . . I've never seen him."

"You telling me, son, that a mystery man you've never seen before comes up on the beach late at night and just starts stabbing you and this young woman? No reason at all?" Balls shook his big head. "You know that's sort of hard to believe, son."

Saliavo bobbed his head. "I know. I can't believe it either."

"And you come walking up here carrying a knife that was almost certainly used in killing this poor woman, and what I guess is part of that poor woman's clothing or bathing suit, and you're telling me you didn't kill her but that some mystery man did?"

Saliavo bobbed his head loosely. "Yes, sir."

Balls puffed out a sigh and looked out toward the ocean. The surf was loud. Then Balls shook his head. "Okay, Mr. Saliavo, tell me some more . . . and make me believe it."

Saliavo started slumping again. The lawmen held to his upper arms. Saliavo winced when the officer touched his left arm.

"Get a medic over here," Balls said. One of the rescue team members scurried over.

"We were lying out on the beach by the dunes down there . . ."

"Down where?" Balls asked.

"About, I don't know, quarter mile, four or five hundred yards, south. Behind the dunes, near where they were staying. I had a big towel spread out."

To Deputy Odell Wright, who had just arrived a short time before, Balls said, "Please check it out, Odell. Take someone with you, and a camera."

Deputy Wright nodded and started south with a young deputy I didn't know.

"So what were you and this poor young woman doing?" Balls said.

"You know, we were making out, I guess you'd say. I mean we weren't really doing anything, you know, I mean . . . not everything." He cringed from pain as the medic cut away the shoulder area of his shirt and began applying a spray of some kind on the wound, and wrapped a bandage around his upper arm, crisscrossing over his shoulder and under his armpit. I noticed an egg-size lump and bruise near Saliavo's left temple. "Cecile was lying on top of me when this guy came up yelling something and grabbed her by the hair and yanked her hard and started swinging that knife."

"What was he yelling?

"Sounded like just a lot of words strung together. I can't

remember 'cept he said something about 'fornicators.' He kept saying that over and over."

Balls remained silent, his eyes boring into Saliavo's face.

"But we weren't, you know . . . fornicating."

"What did this man look like?"

"I don't know. It was dark. All I know is he was tall. Real tall."

"Then what?"

"Hell, he stabbed her. In the back and she screamed and I jumped up and told her to run, run . . ." Saliavo fought back tears. He swallowed, and shook his head. "The guy stabbed me." He glanced at his shoulder. "And I tried to fight him, get the knife and he cut me some more, and turned around and stabbed at Cecile again. I yelled to Cecile to run goddamn it, and she did, and I tried to fight the guy and . . . and he must have hit me." Using the fingers of his right hand, Saliavo gingerly touched the lump on the side of his head. "He must have. Hit me. 'Cause I didn't know anything until I woke up this morning, still lying there on the beach."

"What did you do then?"

"I started walking south along the beach. I was, you know, not walking good and I fell a couple of times, looking for Cecile." He glanced at the officer still holding the knife carefully in his handkerchief. "And I found that knife . . . and then I found the top Cecile was wearing."

"How far did you walk?"

"Shit, I don't know. Then I came back up this way and saw all of you all . . . and . . . and . . ." Staring at the body, he shook his head and tears came in earnest. Balls waited close to a minute. There was the constant sound of the surf and the wind, with distant crackle of police radios. But no one was talking. The officers stood still, waiting for Balls. He leaned in a little closer to Saliavo. "Son, we're going to have to take you in. Check your story. We'll have a doctor look at those injuries."

Very softly, Saliavo mumbled, "Yes, sir. But I didn't do

anything 'cept try to protect her," and he started crying again.

To the Dare deputy, Balls said, "Take him in. Get him a doctor."

"Cuff him?"

"No. No need to."

The deputy put one hand on Saliavo's left elbow and led him to his cruiser. One of the uniforms walked with them.

The woman friend of Cecile's glared at Saliavo as he was led away. Balls, a tired expression on his big face, moved through the brown beach sand to the woman's side. "We're going to need you to give a full statement down at the station. One of the officers will take you. Bring you back, too. He'll get the other friend of yours." Then Balls conferred with one of the Dare deputies, who nodded his head repeatedly.

Balls turned as one of the rescue squad medics approached him. The medic said, "The body? Can we take her?"

Balls said, "Yeah. Dr. Willis will look at her later. Send her to Greenville for an autopsy, I'm sure. " Balls puffed out a tired chuckle-like sound. "Not that he'll be able to tell us a whole lot more than what we already know. Stabbed multiple times, washed up in the surf." Then he seemed to be rethinking what he had just said. "But he or the lab will be able to tell us if that was probably the knife . . . and if there are any traces of blood on it." Talking more to himself, he said, "But State boys will have to do that. See if perhaps— just perhaps—there are traces of blood from two different people . . . and whether she was dead when she went in the water, and didn't drown."

Since the tide was out, it had been rising last night when Cecile and Saliavo were on the beach. And high tide, too. Wouldn't have taken much for the surf to drag her off the beach and toss her back and forth in the waves.

I walked closer to Balls and was getting ready to speak to him when we saw Deputy Odell Wright and the officer coming back up the beach. Odell carried a folded yellow and red beach towel over one arm. Odell came up to Balls. "We got pictures," he said. "Nothing discernible as far as footprints. Wind blowing sand around. Except it did look like there was quite a scuffle going on." Then he moved his arm that carried the towel. "Lots of blood on this. One place really soaked."

"To the lab," Balls said. "See whose blood." Odell nodded and started to the vehicles.

Out of the corner of my eye I saw the medics with a stretcher preparing the sad task of putting the woman's body on it and carting her away, where she would be diced and sliced even more during an autopsy. When they lifted the stretcher, one of her arms dangled out from under the tarp. I turned away and didn't watch them anymore.

I couldn't keep quiet any longer. Moving closer to Balls I said, "The man and woman each stab one another . . . with the same knife?"

Balls looked at me. Raised one eyebrow. "Possible," he said. "They struggle. One gets the knife, then the other . . ."

"Or a tall, very tall, mysterious stranger stabs both of them."

Balls made a dismissive "humpf" sound. "Maybe."

"Another thing, Balls. That word 'fornicators.' Can't really see Saliavo coming up with a word like that on his own."

Balls made another sound in his throat, but it wasn't dismissive. He was thinking. Then he shook his head and sighed. "Jesus, but I get tired of this crap. Always crap. That's all I deal with. Crap and scumbags." He spoke softly, but bitterness and frustration rang out sharply in his tone. "Maybe I've been in it too long."

I didn't say anything.

He looked around. "We might as well clear it up here." Then for what was really the first time, he looked at me, up and down, as I stood there, windblown, ratty old shorts, baggy sweatshirt and soaked and sandy sneakers. "You look like shit," he said.

I shrugged. "Hanging around you." Then, "I'm going home. Keep me posted."

"Yeah, sure." But I could tell he wasn't thinking about me or staying in touch. He did mumble quietly, ". . . a tall stranger who says fornicators."

"A very tall stranger," I said.

Chapter Twenty-One

Walking back across to my car in the Rite Aid parking area, I had to make several detours to avoid deep pools of water and piles of sand. But I noticed how quickly the sandbar we live on was getting back to post-storm normalcy. Heading home in my car, the traffic was still very light, but at least it was not deserted, as it had been twenty-four hours earlier.

One of my neighbors was out in the cul-de-sac clearing away bits and pieces of limbs, leaves, and other debris. I stopped, lowered the window and spoke to him. No damage to his place, he reported, and I relayed the same. We waved and I pulled forward and under my carport. I left my wet and sandy sneakers upstairs on the deck to dry in the sun. Going inside, I spoke to Janey and looked at myself in the mirror. Yes, I did look, as Balls said, like shit. Going to have to get a haircut soon, too, although with my hair this long, wind-blown and unkempt, I have what Elly calls "the tortured poet" look. I stripped off my clothes, threw them aside, and got in a hot shower for a long time.

Standing there in the shower, I thought about the latest murder. Could there be a connection? Certainly not the same as the others as far as weapon used. But one thing did nag at me: Again, it was a couple, like the first one. The second one was a lone male, but he was the deadbeat dad of one of the church members, where the couple was active. The attack on the beach, which according to Saliavo—and how reliable was he?—was totally unprovoked and again according to Saliavo apparently had something to do with "sinning," as in fornication. I tried to shut off my thinking about it: not try to make pieces of a puzzle fit together by bending the edges.

Out of the shower I got dressed again. Glanced at my watch. Decided to call Elly at work, assuming they would all be back at work at the courthouse offices again.

When I dialed Elly's work number, Becky answered and I asked for Elly. I heard Becky, in a sing-song voice, say, "Elly, you've got a very *special* person on the phone, wants to speak to you."

Elly came on the line. "This is a very special person," I said.

She chuckled. "Yes, I figured, Harrison. They like to tease me."

"Everything all right at the courthouse? Downtown Manteo?"

"A few of the businesses got some water damage. Those right on the waterfront. Lower ones. But all in all, we got through in fine shape." Her word "fine" carried that trace of Outer Banks accent. She added, "And I'll bet you've been out again this morning."

"Well, yes . . ."

"Uh-oh. Were you down on the beach? Where that woman was found?"

"How'd you know about that?"

"This is the courthouse, remember? Word gets around fast."

"Well, yes, I was down there with Agent Twiddy." I told her about Saliavo but she already knew he was in custody.

"Mabel said Agent Twiddy was already down here to interview him, or interrogate him further, or whatever it's called."

I wanted to change the subject. "Tonight? Tomorrow night?"

"Let's make it tomorrow night, Harrison," she said softly. I could tell she had turned her head away from her coworkers, who were probably trying to catch her every word. "I'll be home with mother and Martin tonight."

When we signed off, I was pleased that she didn't get into more about my "involvement" in another investigation. Maybe her views on that would come later.

I was busying myself around the house, taking care of Janey, fixing a bite for myself, when the phone rang. Checking caller ID, it read "K. Kessler." I was puzzled. He was calling me?

"Hello, Rev. Kessler," I said. I know I sounded guarded, hesitant, questioning.

"I apologize for bothering you, Mr. Weaver. Please forgive me."

"Nothing to forgive, Reverend," I mumbled, standing there holding the phone and wondering what this was all about.

"The reason I'm making this call is that I'm trying to get in touch with your colleague, SBI Agent Twiddy."

Letting the business of being Balls' "colleague" go unchallenged, I simply said, "Yes?" Might as well let him have the illusion of being colleagues.

"I've called the numbers he gave me, and I get his voice mail. I feel a rather urgent need to talk with him." Rev. Kessler's voice was strained, worried; it didn't have the resonance he used in his sermons. It was the voice of a man troubled, distraught.

I tried to keep my response more or less neutral. "I know Agent Twiddy is deeply involved in an investigation this morning," I said.

"Yes, I suspected he was. That horrible happening out on the beach. It's already on the news this morning, and what I want to talk with him about is not as pressing, I know, and it might not be anything at all, so I don't want to . . . but I do feel I need to talk with him."

"I can try to reach him, Reverend." Then I took a chance: "In the meantime, is there something I can help you with?"

There was a pause of several seconds as he gave thought to what I'd posed. "I appreciate the offer, Mr. Weaver. But I really feel like I should talk with Agent Twiddy. I certainly don't mean any offense by that, and . . ."

"No offense taken at all. Let me see if I can reach him. I'll call you right back." I stood there a moment, puzzled. What was up with Rev. Kessler? Obviously he was very upset about something. But what, I had no idea. Still, I sensed deeply that it was more than just urgent, as Kessler had said. I dialed Balls' cell phone. I didn't expect him to answer, so I was surprised and taken aback when his gruff "Yeah?" came on.

"Didn't think I'd get through to you."

"Just stepped outside the interrogation room. Been having Saliavo go over his story, again and again."

"You believe him?"

Ignoring my question, he barked, "What you calling about?"

"Rev. Kessler called me and—"

" Yeah, yeah. I got a voice mail from him."

"He wants to talk to you. He's concerned about something, and—"

"Yeah, I'm concerned about something, too. I've got four killings down here at your home in Paradise that I'm trying to investigate. Yeah, I'm concerned about something, too."

"Okay, Balls. Give me a quick kick to the kidney. Make you feel better."

He made a sound that could have been a chuckle. Then he was quiet and I could tell his brain was clicking. "What you think he wants to talk about? Rev. Kessler?"

"I don't know, but he did sound, well, desperate."

Another pause, so I added: "I don't think he would have called if he didn't think it was something important."

Balls was silent. I waited. His voice softer, he said, "Naw, you're right. He wouldn't call to pass the time of day. I've been questioning him about his congregation and . . . but

I gotta get back in there with Saliavo." He puffed out a breath of frustration. "Tell you what, call him and tell him I'll be with him either late this afternoon or early tomorrow morning. Find out from him what it is he wants to talk about."

"Not sure he'll tell me anything."

"Tell him I said to talk to you. That you're authorized."

"What the hell you mean, 'authorized'?"

"Works on TV." He spoke away from the phone to someone else: "Be right in," Then to me, "Let me know later what Kessler says."

We hung up and I stood there shaking my head again. "Authorized," I muttered aloud and went out on the deck to look at the sky. I took the handset with me. I remembered my lawn chairs were down in the utility room, so I put the phone in my pocket and retrieved the two folded webbed chairs, one in each hand; I hooked a couple of fingers around my small wrought iron table and struggled back up the stairs with my load, banging the table against my right leg a couple of times. Okay, looking pretty good. I did need to sweep the deck. Well, later. I sat, punched the phone to retrieve Rev. Kessler's number and called him.

The first ring had barely started when Kessler's breathless "Hello" came over the line.

"Reverend, this is Harrison Weaver. I did manage to catch Agent Twiddy for very briefly. He said he would try to see you late this afternoon or in the morning. Meanwhile, he said that I was authorized by him to inquire of you what it is you would like to talk about." I finished my spiel and waited.

He cleared his throat, stalling a bit. "If you are authorized . . . and can you please, please, use utmost discretion about what I tell you."

"Oh, absolutely. Total discretion."

"Mr. Weaver, I'm worried about one of my deacons."

My first reaction was total disbelief that this is what he was calling about: Worried about one of his deacons. Then— duh—it hit me. This could be the key that Balls and I suspected—involvement of someone there in the church. Again, I thought it best to keep it simple at my end, so I said only, "Yes?"

"It's Darien Brody. Not sure whether you remember him. One of the four deacons you and Agent Twiddy met." He cleared his throat again. "His wife, his wife called me very upset. He's missing, hasn't been home."

"Missing?" I know my voice was pitched louder than normal. "What do you mean missing?"

He paused again. Then the words began to tumble out. "I'm afraid, Mr. Weaver, it may be more serious than just missing." He took a breath. "She says he's not taking his pills, and he hasn't slept in days and she doesn't know where he is and she's worried about . . . about his sanity. That's the best way to phrase it."

"His medication?" I lightly chewed my lower lip. "What is it that she thinks or suspects?"

"I knew he needed to take medication. Taking it for years, she said. But I didn't think that not taking it would . . . would lead to something like she says, leaving home and all."

I paused. I wanted to select my words carefully. "What I don't understand, Reverend, is why you feel compelled to talk with Agent Twiddy about this. I mean, I know his wife is upset, and you are, too, but with these other investigations going on that Agent Twiddy is deeply involved in, well I guess I just don't see why—and forgive me if I sound callus —why Agent Twiddy would need to be notified. That is, Rev. Kessler, unless you believe Mr. Brody may in some way is involved . . . involved in these tragedies."

I could hear Rev. Kessler breathing in the phone. He waited so long to say anything further I wasn't sure but that he might simply hang up—offended or embarrassed.

Then he did speak. His voice quivered with emotion. "That's just it, Mr. Weaver. It distresses me almost beyond words, but I wanted to alert Agent Twiddy because . . . because . . . it's possible, and it pains me to the core to even mention it, that Darien, in his confused state, could in some way be involved, involved in these terrible things."

Now I was the one who took a deep breath because that was exactly what I was thinking. I forced myself to stay calm in my questioning, keep it straightforward, analytical. "That's a very serious speculation on your part, Reverend. Very serious." I waited a moment before saying, "What is it that makes you think that Darien Brody might be . . . be involved?"

With what sounded almost like a sob, he said, "I know it's serious. But his wife—and she's an extremely sensible, level-headed woman—said that he's started raving, and that's the word she used, about things like, and I'm para-phrasing what she has said, 'Where's a wrathful God when we need him?' She said, and again these are more or less her words, it's like he's being sucked under with thoughts of vengeance, of trying to set the world aright."

Oh, jeeze, I thought. I spoke quickly: "Rev. Kessler, I will definitely get this to Agent Twiddy, one way or another. And right away." Then, "Do you have any idea where Mr. Brody might be? Does his wife have any idea?"

"None at all. He's taken one of the family vehicles and she hasn't seen him for more than a day. He hasn't been eating, or changing clothes, or sleeping, she said. Just pacing about, or going off on his own. She says she thinks, really, that he's had a breakdown. A complete breakdown."

Promising Rev. Kessler that I would keep him posted, we hung up and I immediately called Balls' cell phone. It went right to voice mail. So I called the sheriff's office and told the deputy who answered that I needed to talk with Agent Twiddy, that it was urgent. The deputy was hesitant but I insisted that he interrupt the interrogation to get Balls on the phone.

I held on and a minute or two later Balls came on.

I gave him a quick rundown of what Rev. Kessler had told me.

Balls was quiet. I thought maybe he believed I was overreacting. But then he said quietly, "Rev. Kessler wouldn't have told you that unless he really believes something is up with that deacon, that Darien Brody." He stopped a moment. "He's probably got even more reasons to be suspicious than he mentioned to you. We gotta locate this Mr. Brody."

"I remember which one he is," I said.

"Yeah," Balls said. "So do I. He's the tall one. The very tall one."

I felt a chill on my spine.

Chapter Twenty-Two

I knew that Balls would ask Deputy Wright or one of the others to be on the lookout for Darien Brody, but I wasn't at all sure how much of a hunt would be conducted. I'd just have to wait, something I knew I'd have a difficult time doing today. I kept telling myself I'd done what I needed to do, except call Rev. Kessler and let him know that Agent Twiddy and others would be seeking Darien Brody. I had asked Kessler to please call me if he learned anything further about Brody's whereabouts. He promised he would.

I paced out on the deck. Tried to concentrate on how blue the sky had turned out to be. When I was perfectly still, I could hear the surf, a quarter of a mile away. There would be dangerous rip tides and undertows in the ocean today, but I knew it would be beautiful and sparkling.

By practicing the bass, talking periodically to Janey, puttering around the house—I couldn't settle down enough to write—I managed to pass the day, resisting the urge to call Balls again. It was not my investigation, and I needed to keep my nose out of it, and I kept telling myself that over and over, that I'd done what I could.

Finally the night came on, and I still hadn't heard anything. I knew I would when something developed, at least I hoped I would. Vowing to do my best to stop thinking about the investigations and Darien Brody, I went to bed early and did try to read a Pat Conroy book I was into, attempting to concentrate on Conroy's masterful use of the language.

I went to sleep with the light on and the book beside me. I waked up once during the night and turned the light off. By five-thirty my eyes popped open but willed myself to stay in bed until at least six.

At six I got up and went into the kitchen and made coffee. I uncovered Janey and went out on the deck. It promised to be another lovely post-storm day. I sat on one of my lawn chairs and tried my best not to think, to just look at the two little puffy clouds that moved across the blue sky, smell the pine trees and the salt air coming off the ocean.

Maybe I put myself in something of a trance, just meditating and letting the time slip by. Later I stood, stretched, and went toward the kitchen for more hot coffee.

And the phone rang.

I frowned, and automatically glanced at my wrist to check the time. Didn't have my watch on. Kitchen clock read five of seven. I hurried to the phone. Probably Balls. But caller ID showed a local number and the name M. Beckham.

I picked up the phone before the third ring. "Mouse?"

"Yes. It's Mouse. I know it's early . . ." There was a catch in his voice. "But Billy's gone, and my car is gone, and I didn't know who else to call."

It took a second or so for me to digest what he was saying, and why. "I don't understand, Mouse. Maybe he's just run to the store."

"No, I don't think so, and he's been so depressed." He paused to take a breath. "We've just got the one car. My Suzuki, and he wouldn't take it without—I mean leaving here before dawn or something and not saying anything. I know maybe it doesn't make much sense, but I'm distressed, really distressed."

"Perhaps he wanted just to be by himself or something, get to feeling—well, less depressed." I sat in the chair by the phone and wanted to be understanding and make Mouse feel better.

"No, it's more than that. I just know . . . just know."

I heard an intake of his breath, then, "Oh, God, hold on a minute, please . . ." The phone made a clacking sound as he abruptly laid it down. Noise in the background as he scurried away. There was a pause and a shouted exclamation of, "Oh, no," from somewhere in his house. I could tell he rushed back to the phone. He spoke loud enough for me to hear him even before picking up the phone. "Oh, my God, oh, my God . . ." He sobbed.

I clutched the phone hard. "What is it, Mouse?"

"My pistol. My pistol. It's gone."

That wasn't good. I had a bad feeling.

Sobs punctuated Mouse's voice as he pleaded: "Will you come help me look for him, Weaver? Please."

"Yes, hold on. Let me throw some clothes on. I'll be there in less than ten minutes."

"Please hurry. I think I know where he's gone."

In about seven minutes, and driving entirely too fast for the neighborhood, I had to swerve around a pickup truck that was parked haphazardly on the edge of the road a half a block from Mouse's place. I pulled into the cracked concrete driveway in front of a small, gray beach-box of a house. I slammed on brakes but Mouse was already outside and opening the passenger door as the tires crunched across gravel and pieces of concrete. His long dark hair hung around his ears and touched the back of his shirt. His eyes were open, wide and frantic. "I'm sure I know where he's gone. Nags Head Woods. That's where we always walked, and . . ."

I was backing out of the driveway before he finished talking. Again, I drove faster than I should have, and headed south on the Bypass. Passed a couple of cars moving at the posted speed of 50 mph. At Pigman's Barbecue I swung a hard right.

Mouse sat rather hunched but leaning forward, rubbing his hands together. "I'm afraid, Weaver. I really am." Something of a sob or gasp escaped his throat. "I don't know what he's liable to do. But I'm afraid."

I nodded but didn't say anything. I concentrated on driving. The paved road gave way to gravel as we passed the Christmas house. My Outback bounced along the rougher road. I had to slow down a bit. Mouse squirmed as if willing me to go faster. We came up on the parking area for the Nature Conservancy, and there was the Suzuki. I slid my car in beside it. Mouse was out of the door before I'd completely stopped. "I know where he would be," he said, as he took off at a run.

I followed him, only a few yards behind him.

At the intersection of another narrow dirt road, he turned right. "He would go down the Roanoke Trail," he yelled back over his shoulder. His hair bounced up and down as he ran. About half way down the trail, Mouse stopped momentarily. "Sometimes we stop along here, but I expect he's gone all the way down to the sound." The trail ended, I knew, with a beautiful view of the Roanoke Sound. Mouse shook his head, pain etched on his face. "My God, I just hope he hasn't . . . oh, goodness . . . let's keep going."

We started running again. I was beginning to sweat, and I knew Mouse was, too. I glanced to my left. We passed the maple trees where the two bodies had been discovered. The yellow crime scene tape was long gone, and the surroundings looked peaceful and serene—except in my mind. The only sound came from the slap-slap of our feet on the earthen path. Mouse tripped slightly once, but regained his balance quickly and we kept going.

I was behind three or four yards when suddenly Mouse stopped. In front of us was the Roanoke Sound, the sun still fairly early behind us so that our side of the water was somewhat in shadowy light. But there stood Billy, his back to us as he stared out toward the water, or toward infinity. His arms hung limp by his sides. In his right hand he had what, from my distance, looked like a .22 pistol, a type used mostly for target practice. His grip on the pistol was relaxed and loose.

Mouse approached Billy quietly. Cautious. Careful. "Billy," he said softly but breathy from the running. "It's me.

Mouse. I've come for you, Billy." His voice was gentle but loud enough to carry the ten or twelve yards.

Mouse stopped a few yards behind Billy, as if he didn't want to approach him too abruptly. I continued slowly, softly, not saying a word. I stood behind Mouse. I could see how his shoulders heaved from the running, and his T-shirt was sweat stained.

Moving as if in a dream, Billy turned mechanically to look back at Mouse. His face was vacant, drained, but tears still streamed from his eyes and glistened on his cheeks. Billy wore sandals and shorts, a baggy sport shirt that was too big for him.

Mouse walked a few steps closer. "Billy, please give me the pistol." His voice was controlled, steady, and as gentle as he could make it.

Billy glanced down at his right hand as if he had forgotten the gun was there. He didn't move his hand, just looked at it. Then he turned his face toward Mouse. Billy's expression was a little less dreamlike. His mouth quivered. I thought he would start crying again. He spoke for the first time, his voice soft, pleading, a bit higher pitched than I had heard before, as if tinged with tears. "I don't like it here anymore, Mouse." His lips crumbled together. "I don't like what people say about me. About us."

Mouse moved closer. "Oh, my goodness, Billy, we can always move. And it isn't what good people say. They don't say bad things. It's only one or two cruel and ignorant people, and we don't pay any attention to them." Mouse held both of his palms outward toward Billy, sounding calm and reassuring.

My presence didn't seem to have even registered on Billy.

Mouse moved closer to Billy. He stood no more than two feet from him. Slowly, Mouse put his hand out and eased the pistol from Billy's hand. Billy didn't resist. Mouse held the pistol by his side, then inched closer to Billy, moving the pistol behind him. I moved forward and put my hand on the pistol. Mouse didn't flinch. He let me take the gun from his hand. With his now free hand, Mouse encircled Billy's shoulder with his arm, and pulled Billy close to him.

"We'll move if you want to, Billy. I don't want you to worry or be unhappy."

Billy nodded, glanced up at Mouse and then stared at the ground. "I'm sorry, Mouse," he mumbled.

"Nothing to be sorry about. I know you've been upset."

I checked the .22 pistol, carefully. I eased the safety on. Jeeze, I thought. It had been ready to fire, fully loaded, a round in the chamber I was sure. Without making any sudden move, I stepped back a pace and slipped the pistol into my right side pocket. It felt bulky and heavy, but it went into my khakis completely. I know I breathed a tad easier, realizing that the T-shirt I'd pulled on was damp with sweat, also.

His arm around Billy's shoulders, Mouse pulled him toward him with a loose embrace. "Let's go home, Billy."

Billy wiped at his nose with the back of his hand, and then rubbed tears away from his cheeks. He tried to smile at Mouse. Softly he said, "Okay."

I let them walk in front of me a pace or two. They both had their heads down, studying the ground, or concentrating on getting their emotions under control. But they weren't looking straight ahead.

I was.

And as the trail made a bend to the right, I saw him, and I uttered the all-encompassing expletive, the one that fits every bad situation. "Shit," I said.

There stood Darien Brody. In the middle of the path. He didn't look at all like he had at the church. His clothes were wrinkled and soiled. His hair, which had been combed neatly straight back, was wild and pitched forward. A half-smile played on his lips. His blue eyes had a bright, unnatural sheen. In his left hand he held a revolver. It looked big and it was pointed more or less at us.

The three of us stopped. We didn't move. I think I

mouthed the word "shit" again.

Darien smirked. "What've we got here? A threesome with you degenerates."

I stepped around Mouse and Billy, moving a foot or so closer to Darien. "Look, Deacon Brody, I don't know—"

He hissed, "Shut up!" Spittle hung on his lower lip. His eyes blazed as if they had taken on an inner fire from hell. He raised the revolver, aimed dead on my chest. I halted.

He smirked, speaking to me, "You were driving too fast coming to his house," and he motioned to Mouse with the revolver, then back on me.

Mouse and Billy stood frozen behind me.

"You three move over there, by those trees." He pointed with the revolver. Then he made a sound that sounded like a giggle. "I'd rather take you up the trail to the other place, but you might try something stupid as I herd you up there."

"You mean where you killed Gladys Chaffey and Dwight Fairworth," I said.

"I told you to shut up. Now move." He waved the gun again.

Mouse and Billy cast their eyes at me as if seeking an answer as to what to do. Terror distorted their faces; put wrinkles that weren't there before.

I stared hard at Darien and noticed the empty knife sheath affixed to his belt. It had held a long knife, like the one Saliavo carried up on the beach.

"Move," he commanded again. "Over that way."

Slowly we began to move. Ours steps were shaky, unsteady. I followed Billy and Mouse off the path toward trees standing about five yards off the trail. They had their heads down, walking close together, shoulders almost touching, their arms now hanging loosely. I kept my right side away from Darien. I didn't want him to see the bulge in my pocket from the .22. There had to be an opportunity, a split second when I could use it—without getting all three of us shot by Darien's revolver. "Now look, Brody, you're not God you know—"

He jabbed me sharply in the left shoulder with the muzzle of the revolver. "I'm not going to tell you again . . ." Then he actually chuckled, "And don't try any of that third grade psychology on me." He made a snorting sound. "Of course I'm not God. There's only one God." He pointed at two trees. "Stop right here." We turned to him. He breathed heavily through his open mouth. "No, no, I'm not God." His upper lip curled. Leaning forward, he hissed, "But I'm His messenger, here to do His bidding."

Waving the muzzle of the revolver at us, herding us in a sense, he barked, "Sit. All three of you sit. Base of those trees."

Mouse spoke, his voice wavering, "Mr. Weaver is not . . . not with us. He's just helping out. He's not . . ."

"Don't talk to me, you fag," Darien said, his voice hoarse with emotion. He stepped closer, the barrel of the revolver only inches from Mouse's chest. "I said sit."

Billy, his small body rigid, fists clenched by his side, screamed, "You go to hell!"

With a quick slash of the gun barrel, Darien Brody smacked Billy across the face. A hard, vicious blow. Billy crumpled to his knees, and then rolled back on his haunches. He put a hand to his cheekbone. Blood oozed out between his fingers. Sitting there, he stretched his legs out in front of him, a dazed expression on his face.

Mouse uttered something and started to move forward, but Brody swung the muzzle of the gun against Mouse's chest, and Mouse stopped. "Sit," he said. Mouse began to ease down beside Billy.

I thought maybe I had missed the one opportunity I might have to get the .22 out of my pocket, and fire. There had to be a chance. And I knew it had to be soon.

Darien stood close. I could smell a sour odor coming from him. The muzzle was only inches from my upper chest, and he had cocked the hammer with his thumb. "Now you sit."

I put my hands along my hips as if I was preparing to sit.

I slipped my right hand into my pocket. It had to be now. It had to be.

At that moment, almost propelling himself forward, Billy kicked out with his left sandaled foot and struck Darien's shin, and struck it hard. I heard the blow and saw Darien almost lose his balance. He staggered to the side and his revolver went off with a loud bang. Bark splintered off one the maples inches from Billy's head.

I had the .22 out, releasing the safety as I pulled it from my pocket and without aiming I pointed it at Darien and fired. He looked stunned and surprised. He started to swing his gun toward me but his arm wouldn't respond and I shot him again. I think this time I hit him just below the chest. He made a sound. Blood came from his left arm and side, and more was beginning to soak his shirt in the front. His arm and hand were useless and the revolver fell to the ground. Just as he started to reach for it with his right hand, I shot him again. This time in the upper chest as he faced me. A puzzled expression on his face. I pulled the trigger a fourth time and nothing. I tried again. Nothing. A spent shell jammed instead of ejecting A bitter, hot anger consumed me. My teeth clinched together, I muttered, "You son of a bitch . . . you son of bitch." I knew in my heart I wanted to keep shooting him. I wanted the gun to keep firing. It was a strange, un-familiar anger in my soul. And frightening.

Darien began to sink, still staring at me, bewildered. He staggered backward and sat, one leg under him. Then he rolled slowly to his side. His eyes remained partly open, like slits, the pale blue of his eyes catching tiny points of light, then fading.

Billy had scrambled up and started to reach for the revolver that Darien had dropped. "Don't touch it, Billy," I shouted. "Don't touch it." My voice sounded like an echo to me. The exploding gunfire had done that to my hearing. Only then did I realize how loud it had all been there in the stillness of the maritime forest.

Billy stood, his fists still clenched. Mouse got to his feet.

He trembled. He put a shaky arm around Billy's shoulder.

I got my cell phone out of my left pocket. My hands trembling, I slipped the .22 back in my right pocket. It felt warm against my thigh. My hands still shaking uncontrollably, I punched in 911 and then the Dare County Sheriff's Department.

When I finished my calls—my voice sounding strained and not like mine at all—Mouse said, "What do we do now?" He stared at Darien Brody's body, then quickly looked away.

"We wait here," I said. "We'll hear sirens in a few minutes."

"Can we go stand over there?" Mouse said. "At the path. Not here . . ."

Billy kept gently touching the place on his cheek where he had received the blow from Darien Brody's gun. Blood had smeared his cheek.

I nodded. "Sure." I glanced at Deacon Darien Brody's body. "I'll stay here."

Mouse and Billy turned to go toward the path, but Mouse stopped and turned to me. "You saved us, Weav. You saved our lives." His lips trembled and tears welled in his eyes. He hesitated, tried to smile, and grabbed me in a tight bear hug.

And I hugged him in return.

I forced a chuckle. "But our real thanks has to go to that feisty little bastard there," and I pointed to Billy. "Hadn't been for that swift kick of his . . ."

Billy managed to grin.

It wasn't long before we heard the faint sound of sirens, then getting louder and louder.

The End

Epilogue

Mouse and Billy testified magnificently at a judicial hearing about my shooting Darien Brody. Clearly self-defense, they said, adding that I had saved all of us by my action. Naturally there was a question about why Brody was shot three times. We fuzzed over the fact that he had dropped the gun when I shot him two more times. I knew I was aflame at the time with such anger that I would have emptied the entire gun's magazine in him if it had not jammed. Still seems like a bad dream to me. Not the kind of thing I want to do, and it does take an emotional toll on you. I tell myself I should feel more remorse for experiencing that much rage and shooting a man who was obviously mentally ill; but at the time, my only thought centered on the fact that he was going to kill us, and that he had slaughtered others. That was enough for me.

During the hearing, DA Rick Schweikert didn't even push against me with much enthusiasm. Maybe, just maybe, he was softening in his animosity toward me. Be a blast if one of these days we actually became friends.

Mouse and Billy did leave the Outer Banks, and moved up to Rehoboth Beach, Delaware, where Mouse got a job playing piano with a group right away. I've had a couple of emails from him, and they're doing well. Billy has been getting some counseling about his depression, which I'm pleased about. They are happy and I'm glad for them.

Rev. Kessler is still struggling to establish his church,

and I hope he does. In a nice twist, he named Delores Willard, the widow of Earl Ray Willard, as his fourth deacon. Darien Brody's widow has moved from the area. Someone said she went back to Arkansas with relatives. In talks with Rev. Kessler, she acknowledged that Darien had suffered for years from various attacks of mental illness before they moved to the Outer Banks. The episodes were under control when he stayed on his medications.

And Balls? He's being his usual self, always deeply involved in his work. He cut Keith Saliavo loose right away. I don't think Balls ever did really think Saliavo was guilty of killing that young woman. Balls and Lorraine are talking about how they'd like to go back to Paris.

Of course Elly and I would love to go back, and I think we will. The fact that we are more of a couple is no surprise any longer to folks here in town. Even though both of us have our own spooks, and are thus mildly terrified about being hurt from getting too close, we definitely are getting closer each day. Who knows? Maybe one of these days . . .